Desolation Argonauts

Clive Radford

Published by Rogue Phoenix Press, LLP
Copyright © 2022

ISBN: 978-1-62420-694-8

Editor: Amanda Armstrong

Cover: Designs by Ms G

Dedication

To all venturers out to conquer their demons.

Well if you ever plan to motor west,
Travel my way, take the highway that's the best,
Get your kicks on Route 66.
- Bobby Troup

CONTENTS

Chapter 1: Harlem 1

Chapter 2: The Proposal 6

Chapter 3: Hicksville 13

Chapter 4: Chicago Skyline 16

Chapter 5: Roadhouse Blues.. 23

Chapter 6: The Banks of the Muddy Mississippi 34

Chapter 7: Swamp and Country Land 43

Chapter 8: Twister Territory... 58

Chapter 9: Making Out in the Twilight Zone 68

Chapter 10: Road Wrecker Felons....................................... 81

Chapter 11: Crossing the Mojave 103

Chapter 12: The City of the Angels 124

Chapter 13: Monterey and Cannery Row 140

Chapter 14: San Francisco Nights 150

Chapter 15: Las Vegas Bound 165

Chapter 16: Bonneville Salt Flats 200

Chapter 17: The Seasoned Sage 218

Chapter 18: A Bolt From the Blue 228

Chapter 19: Big Pain, Bad Karma 240

Chapter 20: Chicago Omnibus 247

Chapter 1: Harlem

Collins made his way along 125th Street, the Duke Ellington classic *Take the 'A' Train* circulating in his head. Ambling the short distance from the Chelsea Hotel to Grand Central Station, he had ridden the IRT East Side Line subway shuttle ten stops north, exiting at Harlem and sidestepped through the crowd heading for the Apollo.

"Hey, motherfucker."

Wrinkling his nose, Collins kept on walking.

"Hey, *motherfucker.*"

Slowing and breathing out heavily, Collins glanced towards the source of the call.

"Yeah you, haircut."

Fully turning around, he came toe to toe with a sassy black man, his face indented with two scars.

"What ya doin' up town, boy? Ya here to cruise black chicks?"

"No."

"*No*! I think you is, motherfucker. I think ya want to get your splice into some black pussy. Well let me tell ya, motherfucker, black pussy is exclusively the domain of the brothers, not lily-white motherfuckers from downtown Manhattan. Ya get your ass back down there for your trim, boy. Ya dig?"

"I'm here on a mission."

"A *mission*!" Placing his hands about his hips, his countenance amassed doubt. "Huh, who are ya, boy? Albert Schweitzer, or one of those other phoney do-gooders? I think you is bullshittin' me, boy. Don't ya know, this is the brothers' territory, and I don't see no stamped visa allowin' you access to our turf." Abruptly changing tact, he grouched, "You sure you ain't scoutin' the sisters for Lower Manhattan clip joints?"

"I'm heading for the Apollo to report on a gig for *Performance* magazine," Collins informed, briefly grinning at the salacious notion.

"*What?*" His eyes became slits. "You shittin' me, boy. And while I'm about it, where the hell did ya get that strange accent from?"

"England."

"*England!* You mean you is an Englishman?"

"Yes."

"What the hell is a scuzzy, blue-eyed, European rhythms magazine like *Performance* sendin' an Englishman to the Apollo for anyway? What the hell do ya know about soul music? Who you gonna see, boy?"

Tempted to reply, 'If you call me boy again, I'll fucking blow your brains out,' he meekly replied, "James Brown."

"*James Brown!*" the interrogator shrieked, his voice straining. "Why does a lily-white, motherfucker like you want to see the Godfather of Soul?"

"I dig his music."

"Dang, now I've heard everythin'." He gawked at Collins again. "Just what do ya call that haircut anyway?"

"A mullet."

"A mullet." Screwing up his expression, he then clocked someone he knew on the opposite side of the street. "Hey, *Leroy*, hey motherfucker." Dipping his shades, Leroy looked in his direction. "Come and see this white boy's crazy haircut."

Pulling his jacket collar up in an attempt to appear indifferent, Leroy sauntered across 125th Street.

"Hey, Jamal, how they hangin'?"

The two Harlem gents hooked thumbs in a dap handshake.

"Say somethin' for my main man Leroy, boy."

"What would you like me to say?" Collins enquired, his dander rising.

"Did ya *hear* that, Leroy?"

"Uh-huh." Producing a surprised grimace, Leroy quizzed, "Say, what part of Australia ya from, boy?"

"Do I look like a criminal?"

"*What?*"

"I'm English. Australia is where we used to send criminals."

Amused by the wit, Jamal hee-hawed. "Say, Leroy, would ya believe me, if I were to tell you, this boy is on his way to the Apollo to catch James Brown?"

"That right, boy?" he yapped, his mug rapt in incredulity.

"Yes."

"No shit. Well, I'll be damned." Staggered, Leroy lifted his top lip. "Say, what does a lily-white, motherfucker like you—"

Jamal cut him short. "I've already hit the dude with that question."

"And the answer?"

"Well, we were just gettin' down to that, when I kinda got distracted by this white boy's haircut, and called over to ya." Gawping at Collins, he advised "The dude says, it's called a mullet."

Taking in the Harlem visitor, Leroy perused his barnet. "I've never seen anythin' like that before. Is that ya own invention, boy?"

"No. Paul McCartney, Keith Richards and David Bowie have been sporting mullets for some time."

"You don't say." Goggling at Jamal, Leroy blustered, "What's this about James Brown?"

"He's gonna catch James at the Apollo and write about it."

"I see." Inspecting Collin's again, he said, "What makes you qualified to pass artistic judgment on one of the brothers?"

"I've been following James Brown's music for years," he mitigated, his intonation flooded with indignation. "That's why *Performance* sent me."

"Well, boy," Jamal began, failing to register the Englishman's annoyance, "I must say, ya have some damned nerve walkin' around here without any apparent fear."

"What have I got to be fearful about?"

Jamal and Leroy exchanged coy looks.

"*Huh,*" Leroy exclaimed. "Ya mean, ya don't know?"

"I know Harlem is a black district, but I didn't see any signs at the 125th Street subway station saying no whites allowed."

"Holy crap!" Jamal rubbed his chin. "This just gets better and better. Hah." Gimbal-eyed, he puckered his lips. "Ya mean to tell us, ya are unaware of the long-standing demarcation lines between the black and non-black parts of New York City?"

"I know about them, but I'm doing no harm, and I have no ulterior purpose other than to do my job."

"I must say, boy," Leroy said, "ya 'ain't like a reg'lar white American. Maybe ya is just naïve, and you've been lucky to run across a couple of liberal brothers, like Jamal and me. But let me tell ya, if you'd run across some bad-ass spades, ya could easily have ended up wasted with a cap in your ass."

"Looks like I've been lucky." In the back of his mind, Collins withdrew a Magnum from a shoulder holster, took aim at the ambushers, and blew them away.

"*Huh*, that's one hell of an understatement, boy. If you'd run into Marmaduke Hackett, you'd have got a very different reception from him."

"*What!*" Jamal bleated. "That poseur ain't heavy. Shit, I've had curries that are more dangerous."

"Are we talkin' 'bout the same brother?"

"Ugly mother with a cleft lip and an overactive mouth. I had to tell the cocksucker, 'You make more noise than a busted chainsaw. Your automatic volume control is defective. Get the fuckin' thing fixed.'"

"You said *that* to Marmaduke!"

"Hell, yeah. He don't scare me none."

"Well, Jamal, as one brother to another, I gotta say you got some brass. As black bad-ass's go, he's always cut a formidable figure to me." As the Harlem gents eyeballed Collins, the outsider symbolically watched smoke distilling from the fired Magnum. "If he'd come across this white boy, they'd be holdin' a wake for him now!"

~ * ~

Not the first time that six-foot-one, surfboard-built Henry Collins had been accosted, comparable incidents happening in Detroit and Pittsburgh, on each occasion the metaphorical Magnum deployed, and in

4

his subconscious, he had blasted the miscreants. Judging the desire not to be unique, he tarried sure other unfortunates had equivalent vigilante aspirations when put under the spotlight by antagonists, the act 'more honoured in the breach than in observance', to quote from Hamlet.

Chapter 2: The Proposal

A quasi-hipster, if he could permanently shake the shackles of the work ethic, Collins had been dreaming about making a Route 66 road trip ever since hearing the Rolling Stones interpretation of the Bobby Troup song of the same title. The urge had happened eons ago, when as a kid he explored his elder cousin Martin's eclectic record collection, stumbling upon a panacea of maven-like rock bands stirred by beat generation luminaries, their subculture vocabulary providing the foundation for a thousand protest songs and a myriad of celluloid creations.

Now, near to twenty-five years later, he had the wherewithal to make the ambition a reality. No longer tied down by a failed marriage and societal convention, he ploughed London's metropolitan bowery looking for like-minded individuals, his senses turned up to eleven on the dial for maximum feeling. Sniffing the air and peering into the distance, his vocation had become finely tuned, his every move and action aimed at fusing with those emitting the same counterculture signals he'd been transmitting since leaving grammar school.

Catching sight of his reflection in store windows whilst pacing down Oxford Street, apart from his mullet, he noticed he'd started to bear an uncanny resemblance to circa early 1950s beat-writer Jack Kerouac. Slowing to scrutinise his image, he pushed his dark hair back, and assumed a quarter turn of his neck exposing his facial flank.

"Must be kismet," he uttered to himself.

At first, Collins mused four guys would suit for the road trip, but being a creature of immense sexual drive, he reconsidered. Three girls would be a male dream, but then not wishing to burn his Debbie-Harry-lookalike girlfriend of three months, Natasha James, he decided two couples to be just as good. It might even peak in some spur of the moment boy-on-girl swapping, just to keep the trip bubbling and alive.

Emanating an incandescent glow tempered with streaks of vulnerability, Natasha fitted the hip girl about town motif, flitting between daytime conventionalities and night-time bohemia. The recipient of a not to be sneezed at monthly allowance from her affluent family, she had elected to forego the trappings of status quo society in favour of something more visceral, her longing to take an extended walk on the wild side surfacing during her stint at St Hilda's College studying ancient and modern history. Graduating, she went to work for the Natural History Museum as a researcher, her employers impressed by her family background and degree qualification, but impervious to her nocturnal exploits.

Collins had broached the subject to Natasha, also suggesting they approach mutual friends Kallen Delaney and Gail Knight to make up the rest of the party. Amenable to the idea, but with a reservation, she pointed out Delaney had a propensity to dive into cocaine at the drop of a hat, amplifying his already peppy personality and thereby could present problems. The perception had crossed Collins' cerebration, but he countered the possible downside by saying Delaney would lend a quota of experimentation to the jaunt, though secretly he knew there had to be an element of danger for the cokehead to even get out of bed, often capping in mishap for the companions Delaney ran with.

Neglecting his shortcomings, with his knowledge of the beat generation, fine-featured Delaney had impressed Collins when they met at Bill Wyman's Sticky Fingers Kensington restaurant. He also exuded a Lord Byron nature, 'Mad, bad and dangerous to know,' to quote Lady Caroline Lamb. Though nominally rational and stable, without warning he could go off on some metaphysical excursion or physical exertion under the influence of alcohol, soft drugs, and especially, cocaine. Whether depressants or stimulants, when he passed the self-control threshold, both caused volcanic reactions, if he felt in the mood for taking liberties and testing boundaries. Consequently, Collins hoped to hook up with beats and pleasure seekers along the Route 66 trail, to see how Delaney might operate when faced with a beast of equal or greater temporary derangement. He figured the interactions ought to layer the adventure with memorable regalia.

A life-long dropout and nonconformist, though possessing off-the-scale IQ, Delaney had been expelled from grammar school during his O-level year for arguing with a classics master to the point of repeated foul language in class. Enrolling at a local college for further education, he completed his O-level and A-level studies before going to the University of Manchester to study drama and English literature. Albeit, during his second year, he quarrelled with a plethora of lecturers regarding their interpretation of the subject matter, and in a gesture of terminal defiance, quit the course during the autumn semester. Since, he'd gone from job to job, sometimes labouring, at other times working in offices and the more creative industries, pushing his vibrant personality as a passport credential qualifying him for the job, but fatally and invariably, finding fault in employer methods and walking out.

When Collins stumbled on him, he occupied the post of A&R man for indie label, Cold Turkey Records, just how he got the assignment remaining vague and nebulous. Via his journo role at *Performance* magazine, Collins knew Cold Turkey CEO, Glen Montague. Assessing Delaney, Montague told Collins he had considered him capable of talent scouting, and overseeing the development of recording artists, based on his overpowering knowledge of the contemporary rock scene, and his apparent aptitude to smooth-talk his way into most things. Naturally, Delaney had winged it, up selling his capabilities way beyond actuality, but being a quick learner, calculated he'd get a grip of the role rapidly, and maybe plant his flag in the music business forevermore. Like Collins, he had become a music afficionado at a fledgling age. In the urban vernacular of the time, he knew his shit, able to differentiate between common ore and potential liquid gold. With his sweet patter and inventiveness, Montague also discerned Delaney could handle the A&R marketing and promotion aspects. Founded more on visionaries and mavericks rather than business graduates and bean counters, pioneering indie record companies tended to look for gutsy, innovative operators inveighed with a silver tongue and an ability to fuse with temperamental rock musicians. Bringing home the bacon, Montague's hunch about Delaney paid off when he signed up a number of up-and-coming acts to Cold Turkey, some reaching the hallowed top-ten slots in the singles and album charts.

Later, Delaney hooked up with Gail, a waif-like creature possessing mesmerising peepers and a hunger for life examination. After matriculating from the Kingston Fashion School, she had laboured endlessly, trying to get her designs chosen for production by one of the major *haute couture* houses. More an issue of being in the right place at the right time, and having an inside champion, luck and fate played huge parts in un-sponsored neophyte designers' finding work, Gail never becoming the recipient of a full-time contract, and having to make ends meet with piecemeal sub-contract work from less gifted practitioners. Nonetheless, she did not relent from her daydream. By the time she fell into Kallen Delaney's arms, she had secured a long-term contract with Sherwood Locke, a fabricator of mid-priced ladies fashions.

Imbued with a measure of common ground and identity, the foursome met up for gigs and hung out in West End pubs, Collins progressively gaining exposure to Delaney's split disposition, and at times having to reel him back from doing the terminally stupid, like tottering along the Westminster Bridge balustrade whilst sozzled, standing the chance of crashing into the Thames, or picking an intellectual fight with some establishment evangelist, leading to violence and bloodshed. Convinced Delaney entertained bravado rather than a death wish, Natasha and Gail hung back, smirking at his antics, whilst Collins performed rescue duties.

Continuing along Oxford Street, Collins headed for Ronnie Scotts, where he had arranged to meet with his fellow iconoclasts to discuss the American venture.

Settling down in a corner booth at Scotts, Delaney asked, "What are we talking about in terms of the route?" a sensation of imminent escapade stimulated.

"*Ahh*, that's the right word," Collins enthused. "Provisionally, we're going to shadow old Route 66 from Chicago to LA, otherwise known as Main Street of America or the Will Rogers Highway, and then either return the same way, or head east from LA to Salt Lake City or Denver, and return to Chicago from the north-west. Might even be a journey of self-discovery."

"Neglecting the esoteric, Henry, how far is that?"

"According to the US Tourist Board, 2,110 miles on the outbound, taking in Illinois, Missouri, Oklahoma, the Texas panhandle, New Mexico, Arizona and California. If we return on the Salt Lake City steer, via Utah, Nebraska and Iowa, about 2,016 miles. It equates to twenty-five days on the road at 165 miles per day, if we stick to the fifty-five miles per hour speed limit, three hours motoring per day, presuming no significant holdups. I've also allowed three days for contingency."

"Twenty-eight days in total then."

"Thirty-one, including flying time."

"And the cost?"

"Around five and a half per person for flights, car hire, accommodation and subsistence."

"Dollars or pounds?"

"The Queen's coin. That's nine-nine in colonial, plus spending money."

"What's it going to be like culture wise, Henry?" Gail raised

"I gauge if we take in the ghosts of the Dust Bowl speakeasies and roadhouses, it's going to be Jack Kerouac meets Tom Joad."

"Well, I gotta muscle me up some action, as the MC5 said," Delaney articulated, "so count me in."

"How about taking in San Fran on the return leg?" Natasha tabled.

"Yeah, why not," Collins supported. "Flexibility should be the nucleus on this sojourn. We'll seek out Lawrence Ferlinghetti and Ken Kesey at City Lights."

"So, we're talking about a fly-drive, are we?" Gail investigated.

"Indeed, we are," Collins confirmed.

"What about the accommodation?" Natasha queried.

"Motels are the way to go. That affords us maximum freedom to do what we like."

"Hah!" Delaney blurted. "Talking MC5 speak, can we hire some muscle cars?"

"Sure," Collins replied. "How about a Corvette and a Camaro, they're not quite what might be deemed to be purist muscle cars, but both are fast and agile. Notwithstanding, they will put a delta increase on my cost estimate."

"Oohh, a Corvette, I like the sound of that," Natasha trilled. "I've fetishized over Corvettes ever since seeing one in *The Gumball Rally*, though it got totalled in the opening scenes of the film."

"Didn't that film have a Camaro in it, as well?" Delaney said.

"Yeah. It got wrecked on the LA Freeway."

"Tell us more about the orbit, Henry?" Gail solicited.

"Just like in the song," he commented, "St Louis, down through Missouri, Oklahoma City, Amarillo, Flagstaff, San Bernardino, and all points in-between."

"And the return leg?" Natasha questioned.

"Well, if you want to head back to Chicago via San Fran, we'll work out a course along the way, perhaps I80 to Reno and Salt Lake City, then on to Laramie and Des Moines, or alternatively, if we elect to take in Denver, it'd be Death Valley and Las Vegas before picking up the interstate for Des Moines."

"Laramie is on I80," Delaney recalled. "I did a visit there to see an old university buddy of mine. The countryside is stunning, valleys and mountains evanescing into the distance, with no towns or villages in-between, just farms and vast grazing lands once teeming with buffalo."

"So…" Collins beamed around his compatriots. "…is everyone in?"

Delaney and Gail nodded.

"Me too," Natasha added.

"That's settled then. I'll book us London to Chicago with BA, and use Hertz to hire the wheels." Brainstorming on the hop, Collins attached, "I'll also book us into the River Hotel on East Wacker for night one. It's only a few blocks north of Buddy Guy's Legends, so we can check out the blues."

The meeting of sparky minds occurred in the depths of winter, snow festooning London's West End, temperatures approaching zero, making for wrapping up warm and utilising waterproof footgear. As Collins made his way home after leaving Scott's, he mentally reviewed what had been agreed, and looked forward to enacting the venture with fervour.

Over the next few months, as the snow melted and the skies cleared, he visioned out the Route 66 road outing into tangible hallmarks, imagining the people they'd meet, and the adventures they'd have along the track.

Chapter 3: Hicksville

Collins had researched the beat genre and established somewhere way out west in downtown USA, they still talked about spaced-out hipsters breaking heads in juke joints, and high-plains drifters trading in their spurs and Stetsons for copies of *Nova Express* and *Doctor Sax*. Hightailing it from rule devotion and surrender to plastic *modus vivendi*, the renegade priests of super-cool had breezed into their docile communities, carving up the forum into contours of their choosing, and redefining Webster's dictionary in terms of beat-poet phrasing. Without fanfare or reveille, the *bone fide* paragons of the *avant garde* arrived unannounced, their rabble rousing stirring up a combustible storm. Seeking refuge from mainstream sorcerers and charlatans, they challenged the shapes in a drape to cast off coherence, and enter the province of original thought. Abstracted from chaos, they contested the mainstream monotonous dirge, their disorderly message becoming the clarion call for the young and the terminally frustrated to throw off the manacles of conformity, and emerge fully transformed into the ranks of hip-cats and bohemian travellers. They got few takers. Convention and fear of the unknown combining to drown the alternative life model in its infancy.

At a time when *Harper's* and *Life* were filled with stories about the Hollister biker riots, often, some general store owner making ten cents on the dollar or a farmer leveraged to the hilt with a mortgage, contested, 'What are you rebelling against?' 'Whaddaya got, daddy-o?' came the rasping reply. No one on post-World War II Main Street had bargained for slouchers and slowpokes contradicting their habitual routines or casting doubt on good old Americana. They'd won the war. Then came the economic boom, fuelled by consumerism. Everything was good. Why put a hampering spoke in the affluence wheel, clogging up their ideals?

Some of the wayward clique pumped gas for a living, others did chores in dime stores and seven-elevens while planning otherworldly ventures, their vision taking in the backdrop, but their minds catapulted into another dimension. When they got time off, they hung out at the local gin mill, hit the bottle, tried narcotics, and acted like birddogs and wolfhounds, sniffing around buttercups and mom's homemade apple pie, but really using it as a front to get to their daughters.

What started out as the occasional juvenile hobo or highbrow beachcomber hobbling into backwater parishes to beg a crust, quickly became a stream of teenage gangs of biker outlaws and clusters of down-and-outs' swaggering into town and leering at the locals. The very few adopting the new creed took their entry as gospel change was underway, their transition from Mister Cleans' to derelict drifters and nomadic sundowners carving out pathways in the American hinterlands with crazed writings and radical art.

Collins had heard of and even fantasised about such hanky-panky going down across the pond, but he never unmasked the equivalent schismatic movement in England. A strikingly US phenomenon, unlike the worldwide migration of other art forms and subcultures founded in the colonies, the rise of the beats failed to gravitate beyond the eastern and western shorelines. Foxing him for a long time, he hit upon the impulse it came down to country scale and newness, the States at least a hundred times larger than England, and not hampered by two millennia of tradition. Put together America's vast open spaces accompanied by a country still finding its character, and the likelihood of a divergent sect became much more possible.

Losing himself poring over beat gen accounts and publications from the era, Collins became absorbed by the substance to the point whereby he lost all track of time, current events and people not registering in his consciousness. For all he knew, the world could have stopped whilst he probed and dug deep into the bewitching genus, his concentration so focused, at times he pictured himself planted in Hicksville, the words he read mutating into discernible properties, including peals and odours. He could almost taste the dust and sweat coming off the disenfranchised as they mooched along Main Street, curling their top lips at Mister America, condemning bourgeoisie vulgarity, and spying about for a desirable doll or easy meat, whilst scribbling a line or two on a scrap of paper to be built into an epic further down the road. Not put off by sneers and spits, the braver operators tried their luck at evangelising the gospel, the sapient regulars saying, 'It's too self-indulgent', really meaning, 'We don't understand or like it', really meaning, 'It's raining scorn on our parade', 'Let's kill these upstarts before their doctrine kills us'. Countering with, 'Take a leap of faith, it's perfectly ambiguous, no answers, only questions', invariably the disbelievers rounded on the adherents, punches thrown, heads kicked, instructions given to leave town. Riding out the beatings and ignoring the putdowns, the disciples didn't so much as evolve, more like mutated into an alternative breed, dashing off poetry and spouting revolution of the mind, their higher plane of knowingness dangling in the theatre of the absurd.

Touchable and vital, the abstractions arrived so quickly, it became impossible for Collins to remember them, let alone transcribe the effigies when he resurfaced into everydayness. He planned an annual homage to the denomination, even considered adopting its principles as a life M.O, but being a creature of dexterous habits with a low threshold of boredom, convinced himself his faith could only be practised when his necessary daytime vocation allowed.

And so it went on, until that crossover point at Ronnie Scotts, when he sold his band of dreamers on the Route 66 jaunt.

Chapter 4: Chicago Skyline

Spring arrived pristine and fresh, and with it the four intrepid explorers touched down at Chicago O'Hare, picked up the cars, and headed for the River Hotel.

"Have you been in the Windy City before?" Natasha quizzed, as the Camaro sped down Lower Whacker Drive parallel to the Chicago River, the antithesis of the manmade and the natural fascinating her.

"Yes, when I was with *Crossroads*," Collins clarified, glancing at her from the driving position. "They sent me to Chicago to interview Phil Chess and report on a blues convention held at McCormick Place. It's not far from the River Hotel."

"Phil Chess, the co-founder of Chess Records along with his brother Leonard?"

"You got it, sister. I went to the famous Chess Records 2120 South Michigan Avenue address, immortalised in the Rolling Stones recording of the same name. Got to see the studio where Howlin' Wolf, Muddy Waters, the Stones, Peter Green's Fleetwood Mac and many others cut ground-breaking blues tracks."

"Just a minute." She frowned. "I thought you worked for *Performance* magazine."

"I do, but after graduation, I first went to *Crossroads*. That's when I also started dabbling in the stock market."

"Resultant from your economics degree?"

"That's right."

Bemused she sought, "So, how did an economics degree qualify you to become a music journalist?"

"It didn't. I knew Danny Petronais, the *Crossroads* sub-editor, from school. He persuaded the features editor to take me on spec. I'd been a music freak since I could walk and talk, and Danny published some gig reports in *Crossroads* I submitted when I was at University College. That helped cement the trial."

"And in tandem, you played the stock market?"

"My late grandfather on my mother's side left me a hundred thou in his will. He did the same for his other grandchildren. Lenny de Kypers, a university contemporary of mine, got taken on as a trader with Credit Suisse. He gave me some steers, and I ploughed my inheritance into stock, Lenny acting as my broker."

"And it came good?"

"Yep. After five years, I'd made half a mill. However, the divorce settlement with Babette put a big dint in my stash."

"Huh, how on Earth did a stock trading jockey like you, ever make the modulation into the world of hipsters and jazz addicts?"

"I guess it's been there since my pre-teens, fostered by an obsession with derivative rock music. The accumulation of money is just the means to live out the dream."

"But, you'll go back to *Performance* when we return to London?"

"Yep, and I'll continue to invest until I have enough collateral to make me liquid. Then I can apply for a permanent exit visa from the music media, and parachute into bohemia for good, set up an artists' colony like the Bloomsbury Group, and just chill out."

"I didn't know you could paint."

"Ah, that's one of my many secrets. I've got an O-level in art, but that bent was put on hold when I went to university. Because of work commitments and the headaches of being married to Babette, it never became unlocked again." He pointed to his head. "But it's all in here, waiting to make the transition from perception to canvass images."

"Was Babette really that bad?"

"French women are meant to be docile and accommodating, but life with Babette was like living with a hurricane. Because I was so consumed with her gorgeousness, and her capacity to fulfil all my sexual fantasies, I never saw it when we were courting. Either that, or she kept it hidden. You'll find a picture of Babette in the French dictionary next to the word, *tempétueux*."

Twisting in her seat, she scanned backwards at the pursuing

Corvette. "Kallen and Gail seem well-suited."

"Uh-huh."

"Do you imagine he loves her?"

"C'mon, Natasha, we've all been down that path and got burnt. Why complicate things by introducing a watershed word with all its attendant implications?"

~ * ~

On reaching the River Hotel, Delaney excused himself, found what he ciphered to be a user in a bar on East Monroe, probed him for directions to a dealer, then headed for a den in New Eastside, acquiring some lunar trajectory grade coke from a pusher. Back at the hotel, he took his fix and by the time the thrill seekers were ready for dinner, he'd entered a euphoric state, energetic, talkative, mentally alert, and hypersensitive to sight, sound and touch.

"Hell," Delaney blustered in Braithwaites, a beanery boasting Eliot Ness connections, two blocks from the River Hotel, "I got a feeling this spree is going to be sensational."

"That's just the blow talking," Collins insisted, "albeit, I've got the same intuition. Picked up on it the moment we jetted into O'Hare."

"Yeah," Gail corroborated, "there's definitely a resonance in the vibe."

"It bodes well for the near future," Natasha endorsed. "Sometimes when I travel overseas, I don't necessarily get flushed with hyperbole, but like you guys, I did feel a distinct blast of anticipation at O'Hare."

"Outside it's America, inside it's America," Collins spouted. "Everywhere you spy, it spells America. Although Canada is similar, there is no other country on Earth comparable with the US idiom and its proliferation of home-grown cultures. And I'm not just talking about jazz, the blues and rock and roll. It's in the very fabric of the country, from its' institutions to its' funhouses. Yes, often its plastic and banal, but mainly it's singular and extraordinary."

"I couldn't agree more with you," Delaney threw into the pot. "The US is just over two centuries old, but in that relatively short epoch, the country has matured into a world leader on multiple fronts. An explosion of talent in the sciences, the arts and in governance has come with that transformation."

"Does go to explain how and why the beat generation arose," Gail theorised. "I mean, using a physics analogy, for every action there is an equal and opposite reaction. In terms of sub-cultures arising out of a dismissal of the mainstream ethic, the beats were more likely to be birthed here, than in any other Western country."

"She's right," Natasha approved, her enthusiasm fizzing. "Every left-field cultural diversity finding life since the late nineteenth century has been founded in America, from new sporting games and business methodologies to rampaging evolutions in the arts. The rest of the world eventually mimics the creations, including England."

"But it's not perfect," Gail consigned. "There are inconsistencies."

"Sure, but what place is flawless?" Collins challenged. "Utopia does not, and will never exist. It's an abstract concept, and could never be populated by real human beings."

"Yes, but why?" Delaney voiced.

"Because man is the most imperfect beast to ever walk the Earth."

~ * ~

Buddy Guy's Legends did not disappoint Collins and co, Champion Jack Dupree, Jimmy Witherspoon and Eddie Boyd delivering a witch's brew of Mississippi and Chicago-style blues, Buddy Guy making an appearance for the combined encore. Leaving the expeditionaries drenched in traditional American repartee, the event set the flood tide yardstick for the tour. Their English heritage confined to the back burner, they became subsumed in the Yankee climate.

"A *dazzling* start to our adventure," Delaney quipped, as they left the club.

"For sure," Collins okayed. "Let's hope the Chitlin' Circuit is as good down south and on the West Coast."

"Whereas London's blues and jazz clubs often arise as rendered,"

Gail inputted, "what we witnessed at Legends had absolute authenticity."

"A little unkind and too far-sweeping," Collins repudiated. "Scott's has as much in terms of ambience as anything in the US, including Blues Alley in Washington and NYC's Birdland."

"You've been to Blues Alley and Birdland?" Natasha prompted.

"With Babette during a vacation in New England."

"*Huh*," Natasha blustered, quivering her brow, "that's something else I didn't know about you."

"Usually, I say very little about my former life, but I seem to have become liberated since stepping off the plane at O'Hare."

"Why is that?"

"Maybe it's because to truly embrace the trip in the style of Kerouac's *On the Road*, it necessitates the sinking of barriers. Even if it exposes my short-comings and failures, I feel pre-disposed to do it."

"To cleanse the soul?" Delaney put forward.

"Yeah, that's it, Kallen. To get the most out of this venture, we all have to lower the defensive boom, and take whatever comes our way without criticism or judgment."

"You mean, the people we meet and the happenstances we have?" Gail suggested.

"I do. Let's have no preconceptions. Let's just go with the flow, see it and feel it."

"Henry is *right*," Delaney backed. "This isn't going to be business-class resorting in 5-star Marriotts and Hiltons, and dining at plush restaurants. If we're going to tread the same metaphysical footsteps as Sal Paradise and Dean Moriarty, we've got to drop the luxury level, and mix with those on the fringes of society."

"That's precisely how I decrypt it," Collins concurred.

"Howbeit," Natasha offered, "don't you deem travelling in a top-of-the-range convertible and a coupe is incompatible with that *modus operandi*?"

"You're right, but—" He grinned. "I reckon if Kerouac and Cassidy were doing it in the late 1980s, they'd ditch their 1950s Oldsmobiles and Buicks for a Vet and a Camaro. After all, the road is about fun, as well as exploration."

"I'll buy into that," Delaney propped.

"Besides, modern American saloons wallow about like nodding donkeys, just as much as they did in the 1950s. That might be fine for driving around a city, but we've got thousands of miles to cover on open roads, and at high speed. The Vet and the Camaro have stiff suspension, and are well suited for our purpose."

Sauntering back to the River Hotel, Delaney getting higher still on the passing nightlife, the girls exchanging quips about the big spenders and fancy damsels in Legends, Collins' psyche drifted to a juncture when after his first year at University College, he'd spent the summer recess as an undergraduate intern at Andersen Consulting in their Fenchurch Street economic services branch. Plastered in formality, the suits ruled the roost, their intransigence to seek beyond the frontiers of the business corral stifling to him. Slicing a demarcation point, it became the watershed moment when he realised fitting into the realms of the blue-chip, corporate business fraternity with all its protocol and paraphernalia, could not be the profession path for him.

Always excelling at mathematics, in particular identifying trends in number sequences, economics seemed to be the optimum forum to forge a career. Accordingly, he had selected economics as a higher education subject, never brooding on its occupational impact *vis-a-vis* his natural, unorthodox lifestyle tendencies. Andersen Consulting smashed the glass ceiling. At every nook and cranny in the business ethic, sprung traps released proclamations designed to impale notions of non-compliance bounding from the aspirant economics professional. Behind his outward cooperative decorum, Collins shrieked internally. To say he cultivated a dole of foreboding became an underestimation of the requirement for complete and unyielding submission to the status quo. Fearing for his free spirit, before returning to University College he made a conscious decision to ditch the economics path after graduation in favour of rock journalism.

Perspiring slightly, he muttered to himself, "Thank God, I did that."

"What was that, Henry?" Delaney inquired.

"Oh, just congratulating myself on a decision made in my late teens."

"Something significant?"

"Put it this way, if I'd taken another option, I'd not be in Chicago on the eve of our grand tour."

Chapter 5: Roadhouse Blues

Way before Chicago, Collins had planned out the pilgrimage in terms of trajectory and provisional stopover points. Lying next to a sleeping Natasha at the River Hotel, he wondered how it'd work out in practice. Having never done a road jamboree before, his only insight came from following promenading bands around England, Europe and North America on behalf of *Crossroads* and *Performance*. Apart from his *ad hoc* interviewing duties and occasional partying with musicians after gigs, the logistics had been regular, his travel and accommodation booked in advance by the magazine admin department. Conversely, Route 66 came into an altogether different regime. With the intention to emulate Sal Paradise and Dean Moriarty, they could count on direction from the dudes they met along the way to send them at right-angles to the proposed itinerary. He'd emitted an erudite standing regarding the junket to his fellow argonauts in London, but behind the front, he didn't know what would happen. Maybe it'd go like a dream. Failing that, the unforeseen might drive them into blank canyons and towering alleys, the unfamiliar having them dig deep to get back on track, or at worst, fighting for survival.

America was huge compared to England. Part of an island in the North Atlantic, she was crossable from Land's End in the south-west to Berwick-upon-Tweed bordering Scotland in less than a day. If they stuck to the fifty-five miles per hour speed limit, a days' car travel from Chicago heading south would barely get them out of Illinois. Immeasurable open near-to flat spaces, colossal mountain ranges, forests and deserts characterised the majority of the United States, accompanied by ice storms, hurricanes, earthquakes and extreme hot and cold, the bulk outside of major cities uninhabited apart from the odd trailer park, honky-tonk, pool hall and motel; the components associated with weird goings-on and the stuff of film fables. Most Americans were passive, easy-going, polite, but one in a million could be a serial killer or a psychopath, out to shoot as many innocents as he could before the police gunned him down. Collins knew the polarity came down to statistical probabilities. The larger the population, the more incidence of bad apples grabbing the headlines and going viral worldwide. But what the hell, he rationalised, risk was an integral element of the Route 66 safari, an adrenalin pumper amplifying the senses. That's what they came for. If they hit upon a Ted Bundy, they'd take him down before he went for his axe or meat cleaver.

~ * ~

Early the next morning the Corvette and the Camaro headed due east on East Whacker to the intersection with Lake Shore Drive, before turning south parallel to Lake Michigan.

"The 1933 outset of Route 66 begins at the intersection of Lake Shore Drive and Jackson Boulevard," Collins notified Natasha, his excitation patent to her. "That's our official start line."

As the two cars pulled up side by side at traffic lights at the intersection, Collins nodded to Delaney and Gail in the Vet.

"Here we go," Collins exalted with the lights on red. "Five, four, three, two, one."

Concurrent with his 'one', the lights changed to green and the sports cars took off, both emitting a meaty exhaust howl in celebration of the jaunt, the Camaro's FM radio providing the complementary soundtrack with Steppenwolf's *Born to be Wild*.

Searching heavenwards, Natasha let out a gulp as the Sears Tower came into view amongst a glut of superstructures. "I had no idea Chicago had *such* an impressive skyline."

"Chicago is the birthplace of the skyscraper," Collins informed her. "When I attended that blues convention for *Crossroads*, someone told me there are more tall buildings in Chicago than any other American City, including New York."

"Did you have much time for sightseeing?"

"Afraid not. The convention schedule had no slack. Apart from the Chess Records assignment, I spent most of my time at McCormick Place, although we did have dinner aboard a floating restaurant whilst sailing in Lake Michigan off the Chicago shoreline, and along the Chicago River, affording some terrific views of the city at night."

"Hah, I've never been anywhere outside of England, apart from holiday destinations in the Mediterranean. Right now, I'm overwhelmed by everything I see in Chicago. It's the sheer scale of buildings, plazas, even people. Last night in Buddy Guy's, I had to catch my breath at times. Some of the swingers and hipsters were larger than life, at least larger to my experience."

"I got caught the same way during my first Stateside trip. Then after a while, I twigged the big cities are synonymous with the unusual, whereas out in the sticks, akin to much of rural England, the people are more down home and unspectacular, just like depicted in Grant Wood's *American Gothic*. Many social commentators say the true America is the bits in the middle where the homesteaders prevail."

"You mean, the Midwest?"

"*Yeah*. By contrast, the sections around the eastern and western seaboards and the Great Lakes are sustained sources for corruption and transformation fuelling modernism."

"I suppose the clash of cultures happens more in the big cities, producing a crucible of screwballs, mavericks and eccentrics creating the latest marvels."

"Oh, definitely. Ninety-nine out of a hundred songs and novels centred on places, feature the big cities around the periphery of the US. It's where the new immigrants gather, trying to acclimatise to Americana, whilst melding their heritage into the melting pot. Invariably it produces fusion, and with that synthesis comes the unconventional nurturing oddballs, Ken Kesey and his band of merry pranksters, typical. It's what I hope to discover in abundance during our expedition."

"Am I right in appraising, once the likes of Kerouac and Burroughs achieved fame, they receded into the outback?"

"You mean the backwaters between the ravines and the valleys?"

"Uh-huh."

"Yes, some of the movers and shakers did take a back seat in obscure locations, principally to find tranquillity away from the hectoring media. But contrastingly, most of the action in the beat generation's writings occurs in the Midwest. Sure, a lot of it is in cities like St Louis and Denver, but there's an awful lot occurring in the back of beyond; those desolate locales in New Mexico and Kansas."

"Just like Dorothy's connection with Kansas in *The Wizard of Oz*."

"Quite. Sometimes the most unlikely of settings can result in significant enterprises."

"So, those cats were like Dorothy?"

"Not exactly," he authenticated, shimmying his noggin, "but they did have a version of the Land of Oz on their radar. However, many of their journeys took place in the mind under the reign of liberating hallucinogens."

"As Timothy Leary prescribed."

"Right."

"So, are we going to go down the psychedelic well, just like Alice did?"

"*Hah*—" He stole a grin at her. "You're really good at catching on with analogies. I take it you're alluding to Jefferson Airplane's *White Rabbit*?"

"Uh-huh."

"Do you want to?"

"Not sure." She blanched. "Have you ever taken drugs?"

"Impossible not to when you're involved in the music business, primarily when touring with a holy rock band, and the pushers are cosying up to them every night after the gig."

"What have you taken?"

"Oh…" His tone became guarded, as if he felt guilty. "Just a little low-grade acid. Nothing to fry the brains, but powerful enough to release perception."

"Are you a music journalist or a music reporter?"

"*Hah*. There's a very similar line in the Humphrey Bogart film *Deadline*. The chap it is said to, says, 'What's the difference?' and the interrogator replies, 'A journalist makes himself the hero of the story. A reporter is only a witness.'"

"So, what are you?"

"Without appearing to be immodest, neither. I'm much more the musicologist, operating within the rock journalism domain. Huh—" He beamed. "It's nothing special. I always deduce, if I can do it, anyone can."

~ * ~

Pulling up in Springfield Illinois for the night, and after checking into the Wayside Motel on Carpenter Street, the adventurers dived into Cleveland Sam's, a South 6th Street juke joint, teeming with farm hands and state government blue-collar workers, pooling a joke or a remembrance, whilst sipping on Miller Lite and Michelob Ultra. To the English arrivals, it had a similar ambience to London's east end hostelries. At any moment, they expected a quarrel to turn into a minor fight, or some cluster to spontaneously break into song.

"Look at that guy in the corner," Delaney cajoled his companions. "Judging by his garb and deportment, I bet you he's a hipster."

Viewing in the given direction, Collin's responded, "Possibly."

"Why don't we go and talk to him?" Natasha advocated.

"Let's weigh him up a bit more before we take the plunge. See if there are any further signs that Kallen is correct in his assertion."

Back in the late 1810s, Springfield Illinois had been settled by Europeans, mainly trappers and fur traders, before commerce and banking moved in. Later, the city became the state capital of Illinois, breeding a substantial white-collar worker population in government administration, medical and higher education services. The gent being scrutinised by Collins and his pals didn't fit the archetype, or the blue-collar set dominating the bar. His rough physiognomy, spread-eagled legs and apparent disregard for protocol made him as much an interloper as they were.

"Okay," Collins began, "let's do it."

Wandering over, he begged, "Excuse me, sir, could we sit down?"

Peeking up, the target replied, "Sure, take a load off."

"You don't look like you come from around these parts," Delaney designated.

"That's very perceptive. I'm just passing through on my way to Columbus Ohio." Taking them in, he mellowed into candor, his features relaxed, his vocalisation frank. "I'm a hobo made good."

"Wow, not heard that one before. How did you manage it?"

"*Hah.*" He grinned. "First, who am I talking to?"

After introducing themselves, Collins outlined their voyage intentions.

"Thank you. My name is Homer Calhoun. Whoever my mother was, soon after my birth, she left me in a cot on the steps of the Sisters of Mary Mother of the Eucharist, in Ann Arbor Michigan, with a note asking them to bring me up," he revealed, shocking the English with his remarkable apportion of openness.

"My god," Gail gasped. "You hear about such happenings, but I've never come eye to eye with someone who has been abandoned at such a tender age."

"I knew nothing about the circumstances until I reached the age of seven. By that time, the sisters had put me in a catholic orphanage, my rearing predominantly based on the teachings of Catholicism, including unconditional obedience, and very regular visits to the confessional. I didn't really take it in when they told me about my foundling status. Nevertheless, it hit home in my early teens at junior high, when I saw all the other kids had parents. Well—" He sniffed as if purging the hurt. "Until then, I'd been an attentive scholar at primary school, but the rebel came out in me, and by age sixteen I'd left the orphanage, and headed for New York, bumming lifts and catching freight trains. Never did make it. Got as far as Morgantown, where I met some travellers going west. Told them where I was headed, and they said they'd come from New York, and the place to be was California. So I joined them."

"When was this?" Natasha probed.

"Oh, 1957. Spring."

"Were the New Yorkers beats?" Collins tested.

"*Hah*, is it that obvious?" Calhoun bayed.

"How do you mean?"

"I saw you eyeing me up. Figured you were trying to place me."

Hesitating, he then shared, "If you gauge me to be somewhat unusual, in let's call it, my demeanour compared to the other folks in this bar, it's down to my education on the road. Some of the New Yorkers were indeed beats, and yes, they did shape my cogitation and world view. By the time we reached San Francisco some six months later, having traversed the beat communities in Kansas City, Denver and other minor epicentres of bohemian chic, I'd embraced their doctrine and could have complete conversations in beat speak, with terms like 'frado', meaning an ugly guy who thinks he's good looking, and 'deck', meaning to be on top of the latest trends. I even tried some marijuana, once called reefer, later superseded by pot and grass, and the odd LSD tab. I was searching for a manifestation I had never known in my formative years. Undeniably, in hindsight, I never found it. The drugs were merely a substitute for the real thing. In my case, a normal life with parents, and perhaps brothers and sisters."

"How long where you with the beats?" Delaney investigated.

"Effectively, six years until I hit twenty-three. Until then I did any job coming my way just to pay the rent and bankroll the lifestyle. Then I got taken on as a roustabout by the Weaver Company at Fresno in San Joaquin Valley, a hot spot for the oil exploration and production industry. Triggering a quantum of possibility, I got the inkling I could make something of myself with hard work and dedication to task. After graduating to roughneck and other intermediary jobs, finally, I became a driller, supervising the rigsite operation. From there, I became a white-collar worker, managing the production of Weaver's field. Did well. Got noticed by other oil companies operating in the San Joaquin Valley. Forged a career in management. Now, I'm on the contract negotiation side of the business, working for the Kosmos Petroleum Corporation out of Houston. I spend most of my time cutting deals with suppliers and business partners."

"But you've prolonged your outsider credentials," Collins observed, his inborn journalist's curiosity clanging against its endstops.

"Yep. Contract negotiation is what I do." He radiated at them, conveying a dash of maturity. "It's not who I am."

"Are you still in contact with the beat crowd you used to run around with?"

"Some have passed...too much alcohol and drug abuse. Like me, others have moved out of the discipline. Nonetheless, there remains a tight-knit core, still jumping freight trains and hanging out in speakeasies. Sometimes, I get a postcard or a call from them, extolling me to re-join their ranks. But being a hobo-come-bohemian became a temporary period in my life, when I was finding myself and putting my birth circumstances into perspective." Pausing, he then delved, "You are probably wondering, despite my apparent migration into the work gang, why my comportment is so contrary."

"It did occur to us," Gail testified.

"Let's just say, if I am travelling on business by myself, I adopt a free-spirit attitude in my body language and semblance. It's a salute to my former life, and those still flying the nonconformist dropout flag. You see, we weren't necessarily put upon the Earth to work for material gain. In peacetime, that's a choice." Suddenly dropping into melancholia, he became sullen. "Regardless, for some people choice became negated from the menu." He shook his head. "I'll illustrate by example. During one business conclave in Ok City, I ran into a Nam vet called Arron Harriman. Affable fellow, I subsequently got to know him quite well, and with that familiarity he opened the emperor's kimono to reveal a sorrowful anecdote." Vacillating, he cast an ambiguous expression at his listeners. "I don't know if this will make sense to you highflyers, but what you have to appreciate, is often, we are not in control of our destiny, the objectives we set ourselves interrupted, or everlastingly curtailed by external forces. Happens to most people in war durations. One time, might have been the second time we met, Arron was telling me a story, laying pipe as they say in the film game, something esoteric, I didn't quite understand. I picked up the meaning of the message on the frequencies he transmitted, but persisted flummoxed by his inability to be cogent. Later, I learnt he'd been mentally invalided in Vietnam, less than a year after being conscripted for the infantry. Some incident involving a vicious firefight had driven him over the edge. Like many in the frontline, he took drugs to give him the will to stand and face the bullets, then other drugs to try to wipe out what he had seen, and been part of. One day, the drugs

30

collided in his brain, the chemical processing factory generating the desired state grinding to a halt, leaving him caught in a crazed world of supercharged adrenalin and cognizance flame-out. Took his CO a while to recognise he was only there in body, his wits floating adjacently. They choppered him out to Saigon. Put him in a medivac facility. Thought he'd recover away from the action and the drugs, but he'd gone. For all they knew, he could have fantasised he was back Stateside. After three months without variation, they accepted he'd had his day as a soldier, and shipped him back to a military hospital in San Diego. Five years later, he got a click inside, and came out of the trance. He had some tests and the doc's resolved he could be released into the community."

"They washed their hands of him?" Collins speculated, his phiz crushed by revulsion.

"Candidly speaking, yes. Local social welfare assigned him to a vet refuge, where he kind of slid back into a fashion of normality, nothing rugged to the extent whereby he could live a conventional life, but sufficient enough for him to get by. I could recount a whole lot more about Arron, but I'm sure your imaginations can do the rest." Dwelling, he prompted, "So why am I telling you this?"

"To instil us with insight."

"Partially, but more to set you straight on what you should deem to be important, and what you should categorise as flimflam. What the beats did is more like flimflam compared to what happened to Arron Harriman. You should wind up your quest with a facility to determine what is crucial and what is immaterial. The beats eluded the horrors of war. Most people do not have the choice. They are predestined to be cannon and work fodder, their dreams nullified from the outset."

~ * ~

Over breakfast, the trailblazers revisited their discourse with Calhoun.

"I'm contemplating what he said about the beats amounted to a reality check," Collins submitted, frowning.

"Yep," Delaney approved, "kinda waters down the folklore and

31

the written word." Leaning forward, he expressed, "There's a parallel with music journalism."

"In what respect?"

"Though *Rolling Stone* has attained some nuance of kudos, question marks tarry over some of their rock music critiques."

"Specifically?"

"I remember as a kid, reading an uninformed and undeserved decimating review of Cream's *Wheels of Fire* album, by founder Jann Wenner."

"*Ohh*, you needn't go on, Kallen," Collins ordained, indignation ascending in his timbre. "Unlike, well-respected and fellow *Rolling Stone* journalist, David Fricke, Wenner has been assessed to be a prize-winning wanker by most of the industry for decades. He's been accused of *riding* on the back of fellow *Rolling Stone* founder, Ralph Gleeson, to acquire reflected esteem, cross-fertilising rock music with radical politics for personal gain, and eligibility favouritism in place of fact for his co-founded with Ahmet Ertegun, Rock and Roll Hall of Fame Foundation. To say Wenner is a tainted commentator and has a loaded agenda, is an understatement."

"Nicely put, but what I'm eluding to is, often we place people on pedestals based on hearsay, impression, even notoriety. Until that unmerited Cream annihilation, I'd viewed Wenner to be the real deal, someone who really knew his onions. At first, I finalised he'd done it for commercial benefit. Knowing the popularity of Cream, such a controversial review would get around, resulting in more copies of *Rolling Stone* being sold. Albeit, over the subsequent years, after reading more of his reviews and articles, I concluded he simply did not know his subject matter. Nine times out of ten, he got it *wrong*."

"So, what are you saying?" Gail interjected, perplexed by the affinity.

"We take what we read about the beat generation in good faith, rarely querying its wholesale validity," he qualified. "*That's* what I'm saying."

"Yes, quite right," Collins backed, more realism distilling in his recognition register.

"Just a moment, daddy-o," Natasha began, "I hope you've not brought us on a wild goose chase."

"No, I believe I haven't, but, it's clear we'll have to temper our theory with practice, as it becomes revealed."

Chapter 6: The Banks of the Muddy Mississippi

Collins had genned up on St Louis before the event, distinguishing when the stock market crashed in twenty-nine, St Louis numbered amongst the biggest cities in the US. With a population of around 820,000, it ranked seventh overall, between Cleveland and Baltimore. Consequently, with many businesses declaring Chapter Seven bankruptcy, the early years of the Great Depression hit St Louis hard, unemployment quickly exceeding the national average by nine percentage points.

Amazed to uncover that, if not for the relative success of the garment industry and the return of brewing post-Prohibition, the situation in the Gateway City might have been even worse, Collins was spooked by the enormity of the tribulation. Desperate to survive, the downside led to tens of thousands joining the ever-growing circus of Midwest migrants snaking along Route 66, heading west in the hope of finding employment, if not salvation, in Southern California. The upshot capped in St Louis becoming a refuge for down and outs, spivs looking to make a fast buck, and worst of all, organised crime, the city authorities struggling to keep order, and the local economy tumbling into further disarray, making life intolerable for those who stayed. Tougher still, on a daily basis, most people stood in long lines to get short-lived work, relief, or a hot meal, many becoming victims of starvation, heat stroke in the summer's baking sun and hypothermia in the depths of snowy winters.

Calling in at several rickety bars and roadhouses located in the Mount Pleasant locale adjacent to the Mississippi River, Collins and his compatriots struck up parlays with blue-collar workers, either the descendants or the survivors of the Great Depression generation, jazz standards blaring from juke boxes in the backcloth anchoring the logic of being transported into a time when Glenn Miller and Duke Ellington held court over the airwaves. One colourful woman working for Ralston

Purina, a manufacturer of animal feed, told them about her baleful memoirs.

"If you folks had been here fifty years ago when I was a girl," Amelia Hart moved, "you'd have seen a city filled with families living in temporary shelters made of scrap wood, packing crates, and other salvaged materials. Now we've got a revitalised downtown, replete with the Gateway Arch, Busch Stadium, home of the St Louis Cardinals, and a whole raft of skyscrapers housing new businesses. *Hell*, we're approaching gentrification." She shook her head. "It was a lot different post the depression, when Roosevelt's New Deal was still to take effect. I remember my mammy telling me, her elder brother Elijah and his family had left St Louis around 1931 in search of a new life. He sent her postcards from along Route 66 for at least two years, him and his family taking time out in places like Amarillo and Gallup where they found interim work, and lived in transient camps under canvass. They ceased coming when Elijah's clan reached Victorville on the outskirts of LA. Later, Elijah's wife, Marylou, wrote my mamma saying her brother had been killed in a freak farming accident. She didn't hear anything after that." Amelia scratched her chin, as if her kin had foreseen the fatality. "Well, what happened to Elijah was par for the times. Often those who made it to the promised land, succumbed to an unanticipated tragedy."

"That type of harrowing saga must be emblematic for wayfarers fleeing from the Dust Bowl," Collins postulated, his appreciation of the catastrophe making for empathetic words.

"*Damn right*," she upheld. "People don't know they're born today. They don't know nothing. They moan they're hard done by if they don't have the latest colour TV, and a new Caddy every other year. *Shit—*" She scowled, her condemnation unambiguous to the visitors. "They're just trinkets. Huh—" Her glower eased. "Of course, Pearl Harbour was a blessing in disguise. It signalled an end to practice restrictions on industry, inducted as part of the New Deal. Washington's response to the sneak Jap attack instituted the mass production of war planes and other platforms spelling the end of the Great Depression."

"Didn't Roosevelt cosy up to Ford and GM to mass produce war planes?"

"Yep. Using blueprints from Boeing, North American Aircraft and other major companies, Ford and GM set up specialised mass production plants. In turn, that fostered a sub-contractor industry nationwide, and gave an injection to other industries like metal producers and even clothing. Wages rose for blue-collar workers. Full employment came by 1943, and after the war America became a major economic powerhouse for the next twenty years, until the repercussions of cheap imports and the rise of automation began to impact job security and wages. Ever since the mid-sixties, blue-collar workers have struggled to retain living standards, and the bottom has fallen out of job security."

"Did you ever meet any of the beats, when they touched down in 1950s St Louis?" Delaney enquired.

She grimaced. "You mean, the likes of Kerouac and Corso?"

"Yes."

"No, but I know some people who did meet them." Again, her lineaments became drenched in censure. "*Sweet Jesus*, they were middle-class college boys playing at being hobos and freight train riders. Sure, they understood the subculture and the nature of the people they wrote about, but they knew nothing about living the life. They could always go back to being a mamma's boy if things got tough. That option was not available to folks who had to make the best of what life threw at them." She took a long pull on her Schlitz, then dragged a hand across her mouth wiping away the froth. "America is the richest country in the world, but you'll still find more poor folks here than in Western Europe, and I don't mean just blacks and a thousand Hispanic and Asian varieties. Working class whites still live near to the bread line, never knowing just how safe their jobs and homes are. It makes me sick how the *noveau riche* and the intellectuals pontificate about supporting the Third World, when the same conditions are prevalent in their own backyards. My mammy told me, at the height of the depression, over 5,000 people were located on a mile-long stretch of land beside the Mississippi River, south of the Municipal, now MacArthur Bridge. Within it were more than 600 shacks and four churches. It even had its own mayor and a suburb called Hoover Heights, named after President Hoover."

"Surely some things have improved for the better?" Natasha

argued.

"Sure, but it's all relative, isn't it?"

"You mean—"

She cut her off. "I mean, whatever the big cheeses and shot callers are getting, blue-collar workers still lag *way* behind them. My brother Duane went to vocational college, and got a job with the McDonnell Aircraft Corporation, later McDonnell-Douglas, as a fitter. He did well, but like me, the rest of my family have always been in semi-skilled jobs. My late husband spent his working life in construction, and all my children are either in the garment business or food processing. Apart from Duane, we've all had to endure tough times when the work dried up and we was on welfare, and that ain't much." She scrunched up her puss. "No, back in the fifties, we had no time to indulge in the beats' pursuits, and despite economic booms, they never last, and we come tumbling down the improvement ladder, the repo man recovering everything on finance. You people are young, and just looking at you, I can tell you're doing fine economically. So you have the disposable income to mix it with the beats." Raising their eyebrows, the English troupe conveyed surprise. "Oh yeah, they're still around, certainly the second and third generation variants, leftovers from the post-beat and hippie movements. I bump into them in the bars done up like 1930s speakeasies, and sometimes they eat in the same cafes I use. You can always fix them as being apart from regular folks. They can't help themselves from trying to cough up leading the bird of passage life."

"How?" Gail pumped.

"Ooohh…their mannerisms, the way they speak. It's like a throwback to when I was growing up, and I brushed up against real wanderers when my mammy took me shopping. The difference is, these fellas are playing at it, and it shows. Sure, there are still real hobos train-hopping and thumbing for lifts, but they have the marks of the real deal. Put them side by side with those guys who are just playing at it, and the difference is all too obvious."

"Do you adjudge we're playing at it?" Collins tabled, concerned for their integrity of purpose.

"No. You folks is tourists, observers of the environment you find yourselves in. You ain't participants or pretending to be neo-beats. Stay that way, and people like me will talk to you. Put on an act, and we'll piss all over you."

Leaving the barrelhouse, Delaney quipped to Collins, "If I'd told her Burroughs was born in St Louis, I doubt she'd have been impressed."

"Especially, if you'd said he came from a privileged background."

"Privileged background," Gail repeated. "How do you mean?"

"William Seward Burroughs II was the grandson of William Seward Burroughs I, the inventor of adding machines for banking functions. He founded the American Arithmometer Company in 1886. After his death, his business partner renamed it the Burroughs Adding Machine Company, later becoming the Burroughs Corporation. A major player in office machinery and later first-generation mainframe computers, it duplicated the rise of IBM, but like Honeywell, NCR and General Electric, remained a distant second to Big Blue in terms of sales."

"So, Burroughs's inheritance insulated him from the scrambles faced by his contemporaries, and the people he wrote about in his novels?"

"It's true to say, he attended Harvard to study the arts, and after graduation received a monthly allowance from his parents, enabling him to avoid regular work and pursue a bohemian lifestyle, at the very time Amelia and her ilk were struggling to stay alive."

Still keen to sample the heady mix of remembrance and nostalgia further, during the evening, the English contingent patronised more gin joints, looking out for Dust Bowl witnesses and beat mavens. Encountering a few candidates, those they engaged either mirrored Amelia's Great Depression viewpoint, or conversely, said it had brought about a cleansing of old regimes and practices when Roosevelt's New Deal eventually kicked in. Finding the progeny of the beat generation proved to be more problematical. They happened on a couple of contenders claiming some interaction, but cross-examination revealed them to be tricksters and imposters, out to con Collins and co into buying them drinks in exchange for genre elucidation. Already stoned on a meld of cocaine and alcohol, Delaney took exception to one faker, entering into a dressing down opposed by his target, and culminating in fisticuffs being thrown, Collins wrestling him away before the cops were called.

They did however happen on one nominee, a long-in-the-tooth, ex-boxer called Mungo Dawson, possessing the mark of credence regarding his interactions with beats landing in 1950s St Louis.

"I didn't meet any of the giants," he told them, "but I did rub shoulders with some of their foot soldiers. What you'd call plenipotentiaries. At the time, I was boxing out of Walter Kincaid's in Hamilton Heights. Some came into the club during training sessions, just to watch, before Walter shooed them away. Then they hung around outside. I got to know some of them. Often, I'd ask what they were doing. Habitually, they'd say, finding themselves. They'd heard or read some of the beat writers, and wanted to take the plunge, ditch regularity, and head out on the highway. See what was out there beyond conformity. They dressed kinda strange and frequently were bedraggled, but in the main, they were harmless. I got a feel for what they were searching for. It was something beyond a daydream, more like a calling. I can't say any of them ever came back, and said they'd found it. I got the impression what they were seeking had few definable peculiarities. You see, they talked in terms of concepts and theories. All very abstract stuff."

"What made you go into boxing, Mungo?" Collins sought, his journo snoopiness getting the better of his diplomatic side.

"I'd just turned nineteen when so-called business progress hit the light-engineering industry in forty-seven, and I lost my job. I'd boxed a bit at high school, so after applying for a whole passel of jobs in engineering, without success, I went to Walter's for a trial. Got through it, and boxed until I was thirty-five. Well, there ain't too many opportunities for a provincial ex-boxer, so I became a trainer. Still doing it."

Spending the night at the Crest Motel by the banks of the Mississippi, and within a few blocks of the Gateway Arch, the travellers reviewed their findings over a night cap.

"I don't know what I expected," Gail revealed, "but the people we met today were so grounded in reality, that it's difficult to believe the hipsters of cool infiltrated their ranks."

"Yep," Collins agreed. "They were representative of most US

working people. Just makes you realise what a small cartel the original beats were. Even if their second lieutenants are appended to the prime movers, I doubt it numbered more than fifty people nationwide."

"It's the same with any fresh coterie," Natasha nominated. "For instance, the Bloomsbury Group and the pre-Raphaelites both tallied barely twenty members. Sure, their admirers were in the hundreds maybe thousands in their lifetimes, and indubitably with the passage of time and word spreading, both have an international following in this day and age."

"Maybe we're still in the embryonic period for the beats," Delaney consigned. "Afterall, it's less than forty years since Kerouac first became published."

"A good point, Kallen," Collins applauded, "howbeit, there is evidence suggesting beat gen culture has spawned few new scintillating talents since the mid-sixties. Unequivocally, it provided the cornerstone for the hippie love generation and stalwart mainstream chroniclers such as Norman Mailer and Gore Vidal to record landmark and turning point events. Even Joan Didion borrowed from the beats, but like as Natasha says, their time was ephemeral, and we are just poking at the ashes hoping to find an ember still glowing."

That night, Collins couldn't sleep, his machinations still grading the personalities they'd met in St Louis. While he lay still, eyes wide open, Natasha slept without a whimper. She had the capacity to turn off the moment her head hit the pillow and be asleep within minutes, nothing bothering her. Collins envied the elusive faculty. Never able to extinguish his cognizance of happenings, and conjure up wondrous eclipses until the right chemicals were released inducing sleep, he had been a borderline insomniac since Babette entered his life. He had loved her dearly, but the waves she caused challenged his sensibilities to the point whereby he couldn't work out how to handle her. Since their divorce, the over-active cerebral syndrome had been sustained, often prompting restless nights. Almost as if she had provided the stimulus, once awakened the tendence to insomnia took on a vivacity all of its own. With her out of his life, he had assumed run-of-the-mill sleep patterns ought to resume. But no, much to his consternation, he found a myriad of totally unrelated matters plagued him on the run up to sleep. They could be anything, from issues facing him at *Performance* to the miniscule in the grand scheme of things. If about to engage in some pleasurable pursuit, he found himself planning it as soon as he shut his eyes, or once in play like the Route 66 outing, occurrences concomitant from the peregrination danced around in his consciousness, as if demanding more attention. Toying with the idea of prescription sleeping tablets, he relented when his GP advised they could be addictive. Though nothing life threatening, having enough addictions and hangups already, he estimated the cumulative sum could present problems downline both physically and mentally, thereby sleep would have to arrive naturally.

By two, he gave up attempting to catch zee's, gently got out of bed without disturbing Natasha, and set out to walk by the banks of the muddy Mississippi. A cloudless night sky and full moon covered his presence as he took in the cavernous river expanse, his senses only interrupted by the odd traffic roar echoing amongst the downtown canyon-like skyscrapers, and a night flight from Lambert International Airport soaring over the city.

Always an avid film buff, movie characters and content often influenced his world appreciation and meditative processes. After viewing John Ford's *The Grapes of Wrath* whilst at grammar school, he had acquired Steinbeck's novel of the same title. Devouring the plot within days, the ramification of the Dust Bowl and the Great Depression hit home, over a million Midwest displaced farmers settling in California between 1933 and 1939, when in 1935 the entire population of California numbered six million, the tumult surfacing in his cognition as the night stole over him on the river's shoreline, giving enormous credence to Amelia's account. Over the next five decades, the west coast state's inhabitants rose to thirty million. Collins knew such economic, political and natural disasters customarily led to massive global migrations, sparking violent unrest and corresponding impoverishment for the indigenous citizenry. California stood alone as being contrary on the score, the state booming with the onset of war machine production for the fight against Japan, and the ever-growing Hollywood film industry.

Forever hankering to increase his knowledge base, Collins had looked into the early history of American film, noting that supplementary to paramount actresses typified by Mary Pickford and Lillian Gish, it supported a relatively steep number of women in key roles, some directors, others, studio bosses. In a fledgling enterprise, no room existed for gender roles, the most able and talented people coming to the fore. Labour relations were loose, demarcation lines far into the vacant distance, everybody pitching into the film process without any notions of constraint. With market take-up and thereby monetary success, the studios started yielding their clout, particularly over the actors. Reacting against the imposition, Mary Pickford accompanied by Charlie Chaplin, Douglas Fairbanks and director D. W. Griffith launched their own production company, United Artists, closely followed by the unionisation of the American film industry, Collins noting the dynamic shifted from employee cooperative to employee uncooperative. Money became the only motivator for all participants, and as in all ventures worshipping the mighty Franklin, once the pioneering studio execs had turned up their toes, Hollywood fell into the hands of the bean counters, knowing the cost of everything and the value of nothing, excellence in art sacrificed on the altar of political correctness and the lowest common denominator.

Occasionally, when music overlapped with film, *Performance* covered the offering in its weekly columns, Collins gaining access to the goings-on in Tinseltown. Dawning on him that the rise of the crass blockbuster series had gained pace in the early 1970s at the expense of quality films, he surmised the go-to-market policy was set to continue and worsen.

Meanwhile, the lingering big puzzle revolved around the music industry going the same way, crowning in the death of rock 'n' roll. Goggling at a lone cargo steamer trundling down the Mississippi, he cogitated on the future, its components indistinct, flaky, and extrapolating trends over the previous two decades, set to become a hive of mediocrities and never-beens, pronouncing on every facet of life, the new masters of the universe driving excellence in all spheres into the dust.

Shaking his head, he dismissed the onerous projection, reversed his step, and ambled back to the Crest Motel. Tomorrow he needed to be on top form again to lead his beat-gen hungry argonauts further into Kerouac's hinterlands.

Chapter 7: Swamp and Country Land

After the hubbub and razz of St Louis, the intrepid expeditionaries took Highway 44 heading south-west to Springfield, Queen City of the Ozarks, and also known as the birthplace of Route 66, though it is 512 miles from the official start in Chicago, Radio KTFN blasting out classic rock anthems on the Camaro's FM band radio, providing the score for the journey.

"Springfield has a chequered past," Collins told Natasha as they hit the city limits.

"In what respect?"

"It's very graphic," he benchmarked, in two minds whether to share the info.

"Come on, daddy-o, *give*."

"Well…after the American Civil War, between 1865 to 1867 the country entered into the Reconstruction era marking a significant civil rights period, gaining more momentum at the advent of the twentieth-century. Never comfortable with the Washington enforcement, in concert with many other states, Oklahoma reacted badly. During 1906, two black men were caught red-handed sexually assaulting white women, and one black had murdered a white man. A 2,000 strong mob broke into Springfield County jail and lynched all three of them at Gottfried Tower which held a replica of the Statue of Liberty, then burned the corpses in the courthouse square."

"You've not shocked me. I've read similar historical narratives and never been able to fathom why when slavery finished in the Americas, the blacks didn't go back to West Africa. As I understand it, the American Colonisation Society created Liberia between Salone, now Sierra Leone, and the Ivory Coast, and the country declared its independence in 1847. Emancipated slaves were returned to Liberia well before the start of the

American Civil War. When the Union prevailed in 1865, and the thirteenth amendment was ratified outlawing slavery, the bulk remaining should have made for Liberia."

"Yes, I've heard that supposition from other people."

"When our ancestors were enslaved by the Romans, they returned home in vast numbers after the Goths sacked Rome in the early fifth century. The same occurred in the nineteenth century, when one and a quarter million European slaves, many of them English, were liberated from the Otterman Empire's North African Barbary Coast by a combined Anglo-Dutch force. If the majority of black slaves chose to stay in the United States, surely they must have known they were in for even more trouble?"

"Someone told me about an Ira Berlin book published in the seventies explaining the dichotomy. If memory serves, when Lincoln gained the presidency in 1861, there were about 480,000 free blacks living in the US, about ten percent of the black population, mostly dispersed in the South. I can't remember the specifics, but Berlin intimated during the Civil War, blacks stayed in the south for economic reasons. Maybe at the termination of hostilities, the option of heading back to Liberia didn't appeal because they'd be worse off."

"Maybe, but surely the prospect of outright freedom should have overwritten any short-term economic gains? I mean, forcing the old South to accept blacks on equal terms was never going to be embraced in practice. Hence the rise of the KKK, and the enigma is still going on today."

"Yes, it seems legislating for disparate ethnic communities to live in the same society does not work. There will always be resentment. Sociology substantiates the only harmonious human societies are ethnically homogeneous in nature. For example, Sweden, Iceland and Israel."

"Precisely, so I guess blacks worked out they'd not be wanted, despite the passing of the 1865 thirteenth amendment. Thereby it made more sense not to look a gift horse in the mouth, and go for the Liberia provision."

"Well, as I say, it abides as a contradiction. Albeit, on the plus side, we wouldn't have had the blues, jazz and rhythm and blues, if all the blacks had left for Liberia."

"Oh, sure thing, rock and roll and all the sixties gen derivative music had foundations in those genres."

"When I got into backtracking the stimulus behind the British blues movement at school, I discovered Robert Johnson, Huddy Ledbetter, Chester Howlin' Wolf Burnett, and a whole host of black American blues legends from the 1920s right up to the 1960s. Back then, I took it for granted the blues had been wholly hatched by black Americans. In later years, when I became a fully-fledged music journalist, I dug deeper into the blues. In all probability, the blues was founded on English, Scottish and Irish folk songs played by the early settlers. What gives further credence to the premise is blues instruments and musical timings are of European origin, and most assuredly, the language is English."

"What else do you know about Springfield?"

"Only what I picked up back home. From my world, Springfield has a deep connection with country music, notably, the Ozark strain. The Ozark Mountain Daredevils hail from Springfield."

"Speaking of country, how far are we from Memphis and Nashville?"

"Ohh…both are to the south-east of Springfield, way off Route 66. Memphis must be about 300 miles, Nashville even further."

"Too late to build them into the schedule?"

"When I first conceived this sojourn, I looked at all the music and historical places peripheral to Route 66 within fifty miles. There are so many of them, that to take them all in, I figured we'd need to make this a two-months holiday. Don't forget, we're deviating well off the primary return traipse by taking in San Fran. I reckon to get back to Chicago in time for the return flight to Blighty, we're going to have to motor like a bat out of hell across the east-bound leg."

"Maybe next time we'll take in Memphis and Nashville."

"You got it, girl." He'd been hoping she'd produce the proposal. "We could make a second hike centred on Tennessee, Alabama and Louisiana, taking in Graceland, Muscle Shoals Sound Studio and New

Orleans jazz, as well as Memphis and Nashville. I mean, hey, for a musicologist like me, the opportunity to check out Sun Records and Florence Alabama Music Enterprises, and maybe talk to Sam Phillips and Rick Hall, would be an awesome good fortune."

"I wonder if Kallen and Gail are having similar fancies about deviating off Route 66 to take in outlying attractions?"

"Conceivably, yes." Pondering, he counselled, "We'll talk about it when we stop. If the consensus is for extension, then we'll have to re-schedule the return BA flight, and beg more time off from our employers."

"The last part could be difficult."

"For sure."

~ * ~

An altogether more relaxed environment than St Louis, after the jetsetters parked the Camaro and the Vet, they strolled around Park Central Square in downtown Springfield taking in the ambience. Never absolutely sure of what they might find in way station places, they kept an open mind and sharp eyes, always on the lookout for a sliver of the beats' pathway. Covering over 500 miles since leaving the Windy City, they had chased their noses, never prejudging people and places. Enduring eternally open to any circumstance falling into their path, they had basked in bohemian and blue-collar districts, sensing for a nugget of beat gen antiquity like they were pursuing the Holy Grail. Little had been harvested in terms of gold-standard leads, but they had immersed themselves in Americana and picked up first-hand accounts from the descendants of the Route 66 migration west after the twenty-nine crash and the Midwest Dust Bowl took hold. Juxtaposed to the commercial sightseer trail, characterised by Walt Disney World, the Johnson Space Centre and Universal Studios, they were unwrapping hidden America, the parts the politicians didn't want holidaymakers to see.

"Natasha and I were mulling over the possibility of expanding the trip to take in more places subsidiary to Route 66," Collins briefed. "What do you think?"

"Hah, must be providence," Delaney retorted. "Gail and I have discussed the prospect."

"Well, as I see it, the major hurdle to overcome is being accorded more leave from our employers. I could perchance swing it with *Performance*, by engaging in some journalistic work along the way. What about you guys?"

"I might be able to secure a further two weeks," Gail advised.

"Yeah, I could do the same," Delaney notified.

"How about you, Natasha?" Collins prompted.

"With a lot of cajoling, I could negotiate an extra fortnight."

"Right," Collins began, "I'll contact BA and trade in our return tickets for two weeks further down the trajectory. It will cost us more, but it will be worth it."

"So additional to San Fran," Gail began, "we could take in Roswell and Area 51."

"Plus the Bonneville Salt Flats," Delaney annexed.

"Yep, we can do all that," Collins confirmed, "and more besides as it comes into our focus along the way."

When the girls went off to do some girly things, Delaney struck up a conversation with Collins about Cold Turkey.

"You might deem this uncharitable," he allotted, looking pensive, "but I'm considering leaving the record label."

"You astound me. I *believed* you'd found your niche with Glen Montague."

"Yeah." Shrugging his shoulders, he conveyed an aura of self-loathing. "Glen's been good to me, but I'm getting itchy feet. Not so long ago, I got an approach from 4AD, but the label that really interests me is Creation. Alan McGee tells me they are surfing the club scene searching for power-pop bands to sign-up."

"Yes, I did hear that."

"Cold Turkey are going in a contrasting direction. Montague is keen to sign up a power-ballad band."

"*Really*! Hardly in keeping with Cold Turkey's art house indie roster."

"No, he's spreading his bets. Doesn't want to put all his eggs in the indie basket. *Hell*, soon he'll be bringing in the suits, dispensing with go-getters like me, and going corporate."

"Never. Glen is too much of a control freak to let a boardroom make decisions for him. It's much more likely Cold Turkey will be the target of a corporate predator, and he'll sell the company also demanding a place on the board."

"Hah, maybe. Anyways, he calculates indie bands might be on the wane, though my own research indicates American grunge fathered by Neil Young and Crazy Horse will become a major market, and the British indie market is yet to peak."

"Hhmm, I can empathise with his strategy. Power ballads from heavy rock outfits have surged up the singles charts in the 1980s. Foreigner's *I Want to Know What Love is* and Bonnie Tyler's *Total Eclipse of the Heart* both hit number one in the worldwide singles charts."

"I gather Montague is more partisan to taking a classic ballad, and applying a Phil Spectre-like wall of resonance production to it."

"In the right hands, it'd work beautifully. Neil Young instilled his own particular brand into the Drifters ballad, *On Broadway*, included on last year's *Eldorado* EP, turning the song into a *tour de force*, and keeping it in tune with grunge market expectations."

"Yeah, I can see that, but I can't see a major player like Neil Young ditching Reprise for Cold Turkey."

"No, Glen will have to come down the food chain to attract an established mainstream rock artist, and even then, persuading them to perform a classic ballad in a rock style might be difficult." Dwelling, he added, "If I had to make an educated guess as to the next gamechanger in terms of worldwide record sales, I'd be inclined to say it will come from grunge."

"Why?"

"Because I have the intuition there are legions of disenfranchised teenagers out there not remotely captivated by mainstream pop, and what has become 'corporate' rock. They are hoping for a new messiah in the mould of Jim Morrison or Ian Curtis, someone out on the periphery of the rock spectrum who can feel and feed their emotions, even inspire them."

"Know you of such an up and coming icon?"

"Last year, *Performance* sent me to Seattle to check-out the evolving grunge scene," he recapped, his enthusiasm not lost on Delaney. "Sub-Pop label founder Bruce Pavitt had called the office, saying they had signed several new Seattle bands including Mudhoney and Soundgarden, and that the local rock scene was about to explode. I saw Mudhoney, Screaming Trees, Alice in Chains and Soundgarden. Liked some of the material, but didn't assess it to be all that different to existing variations on the heavy metal formula. Then someone said I should go see Nirvana at the Central Tavern. At first, they seemed to be the same as the other bands I'd seen, then they played more piquant stuff, a cross between the fast and slow components of a Pixies song, and the raw energy of the Stooges with a Beatles flavour to the lyrics. I stayed until the end of the gig and talked to some of the audience. They told me the band's leader Kurt Cobain hit the spot perfectly because his songs bled emotion as well as energy. Got me ruminating."

"About a possible new king of kings, a good shepherd?"

"Yeah. Then later in the year, Sub Pop released Nirvana's first single *Love Buzz*, a cover version of the Shocking Blue prototype. I reviewed the single with positivity. It had been one of the standouts from the Central Tavern gig, but the studio had refined it into a potent anthem. Made me call Sub Pop, and Pavitt told me Nirvana's *Bleach* debut album of like songs was set for release June 1989, and the band were due to tour England in October. By the time we get back home, *Bleach* will have probably entered the charts."

"And you adjudge Nirvana could make it big time?"

"Like I say, there is a ready-made, as yet untapped teenage market for their kind of music. Could be they will be the next big thing."

"Maybe. Let's see."

"So, what you gonna do, Kallen?" he asked, his tone unmistakably critical. "Move on, or stay loyal with Cold Turkey."

"Well, *hah*...the other factor is," Delaney defended, "I've blown up a couple of times after ingesting too much Columbian marching powder, and it's come to Montague's attention. Behind that hip trendsetter façade he projects, he's quite a stickler for professionalism, even in the assemblage of badly behaving clients. So, before I get the push, I might elect to jump into McGee's arms."

"You might find McGee is of the same ilk. Whatever happens, you need to clean up your act."

"Meaning?"

"Quit behaving irresponsibly," he spat out without soothing colouration. "Control the cocaine habit."

"You've been known to indulge."

"True, but I don't let it run my life."

~ * ~

Swinging into Tulsa, the globetrotters were immediately struck by the city's rarified ambience, the downtown area carefully sculptured to mix megaliths and boulevards with landscaped municipal parks and an abundance of water monuments. Like all Oklahoma cities, Tulsa had become a bastion for the oil exploration industry, housing many corporate headquarters, and thereby maturing a thriving middle-class, with relatively few blue-collar workers. A modicum of tranquillity prevailed, as if the great god in the skies had bestowed the city with reverential status, it's citizens much more upbeat than the residents of St Louis and Springfield Missouri.

"Resplendent city," Collins complimented to a man sat at the bar of The Old Canteen, a once bedraggled honky-tonk blanched in beer and tobacco stains left over from the Great Depression, now revitalised via an extensive makeover.

"Oh, she's luscious," he commended. "Back in the 1950s, *Time* magazine dubbed Tulsa as America's most beautiful city. This is the buckle of the bible belt, son, Southern Baptists and all manner of evangelical offshoots, but what they have in common is an unbreakable faith in the Lord. For most workin' folks, when they're not sweatin' in the oil industry, they're prayin' in churches and the gospel houses, either that, or listenin' to the swamp and country music of J J Cale and Elvin Bishop."

Way before his music journalist career took off, Collins had caught the American blues and roots bug, delving into the oeuvres of

Sonny Boy Williamson, Jimmy Reed and Woody Guthrie, amongst a plethora of mahatmas energising the Rolling Stones, the Yardbirds and Bob Dylan. Diving further into the Yankee backwaters, he uncovered Ry Cooder and J J Cale, masters of the slide and Tulsa-style guitar, the former contributing to the Rolling Stones *magnum opus* album *Let it Bleed*, and the latter having a direction-changing impact on Eric Clapton, post the breakup of Cream. Throughout the seventies, Collins collected just about every Cooder and Cale album, never failing to be seduced by the sincerity and elegance of their work, the catchiness of the music coupled with down-home themes striking a chord with his ever-expanding valuation of American blues and roots music. Bishop too had drawn his admiration, his guitar workouts with the Paul Butterfield Blues Band and collaborations with Dylan stalwarts Al Kooper and Mike Bloomfield very much in tune with his blues-rock leanings.

"My name is Henry Collins."

"Bert Browning." Scrunching up his mien, he pronounced, "You ain't from Tulsa, is you?"

"No, England. Me and my band of buoyant beachcombers..." He indicated to them sat in a nearby booth. "...are checking out Dust Bowl survivors and searching for traces of beat generation ghosts."

"*Hah*, you don't say."

"We've been on the road since jetting into O'Hare International. Picked up some scents on I55 and I44. Beginning to get a first-hand account feeling for the debilitating aftermath of the Great Depression, and the spirit of the beats crusade, especially the personalities driving it."

"Well, your beats enterprise has fallen on stony ground with me, son. My knowledge of them is minimal, but I do know about the Dust Bowl." Ceasing, his frontage dropped into a venerating register. "With one hell of an effort, my parents dealt with the bugbears of the 1930s depression."

"They told you about it?"

"*Hah*—" He took off his Stetson, then wiped his brow with a neckerchief. "Just about every day from the moment they perceived I'd grasp it. My brothers and sisters got the same treatment. We were taught to count our chickens, always keep an eye on the economic barometer, and never to get into debt. I still abide by those constraints, and have relayed them on to my offspring."

"We've been hearing similar approaches about staying solvent from folks in Missouri and Illinois."

"Doesn't stagger me. Great Depression legacy will never be ignored in these parts." Breaking off, he scanned around the bar area. "You should really have a word with Gawen Trescothick." He pointed to a tall, slim fellow with greying hair, dressed in a pinstripe suit and shiny brogues, sipping a tumbler of rye, at the opposite end of the bar. "We call him 'The Seer'. He's an educated man, and can converse in Latin. He's also a regular Anglophile, and has a good comprehension of beat culture."

"You don't say," Collins reacted, his inquisitory juices beginning to flow.

"Go ahead," Browning bolstered. "He won't bite you, and he can tell you things that the rest of us can't."

Summoning his cohorts, Collins and co sloped off in the given direction, arresting short of their target.

"Excuse me." The slender gent half-turned to eye Collins. "Mister Trescothick?"

"At your service, sir. And who might you be?"

"Henry Collins."

"Robust moniker, and judging by your intonation, you come from Blighty." Scanning Collins' contingent, he nominated, "I take it the rest of your brigade are also English?"

"All born and bred in Albion."

"Good to meet you," he exalted with good heart. "Complementing your lineage, I can trace my own ancestry back six generations to Cornwall."

"Not surprising. You have a traditional Cornish Christian and surname."

"Inherited from my grandfather, on my father's side. His great grandfather Tristan Trescothick and his family came ashore at Cape Cod in 1798 to escape the clutches of the excisemen at Porthallow."

"Some chicanery in your bloodline then?"

"Just let's say —" A touch of devilment distilled in his dial.

"Tristan was a gentleman farmer, who had a side-line in importing French brandy. He went toe-to-toe with being caught by the excisemen for several years. Then a set of unforeseen circumstances led to him and his family liquidating their assets, and sailing for the New World, before the revenue officials could catch him in the act. It's a hereditary tale I've always been proud to recount. Can't say I've ever been an admirer of the establishment, so I suspect monkey business runs in the family."

"Sounds like you are a rebel."

"Only in the nicest possible way," he assured, grinning. "I just like to tweak the tail of authority. That's been an English trait since time immemorial."

"True."

"I adore English audacity, from Lord Nelson to the Scarlet Pimpernel, Winston Churchill to George Smiley. There's a uniqueness about the English temperament, readily lending itself to daring, valour and fearlessness, regardless of overwhelming odds. Admiral qualities, rarely found beyond the English."

"Maybe it's because we're an island race."

"Yes, *that's* it." His visage broke into a radiant veneer. "*This royal throne of kings, this sceptered isle. This earth of majesty, this seat of Mars. This other Eden, demi-paradise. This fortress built by nature for herself against infection and the hand of war. This happy breed of men, this little world. This precious stone set in the silver sea which serves it in the office of a wall or as a moat defensive to a house against the envy of less happier lands. This blessed plot, this earth, this realm, this England.*"

"The Duke of Lancaster's speech from Richard II."

"Indeed. I can't remember the remaining sixteen stanzas."

"Nonetheless, a sterling effort."

"Thank you." Adopting a curious demeanour, he probed, "What brings you to Tulsa?"

"We're adventurers, hot on the beat gen trail and seeking sources of illumination."

Peeking at Browning, he checked, "And Bert pointed you in my direction?"

"Correct."

"How much time have you got?"

"Ohh, time does not lay heavy on our shoulders for a few hours."

"The reason I table the question, is because I've been known to waffle on about the beats for some time, dependent upon what arises from the vaults."

"We're all ears."

"Well, children…sorry that's a bit condescending. Well, questers…is that better?"

"It suits us."

"As a young man at prep school and college, I devoured Blake, Shelley and Keats before moving onto Forster, Waugh and Somerset Maugham. Automatically, in parallel, I delved into American literature, explicitly Sinclair Lewis and Jack London. My fascination with English writers continued into my late twenties, then I happened upon Jack Kerouac's first novel, *The Town and the Country*, and refereed it to be highly inspired by Thomas Wolfe, and nothing that special. Albeit, I was sufficiently attracted by Kerouac's approach that I bought *On the Road*. Employing an altogether more innovative writing technique, it had me mesmerised, and I made it my goal to find out a whole lot more about Kerouac and his clan of beat writers and poets. Over the subsequent years, I attended readings by Kerouac, Ginsberg, Burroughs and a whole host of beat crackerjacks. Got to chat with a lot of them. Found out what made them tick. By 1970, I'd accumulated over forty beat generation works. To me, the undivided beat ensemble resonated with a passion for finding the obscure and the enigmatic as sources for writing. In many ways, the evolution of English and American literature from the seventeenth century onwards, has been an exercise in distilling writer autobiography into glorious fiction. The beats continued that tradition, but enhanced its baseline model with writing styles and subject matters outside of the recognised norm, enabling a tandem strand of beat gen works to provoke writers like Charles Bukowski and Anthony Burgess into action. Undeniably, it all started at Columbia where Kerouac met Ginsberg, then transferred to New York, principally Greenwich Village, where Burroughs came into play and the burgeoning syndicate horsed around with abstract impressionists' de Kooning and Pollock. Then the West Coast joined the circle when Ginsberg visited Neal Cassidy in San Fran, and Ferlinghetti, McClure and others became fused with the New York set. That embryonic cartel derived a singular lifestyle based on sexual freedom, drugs, jazz, French surrealism and the English romantic poets."

"You mentioned jazz," Delaney remarked. "Isn't it true the word 'hipster' ultimately replaced the slang 'hepcat', pretty much meaning a jazz subculture devotee of decades earlier?"

"Unequivocally. Hipsters were in constant pursuit of whatever was deemed to be 'cool', and the slang term survives to this day. In the late-1940s, that included a combination of jazz and bebop, or bop music, a take-off on jazz, but with a quicker beat and lots of improvisation. Many beat poets used the bebop tempo and improvisation mode as a basis to create their work, and in the sixties, rock outfits like the Byrds, the Grateful Dead and Cream took jazz improvisation as a tool to extemporise on their studio work for live performances, four-minute gems becoming five or six times longer via improvised instrumental breaks."

"Yes, Roger McGuinn has gone on record stating the Byrds acid rock classic *Eight Miles High* instrumentation was highly influenced by jazz saxophonist John Coltrane. When played live, the song developed a life all of its own, the Byrds often jamming on the instrumental break for over ten minutes."

"That number was also touched by Dylan's *Blonde on Blonde* album; applauded as a pathway to a higher consciousness of spectral awareness, and worshipped by hippies. Inevitably, though McGuinn and Gene Clark maintained *Eight Miles High* was about a flight to London, the establishment perceived the lyrics centred on drug abuse, and it became banned from radio airtime, it's meagre success as a single chiefly resulting from word of mouth to those in the know."

"Another beat-speak borrowed by sixties rock artists and acid rock adherents meaning an incredible amount of fun was 'a gas'," Natasha commemorated, "as in the Stones *Jumpin Jack Flash it's a gas, gas, gas*."

"Quite correct, young lady. There's a whole vocabulary of beat words and phrases enabling its purveyors to have an entire dialogue without resorting to Webster's dictionary and conventional conversation." He sniggered. "One that always beguiled me revolves around a woman rejecting a man's advances. If the chick nixes the 'back scat bingo', a phrase devoted to the fine art of kissing, or making out with a girl in a car, she'd be 'bad news'. Howbeit, it's important to note that it's not the act of rejection, but the person themselves who is the 'bad news'. You follow?"

"Yes," Natasha affirmed.

"There are many others, for example, 'Yo, I heard on the clothesline that she is sleeping with Tommy. She is such a chipper.' Clothesline meaning gossip, and chipper, a woman that's easy. And 'I don't know what her problem is, but she gives me the frigidaire every time I see her.' Frigidaire, meaning cold shoulder."

"Yes," Gail verified, "we've been hearing the odd hipsterism en route, namely, 'juicer', 'kale', 'frado' and 'tassel'."

"Well, if you've heard those terms, your quest is indisputably hitting the right ballpark."

"Isn't it also true," Collins initiated, "that the beats took onboard the precepts of Buddhism and Daoism?"

"Indeed, and the practices were embraced by beatniks, hippies, and dominant sixties rock icons the Beatles, the Doors and Donovan."

"Have you ever experienced any downside within the beats movement?" he tentatively asked, as if the question implied a negative.

Pondering, Trescothick retraced, "I once met some grifters in New Orleans alleging to know William Burroughs and Jack Kerouac. Playing along with them, it soon became patent they'd heard the names, but were entirely in the dark regarding their occupations."

"How did that come about?"

"Ohh, I was in Orleans on business, the details I will not bore you with, other than to say it involved a humongous amount of Franklins. Now—" Inherently vexed by the tale, he blanched. "When you've got money to invest in a vibrant, succulent city like New Orleans, word soon goes around, and the hawks and vultures begin to gather, including cardsharps and bunco booth bandits, like the grifters I ran into. I'd been talking to a local dignitary having a penchant for Thomas Pynchon and Tom Robbins, both swayed by 1950s beat literature. After that most pleasant interlude, they purloined me under the guise of intimate relations with Burroughs and Kerouac, but really it was an intended softening up exercise before relieving me of my money. I saw it coming, so engineered a withdrawal course, leaving them looking for another mark to suck dry. The incident taught me that professed association with the superintendents of any genre can loosen the defences culminating in calamity. Fortunately, I had my predilection for rye under control and my wits about me on that occasion."

Hypnotised by his recollections, Trescothick went on to entertain the Collins congregation before he had to crave their indulgence to depart because of a set-in-concrete engagement. Leaving an everlasting indent on their beats appraisal, they hoped for further productive interactions with beat savants during their Route 66 junket.

Chapter 8: Twister Territory

Collins had established Oklahoma City fared no better than St Louis during the Great Depression. Although the state agriculture had been in the doldrums for a decade, signs of the economic downturn only emerged in 1930 as drought hit the region creating the infamous Dust Bowl, rural Oklahomans seeing farm income fall by sixty-four percent. It coincided with the East Texas oil field opening, creating a petroleum glut and rapidly falling oil prices in the existing Oklahoma oil exploration industry causing extensive layoffs. By the winter of 1932, joblessness exceeded 300,000. Relief came a few years later from Roosevelt's New Deal programme, but by then the city had its own 'Hooverville' community camp along the North Canadian River, a sustained feature during World War II until the economic boom of the 1950s.

Rolling into Mondales, a bar on rundown South-West 25th Street in the Capitol Hill district of Oklahoma City, stacked out with blue-collar oil workers ravenous for refreshment after a gruelling shift on the rigs, Collins and his buddies got friendly with Grenville Draper, a grizzled well-driller of thirty-years standing with a limp left eye resultant from an oilrig blowout, asking him about his episodes.

"My pappy told me, back in the twenties" Draper footnoted, "Capitol Hill boasted top-drawer departmental stores and solid citizens. When the crash came, it went downhill fast and stayed that way. Got even worse when the Crossroads Mall opened in seventy-four, but that's typical of most urban city locales. The upwardly mobile want to live in the exclusive enclaves on the periphery of Ok City, so what's left is a kinda glorified shanty town for workers. It's also a refuge for down-and-outs and the odd weirdo breezin' in to check out for juke joints, barrelhouses and clip joints." Issuing the English contingent a suspicious look, he posed, "Say, you boys and girls aren't freaks are you?"

"No," Collins replied, breaking into a grin. "We're argonauts."

"*Argonauts*," Draper lustily repeated. "What you searchin' for?"

"We're tracking down the beats' shadow."

"Oh."

"You know anything about the beats?"

"Some."

"Got any personal exposure to them?" he investigated, sensing another rewarding source of elucidation.

"Well, *huh*…when I was at high school, Jim Thompson…you know him?"

"Writer of *The Killer Inside Me* and *The Grifters*," Delaney supplied.

"Yeah, I believe you're right. Well, Thompson gave a lecture to my high-school student fraternity. I don't know if you can call him one of the beats?"

"He was decidedly in the ballpark in terms of his expositions, and the style in which he expressed himself in the written word," Collins qualified.

"Well, he did have an impact on some of my classmates, because a couple went off to New York after graduating with aspirations to become writers. I don't know what happened to them, but I've never seen their names in print."

"What about you, Grenville?" Natasha enquired. "Were you tempted by Thompson's words?"

"Ohh—" He half-smiled, his head drooping. "I come from a poor background. My folks couldn't afford to send me to college. I was always destined for the oil rigs, just like my two older brothers and my pappy. I started off as a floorhand, assistin' riggin' up and down, layin' rods, tubin' and casin', and doin' the odd bit of crew truck drivin'. Then I became a derrickhand doing much the same thing, with the addition of well servicin' tasks. Right now, and for the past ten years, I've bin a rig operator for the Broadbent Corporation, managin' the rig and the crew team. It's where the real money is on the rigs. That's my crew, you've bin eyeballin'. Bin comin' to Mondales all my workin' life. Though I could go upmarket, old habits are hard to break." Gawping away he fell silent, wrinkled lineaments forming around his eyes, as if he had accepted his fate, but way back when had ambitions elsewhere.

"We met another oil man in Cleveland Sam's, Springfield Illinois," Natasha outlined, breaking the awkward impasse. "Homer Calhoun, working for the Kosmos Petroleum Corporation out of Houston."

"Doesn't startle me. There are more people workin' in the oil industry than most other industries in the US, and most frequent speakeasies and roadhouses."

"He's an ex-beat made good."

"That so." Unfolding a mischievous grin, he babbled, "Bet you didn't know Thompson was born in Oklahoma."

"No," Delaney admitted. "I always conjectured he came from California."

"Yeah, well that's a damned sight more fashionable than Capitol Hill, or any other Oklahoma boondock."

Carrying on chewing the cud with the affable oilman, Draper recalled more about his life journal, the English contingent building their knowledge of blue-collar working life, first hand. Transpired for various family-related reasons, he'd never been out of the state, never seen the ocean, Lake Texoma south of Ok City the closest he'd got to a mass of surface water, though one of his sons had sent him a postcard from Santa Barbara, showing the Pacific.

"Actor Lon Chaney Jr came from Oklahoma City," Draper almost boasted. "He played the role of Lennie Small in *Of Mice and Men*. My pappy went to see the movie. He told me, he looked just like the men who headed west during the Great Depression."

"Yes, a lot of people maintain," Gail began, "Steinbeck's novels and films based on his work captured the zeitgeist perfectly."

"I've got some old brown and white photographs from that era, some my pappy took of Dust Bowl families holed up along the Canadian River, livin' like sewer rats, scroungin' about for a few hours work and a crust before finally throwin' in the towel, and headin' out on Route 66."

Later when the Collins entourage checked into the Slattery Motel on South-East 44th Street, they re-examined their confab with Grenville

Draper.

"I can't even begin to imagine not seeing the ocean in a lifetime," Natasha lamented.

"It's just another thing we take for granted," Collins deciphered. "There must be millions of working-class Americans like Grenville, who will spend their plenary lives in the state they were born into, particularly in the Midwest. Makes me appreciate more than ever, the worldview image of the United States, where everybody lives the upper crust life, is simply incorrect. I got my first contact with the reality driving from Anaheim to Oakland when I covered the 1978 Rolling Stones US tour for *Crossroads*. Instead of taking I5 all the way, I branched off at Kettleman City and took in the boonies whilst continuing to head north-north-west. The artery snaked into rundown small towns and settlements, distinguished by chaparral, near desertion, and meagre facilities. Here I was in the richest state of the richest country in the world, and if not for knowing my actual whereabouts, I could have taken it for some desolate Third World acheron."

"So, the people looked poor?"

"Yeah." He pursed his lips, the remembrance charged with misgivings. "Like throwbacks from a Steinbeck creation set in the 1930s. Beaten-up trucks and fifties sedans littered the streets, most of the general stores, still family owned. Old men and kids sat out under porches, reading aging editions of *Automotive News*, and kicking tin cans. It was like corporate America had passed them by, concluding there was no business to be had here."

"What did they do for a living?" Delaney pressed.

"As I motored through the communities, I postulated the same mystery to myself. I guessed they were mainly farm hands."

"Just goes to show," Gail put forward, "the capacious chasm between the mega-rich and those not even on the politicians' radar."

"For sure," Collins yielded. "It's a bipartition the beats regularly ran into during their jaunts overarching the States."

"Hhmm, we don't seem to be finding too many people directly connected to the beat generation," Delaney recounted. "Most we engage are workers with heritages going back to the turn of the century. In that respect, we're in the lap of the gods. If we do crash into the real McCoy, it will be happenstance, kismet."

"Yep, you're right, Kallen," Collins consented, "but on the positive side, we're gaining a discernment of the real America few holidaymakers undergo, and having a splendid time in the process. What say you girls?"

"Absolutely," Natasha agreed. "It's the freedom of the road that is really setting this excursion apart from past ventures."

"Yes," Gail backed. "We have unabridged *carte blanche* to do whatever we like. Even if we don't run into prime time, *bona fide* beats, this venture is still providing a whole host of highs. It's the sheer exposure to the American hinterlands that fascinates me. Our choice to eat at honky-tonks, drink in gin joints and stay in motels is giving a wholly multifarious dimension to the Route 66 crossing. I wouldn't change anything."

"Yeah, that's it," Natasha endorsed. "Let's just go with the flow."

Approaching midnight, Collins and Natasha were sat up in bed watching Johnny Carson interview Joan Rivers on his NBC show, their attention wafting in and out dependent on River's hilarious retorts to Carson's judicious pumps.

"Harking back to our earlier debate about the likelihood of meeting real beats," Natasha begun, "if we do, will we be either impressed or disappointed?"

"Jesum crow! That's a loaded paradox. I hadn't considered the possibility of either being elated or disillusioned." Pondering, he appended, "I suppose I'll be more persuaded by what they have to say, rather than how they dress, or come over."

"And running into one of the greats is off the scale?"

"Apart from if Ferlinghetti and Kesey happen to be hanging out at City Lights when we put down in San Fran, I'd say we have a better chance of happening upon newly elected President Bush than say Ginsberg, Corso or Burroughs. You see, after becoming acclaimed, many of the beat generation writers and poets tended to fade away into obscurity, some because they craved solitude, others because they were burnt out, but their status, their prestige and distinction has survived."

Pausing, he offered, "It's like *Ready, Steady, Go* has everlasting cult status, whereas lesser TV music shows fail to achieve kudos."

"That's an enticing comparison." She swivelled her head to address him. "What *happened* to *RSG*?"

"That conundrum has foxed pundits over many a year," he shared, his own incredulity at the show's demise transparent to her. "When I first joined *Crossroads*, Grady Melrose, a much more seasoned journalist told me, in December 1966 just before Rediffusion pulled the plug on the show, the magazine interviewed teenagers regarding why their love affair with *RSG* had waned, crowning in falling studio audiences at the Associated-Rediffusion studio in Kingsway. *RSG* had become patronised by rhythm & blues and rock junkies, plus the Mods, after the likes of the Who, the Kinks, the Rolling Stones, the Small Faces and the Yardbirds first set down on the show. Then producer Vicki Wickham started to fill the schedule with Dusty Springfield and American soul acts, much to the displeasure of the original core audience, who seeped away."

"Vicki Wickham is a lesbian, isn't she?"

"Just so, as is Dusty Springfield."

"Surely, with her actions killing off *RSG*, Wickham must have felt like a real horse's arse?"

"Well put it this way, she never worked in television or any media again, whereas anchorman Keith Fordyce ripened his career in both tv and radio, and is still at the forefront of rock, fellow presenter Cathy McGowen to a lesser extent."

"So, the Wickham-Springfield duo scuppered England's premier music show?"

"Well, apparently Wickham might have been having an affair with Springfield accounting for her grabbing the limelight on *RSG*. Certainly, the Wickham-Springfield combination transposed the whole ethos of the show to soul, and with that the nucleus audience melted away. On the back of the American soul artists appearing on *RSG*, Motown Records organised a nationwide UK package tour. Grady told me the junket was a washout, poorly attended and Motown lost a bundle of the folding stuff, but more significantly, the soul artists claimed that by not attending their gigs, British audiences were being racist."

"*What!*" she yapped, her veneer dimmed in disbelief. "That's ridiculous. Good god, the number of rock bands suffering near-to deserted gig venues in their formative years is legion, and includes the Rolling Stones and John Mayall's Bluesbreakers. Why should those uppity soul artists have the gall to smear British youth of the time, just because they didn't like their music?"

"Yes," he morosely regretted. "Disingenuous is an understatement. Using current vernacular, I have to say it was a case of bmw - bellyaching or bitching, moaning and wailing, and highly insulting to the Zoot suit and Mod generation."

"So, Ms Wickham tried to indoctrinate them by pushing her soul agenda down their throats, hence the kids looked elsewhere, and *RSG* went into decline."

"Precisely. However, the odd thing is Fordyce and McGowen were hip to the London scene, and in 1966 British blues took off at Eel Pie Island and the Marquee, plus psychedelic music had arrived, all attracting *RSG* onlookers. After Rediffusion terminated *RSG*, most of their audience fled to the West London blues clubs, and the UFO Club on Tottenham Court Road to see Pink Floyd. If Rediffusion had been smart, they'd have celebrated the trend with say 'RSG2' hosted by Keith and Cathy, and caught the bourgeoning progressive-underground movement with Cream, the Jimi Hendrix Experience and Peter Green's Fleetwood Mac, leading to Led Zeppelin and King Crimson."

"Yes, I see your reasoning. Mod aroused psychedelia and progressive."

"Uh-huh, and with it, the compression of ideas and musical themes into three-to-four-minute songs."

"Such as *I Can See for Miles*, *Purple Haze* and *Tales of Brave Ulysses*?"

"Affirmative. Albeit, irony of ironies, *Beat-Club*, the weekly-screened German equivalent of *RSG* with Cathy McGowen lookalike Uschi Nerke, became inaugurated in 1965 and went on until 1972. They had all the English bands on the show that the quintessential *RSG* gallery liked, and went on to cover the progressive rock genre with the MC5, the Doors, Frank Zappa, Captain Beefheart and an additional raft of evolving

American and British rock artists. Meanwhile, the televised rock scene in the UK persisted mainly dormant, apart from the odd very fleeting show like *Colour Me Pop* and *Disco 2*."

"Yes, neither the BBC nor independent television really caught onto the blossoming rock market, not even after the blistering success of Woodstock and the Isle of Wight Festivals."

"No, once again the Germans took the torch with *Rockpalast* launched in 1974, and set to go on *ad infinitum* as the world's premier rock show screening weekly, hour-long in concert performances by Steve Miller, the Patti Smith Group and Spirit, to name but a few rock headliners." He dwelt. "Anyway, we digress. Just coming back to beat spotting, it's going to be a matter of the stars aligning."

"Meaning?"

"Being in the right place at the right time, and that will come down to pure coincidence."

~ * ~

Continuing their venture into Oklahoma, I40 took the pilgrims into a series of small towns, most characterised by an abiding dependence on state farming support for their continued wellbeing. General stores come seven-elevens, rundown restaurants, pool halls, gas stations and roadhouses, their Wurlitzers still playing Hank Williams and Johnny Cash, served the sharecroppers and cattlemen, as well as those in transit, heading east or west. But for the Vet and the Camaro, Collins and his troupe could have entered the 1930s Dust Bowl, little to differentiate that grievous time from the present in terms of modernisation.

Giving way to billowing clouds and strong winds, the early morning's clear skies became grey, rain and hailstones pelting into the muscle cars.

"Our first bad weather day," Collins reviewed, now in the Corvette with Natasha, and flashing by water-towers and telegraph poles at a steady seventy-five.

"We've been lucky so far."

"Better slow down to fifty-five." Easing off the gas, he spied in his rearview mirror, Delaney and Gail in the Camaro looming large before decelerating.

Occasionally, juggernauts and farm vehicles passed them by on the opposite carriageway, the turbulent downpour hitting the Vet's windows making the traffic into irregular shapes. With the potent gale sucking and blowing, the occupants sensed the car's suspension dipping and jerking, Collins slowing to forty, Delaney following suit. Then it decayed, the torrent ceasing and the chinook dropping, the drivers increasing speed back to fifty-five. Soon after, Collins heard the Camaro's horn, it's signal Morse-like, as if intended to convey a message.

"What's up now?" he reacted, checking his mirror again, and seeing the Camaro's lights flashing.

Peeping over her left shoulder to the south-east, Natasha blurted, "*Good god*, there's a twister coming up on us."

"*What!*" Spying into the mirror again, he clocked Delaney gesturing for him to get a move on. "That peppering cloudburst and blustering front must have been the forerunner."

With the road ahead empty, he floored the accelerator, Delaney replicating his action, Vet and Camaro streaking along the highway, Natasha and Gail monitoring the track of the twister.

"Oh, it's not a big one," Collins adjudged, glancing behind. "We should be alright."

"Looks *big* enough to me," Natasha contradicted.

Ploughing on, they kept ahead of the advancing menace, though its attendant driving deluge and gusting squalls consumed them again.

"Might deviate off," Collins stipulated. "Often they do."

"No, it's getting closer, but appears to be running contiguous to the road."

Inspecting ahead, Collins scanned the landscape for a refuge, but it resided as a matrix of undulating fields and scrubland.

During a flight from Washington to LA years earlier, the 737's captain had come on the intercom extolling passengers to look down at three mid-sized twisters, thirty-thousand feet beneath them, moving across Oklahoma. To Collins, their funnels behaved like graceful rotating chimneys, but they hid a package of death and destruction. Beginning in the spring, from Indiana to Texas encompassing Oklahoma, the Midwestern States are often hit by tornadoes until summer's end, due to warm air masses moving northward from the south-eastern states bordering on the Gulf of Mexico, and combining with colder air masses wavering southward from Canada.

"We're going to have to out-run it."

"Oh, Henry. Is that going to be safe?"

"We don't have any other choice. If we slow or stop, the cars could be sucked up into the twister vortex."

Not the only ones fleeing from the typhoon, ahead Collins saw a parade of vehicles hightailing it, within tens of seconds the Corvette and the Camaro catching up with the traffic. The chase continued for several miles, the twister weaving to and fro, its path sustained near-to parallel to the highway, less than a mile away. Then Collins saw a placard on the side of the road proclaiming, 'You are now entering Texas, the Lone Star State. Drive carefully'. Miraculously, the twister slowed then veered towards the highway, heading north, Delaney watching it in his rearview mirror dance across I40 in the direction of Dodge City. As they sped into Texas, it faltered and broke up, ferocious sleet and monsoon winds ceasing.

"Who'd have thought it!" Natasha chuntered. "Chased out of Oklahoma by a hurricane."

Chapter 9: Making Out in the Twilight Zone

Hanging out in Josiah's Surf 'n' Turf diner in downtown Amarillo, Collins and co recovered from their twister escapade, then discussed calling in at Roswell. Made internationally famous by the 1947 'Roswell Incident' alleging a UFO crashed at nearby Foster ranch discovered by foreman Mack Brazel, the locale had achieved cult status.

"If we do elect Roswell, we'll miss out on the Cadillac Ranch," Collins alerted.

"Just remind me what that is, daddy-o?" Gail requested.

"It's a public art installation and sculpture, comprising ten successive generations of brightly painted caddies, 1949 to 1963, buried nose-first in the ground, defining the evolution of their tail fins."

"And it's on I40, west of Amarillo?"

"Yes, whereas we need to take I27 for Roswell."

"I suppose, something's got to give," Natasha articulated, "and given the option, I'd still plump for Roswell."

"Inspecting the map," Delaney advised, "Roswell is about 175 miles south-west of Amarillo." Pausing, he supplemented, "And…." He beamed. "….Lubbock, birthplace of Buddy Holly, is 160 miles due south of Amarillo."

"Much as I admire Buddy Holly," Collins responded, "if we take in both, it will add two days to the outbound leg. How about a compromise, and we do one out of the two?"

After some four-way debate, the vote came down in favour of Roswell.

"I'm not interested in the town or the UFO museum," Gail weighed. "It's the actual site I'd like to see."

"Yeah," Delaney approved. "Just getting a look and feel could provide a rush. See if there are any traces left in the landscape."

"Well, if it really did happen," Collins conditioned, "it's said the military authorities removed all UFO evidence from the crash site, including alien bodies, and transported both to top-secret Area 51 in Nevada, though the official line centred on a crashed weather balloon."

"True," Delaney okayed, "but the ranchers who pored over the crashed UFO are still about. Be good to talk to them."

"*If* we found them, Kallen," Natasha cautioned, "would they really open up to us?"

"There's only one way to find out. But before we do that, I need a fix."

"You'll never find a cocaine dealer in Amarillo," Gail predicted.

"Watch me."

Twenty minutes later, Delaney rebounded, his face emblazoned with zest, his pupils already dilating.

"I don't believe it," Natasha jabbered.

"Have cocaine, will travel," Delaney snapped out. "Snow is so ubiquitous, especially here in the US. As well as in the giant metropolis's, it can be obtained in just about every backwater, even in the staunchly conservative Texas Bible Belt."

"One day, you're going to get caught receiving, or busted for possession," Collins warned. "If that happens during our road trip, it won't be a smack on the wrist like in Blighty. You'll get a hefty fine, and time in the slammer."

"Look—" He nonchalantly fanned out his hands in a gesture of contempt. "Cocaine users number the millions in the US. If the authorities jailed every user, they'd have to build a whole new raft of prisons. The costs are prohibitive. That's why most of the DEA efforts go into nailing the producers and the major dealers."

"True, but it's the local cops who target users. Caught, and we could be saying adios to you for some time, and Glen Montague would fire your arse from Cold Turkey."

"Ooohh, man, you're making with the bad vibes," he complained, his peepers blooming even more, "just when I'm hitting lunar orbit. Come on, let's head for *Twilight Zone* territory."

By mid-afternoon, the Camaro and the Corvette were winding

their way along a minor road north-west of Roswell to the Foster Ranch. Before reaching the destination, they saw a man on horseback rounding up some strays. Desisting, Collins got out of the Corvette and waved to him. Dressed in archetypal cowpoke mode and displaying an unfettered moustache, he glanced at Collins, then sauntered over to the outsiders.

"You goin' up to the ranch house?" he questioned.

"We er…want to talk to Mister Brazel."

"About steers?"

"No, er…about the Roswell incident."

"You reporters or from the government?"

"No, we're just vacationers."

"Curious about somethin' that happened long ago?"

"That is the truth of it."

"No need to bother Mack. He's gettin' a bit long in the tooth to receive inquisitors." Swivelling in his saddle, he pointed to a distant gorge. "You see that hollow?"

"Uh-huh."

"Take a walk around there. That's where it crashed, but you won't find a damned thing. Government men took away all the evidence back in forty-seven."

"Did you see it?"

"No. I was a saplin' at the time, but the legend is folklore around these parts. Though the government men didn't like it, I know the folks who saw the crash site, including Mac, did their own investigations."

"About where the spaceship came from?"

"More about why the government tried to hush the whole damned thing up. But by then, the entire state knew about the wreck and the impact site, so the military patrollin' the area couldn't do anythin'. The cat was out of the bag."

"You mean, why the government officials took the crash site debris and maybe extraterrestrial bodies to supposedly Area 51?"

"Yeah. Mac's theories didn't arise out of a vacuum. They arose out of a scientific and political context born out of the mainstream. He remained categorical that the military were intent on reconstructin' the spaceship and analysin' the bodies. You see—" Shifting his Stetson off his forehead, he adopted a submissive disposition. "Back in forty-seven, the US was just gettin' into supersonic flight and missile technology. After Roswell, those initiatives came on by leaps and bounds. Then more recently, we heard about the Majestic Twelve, a coalition of scientists, military leaders and government officials formed in 1947 by an executive order from President Truman to cover up the Roswell incident."

"So the locals still think it really happened?"

"They *know* it happened. Anyways, go see the hollow."

"Thanks, we'll take a stroll over."

"Just don't scare this prime American rib. They don't take too kindly to strangers."

To the English, they could have been spying at a crevice on the dark side of the moon, the landscape barren of anything apart from sun-brazed shrubland and the odd shoot of green, as far as the eye could see. Engendering feelings of anti-climax and disappointment, they reckoned the detour had been a waste of time, and wished they'd gone for the Cadillac Ranch option.

~ * ~

Along with speakeasies, Collins knew after prohibition ended juke joints, pool halls and taprooms became the epicentre of life for Route 66 travellers as far back as the 1930s, when the Dust Bowl took hold in the Midwest farming lands, sending sharecroppers in search of a better life in California. Some failed to complete the safari, instead settling along the way in minor towns like Winslow and Kingman, or headed off Route 66 for Phoenix, Lake Havasu City, and even Las Vegas. Routinely, journeymen stopped off at watering holes for sustenance and refreshments during their odyssey to the land of milk and honey. Those electing to settle in the south-west invariably used them as meeting places and for social events, the roadhouse becoming the locus of choice for uncut communities to gather and talk.

When Collins and his pals sloped into Taco Bell in Clines Corners, midway between Santa Rosa and Albuquerque, they were befriended by a descendant of the Dust Bowl generation, introducing himself as Bill

Tansey. Weather and sun-beaten, and looking to be in his early sixties, Bill told the listeners his extended family had set off from Tupelo Mississippi with the intention of becoming fruit pickers in Orange County Los Angeles. They never made it. After over a thousand miles of heading due west, their rickety old truck engine coughed its final combustion cycle outside Santa Rosa. Down to their last few dollars, after being told by a local cattle man the railhead were looking for casual workers to load freight trains, they abandoned the vehicle and walked sixty miles in the searing summer heat to Santa Fe. Bill's father carried his three-years-old son on his shoulders, the rest of the family edging their way along the dirt track, in later years becoming Highway 285. By the time the Tanseys had raised enough money to repair the truck, it had been towed by the Highways Department and crushed. Left with no option but to continue with their casual endeavours loading freight, they never left New Mexico.

"Part of a workers community by the side of the rail terminal, we lived in a tent," Bill advised. "Huh—damn." He glowered. "They were rough, tough times. Then the war came. Daddy went off to fight the Japs, and my elder brothers and sisters went to work in a munitions factory. When daddy came back in '45, things got better. Santa Fe expanded. There was work for everyone. Eventually, my parents bought a small wooden house at Seton Village, and I went to St John's College to become a graphic designer." Terminating abruptly, he became reflective. "Lot of water under the bridge since we first came to New Mexico. Often, I calculate it's a miracle the family survived the 1930s."

"What brought you through?" Collins catechised, his ever-burgeoning awe of Dust Bowl survivors' tales breeding more curiosity.

"Sheer stubbornness and willpower," he asserted without reservation. "If you let your head drop, you're done for. That's a lesson everyone learnt on the road. It's a harsh, unforgivin' existence. If you don't heed its warnin's, you're doomed, and I knew many who didn't make it. They simply lost heart, curled up into a ball, and waited for the reaper to take them." Blossoming a more optimistic countenance, he said, "I heard you folks talking about Kerouac and the beat generation. That's why I came over and introduced myself."

"You met Kerouac and the beats?" Natasha propositioned.

"Naw, but I've known people who did meet them. Guys older than me, travellin' coast to coast in the fifties, lookin' for all kinds of action. Drifters, grifters, down and outs, writers seeking inspiration, even adventurers like you folks. They told me stories about the characters they encountered along the way. Some had met Kerouac, Neal Cassidy and Burroughs, plus a whole passel of dope fiends and alcoholics subsuming the wanderers' inclination. I'd heard about the rise of the beat generation when I was at St Johns. Some students I knew got all light-headed about the fable. They mimicked the same path, but I know only a few found what they were looking for. For most, it was a youthful rite of passage before settling into grafting."

"Hah," Gail retorted, "sounds familiar."

"What you folks have gotta understand, is the romance of the road associated with Kerouac was, and still is, much more like the ventures of Woody Guthrie. Howbeit the backdrop has altered since Kerouac bummed lifts along the Mother Road, and Woody jumped on freight trains, not much else has changed for workin' people. America is the most affluent country in the world, but you wouldn't certify it, if you saw how some folks live round here. Poverty is still rife."

"Yeah," Henry supported, "I told my compatriots about me driving from Anaheim to Oakland via Kettleman City and the boonies. It was as you describe. And a few years back, I took the scenic option from Sacramento to San Fran along Highway 84. Pulled in at Five Points to look out on Prospect Slough. The whole place resembled a ramshackle set from a cowboy movie. Broken wooden buildings and bleak thicket in every direction I scanned."

"Huh, we got those sights in New Mexico as well," Bill grumbled. "And I'm not talking blacks or wetbacks. These are white folks, who've never been able to escape the trailer parks and existing on low-paid, part-time jobs. Sure, America exhibits a glossy corporate image to the world at large, but that only exists for those at the top of the pyramid."

"Just returning to what you said about roamers," Delaney began, "it's true to say, whereas for Guthrie the rail track became a lifelong mission, for the beat writers the road rendered a source of inspiration. Once that had been distilled into works, most of the beats settled into metropolitan regularity."

"Without doubt," Bill acknowledged. "Though Kerouac and Burroughs did visit Morocco, and incontrovertibly, all of them took rambles into Mexico."

"Were you ever tempted by the wanderlust bug, Bill?" Collins queried.

"Huh." He vacillated, his hesitancy plain to the listeners. "I kinda embraced the ideal in theory, but having come from fragile beginnings, I felt duty bound to contribute to the family household budget as soon as I graduated from St John's. That was back in fifty-one, when the consumerism boom began in the States. Advertising agencies were crying out for ideas men to come up with graphics and one-liners to sell their clients products, and they paid top dollar."

"So you headed for New York?" Henry suggested.

"I did. Became a Madison Avenue man for fifteen years before coming back to New Mexico to work for a branch of Grey Advertising in Albuquerque."

"Are you still in the game?" Delaney enquired.

"No. I retired eighteen-months ago. Hung up my graphic designer credentials, and now I mainly look after the grand-kids, and walk the desert."

"That's some transition from Dust Bowl refugee," Gail saluted.

"It is. I was one of the lucky ones. I had a little bit of artistic talent and a cranium full of visions. Without that, I'd have ended up as factory or sharecropper fodder."

"Your success story is rare amongst the glut of sad tales we've been hearing from Chicago to Ok City," Collins observed.

"You betcha." A sheen of gratitude ingrained his phiz. "Say—" Near-certitude overtook him. "I take it you folks are dogging old Route 66 in your quest to tread in the footsteps of the beats?"

"Got it in one, Bill."

"Well, the trails gone cold, but you can still sniff out the ghosts of yesteryear, if you know where to look. When you get to Kingman, ask for a guy named Luke Berringer. He used to live out at Yucca, further down I40, maybe still does, but he socialised in Kingman. Luke met Burroughs in the early 1960s when the beat generation ethic had largely been superseded by Kennedy's liberalism germinating the love generation. He's not everybody's cup of tea, but Luke will be able to clue you in a lot more than I can regarding the principal beat luminaries. However, be careful, he can be waspish and ornery, so tread lightly."

Cruising back on I40, Natasha said to Collins, "So how many times have you been to California?"

Glimpsing at her from the driving position, he replied, "Too many to count."

"You never tell me anything unless I drag it out of you," she whined, grimacing. "Why is that?"

"Naturally unpretentious, I'd say."

She smiled. "I like that, Henry, but you don't have to hide your light under a bushel with me. I won't condemn you as boastful. It's not in your makeup."

Tongue in cheek, he blessed, "I need every accolade I can get. Thanks."

"How did that scenic passageway from Sacramento to San Fran come about?"

"I covered the three-day Retro Revolution Festival in Frisco for *Performance* last year. Took a couple of days' vacation, hired a motor and went up to Lake Tahoe. Its nearly all freeway, so coming back, I decided to take the dishy carriageway south of Sacramento. That's what really rekindled my desire to do Route 66. What with the job, and sorting out Babette, the opportunity had eluded me for a long time."

"If you eventually jack in being a music journalist, will you continue writing?"

"You mean fiction or non-fiction?"

"Both."

"Oh, fiction is a diverse discipline to writing the facts and impressions in a record review, or reporting on a concert or interview. Non-fiction maybe, and it'd be based on my time in the music industry…but I'm not sure that's in me."

"More modesty. You know damn well you could turn your writing talents to anything. We've all read your *Performance* pieces, and they stand up alongside any musico journalists' work."

"Not like you to be so forceful."

"Hah, I do have an aggressive side, even a dark side. Doesn't materialise very often, but when it does, usually its indifference that sparks it."

"Wasn't it Bukowski who said something like, as we live, we all get caught and torn by various groups. Writing can trap you. Some writers tend to write what has pleased their readers in the past. They hear accolades and believe them. There is only one final judge of writing and that is the writer. When he is swayed by the critics, the editors, the publishers, the reader, then he's finished. And axiomatically, when he is swayed with his fame and fortune, you can float him down the river with the turds."

"And that's how you see yourself ending up?"

"Maybe." Without notice, he then professed, "Like you, I do have a dark side."

"*You*! Oh, Henry—" Her cheeks lifted in defiance of the claim. "You're one of the nice guys, placid, even-tempered, a natural peacemaker."

"Surface gloss," he rebutted. "Underneath, I nurture a *Death Wish*-like vigilante persona, out to right wrongs."

Recapping the two Harlem gents episode, Natasha countered saying most people had a latent thirst or fantasised about evening out such loaded interludes with the ultimate payback.

"Yes, but if I'd had a handgun, vengeance might have got the better of my white angels."

"Henry, darling, you're just trying to wind me up. You haven't got a rotten bone in your body."

"Maybe, but perhaps one day, the levee's going to break my restraint, and I'll let fly."

"With a Magnum?"

"The Magnum was a metaphor. All the same, if I'd been armed, perhaps my self-suppression would have been breached, and I'd have ended up in Sing-Sing for wasting two uppity Harlem gents."

"You mean, the only thing holding you back was being

outnumbered in bandit territory?"

"Often, I've watched people in some volatile situation getting angry, or simmering while keeping a straight face, and I could tell if they'd had a weapon, it would have been used." Sneaking a peek at her, he surmised, "Why should I be any different?"

~ * ~

Albuquerque provided a pleasant surprise for the trekkers. Taking rooms at the Quigley Park Motel, they dialled a billboard in the lobby advertising the Sunshine Theatre concert by alternative rock band, the Pixies, Collins calling the theatre and booking four tickets charged to his American Express.

"Oh, wow," Delaney gushed, "I've never attended a Pixies gig, but I've got all their records. Round for round, pound for pound, there ain't no better band around."

"For sure," Collins warranted. "Zep's gone, the Stones are in limbo, the Who are in and out, and Paul Weller's producing soft soul crap with the Style Council. First time I heard the Pixies *Come On Pilgrim,* I knew it marked the dawning of a new age of rock innovation. *Surfer Rosa* was even better. Evidently, there's a lot of mileage in this band. They're gonna be around for a long time. And—" He bared his teeth in a show of delight. "It presents an opportunity for me to review the show, and fax it into *Performance.*"

Delivering an awesome blend of their trademark, dynamic, loud-quiet-loud shifts and unusual song structures, the Pixies pasted the packed Sunshine Theatre audience with crowd pleasers *Bone Machine, Gigantic* and *Monkey Gone to Heaven* amongst a plethora of superlative songs about extra-terrestrials, incest and biblical violence. Despite air-conditioning, Collins and his crew came away from the gig dripping perspiration, the heat generated by the packed gig-goers and the band's audio set up driving the inside temperature into the red zone.

"Not knowing quite what to expect," Gail reviewed, "I've become a Pixies convert. Haven't heard anything as powerful and vibrant since I saw the Who at the Rainbow Theatre in 1971." She stopped and gasped.

"Great heavens, I was eleven then!"

"You're right," Natasha agreed, "the Pixies blew away the cobwebs of some very mediocre gigs I've attended in recent years." She narrowed her eyes at Collins. "Don't tell me you've played me some Pixies records, and it's gone straight over my head."

"Yes." He grinned. "No, actually that pleasure is yet to come, albeit, I have abused your ears with Husker Du, Butthole Surfers and the Minutemen."

"The audience reaction was as visceral as anything I experienced at the height of punk," Gail exclaimed. "And this is New Mexico, not too far removed from Texas in terms of conservatism!"

"Oh, I'd not dismiss Texas too lightly," Collins encouraged. "The Lone Star state has produced many a good rock outfit. ZZ Top, Sir Douglas Quintet and the Thirteenth Floor Elevators were all founded in Texas."

"Yeah," Delaney supported, "and don't forget Buddy Holly and the Crickets, members of the first-generation masters."

"What about New Mexico?" Natasha asked.

Exchanging a dubious look with Delaney, Collins answered, "We'll pass on that one."

"Anyway," Gail began, "if we see any bands on this outing coming anywhere close to the Pixies, I'll be astonished."

Returning to the Quigley Park, Collins left his comrades and scribbled out a thousand- word Pixies concert review, faxed it to *Performance*, then joined them at the bar.

"How about a burritos and margaritas supper at a Mexican?" he proffered.

Receiving the thumbs up, the troupe made for Los Colima Mexican Kitchen, a few blocks away, their antennae tuned into the Albuquerque night awash with Stetson-wearing ranchers and cowpokes. They'd traded in their palominos for pick-up trucks, parking them outside seven-elevens and bars. Half anticipating pistol shots to ring out in celebration of ending a cattle drive or fencing campaign, instead the expeditionaries heard the occasional hoot and holler. Inevitably, by the time the beats were steamrollering over the American outback, the steers were a minor part of the local economy. Gentrifying the city, technology and military elements had taken root in the form of the Sandia Laboratories and Kirtland Air Force Base, boosting local revenues and employment. By the time the Collins collective came by Albuquerque, a whole lot more science and technology companies had arrived, much of the old wild west town torn down to make way for glass and steel edifices.

Observing the deviations, the visitors envisaged the trend continuing over the next hundred years, the sight of a longhorn on Albuquerque's streets rarer than tumbleweed, the desert encroached upon by an expansion of state-of-the-art combines, the prospect alien to their sensibilities.

"I suppose that's so-called progress for you," Delaney critiqued. "Tradition sacrificed on the mighty alter of moving onwards and upwards."

"It's a never-ending phenomenon in the developed world," Collins categorised. "But for preservation societies and museums, much of the past would have been forgotten."

"That does seem to be the fate for buildings, in particular," Natasha advanced. "Unless they have a significance, most are torn down to make way for the new."

"Yes," Gail concurred, "we treasure the arts and sciences far more, at least over the past 500 years. It can be argued Mozart is just as alive today, as he was in the eighteenth century."

"Coming from the music industry, I'd sanction that supposition," Collins acclaimed. "Just about every momentous signature arriving in the twentieth century has been thoroughly indexed and catalogued for prosperity, even those not necessarily in the forefront of the public eye."

"Embodied by?"

Cogitating for a moment, he declared, "I'll quote two examples, both of whom I met at a party given by Columbia Records in New York when I was still with *Crossroads*; bassist-guitarist Carol Kaye and producer Tom Wilson. Not many people outside of the industry are aware of Carol Kaye's axiomatic role in the Wrecking Crew, a loose collective of LA-based session musicians, whose services were employed for thousands of studio recordings in the sixties and seventies. Carol played on ground-breaking tracks, inclusive of the Beach Boys *Good Vibrations* and the Mothers of Invention eponymous album, *Freak Out!* Black man Tom Wilson, a rare sighting in the rock world, produced on a host of Dylan albums, the first two Velvet Underground albums, and *Freak Out!*"

"What were they like?"

"Unassuming, gracious." He raised his eyebrows in respect. "Typical of many behind-the-frontline operators I've met."

"And as you say," Delaney validated, "Carol and Tom are already canonised in the annals of rock history."

"Pity the same echelon of recognition does not apply to other walks of life," Natasha said.

"Yep," Collins corroborated, "we'll never know for example, the names of the caddie designers at the Cadillac Ranch, who was responsible for the St Louis Gateway Arch, or the architecture of Philtower in Tulsa."

"You know," Delaney began, frowning, "when it comes down to it, not many lives are aggrandised."

"A salutary reflection," Collins backed.

Chapter 10: Road Wrecker Felons

Though the two couples regularly took turns to drive the Camaro and the Corvette, increasingly when Delaney got behind the wheel of the latter, the devil in him prompted by cocaine sniffing resulted in some hair-raising incidents along the quieter sections of Route 66. Without doubt the muscle cars strained to get off the leash as soon as the driver went anywhere near the gas pedal, their natural constituency way above the nationwide fifty-five miles per hour speed limit. Constrained by both traffic and an abundance of highway patrol and city police monitoring the interstate freeways in the high-population conurbations, the same constriction to speed did not apply along the stretches disappearing to infinity between major cities, patterned by innumerable open spaces including croplands, grasslands and desert, sparsely inhabited by farmers, hamlet communities and native American Indians. A speed-freaks paradise, such adrenaline-inflating, fun-filled, merry-go-rounds offered the opportunity to floor the gas pedal, and watch the speedometer rise from fifty-five to over a hundred and thirty in seconds.

Delaney had partaken the whirlwind rush at least a half-dozen times between Chicago and Albuquerque, Collins on his tail, the pair zinging along the near-to deserted highways at a steady hundred-plus miles per hour with FM radio chugging out Blue Oyster Cult, Boston and Lynyrd Skynyrd classics for company. Collins had told his companions, during previous Stateside visits, he had charged along such desolate interstate roads in the hope of being chased and pulled over by the local sheriff, and the said bastion of the law letting him off scot-free when presented with a British driving licence, and thereby all the red tape it involved in sentencing the culprit. Notwithstanding, though exceeding the speed limit, time after time in the Mojave Desert, Death Valley or Joshua Tree National Park, not once did a smokie latch onto his flagrant lawbreaking. Delaney had assured him his duck would be remedied during their Route 66 sojourn, Collins assuming if caught, a fixed speeding fine to be the limit of the penalty paid.

After charging through Gallup, home of the historic El Rancho Hotel used by John Wayne, Gregory Peck, Spencer Tracey and other leading actors while on-location shooting Westerns during the 1940s and fifties in rugged terrain surrounding the town, and crossing the state line into Arizona at Lupton, they gassed up at Chambers on I40, known as the Purple Heart Trail in the section between Allentown and Holbrook. Soon after, the pathfinders entered the Petrified Forest National Park, the road ahead becoming straight as a die and virtually free of other road users, the mid-afternoon sun exciting haziness on the horizon. His vision lighting up at the prospect of the need for speed, Delaney stamped on the Corvette's accelerator pedal, and she took off like a bat out of hell, Collins quickly catching up in the Camaro, both tuned into FM Albuquerque blasting out Steely Dan's *Pretzel Logic*. Now seasoned practitioners of the two-car Route 66 race, they flashed over the landscape, the two drivers and their passengers solely concentrating on the road ahead, the Petrified Forest's boulders, sharp stone rises and shallow canyons not registering in their field of regard. All went well until they passed a giant billboard advertising an off-roading event at nearby Sun Valley. Hid on its blindside, a Highway Patrol black and white Mustang crouched in a lair awaiting road law transgressors, it's onboard radar scanning I40 for prey. As the speed-freaks sprinted by, they caused the radar annunciator to blip, awakening the half-asleep patrolman. Quickly radioing into base that he was in pursuit of two racers, the officer then engaged drive and the Mustang leapt onto I40, lights flashing, siren squawking. Oblivious to the speed-trap, the hypnotised drivers still only had eyes for the road ahead until Natasha tuned into the wail, turning around to see the black and white closing in fast. Alerting Collins, after checking his rear-view mirror, he twigged at length his ambition to be hauled over by a state sheriff was about to be fulfilled. Gail had also latched onto the penetrating siren, Delaney consequently beholding the Camaro slowing in his rear-view mirror. Tempted to outrun the law, just for the buzz, he knew the action would leave his buddy in hot water. Easing up on the gas pedal, within a quarter mile, the Corvette pulled over to the side of the road, Collins replicating the action, the Mustang arresting behind the Camaro.

"Turn off your engines," they heard from the cop car's public address.

"Well, here's where we learn to take it," Collins quipped to Natasha.

Recalling his confessed craving, she shot back, "Enjoy it."

Wrought with trepidation, as he lowered the driver door window, Collins watched the looming law enforcement officer in his rear-view mirror. A large, bulky man with a face seemingly splayed in every direction, he toted a handgun that would make Dirty Harry proud.

"What you got underneath the hood, boy, a Saturn 5 rocket? What are you? Ben Hur?"

Not foreseeing the sardonic, Collins mumbled, "Erm..."

"Never mind. Driving License."

Collins handed over the document.

Examining the permit, he narrowed his eyes. "You're from England?"

"Indeed."

Glancing ahead, he pinpointed the Corvette. "And your fellow road wrecker is also English?"

"He is."

"Get out of the car, boy, and don't move."

Ambling down to the Corvette, the lawman subjected Delaney to the same routine before the pair joined Collins beside the Camaro.

"I suppose you boys imagine just because you are aliens with alien driving licenses, that makes you immune to Arizona State laws?" Before they could reply, he carried on. "Well, this is not your lucky day. When it comes to lawbreakers, Deputy Sherriff J D Jackson, that's me, does not make exceptions. I clocked you boys doing a hundred and ten back at the Sun Valley billboard. Now, here's what's gonna happen. You two are going to climb back into your speed machines, and follow me to Holbrook Police Station. Clear?"

Definitely not a time to lose his cool, withdraw the metaphorical Magnum from his shoulder holster and blast the lawman, instead Collins gritted his teeth.

"Clear," they chimed.

Illustrative of small towns to be found on the south-western stretch of Route 66, Holbrook Navajo County was dusty, flat and tumble-weed bound. Born when the Atlantic and Pacific Railroad dropped anchor to use it as a staging post for construction back in 1882, Holbrook had gained a reputation as a frontiersman town, women and churches rarely surviving it's early incarnation as a whiskey branch line for cattlemen and railroad construction crews, the hardness surviving into the late twentieth century.

"What have we got here, J D?" pumped the policeman manning the front desk, when the Deputy Sheriff escorted the offenders into the police station.

"Oh, just some alien hotheads, Clay, reg'lar Ben Hurs' from England."

"*England*," he echoed. "You don't say. What have they been up to?"

"Well, what we got here is a couple of limeys with defective eyesight, and their molls."

"Ahh, can't read the speed limit signs?"

"Damned right. These melon-heads were churning up I40 at a hundred-and-ten."

"Ooohh-ee." Clay sucked in breath. "Judge Carson is gonna tear them to shreds. Probably end up in the State Pen for a thousand years. Don't you boys know it's a hanging offence in these parts to break the speed limit?"

Perceiving the encounter not to be the picnic he dreamt up, Collins pleaded, "We didn't realise we were going so fast."

"Yeah," Delaney supplemented, "these highways are so long and straight with little traffic that you just don't notice the speed."

Grinning, J D turned to Clay. "Now where have we heard that before? Alright, take their names and licence details, then lock 'em up."

"*Lock us up*," Natasha blurted.

"Oh, not you and your lady friend, miss. Just your menfolk are for the slammer. You can wait here, or mosey around Holbrook, until Judge Carson has passed sentence on the felons."

Resigned to their fate, Collins and Delaney followed Clay to the cells, unsure of their continuing liberty. Not alone, when Clay locked them in, they saw a fairly well-dressed man lying on a bunkbed, snoring and burbling as he slept.

"Must have been booked for drunkenness," Delaney conjectured.

Not really taking in the comment, Collins bleated, "Jesus, did I underestimate the ramifications of being busted for exceeding the speed limit."

"Oh, relax, Henry. At worst, we'll get endorsements and a fine. *Hah*, but it will be worth it. The buzz of flying down I40 for mile after mile, at well over a ton, was phenomenal. Can't do that in England."

"No, the motorways are far too busy, and police constantly monitor them. Huh, I recently heard speed cameras will soon be introduced."

"Speed cameras!"

"Yeah, an article in the London Evening Standard mentioned the Department for Transport were testing devices with a view to installing them first on motorways, then on other roads."

"My *god*, England really is becoming a police state. They'd never stand for that here in the US."

"No, they'd machine gun the bloody things, claiming they were un-American and contravened the Constitution and the Bill of Rights."

"Oooohh," the Englishmen heard emanating from their prostate cellmate. "Ohh…what happened this time?" Licking his lips to find moisture, and placing an arm over his eyes to blot out the light, the drunk stirred. "Wow…have I got a humdinger of a hangover." Staring to the heavens, he petitioned, "Lord, don't let me near a bottle of bourbon ever again." Sensing he didn't have the cell to himself, he took in his fellow inmates. "Who are you?"

"Globetrotters, making for LA."

"Globetrotters! You mean, you're on the road?"

"We *were* on the road."

"Hah…don't tell me. Deputy Sheriff Jackson caught you speeding."

"Yep," Collins confirmed.

"Haaah, J D's bust me a few times as well. How fast did he clock you at?"

"A hundred and ten."

"*A hundred and ten*! Boy, Judge Carson is gonna throw the book at you. J D trucks in transgressors doing *fifty-six*. They get a fine, but a hundred and ten…holy mackerel, that'll get you a thousand years."

"That bad, hey?" Delaney inferred.

"Well, it depends on the Judge's mood. If he's just had an assignation at Miss Lacey's whorehouse, he'll be more charitable. If he's been dragged over the coals by the county DA, or worst still, the state governor, his vengeance will be turned on you boys."

"Sounds like a colourful customer," Collins attributed.

"Oh, Vern Carson has a chequered history, just about stayin' on the right side of the law long enough to sit the bar examination, but he's well-connected, any peccadillos swept under the carpet. He's in his late sixties now, and apart from the occasional rendezvous at Miss Lacey's, his horsin' around tendencies are a thing of the past. Now he gets his kicks from applyin' the full extent of the law. If it hadn't bin for the intervention of my daddy, I'd have come in for some harsh sentencin' from Carson."

"You rich then?" Collins presumed.

"Huh—" He winced. "That's a sore point. My family is rich, but they consider me to be a liability, so all I get is an allowance. I gotta hunger for the booze and other delicacies which are incompatible with my family's Arizona State standing."

"What's your name?"

"Oh, do forgive me." Managing to rise and sit on his bunkbed, he dialled some steak and fries leftovers on his jacket lapels and brushed them off. "What with feelin' like a herd of steers have trampled all over me, I clean forgot my manners. Wade Gardner."

"I'm Henry Collins and that's Kallen Delaney."

"Say, I'm starting to detect an unfamiliar accent. You boys aren't from around these parts, are you?"

"We're from England."

"England. Well hell, my great, great, great grand-daddy hailed from England."

"You live in Holbrook, Wade," Delaney nominated.

"Ohh." He grinned. "I live all over the state, but nominally my domicile is Phoenix. That's where the family are based."

"How do you happen to be in Holbrook?" Collins tested.

"Ahh." He rubbed his chin. "I could have difficulty rememberin' the specific reason. Usually do when I end up behind bars. Suffice to say, they know me here."

"Are you due to come up in front of Judge Carson?"

"Oh, I doubt it. Clay on the front desk knows I have an inauspicious predilection, so when they brought me in, he'd have made some calls to Phoenix. So long as I didn't do too much damage to whichever nightery, clip joint or cocktail lounge I was frequentin', when I felt the need to become boisterous, money will be being wired to the plaintiff's lawyer to settle any wreckages."

"So the Holbrook Police allow you to sleep it off in a cell?"

"They tell me, it's for my own good." Beginning to establish a *compos mentis* shape, he said, "Say, what brings you fellas stateside?"

"We're on a Route 66 road hike from Chicago to LA."

"You don't say. Wow. *Huh*, the number of times I've set out both east and west by road, intendin' to explore the world beyond Arizona, and never gettin' across the state line —" He shook his noodle, Collins fathoming they had an eccentric in their midst. "Well, I've lost count of the number. However, I have extensively flown out of the state, mainly in private jets, chiefly down to the pueblo. I have a hankerin' for desolate but exotic places like Juarez and Durango." Wrinkling his nose and scratching it, he then asked, "Say, what you bin doin' along the way?"

"We came with the intention of finding the beats' spoor, and meshing in with people surviving the Dust Bowl."

"Rings like you boys have a vocation."

"Kind of."

"You er, you mentioned the beats."

"Uh-huh."

"You mean Kerouac, and er, Cassidy?"

"Yep, and a whole host of other 1950s hepcat guiding lights."

"I see. Might interest you to know, I once met Ferlinghetti."

"*Really.*"

"Yeah, in a Flagstaff juke joint, about a decade and a half ago. I've always been fascinated by American literature and poetry right from Walt Whitman and Emily Dickenson to Robert Frost and Allen Ginsberg. Recognised Ferlinghetti from his photographs. Marched right up to him, told him I'd read his *Tyranus Nix* and *The Secret Meaning of Things*. The former is a satirical tirade on Nixon, deliciously deceptive, but the hammer points are driven home with venom. We talked about it at length. Very cordial guy. Bags of charisma. Needless to say, he knew all the beats. Over the span of the engagement, he told me lots of stories about them. Damned if I can remember any of them now." Breaking off, he rose from the prone position and took a few steps around the cell. "So you fellas are going to LA?"

"Providing Judge Carson doesn't lock us up, and throw away the key," Collins jested.

"Say, how'd you respond to the proposition of a fee-payin' passenger?"

Collins exchanged arched shoulders with Delaney. "You're welcome."

"That sure is nice of you guys. On the basis the family attorney has done the business with the plaintiff's lawyer, they should let me out of here pretty soon. I believe—" Thoughtfully, he scratched his chin. "I'm stayin' at the Wigwam Motel on Hopi Drive. Why don't you meet me over there when you're through with the Judge? They'll take you to the magistrates court on West Buffalo. It's just a few blocks from here. Even though you've been busted for doin' a hundred and ten, I doubt Carson will do anythin' other than fine you, once he's been acquainted with the rigmarole of incarceratin' alien drivers by the police."

Soon thereafter, Gardner was released, Collins and Delaney assessing quite by off chance, they might have stumbled on a fount of beat gen lore.

As the sun tumbled into the western skies, Deputy Sheriff Jackson took the felons over to the courthouse for their hearing, Natasha and Gail shadowing them into a building more resembling a glorified cattle shed than the regal, neo-Georgian buildings associated with east and west coast law courts.

Standing in the dock together, Collins and Delaney awaited Carson's arrival, Jackson at their side looking deadpan, the court recorder ready to transcribe sentencing. As he entered the court, the usher commanded, "All rise. The Magistrate's Court in the county of Navajo Arizona, is now in session. The honourable Judge Vern Carson presiding."

After taking his post, Carson bequeathed, "Be seated."

Reminiscent of the actor Burl Ives in stature from his role as Big Daddy in *Cat on a Hot Tin Roof*, and emanating an aura of implacable intolerance to lawbreakers, the Judge cut a mean, uncompromising figure.

"What you got for me this evening, J D?"

"Couple of alien reprobates, your honour."

"So I see from the charge sheet," he acknowledged, scanning the said document before him. "Mister Collins?"

"That's me, your honour."

Glancing up at the miscreants, the Judge deduced, "So that makes you, Mister Delaney."

"Yes, your honour."

"Gentlemen, I can't begin to tell you how much I abhor road users breaking the speed limit. Usually, the excess is no more than twenty to thirty miles per hour, but being indexed at a hundred and ten, you two have set an all-time record. Just because you are not US citizens, you might have speculated having immunity from the law. Albeit, let me underwrite, anyone brought before me, no matter what their native country of residence, will be subject to the demands of law enforcement. Have you anything to say in your defence?"

Agreeing to plead guilty in advance, on the basis any limp-wristed excuses would only serve to increase their sentences, Collins substantiated, "We are guilty as charged, your honour."

"No mitigating circumstances then?"

"Unfortunately, no, your honour."

"No life or death excuses?"

"I'm afraid not, your honour."

"Very well. Normally, those caught for the first time breaking the highway speed limit by up to thirty miles per hour are fined a hundred dollars." He scowled. "*You two* have exceeded the limit by twice the maximum allowable speed. Thereby under the authority granted to me by the Navajo County legislature and under Arizona State law, I hereby sentence both of you to pay a fine of 250 dollars. Pay the clerk of the court on your way out, and your licenses will be returned to you. And gentlemen—" He eyed them sternly. "While you are in the United States, I'd advise you not to contravene the speeding laws again. A second offence with a less liberal judge than myself, could see you not only fined, but also imprisoned. Do I make myself crystal?"

"Yes, your honour," Collins affirmed.

"Case found," the Judge declared, slamming his gavel sharply down on its hardwood sound block.

~ * ~

A tribute to the Navajo, Hopi, Apache and a host of other Arizona State native Indian tribes, the Wigwam Motel literally comprised fifteen non-connected, accommodation tepees fashioned in the manner of the Plains Indians, and laid out in an open rectangle to resemble an Indian village. After inquiring at the conventionally styled, once a filling station reception, the English troupe made their way to wigwam six, where they found Wade Gardner spaced out in a chair watching cable TV, and sipping on a bottle of Wild Turkey.

"Well," he yelped as they entered his tepee, "since you boys are foot loose and fancy free, I guess Judge Carson must have been in a generous mood."

After making all-round introductions, Gardner probed, "Where are you folks stayin' tonight?"

"We'll find a motel in Holbrook," Collins cited.

"Ohh, I'm sure I can get you a couple of wigwams here. I know Albert Tucker. He owns the Wigwam Village chain."

Getting on the horn, he spoke to reception, the man on the desk duly obliging with two wigwams.

"Now we got that sorted, why don't we mosey on down to

Eduardo's for some tacos and tequila gold."

During dinner, Gardner opened up further regarding his chosen life pattern.

"I never was a dedicated scholar. Very little of the school curriculum absorbed me. My mama wanted me to go to the University of Arizona at Tucson to study law and politics. It's a kinda family tradition, but I knew after flunkin' most subjects, apart from English and American Literature, I'd never make the grades to be accepted for the course."

"What did you do then?" Natasha explored.

"Hah." He broke into a radiant smile. "Well, I'll tell ya, Miss Natasha. When it became lucid I wasn't law and politics degree material, I said I intended to study literature, but er, huh, my family deemed it to be incompatible…there's that decimating word again…with their expectations."

"So they didn't let you go?" Gail envisioned.

"Not exactly, Miss Gail. They informed me, the family wouldn't be pickin' up my tuition fees, and I'd have to work to subsidise my studies. Well, hah…work and me have never been the best of associates. I could never hold down the nine to five slog in a drug store or an office. Oh, I enrolled at Arizona State to study literature, and became a member of the nine to five club the summer after graduating from high school, the purpose being to save enough dollars to bankroll my first-year costs. How-ever —" He grinned. "The work ethic hit me like a sledgehammer. I found it impossible to buckle down to the regularity the task demanded. After arrivin' late for the fourth time at Reed Harris, a farming equipment leasin' firm, they fired me. Well, after that, my bolt was shot. I imagined I could never get back on the treadmill. Then it became one long, lingerin' road of maybe's and possibles, furnished by family connections, but er…nothin' ever lasted. So by the time I reached twenty-one, I had a whole passel of failures behind me with little to no prospects. Naturally, the family couldn't see me destitute, bad for the image you know." Simpering mischievously, he relayed, "So, they assigned me an allowance on the proviso none of my peccadillos wound up splashed in the front pages of the Arizona Daily Star or some such journal."

"So ever since, you've been a kind of bohemian adventurer?"

Collins postulated, his admiration for the genial pleasure-seeker escalating.

"Oh, that's a posh way of sayin' it, Henry, more like a saddle tramp or a bar fly, and if you're bein' really uncharitable, a playboy." Grimacing, he confided, "Tried my hand at marriage once. Nice girl. Good family. But patently preselected by my own family, with the intention of drawing me back into line. Well, I held out for all of three weeks before I hightailed it out of Phoenix, and indulged in one hell of a binge outin' for at least two months. Met some real interestin' dudes beyond the bounds of Arizona *haut monde* during that period of let's call it, enlightenment. Anyway, when I came home, she'd gone back to her mama, and I got a writ citin' 'unreasonable behaviour' as the pretext behind her requested divorce. As I anticipated, Daddy went wild. Told me I'd let the family name down, and indulged in disgraceful etiquette. Well, it all got handed over to the Gardner family lawyer, Clint Howard, my mother's brother. He cut a deal with my ex-wife's family to hush it all up. So—" He beamed. "You folks know just about everythin' about me now. I've told you all this, so if you find my conduct beyond the pale, you can bale out on taking me with you to LA."

"We're not in the business of making judgments on preferred lifestyles, Wade," Collins guaranteed. "None of us is a hundred percent squeaky clean in terms of moral virtue."

"Yeah, that's right," Delaney backed. "Part of the motivation to take Route 66 was to meet people from disparate backgrounds and familiarities. We're not seeking devoted church goers and bulwarks of regular society. There's plenty of that back home."

"Well," Gardner began, "it appears I'm in the company of fellow free-spirits and mavericks." Hesitating, he enquired, "Say, did you happen to stopover in Gallup?"

"No," Collins advised. "We haven't got the time for an overnight in every famous location."

"Well, that's a blessin' in disguise."

"Oh."

"Gallup's gained a wretched reputation in recent times for violent crime includin' murder, rape and robbery. It's not the same affable place the Hollywood set knew thirty to forty years back. By all account, a bad element has taken stage centre. Just recently, I watched an NBC special on Gallup's lawbreakin'. Couldn't believe what I saw. Town's hit the buffers since a barrel load of Hispanics moved in, and made it into a drug dealers paradise. The stuff is being flown in under the radar from Columbia in the dead of night, parachuted into some canyon south of Gallup, then loaded onto a waitin' truck. After that, the distribution chain comes into play, other drug gangs coming into Gallup from Harlem, Black Bottom and DC to make their collections. Native American Indians still form the town's majority, and they don't want their young folk to be corrupted by dealers. That's led to some confrontations, and the accompanying crime wave."

"Knowing the scale of the problem, it's bound to happen somewhere along our chosen orbit," Collins admitted.

"You're right, its prevalent in many places these days, but most goes undetected because the drug barons are smart enough not to draw attention to their operations. Gallup hasn't been fortunate in that respect."

"Now's a good time to admit I'm a cocaine user," Delaney admitted.

"Well, that's you and about another five million consumers, just here in the US. I don't mean to be judgemental, *hell*, I've got into a lot of shenanigans myself, but er…the next time you take a dose of pearl, just remember behind the facade lurks a lot of misery, and that includes murders."

~ * ~

Over the next few days, Wade Gardner and the English contingent talked about all things of a bohemian nature, his experiences of interfacing with a myriad of hipsters and hippies providing forums to discuss the nature of the nonconformist fraternity.

"Inevitably, no one I ever met on the road could articulate precisely why they chose the rebel path," Gardner shared during lunch in a dilapidated dice joint at Seligman. "Invariably, they'd hunch their shoulders, or gaze into the distance like they'd been whacked, their recall ability irretrievably curtailed."

"Have you ever met someone coming from a rich background like yourself rejecting the trappings of privilege?" Delaney checked.

"That's a problematical question. Huh." He lowered his head, as if wrestling to fetch up a candidate. "Can't say that I have, though I'd assume outside the godly state of Arizona, there must be rich boys like me on a similar trek. You see, Arizona is very conservative. Nonconformity is an anathema, a black mark so deep that it has been virtually struck from the record. You could say, it's the tyranny of the mainstream. Those metropolitan states like Pennsylvania or New York breed more affluent discontents, the incidence down to an immersion in let's call it, the murkier, wild side of Americana. Arizona is principally desert. It begets cleanliness in nature, mirrored in its citizens. You see, due to wholesale immigration since the end of the Civil War, the northern east and west coasts have been in an unwavering state of flux. The bits in the central south, meaning Texas, New Mexico, they're mainly desert or plains as well, and Arizona, have sustained a more or less changeless demography since the early British settlers arrived in the mid-eighteenth century. The population density for all three states is less than one thousandth that of New Jersey or Maryland. So we're not jammed in like sardines. Got room to move and stretch without elbowing our neighbours. And…we all look pretty much the same. This is a white state, and most folks want to keep it that way. Hence, the probability of finding another dropout from the highest social stratum like me, is remote."

"You mentioned Arizona being a white state, Wade," Collins began. "What about the influx of Mexicans?"

"Oh, they're no trouble, daddy-o. They're just happy to have a job, any job from Monday to Friday, before hoppin' back over the border into the pueblo."

"But we comprehend most of them are illegals."

"Yep. I'll admit that is an issue, because unlike the cross-border, legal workers, they don't go home, can't work legally, and are a ceaseless drain on social welfare. It's a problem effectin' California, New Mexico and Texas, as well as Arizona, upsettin' taxpayers forced into fundin' their unproductive existence. Not wishin' to be superior, unlike *that* particular groupin', most hobos and nomadic trailblazers like me, are decadent, degenerate, even depraved and debauched, but we 'ain't a drain on the public purse. Our hedonistic, libertine and pleasure-seekin' outlook maybe despised by Joe Clean, and levied to be unprincipled, wanton self-indulgence, but we move through society near-to transparently, demandin' nothin'. That's why we're tolerated as apathetic oddballs and dodgers."

Since exiting Holbrook, they had explored the depths of Winslow and Flagstaff, Collins knowing the former had been made neo-famous in the lyrics to *Take it Easy*, recorded by the Eagles, and renowned for the Canyon Diablo Meteorite, a gigantic meteor crater, three-quarters of a mile across and 560 feet deep, the latter boasting the historic 1888 Babbitt Brothers building, a trading emporium still in business, and a lively café society hallmarked by Parisian ambience. Bringing credibility to Wade Gardner's sociological perspectives, compared to the densely packed and diverse St Louis conurbations and other interracial cities perennially bristling on the edge of societal breakdown, Winslow and Flagstaff exhibited the calmness and tranquillity associated with homogeneous communities. Everyone said 'Howdy' and smiled. Unlike in Illinois and Missouri, the bartenders didn't hide a Colt beneath the counter to deal with robbers and rowdies. Even the police were relaxed. None of the locals were going to indulge in hijinks, and those in transit seemed to segue into the nonconfrontational regime. These were places to find serenity, far away from big city commerce, out of control crime and burgeoning civil unrest.

Trekking to the Canyon Diablo Meteorite, eighteen miles west of Winslow and south off I40, they were treated to the rare sight of mustangs in the wild.

"You folks sure are lucky," Gardner quipped. "Not many people get to see those magnificent beasts in their natural habitat, this far north. Usually, mustangs can be found in and around the Tonto National Forest, north-east of Phoenix."

Standing on an observation platform on the edge of the Canyon Diablo Meteorite, affording aspects due south into the heart of the crater, Natasha exclaimed, "My God, it's *huge*."

"Yep," Gardner assented, "when that baby hit 50,000 years ago, it sure as hell must have devastated the locale. Not even the Manhattan Trinity A-bomb test in the Jornada del Muerto Desert New Mexico yielded a crater this deep and wide."

"For sure," Collins agreed, "but this is a mere dent compared to the Cretaceous-Paleogene extinction event caused by a massive comet or asteroid, possibly up to nine miles wide, striking the Earth sixty-six million years ago. Its subsequent upshot wiped out seventy-five per cent of species, including all the dinosaurs."

"Oh well," Gardner began, "that raises the whole panacea of another like-sized intergalactic piece of space debris collidin' with the Earth. That's the biggest threat to life before our Sun becomes deplete of all its hydrogen and helium, collapsing into a white dwarf in about four-point-five to five-point five billion years. Nevertheless, before that cataclysmic event, in one-point one billion years from today, the Sun will be ten per cent brighter than it is now, the increase in luminosity amplifyin' heat energy absorbed in Earth's atmosphere resultin' in runaway warming. But that's not the end of it. In three point five billion years, the Sun will be forty per cent brighter, causing the oceans to boil, the ice caps to permanently melt, and all water vapour in the atmosphere to be lost to space. By then our Sun will have entered the Red Giant phase of its evolution, encompassing the orbits of Mercury, Venus, and even the Earth, before eventually cooling and becomin' a white dwarf, then possibly a stellar black hole."

"You're talking about the end of all life on Earth," Gail summarised.

"Oh yeah, it's an inevitability, reinforcin' the philosophers gloomy standpoint; all human endeavour is futile."

"Yes," Delaney approved, "the picture of all of man's majestic inventions, works of art and social structures becoming vaporised, is a salutary admission."

"Doesn't make for pleasant cogitation, does it?" Gardner tendered.

"Absolutely not," Gail concurred.

"Howbeit, between now and then, it's another gigantic-sized

meteorite that presents the greatest threat to life on Earth. Someone from CALTEC told me, Reagan's Strategic Defence Initiative programme, known as 'Star Wars', could also be used to destroy inbound space debris."

"Speaking of nuclear detonations," Collins began, "we were considering taking in Las Vegas and the Nevada Test Site on the return trek to Chicago."

"Not sure you'll get too close to that covert installation, before the military police shoo you away. The whole area has become very politicised by anti-nuclear protesters. Lot of people arrested."

"I read in *Life* magazine," Natasha elicited, "during the 1950s, mushroom clouds from numerous atmospheric tests could be seen a hundred miles away in Las Vegas, and the prevalence of cancers markedly increased in Nevada."

"That is all true," Gardner verified, "and the Department of Energy continues to detonate nuclear devices in the Nevada Test Site. Nellis Air Force Base, just north of Vegas is so concerned, they perform regular radiation tests on air force personnel. Comprehensive national outrage beyond the protesters prompted Washington to act on the matter. Consequently, government contractors are endlessly engaged on aerial radiological surveys, analysin' particles for man-made radioactive isotopes, such as cesium and cobalt, and measurin' gamma ray concentrations."

"What does the site comprise?" Delaney examined, his appetite for zeal triggered at the prospect of out-foxing the military.

"Well, it's real estate has become a matter of public record. My understanding is the site incorporates over twenty-five sub-areas, each used for assorted nuclear evaluations, at least a thousand buildings, multiple heliports and two airstrips in Nye County Nevada. Oh yes, and talkin' of craters, the Sedan crater created in 1962 by a thermonuclear device buried over 600 feet beneath the surface, has a diameter of 1,280 feet and a maximum depth of 320 feet, but that is less than a third the size of the Canyon Diablo Meteorite."

"You seem to know a lot on a wide variety of subjects," Collins complimented.

"Oh, I'm well read, but knowledge is one thing, application is another."

"We also kicked around the premise of reconnoitering Area 51."

"Ahh. That's another no, no."

"Unapproachable?"

"There's only two ways of gettin' into Area 51. Using the road system created by the military connecting other hush-hush facilities in the locale, or landing at Homey Airport, a.k.a Groom Lake. Homey is administered by the USAF's Edward's Air Force Base in Kern County California, so unless you are authorised, there's no way you can fly into Homey."

"Presumably, the road system is not open to the public?"

"You've got it. You can go as far as Mercury on the south side of the base, but security officers bar you from goin' any further."

"What about going cross country?" Delaney interjected, still keen on outwitting the authorities.

"Area 51 is located between I95 to the west, I93 to the east and Interstate 375, known as the Extraterrestrial Highway, to the north, some eighty-three miles north-northwest of Las Vegas. Looking at your Corvette and Camaro, manifestly they are incompatible with the terrain. Off-road vehicles are needed, like the army uses. And don't go thinkin' you can walk there. Area 51 is at least fifty miles from Amargosa Valley on I95, right on the edge of Death Valley National Park. The heat at this time of the year is cripplin'. You'd die from sun exposure."

"And I'd guess, even if we did attempt walking, we'd be detected?"

"Conclusively, Kallen. Fly boys patrol the region in army copters, and surveillance cameras are supplemented with buried motion sensors and boundary warning signs. Even if you reached the base, you'd never breach the security and get inside. You see, additional to Area 51 supposedly housing the Roswell incident spacecraft and alien bodies, it's used as a military facility to support the development and testin' of experimental aircraft and weapons systems, typically, the Lockheed U-2 and SR-71 Blackbird spy planes. Nonetheless, permanence of the base has never been formally corroborated by the Pentagon or the CIA."

Halting briefly, he then added, "I do have some personal experience of being shooed away from such sensitive installations.

"Way back when, I used to go down to Yuma City, and hang out on I95 watching the Huey and Cobra attack helicopters and the M1 Abrams tanks pummelin' ground targets at the Yuma Proving Ground. Like Area 51, substantially, it's on open ground. One time, I decided to get closer to the action, and wandered into the restricted zone. Boy, was that a *big* mistake. Before I knew it, I'd been surrounded by a pack of Humvees. Seemed to come out of nowhere. The lead officer told me in no uncertain terms to go back to I95. Made me appreciate, though Yuma looked undefended, it is unremittingly monitored by the military. Same goes for Area 51. You won't see them comin', but they sure as hell will see you."

"Isn't it true there's some credence to the notion that the Lockheed skunk works have a successor to the SR-71?" Collins raised.

"You must mean the Aurora Black or the SR-91 triangle," Gardner specified. "Earlier this year, The *Journal of Aeronautics and Aerospace Engineering* suggested Aurora flies at 135,000 feet at Mach six, and is powered by a pulse wave detonation engine. Nonetheless, accordin' to the US Government, Aurora is not real, just a speculator's fantasy. The *Journal* went on to say, at the end of the SR-71 spy plane programme, the US was left with no spy plane to patrol the world, and a future SR-72 is decades away, leaving the US Air Force flying blind, hence the conjecture regardin' Aurora being real."

"But surely Mach six is beyond conventional turbofan technology," Collins submitted.

"Yeah, again, if memory serves, quoting from the *Journal*, to reach this speed, the aircraft would either have a ramjet or a scramjet, or a very unique propulsion called the pulse wave detonation engine. Basically, it uses small detonations of fuel to push the aircraft forward, constantly chain-reactin' until the aircraft reaches the required speed. Normal jet engines and rockets work on the deflagration of fuel, that is the rapid but subsonic combustion of fuel. The pulse wave detonation engine works on the supersonic detonation of fuel, providin' constant volume combustion, and is much more efficient than open-cycle designs.

Like gas turbines, it leads to greater fuel efficiency and top speed."

"So, if Aurora does exist, it must fly higher than any anti-aircraft defences, while offering a range considerably greater than the SR-71?"

"You got it, Henry. The *Journal* said Aurora is set to be built in the early 1990's. *But*, and this is where reality parts company with truth, just last month, your own government questioned our DoD after a North Sea oil rig engineer reported seein' a triangular-shaped aircraft refuellin' from a KC-135. DoD told them; no such aircraft existed."

"If Aurora does exist, Wade," Natasha mused, "where would it operate from?"

"Probably the China Lake Naval Air Weapons Station, twenty miles north of Edwards AFB. You see, the term Aurora comes from a 1985 budget report in *Commerce Business Daily*, a classification of procurement notices freely available from the US Government Accountability Office. It delineated a 450 billion allocation for aircraft construction in 1987 for black-op planes. China Lake became home to black-op planes in the 1950's. The *Journal* guessed the appropriation was for the Lockheed Aurora."

"And all this Aurora stuff," Collins began, "is independent of the official SR-72 'Son of Blackbird' programme?"

"Indeed it is. So, when you boys and girls are ploughin' through Death Valley on your way back east, don't be surprised if you see a flyin' triangle in the skies heading south-east from the Palmdale skunk works to China Lake."

~ * ~

Arguably, the finest sight on the North American continent, on leaving Seligman, the Corvette and the Camaro journeyed along original Route 66 to Peach Springs, the thrill-seekers decamping on foot to a viewing station affording breathtaking views of the Grand Canyon.

Previously, whilst on assignment for *Performance* covering the American punk band NOFX gig in the desert just outside Las Vegas, Collins had used the opening to take a helicopter tour down the Grand Canyon tracking the passageway of the sandstone quenched Colorado

River. On the formative occasion, he had extensively photographed aerial views of the canyon and surrounding landscape, including the Grand Canyon National Park and the Kaibab National Forest. Jaw-dropping in terms of impact, the chapter left a perpetual imprint, the sheer vastness of the spectacle overwhelming his sense of proportion, the intricacies and broad colouration of the steep-sided canyon and near-to marooned hill shapes excavated by the passage of the river saturating his optics.

"You must have been here before," Gail posed to Gardner.

"Oh, many times, but it never fails to amaze. After my first visit while still at high school, I did some research on the canyon's foundation. Established it comprises Proterozoic and Palaeozoic strata and the meanderin' pattern was forged by the Colorado River windin' its way makin' crevices and gullies, before ventin' into Lake Mead and ultimately the Gulf of California." Halting, he spied the English with a wary expression. "It's a dangerous place as well, not to be underestimated. Dehydration, hyperthermia, lightnin' strikes, rock falls and flash floods taking their toll on the curious, and foolhardy amateur and professional geologists alike. Because of the approachin' perpendicular incline of the canyon walls, if the unexpected happens, there's no escape. Plus, the river is also unforgivin'. White water rafters have had their final moments when a surge occurs upriver in Utah after heavy rain, sending a tsunami-like bore downstream. It gathers pace in the constrictin' canyon section, risin' in height and devouring anythin' in its path."

"Definitely not a place to wander into uninformed then?" Natasha voiced.

"Put it this way, Miss Natasha, once I'd identified the risks, despite the obvious attraction of hikin' along the canyon side by side to the river, I have never been inclined to test the gods."

"But notwithstanding," Gail chanced, "people still go down into the canyon?"

"Verily they do," Gardner certified. "Park rangers erect warnin' signs on the road accesses to the canyon and patrol the locale, but it is so vast, and their few resources spread too thin to cover every possible entry point, seven by twenty-four. Usually, their job is to recover the bodies."

"It exemplifies the juxtaposition between beauty and jeopardy," Collins stationed. "Like a gigantic Venus flytrap."

"That neatly describes it, Henry," Gardner lauded. "Look but don't touch."

Chapter 11: Crossing the Mojave

In need of sustenance, Collins and co pulled up at Daily's Steakhouse in Kingman, a roadhouse first launched in the 1920s, primarily to service the needs of truckers and traveling salesmen en route to California from all points east, and about to cross the Mojave Desert. Faring well until the twenty-nine crash, core business significantly reduced in parallel with a continuous stream of dispossessed Dust Bowl migrants traveling west, calling in to buy a single coffee to meet the needs of an archetypal extended family of eight. After Roosevelt's 'New Deal' took effect, commercial business soared again, continuing to do so right up to the late 1950s, before flattening out due to competition from a myriad of similar roadhouses springing up in the Kingman locale on I40.

"Excuse me," Collins called, attracting the young bartender's attention as he served them chilli and cold beers. "Do you happen to know a gent going by the name of Luke Berringer?"

"Luke Berringer. Hhmm, doesn't strike a chord with me, friend. What's the age of this fella?"

"Erm, probably in his late sixties."

"Oh, heck, I don't believe I know anyone that old apart from my grandmammy and grandpappy." Rubbing his chin, he pleaded, "Just a minute, Pikey Brown has been here since before I was born. I'll see if he knows this Luke Berringer."

A couple of minutes later, an elderly man dressed in chef's gear and wiping his hands on a tea towel trundled up to the Collins coterie.

"You folks after Luke Berringer?"

"Indeed, we are, sir," Collins validated.

"Might I ask your business with Luke?"

"We got talking with a guy named Bill Tansey in a Taco Bell midway between Santa Rosa and Albuquerque about Luke's interactions with the beats. He recommended we contacted him."

"After his yesteryear remembrances, are you?"

"Something like that."

"Where are you folks from?"

"We're from England, chasing the beat's ghosts on Route 66, but our newly acquired compatriot here," he annexed, gesturing at Gardner, "is from Arizona."

"You don't say."

Delivering his usual radiance, Gardner introduced, "Wade Gardner of Phoenix."

"How did you happen on these English folks?"

"Oh, they took pity on me in my hour of need."

"My," Brown began, bypassing Gardner's explanation, "it's quite a while since I met anyone making out like Sal Paradise and Dean Moriarty. Me and Luke used to play pool at Elmo's Pool Hall on Airway Avenue. Had some rare ol' times. Mind you—" He pursed his lips. "Luke could get a bit finnicky if someone sounded off when he was about to take a shot. Bin known to blast offenders." Glancing right and left, as if the action provided scope for cogitation, he then divulged, "These days, Luke's livin' in Desert Hill, just north of Lake Havasu City, at 42 East Troon Drive. Tell him Pikey sent you, or you might get a hostile reception."

~ * ~

"Who *the hell* is it?" Collins heard, after knocking on the front door of 42 East Troon Drive.

"Mister Berringer, Pikey Brown from Daily's Steakhouse sent us."

"*Us*, how many of you is there?"

"Three guys including one American and two gals."

Seconds elapsed before the callers heard someone moving inside the property. With a crack, the front door burst open, and a grizzled man with a face like a clenched fist and piercing blue eyes popped his head out.

"What do you want?"

"If you have a few moments, Mister Berringer, we'd value talking to you about your exploits on the road with the beats."

"*Hah*, scummy bastards who'd do anythin' for notoriety." Halting, he became a mass of remorse. "No, I didn't mean that." Screwing up his phiz, as if suddenly educing events faded from recent memory, he barked, "You say Pikey sent you?"

"That's right, but Bill Tansey, a man we met in Clines Corners, said to look you up."

"*Bill Tansey!*"

"Yep."

Scratching his chin and wincing, he declared, "I thought that old buzzard had passed long ago."

"Well, I can assure you, Mister Berringer, Bill is very much alive and kicking."

"What's your name, boy?"

"Henry Collins." Outstretching an arm, he attached, "These fellow venturers are Natasha James, Gail Knight and Kallen Delaney. The gentleman at the back is Wade Gardner, a native of Arizona."

"Gardner?"

"Yes, sir," the American ratified.

"You related to Milt Gardner, the attorney of law?"

"Yes, sir. He was my grandpappy on my father's side."

"I guess he's passed."

"Back in seventy-six, at the ripe old age of eighty-seven."

"I had dealings with Milt in 1960. Some land speculators were trying to roust me of the property I owned, *hah*, more like a shack, and Milt represented me in court. Did a fine job. Sent the shysters packing." Peering at Collins, he jabbered, "I'll give you fifteen minutes."

Inside the house, the Collins faction quickly realised Berringer must be conducting a monastic existence. Though furniture tops were adorned with photographs and mementos of former years, it became palpable he lived alone, his introductory words making no reference to family or friends, reinforcing the belief.

Softening to Collins' courteous and respectful manner, Berringer obliged the curious pilgrims with remembrances of meeting Burroughs, Kerouac, Ginsberg and Ferlinghetti, whilst bumming around in the Midwest and stealing rides in Union Pacific Railroad boxcars. The second son of a pan-handle cattle rancher, Berringer had traded a sheltered but highly regulated lifestyle for the freedom of the road, his innate essence of rebellion against four generations of family devotion to raising Texas Longhorns forging the desire to cut loose. Along the haul, he had married and divorced a cocktail waitress twice, reared a bunch of offspring, and had numerous affairs with beat culture women, searching the juke joints and barrelhouses to excite their middle-class *modi vivendes*. From Memphis to Tucson and all points in between, work became a drag to him, his casual jobs in factories and stores lasting only a matter of months before he quit, or the boss fired him.

"Well, Mister Berringer," Gardner inaugurated, "we have a lot in common. I too forfeited my roots for the road and have had considerable problems adapting to the rules and statutes of the workplace."

"You mean, you haven't trod in your grandpappy's footsteps?"

"Neither my grandpappy's, nor my father's. What you see before you is a dissenter to regular protocol, an unorthodox heretic forsaking the accoutrements of Arizona aristocracy for the Romany life."

"Sounds familiar."

"Perhaps you can recall some of your associations with the beats?" Collins gently tabled.

"Well, let's see…While I was in Kansas City working as a press operator, *holy kamoly!*" He shook his head. "That's a soul-destroying occupation. Anyways, I ran into Burroughs in Linskys, a bottom of the barrel bar backing onto the Kansas River. It's not the kind of joint you find in Yellow Pages. I was twenty-five and looking for a way out of ranching, when I read his *Junkie* and Kerouac's *The Town and the City*. They part stimulated me to extricate myself and discover other worlds. I'd seen photographs of Burroughs, so I knew it was him. I kinda sauntered up to him and opened a conversation. He took to me right away. Later, I met Ginsberg, Kerouac and Cassidy, all beat generation romantic figures. *Aahh—*" He sneered. "But most of that turned out to be a front. Beneath the cool hipster veneer, they were full of human frailties, and as vulnerable and scared as anyone else. Ferlinghetti was the same, but Ken Kesey was built from sterner stuff. Little fazed him. In the end, those cats turned out to be like any other *avant garde* sub-culture. They burned brightly, but they burned out."

"Like the Pre-Raphaelites and the Bloomsbury Group?" Gail suggested.

"Yes, but the difference is, though the collectives you table had imperfect human conditions, howbeit, they were taken into the brotherhood of the arts by later generations. In many ways, the jury is still out on the beats."

"Yes," Delaney okayed, "but they did influence Dylan, and a whole host of rock artists."

"True, but so did Woody Guthrie, and he was the real deal, the archangel who lived continuously amongst the down and outs and hobos. His currency has wider appeal than most of the beat writers, and, the Government canonized him."

"Isn't that because Kerouac and his cohorts incited discontent with the Establishment," Collins put forward, "and promoted disobedience, if not outright insurrection."

"Certainly, that creed became instrumental in virtually all of them and their partisans, ending up under CIA surveillance," Berringer authenticated. "But the crux I'm trying to make is most of them didn't give a damn about anything. They just rolled and buffeted from situation to situation, picking up stopgap lovers along the way, even shelved away wives and children, but in terms of accomplishing satisfaction, it rarely or never happened. Most were really street hustlers and ex-Andy Warhol acolytes, out for a free ride, always envisioning the grass to be greener just a few miles further up the railway and over the embankment. It never was. It was just different. That's why most of Kerouac's oeuvre covers the same themes to be confronted. He found St Louis and Denver were no different to New York City. Sure, the people he met had their own personalities, and the backdrop differed, but fundamentally, outside it was still urban America."

"Can't that be essentially explained by virtue of the fact," Natasha began, "Kerouac and the other beat writers more or less moved strictly among those on the periphery of society, rarely if ever distilling on regular people and in status quo meeting points?"

"Oh *yeah*," Berringer agreed, "and you can count me in that insular camp. But the point I'm making, and it took me over thirty years to recognise, is the beats were petrified of becoming involved in the institutions and norms of middle America. They fancied it'd infiltrate their beings, and they'd become suits, engaging in customary pursuits, paying taxes, voting and embracing a responsible attitude. All that went against the beats' medicine. So tellingly, they were constantly marooned in a sub-society of their own making, only condensing on drifters, grifters, street entertainers, drug peddlers, and empathetic intellectuals. In reality, it engendered a lot more dirt than romance. Contrastingly, the spawn of the first gen beats, meaning the hippies, were fickle, capricious, their embracement of the counterculture, fleeting. The descendants of the Summer of Love reversed to their middle-class habitats becoming corporate lawyers, bankers and politicians. Haight-Ashbury in sixty-seven was just a youthful distraction to them, not a vehicle to promote an alternative lifestyle. Yet at the time, the authorities ran scared of the potential for wholesale revolution, sponsored by this dippy consortium."

"So you split from the beats?" Delaney hypothesised.

"Well, it'd be pretentious to say I saw the light and returned to the ranching fold. Much more the case, after traveling the highways and byways of mainly the Midwest for too many years, my yearning to see what's out there fell apart. Like for the beat writers, within the sub-strata's I moved within, I found the same types everywhere, and I became one of their order. I remember being at a Frank Zappa concert, can't remember where, when some yahoo in the audience gave Frank verbals about selling out to the establishment and becoming conformist. Frank replied, 'Everyone in this room is wearing a uniform, and don't you forget it.' That retort stuck with me because within my naturalised clique, we all dressed the same, had the same speech patterns, and behaved the same way. We were wearing not only the uniform of the disenfranchised, but its standard persona and its mask as well. We were no different to any other society or social federation having its own definitions. We were kidding ourselves that we were different. In practice, we were just an assemblage of compatible advocates, scurrying around on the bottom layer of the social structure, pretending to be hip by tuning in and dropping out, as Timothy Leary preached."

"Leary also promoted turning on, meaning taking mind-expanding drugs," Gail cautioned. "Did you indulge in the forum?"

"That came later for me when LSD could be bought over the counter in San Fran. Sure, I experimented, but I was lucky. I came out of the other side intact. Many I knew got their brains fried, ending up in mental institutions. Others emerged from the void inexorably regenerated, and unable to retrieve their former selves. They kinda traipsed around in a coma, unable to resolve what had happened to them. I easily get bored, so for me, lysergic acid became a vehicle to experience the otherworldly. Eventually I quit, because the inner-space voyages became repetitious in terms of the baseline constituents, a bit like dreams."

"What did you do after that?" Collins asked, starting to distinguish an unwholesome finish to his yarn.

"My father passed in sixty-nine leaving the ranch to my brother Mason, but he bequeathed me the princely sum of 500,000 dollars. I'd just got over my second divorce, so I needed a place to get away from everything. First, I went to Kingman where I met Pikey Brown, then moved here to make my peace with the world." Squinting at them as if undecided on an action, he then said, "If you go by way of Cheyenne on your way back to Chicago, look up beats' sage Rope Fisher. He's got a pretty wife named Hannah. He can tell you a whole lot more about Kerouac and Ginsberg." Going to a dresser he returned with a scrap of paper. Faltering, he handed Collins Fisher's address, then goggled at them with inflexible features. "Well, that's it. You've got my take on the beats. Sorry if it burst your bubble." Scrutinising them without regret, he cawed, "Your fifteen minutes is up."

~ * ~

Heading north to the I40 in the Camaro, Radio KTAR filling the interior with the Flying Burrito Brothers country cacophony, Natasha disclosed, "I didn't expect him to be so crotchety."

"No," Collins concurred. "Distinctly, he'd anticipated adhering to the beat's outlook to be both intellectually liberating and life fulfilling. But it didn't totally happen for him, the seed change not quite working out as he foresaw at its outset."

"Any acquired creed has a downside," she nominated. "Nothing is perpetually full of highs."

"Yep, but I was under no illusions before we set out on this trek."

"Oh. How?"

"In my youth, I'd have been entirely consumed by the romance of the road and meeting seasoned beats, but with creeping years comes a modicum of prudence."

"In what respect?"

"Ohh…a kind of predetermination that nothing on God's green Earth is free from inconsistencies and disappointments. Luke Berringer confirmed the supposition."

"I see."

"My motivation centred more on seeing the places Burroughs and his cohorts hung out at. I kinda knew at least some of the people we met would be disillusioned, even spiteful, but that's not to say their views would not be valid and informative."

"Hhmm, I got the express impression Berringer got his fingers burnt on the trail."

"Doubtlessly. Anyway, let's file it under ex-beat with an anti-climax complex."

"Quite right," Gardner endorsed. "No profit in seeing nirvana where it doesn't exist."

"What was your take on Berringer, Wade?" Collins sought.

"Far be it for me to cast doubt on his findings and conclusions, nonetheless, I detected resentment brought about by other factors, he unequivocally was not going to field to us. I can visualise why. I mean *hell*, we turned up on his doorstep out of the blue. It's only natural to open the emperor's kimono so far in the fellowship of acquaintances. I didn't tell you my whole story durin' that first encounter in the Holbrook jail. A lot of it has seeped out since. If we revisited Berringer, forewarnin' him in advance, he might be more receptive on a second occasion."

"Maybe," Collins qualified, "but candidly he gave us the uncensored thumbnail sketch, in the hope we'd be put off from another get-together."

"Well, I admit patently he reviewed everything in black and white, whereas I suspect durin' his time on the road, though aware of the contradictions, he assessed the backcloth in shades of grey."

"Yes, I can see that. When you've first made a monumental life transformation, you need to blank out the downsides and revel in the brightness."

"Well, Henry, I gotta admit, that is precisely what I do."

~ * ~

Throughout the trek, the English had been photographing anything and everything; people, places, predicaments, and natural wonders. Even so, once they entered the region commencing at Albuquerque, what astonished them more than anything centred on sun rises and sunsets, especially in the desert zones north and south of Route 66. Often, they'd rise early to catch the sun breaking over background mountains or flat plains, the complementary evenings providing a collage of vivacious colours as the sun descended into the western horizon, highlighting foreground objects. Cactus, tumbleweed, and irregular fashioned rocks appearing as dark to black icons against desolate but intrinsically beautiful landscapes.

Resuming on I40, they headed for Needles and the final trek along Route 66 across southern California to Santa Monica. Back in London, Collins had mentally mapped out the major stretches of the road, identifying Needles marked the beginning of the metaphorical outbound epic downhill slope. Before the linchpin demarcation point, he had envisaged predominantly gaining what they set out to do between Chicago and Kingman, ostensibly still the workhorse section of Route 66, replete with Dust Bowl, Great Depression and inflated beats legacies.

Symbolising the 'promised land' to generations of sanguine Americans both pre and post the twenty-nine Wall Street crash, in his mindset he foresaw the United States third largest state by territory behind

Alaska and Texas as a near-to utopian province, overflowing with milk and honey, the hard luck stories, bad times and tragedies stamping the Midwest replaced with tales of prosperity and success. His previous jaunts to California had imbued him with a sense of 'if you can't make it here, where all the economic provisos are ripe for attainment, then you won't make it anywhere'. True, Washington DC, Maryland and Massachusetts regularly topped the household income charts, nevertheless, distinguished by new money enterprises, notably in aerospace and computers, California typified a young person's paradise to hit the heights in terms of becoming liquid, and enjoying a healthy lifestyle away from the east coast ghettos, Mafia-controlled streets, and urban overcrowding.

Over the years, Collins had met a myriad of career-enhancement seekers, entrepreneurs and visionaries, originally from backwaters and boondocks caked in insularity and parochialism, such as in West Virginia and New Jersey, who had wended west to the vibrant and pulsating 'Golden State' and made it big time. Often such go-getters said to Collins, it they had stayed put, only frustration and failure awaited them. Though they quite rightly foresaw taking the bold step equated to an all-or-nothing strategy, the potential rewards far outstripped the relative safeguards of irrevocably planting their flags in Charleston or Hackensack. Collins admired their pioneering spirit, self-belief, and will to go on when the going got tough. In their psyches, nothing prevented their drive and determination to make the best of their lives, and steadfastly they'd negotiate setbacks coming out even stronger, and boldly go on, setting themselves higher objectives. Equivalently, to Collins, they matched first to sixth generation English ex-pats from Australia, New Zealand and South Africa, overcoming tremendous problems, grit and guile their bywords, empowering them to plough furrows in the hinterlands of new enterprise opportunity.

Without fail, the native Californians he met, and most of them were young, acknowledged they had been fortunate to have been born in a state offering open-ended prospects and scope for those with nous, and willing to put in the hours.

He had also noted Silicon Valley seemed to be mainly populated by magnates and tycoons in their twenties, quickly creating enterprise-scale businesses on the back of NASA space programme technologies and spearheading the world in terms of derived computer operating systems and industrial strength platforms and applications. These just past puberty, still learning to shave dreamers challenged long-established business support systems giants IBM, DEC, UNIVAC and Honeywell, not only gaining mindshare in the business community, but also permanently altering the complexion of the computer business away from mainframes to distributed departmental servers, a trend indefinitely sustained and owned by Silicon Valley. Often, Collins asked himself if such far-reaching steps could have been achieved in the business conservative heartlands of New York and Boston. He deduced not.

Cardinally created in the seventeenth century, the thirteen founding New England east coast states became the backbone of everything American for over three centuries, thereby breeding a closed shop to anything upsetting the status quo. Contrarily, California was a new state, joining the union in 1850, only peripherally involved in the American Civil War, and until the advent of the twentieth century, virtually unpopulated by pioneers apart from in the major conurbations of Los Angeles and San Francisco. Most nineteenth century, east coast observers, viewed California to be virtually a foreign country; remote, backward, unsophisticated, underdeveloped, and lacking the governmental structure necessary for business. Despite the rise of Hollywood as the film-making capital of the world, the blinkered view became perpetuated well into the twentieth century until a myriad of natural resource exploration and engineering companies, principally in aerospace, set up major concerns in California, particularly Los Angeles, attracting huge investment from east coast backers. Post the depression, California GDP boomed, ratcheting up many more notches after Pearl Harbour when the state provided armament for Uncle Sam to wage war on Japan, and eventually Germany. Enhancing industry, embryonic, cutting-edge enterprises showed green shoots even before termination of hostilities in the Pacific, the fascination of the new cultivating an adventurous ethos, California the place to be for men with ideas, specifically when those designs could be translated into gigantic money-spinners.

"You used the phrase, 'the tyranny of the mainstream' back in Seligman," Collins reminded Gardner, as the lower reaches of the Sierra Nevada's reared up in front of the convoy.

"Indeed I did."

"Got me ruminating about its implications."

"How?"

"If I understood you correctly, you were implying the mainstream constitutes majority consideration, and anyone casting doubt on its veracity, or donating a poles apart viewpoint, is deemed to be a heretic."

"Yeah, it's induced by fear. If a dominant combine is faced by dissention, it sparks doubt in the creed, leadin' to defence in the form of threats, castigations, intimidation and scorn."

"That's the way I see it. But there again, the world would be extremely boring, if everyone deliberated exactly the same way, and held the same opinion on every subject."

"Undeniably accurate, Henry, but what you gotta understand is most folk don't like their standpoint being queried, noticeably when they align with the mainstream. We all do it to a greater or lesser extent, yours truly included. By way of paradigm, in my humble opinion, the works of F. Scot Fitzgerald cannot be bettered in terms of reflectin' American society in the 1920s. Having devoured his oeuvre, I concluded the tribute to be without variance. All the same, I've read published critiques decimatin' Fitzgerald's take on the bigwig's double standards and hypocrisy, delineated in all quarters of his works. What ignites such an opposed and vitriolic treatise, I can only guess."

"Do you estimate the tyranny of the mainstream holds sway in California?"

"Ahh, you're pressing a native of Arizona, a state pre-eminently subscribing to the concept of mainstream views representin' the bulk, to comment on a state singularised by a wide variety of societal norms, and where virtually anythin' goes, from free love to campin' in Death Valley. Irrefutably, Californians see themselves as the *avant garde* mavens of American society, wantin' to steer the country into realms, often dismissed and ridiculed in the Midwest and on the eastern seaboard. It'd be easy to say they are natural democrats with little interest in republican principles, but like most states, the political pendulum swings both ways consonant with prevailin' instruments. I apologise if that peals like a lengthy intro to answering, but it's essential to accredit that often California sets itself apart from the American collective. Havin' said that, the tyranny of the mainstream still comes into play, but in domains you might not find elsewhere."

"Because the current corporate music business is paramountly centred on the West Coast," Collins identified, "I've probably spent more time in California than any other state. Whereas, immutably, I've found New York, Boston and Chicago to be stifling in demographic terms, often exhibiting an underlying layer of unrest on the verge of detonating. West Coast cities, exemplified by LA, are laid back in comparison. You get the feeling soon after leaving LAX, and heading north on Lincoln Boulevard towards Marina del Rey. Everything feels so spaced out, plenty of room to move, few societal restrictions, park anywhere, do anything. Does that ring a bell, Wade?"

"Well, as you know, I've never been outside of Arizona by road before, and California will be a first for me, but your valuation resonates with what I've discerned readin' and talkin' to people."

"Mmmm, I thought you'd assent. Notwithstanding, again from a music journalism slant, both the east and west coasts have thrown up a myriad of sensational rock acts since the mid-sixties, the east responsible for the Velvet Underground, the Patti Smith Group and Television, the west nurturing the Doors, the Mothers of Invention and the Byrds, to name but a few."

"Well, you'd know a whole lot more about that than me, Henry. In my youth, I saw the Seeds and the Thirteenth Floor Elevators at the Phoenix Auditorium. I might have caught Bob Dylan as well, but after that, I kinda left contemporary rock music behind, preferrin' other pleasures. These days its good ol' Johnny Cash and Waylon Jennings I tune into."

~ * ~

After checking out the Kelso Dunes Trail and Edgar Peak in the Providence Mountains on the southside of the Mojave National Preserve, the intrepid explorers holed up in Ludlow for the night at the High Desert Motel. Founded in 1882, Ludlow became a water staging post for the Atlantic and Pacific Railroad. Soon thereafter, pioneers unearthed ore in nearby hills containing precious metals and silicates, the settlement booming. During one of his early American assignments for *Crossroads*, Collins had met Josh Elderberry, a session musician working for MCA Records. A son of Ludlow, during their conclave, Elderberry had waxed lyrical about the town's history, saying despite its railroad and natural resources economic cornerstones, by the 1940s both had ceased, the town surviving by supplying the needs of commuters on the National Old Trails Road, an integral part of Route 66. Albeit, when Interstate 40 was built bypassing the town, it left little business for the residents, most departing, leaving a ghost town of decaying buildings, caressed by wilderness boscage, and inhabited by desert critters. Those left migrated to form service businesses adjacent to I40, Elderberry's parents inclusive in the move. His recital had indented Collins with a salutary recognition that remote settlements are often transitory, here today, gone tomorrow, dependent upon dominating economic circumstances.

Observing the 'new' Ludlow from the High Desert Motel, Collins sealed compared to what he knew about 'old' Ludlow, it was akin to an expansive service station on the English motorway network, dignified by little character, it's saving grace, magnificent views of the Mojave Desert and hills to the north, and the Sheephole Valley Wilderness to the south.

Earlier in the afternoon, the touring party had experienced breath-taking panoramas on the Mojave, the sun reflecting off hills, mountains and terrain irregularities producing a montage of vibrant pastel shades merging into the darker hues of the landscape. Howbeit, like for all desolate desert zones north and south of Route 66, sun rise and sunset provided the most photogenic spectacles, expressly the twilight period, when the descending sun silhouetted cacti and flowers, strikingly defining their physicality in high-fidelity black contours.

"You know," Gardner began, when Collins joined his cabal in the motel lobby, "some of the beats you are pursuing could have overnighted in Ludlow on their way to the West Coast."

"Yes, an explicit possibility," Collins concurred. "I wonder what they made of this oasis halfway into the Mojave Desert."

"Five'll get you ten, Ludlow hardly registered, if they did happen upon this neck of the woods."

"Oh, why do you say that, Wade?" Delaney investigated.

"Well, what you folks have gotta grasp, is most transients purportin' to be beats fell well short of the archetype portrayed in *On The Road*. Many clung onto the uniform and wore the badge in an attempt to be gauged as the genuine article, when in reality they were hillbillies and townies masqueradin' as hipsters and bohemians, out to prise a few bucks from gullible passersby."

"Are you saying," Natasha propounded, "the likes of Kerouac, Ginsberg, Burroughs and the other published beat gen writers and poets were the cream of an erudite crop, and most of the so-called beat afficionados were tricksters, hanging on the coattails of the movement's most renowned operators?"

"Well, Miss Natasha, if history teaches us anythin', as sure as eggs are eggs, new factions have their prime mover vanguard discriminated by invention and dedication, and their follower imitators. Often this latter alliance are locust-like charlatans, feedin' on the primary inaugurators' harvest, but contributin' little to nothin' or merely wearin' the clothes of the genre on the basis the same kudos will be bestowed upon them."

"What Wade says has credence," Gail lauded. "The hippie creed became international in terms of music and dress trend, but in the context of corresponding spartan lifestyle, few of those flying the hippie flag broke ranks with societal conformity and consumerism. It must have been the same with the beat generation."

"Right," Gardner sanctioned. "Luke Berringer alluded to the same point."

"We idolise what we perceive on the surface to be a better faith," Collins postulated, "but remain blind to the warts. Our colourisation only paints the positive symbols and icons with radiance, whilst subconsciously, we relegate the clashes to fading greys." Hesitating, he then inserted, "I hope we've not been adopting rose-tinted glasses to look at the places and people we have met during this Route 66 sojourn."

"Don't beat yourself up, Henry," Gardner encouraged. "I do not detect any unduly sentimental or wistful perspectives. On the contrary, in the short time I've known the four of you, it has become evident you all exhibit a clinical detachment, and do not froth at the mouth when you come upon beat gen leftovers, like Berringer." He grinned at them. "Anyway, no more self-recrimination...let's go get some tacos."

After wolfing down a wide array of Mexican dishes washed down with margaritas at Delgado's Taco Shack, the wayfarers segued into the night.

"Man, just look at that stellar array above," Gardner urged. "You can't see such faraway galaxies in the cities. Ambient light blots them out, but out here in the desert, all is revealed. The only time it's gonna be 'starless and bible black' to quote from *Under Milk Wood* is when the sun finally engulfs the Earth, as per my cataclysm account at the Canyon Diablo Meteorite."

"Clear skies dappled with the constellations have always been an inspiration for artists and writers," Collins opined. "Without the glories of the firmament, I'm sure most of the world's revered artistic treasures would not have been fabricated."

"We've been marvelling at the night sky since leaving Ok City," Natasha supplemented. "Living under London's bright lights, most of the heavens are lost to view, as they were in Chicago, St Louis and Oklahoma City. Asymmetrically, in the sparsely populated run between Amarillo and it looks like Barstow, manmade light is thinly dispensed, affording an un-diminished view of the stratosphere."

Night time had always been an enchanted event for Collins. Marvelling at the wild blue yonder since childhood and possessed with notions about men on the moon and beacons emanating from faraway Mars, the galaxies embodied a captivating playground for him. Whereas daylight exposed nature's singular beauty, it lacked the inherent mystery of the nocturnal hours. Darkness illuminated by the moon heralded the possibility of the paranormal and the supernatural, the witching hour recorded by the chiming of grandfather clocks striking twelve, signalling the entrance of sorcerers' wizardry, maybe even the occult. Never a fan of Tolkien's childish 'Middle-earth' mythology, his preference erred towards Weston's *From Ritual to Romance* and Frazer's *The Golden Bough*, both highly influential on Eliot's *The Wasteland*, as sources of Arthurian legend and psychic myths, their best manifestations occurring during the night. Fleetingly, he had dabbled with the machinations of occultist Aleister Crowley, but dismissed the bombast as farfetched. Often during his teens, he found a remote location well away from city illumination to view the celestial sphere, his ingenuity fired by the boundless star array. When his relationship with Babette turned sour, he sought refuge in the endless night, trying to decipher the problems of two specks of dust meandering the Earth, against the expanding magnitude of the universe, his dilemma put into cogent context.

Before setting out for their 'New World' adventure, one February evening, he had gazed at the vault of heaven conjecturing if the same star configurations were visible from Chicago to LA. So absorbed by his job assignments and personal factors, not once during previous visits to the colonies had he taken the trouble to make the check.

Now in the cradle of uncluttered, astral observation offered by the Mojave, he revisited the earlier impulse, determining the heavenly raiment above to be a key reason for those with an artistic bent to make the desert their home, nightly lunar field inspections providing the stimulus for universal creation.

~ * ~

"So, boys and girls" Gardner initiated, over breakfast at Denny's, "how's your appointed road excursion treating you?"

"It's the ambiguity of happenstance that makes it alluring," Delaney attributed. "You're never absolutely sure what's going to happen."

"Primarily way out west," Natasha attached. "The frequency of running into oddballs is more prolific than in Illinois, Missouri and Oklahoma."

"Yes," Gail accepted. "If I had to make a demarcation point, it'd be at Amarillo in the pan-handle."

"How do you explain that, Wade?" Collins probed.

"It's down to wide open spaces grantin' a bountiful playground for disenfranchised thrill-seekers like me." Pausing, he then volunteered, "Since you are all such affable folks, I'm goin' to share a confidence with you. After Holbrook, I said I hadn't met anyone with a similar background to me on the road. Wasn't quite true." Entering into a judicious comportment, he delineated, "Ethan Stone, a fellow wanderer of my acquaintance, is the best example of a totally free spirit I have ever witnessed. We have much in common. Born into a fairly affluent family in Tucson, he traded the trappings of comfort for walkin' the Earth like *Kung Fu* David Carradine, substituting the Shaolin monk mantle for that of a zingaro, what you folks call a gypsy. Whereas I went into a kind of arrested development phase, gingerly findin' my way in the unfamiliar zones, Ethan seemed to have been everywhere and done everythin' all at once, without breakin' sweat. He's a shape-shifting eccentric, comin' up from a varyin' hole every time. You never know where he's going to pop his head up, and engender astoundment or havoc. Anyways—" He shone as if mesmerised by the recall. "Of all the people I've met during my wanderings, Ethan Stone is the epitome of the disenfranchised thrill-seeker clan. Unequivocally, nothin' fazes or shocks him. He takes everythin' full-on as the road rises up to meet him. Got him hospitalised a few times, but that didn't prevent him from goin' for infinite exploration. *Hah*—" His glint broadened. "Just for kicks, whilst workin' as a gofer at Turf Paradise, a horse track, pari-mutuel betting exchange, he engaged in a bit of free enterprise, running his own book. Worked well for a few weeks, then the accountants noticed a consistent drop in betting receipts, when he was on duty. Now I don't know how English bookies react to such goings-on, but er, here in the United States, the gee-gees are big business, cartel-like in their structure and very, very possessive about every placed dollar. When they caught Ethan in the act, instead of turnin' him in to the city police, they administered a solid beatin' to him, and he was banned from entry into any racecourse, country-wide."

"Did he suffer bad injuries?" Delaney enquired.

"Put it this way, Kallen, he got hospitalised for a month. Nothin' broken, but he was a mess of lacerations and bruises from head to toe."

"So the kicks were provided by him getting away with it, at least for a while?"

"Yep, but he paid a heavy price. Nonetheless, Ethan's got in worse scrapes, but managed to avoid retribution. I suspect he knew the Turf Paradise caper was fatally flawed, but just couldn't resist seein' how long he could get away with it. On the flipside, inescapably, he's a consummate experimenter on the social front, and has been known to buy into Dr Leary's prescription for cerebral expansion, leadin' to intense insight. If the occasion demands, he's also an opulent conversationalist and orator, on a wide range of philosophical and scientific disciplines."

"Reverberates like a powerful piece of manpower," Collins quipped.

"For sure, but what really sets Ethan apart is his capacity to dovetail into any diverse grouping, and materialise as a gifted guru on whatever subject they have tied their colours to. I mean hell, if he hadn't chosen the itinerants' path, he could have become a university professor, or an industry megastar. There's that much substance to the man. First time I met him was in Tombstone."

"Legendary town," Collins acclaimed, "now close to a ghost town apart from tourism."

"Oh, that's the truth of it. The barometer population of Tombstone has gone up and down accordin' to prevailing economic conditions. It became one of the last boomtowns on the American frontier, meanin' the Old West or the Wild West, when local silver mines produced up to eighty-five million dollars a year in silver bullion in the mid-1880s. Then, over 14,000 lived in and around Tombstone, but when the silver minin' became uneconomic, the population gradually shrivelled to less than a thousand by 1940. Anyways, I digress. When I ran into him in one of the few remainin' saloons' selling liquor, he blew me away with his physicality and rhetoric. Well over six feet with broad shoulders and a Wild Bill Hickok hairstyle with penetrating eyes, he cut an awesome effigy. *Huh*, looked like he'd just done battle with the McLaury-Clanton gang in the guise of Doc Holiday or Wyatt Earp at the O K Corral.

However, when I opened chitchat with him, I quickly discovered his intellectual prowess far exceeded his mighty physique. He had me enthralled by his take on a wide variety of disciplines and philosophies, so unique, I became tempted to write them down, but er, hah, by then we'd drained a quart of rye and I found my writing hand incapacitated."

"Just advise me, Wade," Delaney interjected, "where is Tombstone located?"

"It's south-east of Tucson, and only forty miles from the Mexican border. If memory serves, I was hitch-hikin' on I10, heading for Tucson when this guy picked me up. He was goin' to South Bisbee. I knew Tombstone was on his scheme, so I updated my plans and he turned me loose in Tombstone. I didn't know what my intentions were, other than checkin' out the town. So pure off-chance trumpeted my meetin' with Ethan Stone."

"When did you last see him?" Natasha pumped.

"Ohh...let me think." Rubbing his unshaven chin, he authenticated, "It must have been in Gray Mountain two years ago. He'd been up in Mount Pleasant Utah, moseyin' around a carnival, and was goin' to Flagstaff to see some old buddy of his. I'd been holed up in a tradin' post for a few days, when in he walks, larger than life, shinin' like a sapphire. We talked for quite a while, in fact, he stayed the night, but left early the next mornin'. Hah—" He gleamed. "They don't make em like Ethan Stone anymore. All that free-wheelin' has been socialised out of the latest two generations of Arizona aristocrats."

Crossing the balance of the Mojave became memorable for the adventurers, the contrasts between flat sections and those littered with sand dunes with single hills or ranges poking skywards before and behind them, serving to amplify an intuition of isolation in a state containing some of the biggest cities in the world. Its legends were legion. After taking acid, this was the place where Jim Morrison and the Doors had visions of a Navajo medicine man directing their creative juices, the sanctuary where Gram Parson's close associates had immolated his body after he had died from an overdose of morphine and alcohol, and LA's backyard where countless writers, artists and musicians pilgrimaged for inspiration, and periodically, respite from the million miles per hour city.

Emerging from the winter hiatus, the Mojave was beginning to burst into bloom, the Collins posse intermittently stopping to photograph vibrant flora, in particular blue palo verde, desert holly and chuparosa, driving home the rationale that even the most hostile environments have their golden patches.

Just like in Bobby Troup's famous song, they had passed through Gallup, Flagstaff, Kingman and Barstow. By nightfall, after cutting into the Angeles National Forest at Cajon Junction, the convoy entered the outskirts of San Bernardino. Soon, the glowingly lit downtown skyscrapers of Los Angeles loomed into the foreground, signing the rundown to the termination of Route 66.

Chapter 12: The City of the Angels

A perennial favourite for Collins, of all the major cities attracting touring rock bands and thereby the musical press, Los Angeles held pride of place in his reckoning. Not simply based on Hollywood's glitz and glam and the vivacity dripping from high-octane output recording studios, the city vibrated with energy and pizzazz raising his heartbeat and sharpening his senses. Whereas, in the main, most of the east coast whistle stops were predictable, there always seemed to be a fresh experience around every LA corner, an unexpected sight or a new take on an established formula he marvelled at with wonderment. Better still, the residents set themselves apart as well. Certainly New York, Boston and Washington DC boasted their fair share of intellectual buffs, but beyond this fringe fraternity the general populace were dull. In comparison, LA folk never lacked for dash and gusto, the cream of its intelligentsia often surpassing the oft cited masters of highbrow chic holed up in Brooklyn and Cambridge.

First setting foot in Los Angeles whilst reporting on the 1975 Led Zeppelin tour of North America for *Crossroads*, Collins had stayed at the Marina del Rey Marriott to also checkout Nils Lofgren at the Whisky a Go Go, Tom Petty & the Heartbreakers at the Roxy, and the Flamin' Groovies at the Troubadour. Affording him a weekend stay, after the Saturday night Nils Lofgren gig, he picked up Sunset Boulevard from the Sunset Strip in his rented Mustang convertible, eventually merging onto Mulholland Drive, and journeying all the way to Autry Overlook vaunting panoramic views over Bel Air and Beverley Hills.

As the shimmering night passed by during the drive, he pondered on his impressions of LA. Arriving charged up with imprints of the celebrated Doors, Love and the Byrds, during the days, he took the opportunity to cruise the Strip searching for the ghost of Jim Morrison, and noting forthcoming music attractions on the billboards towering above the rock joints. By night, the City of the Angels downtown locale metamorphosed into a hive of pleasure seekers, drug pushers and hipsters, the insanely nouveau rich parading down from Beverley Hills into music halls, bars and bordellos, intent on getting high on some libation or another, fooling around with hookers or chancing a shot of white line fever. Collins took in the twenty-four-hour cycle like a sponge, absorbing everything entering his sensory systems, the observance providing the backdrop to anchor and position his accounts of the bands he'd witnessed strutting their shtick on stage.

Pushing the driver door shut behind him, and taking a few steps to the edge of the overlook, he goggled at the sweeping cityscape in the background filtering into the suburbs of Laurel Canyon and Beverley Glen in the middle-ground, the swanky districts then seeping into the lower reaches of the dense tree formations, winding their way up into the hill top shrubland in the foreground. Gaining the manifest hunch of being a minor player in a widescreen Cecil B DeMille production, he put the illusion down to the nearness of the Hollywood film studios and the knowledge that much of the Los Angeles conurbation had been used for shot-on-location epics since the 1920s. Comparing the vista with remembrances of Harlem, Detroit, Trenton and Cincinnati only served to reinforce the hypothesis that LA differed markedly from east coast and Midwest industrial heartlands, mainly because of their geographical limitations. Unlike the Hollywood Hills and the vast Pacific giving counterpoint to the central Los Angeles basin, most eastern seaboard and central US cities lay in flatlands with no topographical respite affording relief from their insular domains.

Mulling over the disparity for several minutes, he then heard someone say behind him, "Quite a spectacle."

Wheeling about, he became confronted by an elegant young woman, the distant city lights reflecting off her deep lapis-blue eyes.

"Yes," he agreed.

"It's pretty in the daytime, but at night it has much more aura."

"Have you walked down Mulholland Drive from Laurel Canyon?" he gambled, after noticing the Mustang had not been joined by another car.

"Yes, I'm on my way back to Coldwater Canyon Drive. Been at a party given by a famous English blues musician." She took him in more fully. "You're English, aren't you?"

"Is my accent that much of a giveaway?"

"Hah, as soon as you spoke, I knew you were English."

"I'm a journalist for *Crossroads*. Out of professional curiosity, may I know the name of the English blues musician?"

"John Mayall."

"Oh, very impressive. I've never met him, but I do admire his music, notably the 'Beano album' and *Blues from Laurel Canyon*."

"I've also met Frank Zappa, Joni Mitchel and Roger McGuinn."

"In Laurel Canyon?"

"Yes." She twinkled at him. "What's your name?"

"Henry Collins, at your service."

She smiled. "Very gallant. I'm Carrie Carter."

"Mmmm, catchy. Is that your real name, or your stage name?"

"Stage name?"

"Yes, with your good looks and connections, I speculated you must be in the film or the music business."

"Ohh, it's my brother who's in the music business. He's an A&R manager for Capitol Records. I'm a contracts officer at Lockheed."

"What, the Burbank skunk works HQ?"

"Indeed."

"Wow, a very hush-hush establishment."

"Quite."

"So it's via your brother you get to meet these music superstars?"

"Yes, he knows a lot of people in the LA music business. He signed Linda Ronstadt, Grand Funk Railroad, Quicksilver Messenger Service and the Steve Miller Band to various Capitol and EMI labels."

"Impressive."

She ventured nearer to the edge of Autry Overlook. "I never get tired of this view. Sometimes I've stood here for hours gaping into the diorama and picking out places, even buildings I know. With all the mega-rich residents, the cops patrol the canyons in the wee-small hours. They've checked me out several times when I'm here in the middle of the night." Swivelling on her heels, she informed, "We had some murders here six years ago at nearby Cielo Drive Beverley Hills."

"Sharon Tate and colleagues butchered by the Manson ring."

"That's right. Paranoia ran rife for a while, prominent home owners demanding police protection."

"Made worldwide headlines."

"I was still at high school when the Cielo Drive murders occurred, but they left a permanent fingerprint in terms of how people reacted. Some petitioned the mayor of Los Angeles to beef up the policing provision. There were demonstrations as well outside City Hall by Beverley Hills and Laurel Canyon residents. It became a big issue at the time. Hence the cop patrols." She shrugged her shoulders. "It's cosmetic anyway. There's only one cop car patrolling the aggregate Beverley Hills and Laurel Canyon districts."

"Doesn't it bother you that maniacs target this area?"

"I figure if you're in the sights of a killer, they are going to get you one way or another, so there's little advantage in hiding away. Besides, you shouldn't spend your life in the grip of fear, when there are so many positive things to appreciate."

"Like this view?"

"Yes."

~ * ~

Nearing West Covina on I10, Carrie Carter seeped into the forefront of Collin's cognition. Additional to the Autry Overlook interlude, he had experienced other chance meetings with diverting people on Venice Beach and Redondo Beach, at Griffith Observatory and in a multitude of hotels in West Hollywood and Inglewood. Albeit, Carrie stood out because she emanated a *laissez-faire* attitude to all phenomena, including the Cielo Drive murders. He had surmised it to be an American, or more precisely, a Californian trait, signalling with the freedoms on tap to the anything goes west coast society, she accepted some bad eggs germinating in the environment. That concept bothered Collins because it acknowledged homicidal maniacs like Charles Manson were inherent in the 'land of the free', the very nature of the doctrine allowing crazed killers to refine their evil arts without restraint, until finally apprehended. Whereas English society was horrified by 'Moors Murderers' Hindley and Brady and other serial killers, not only Carrie but other Americans he'd met seemed to bear their own lunatic slayers as an everyday hindrance, placed in the same risk category as contracting an incurable disease or inadvertently walking in front of a speeding Greyhound bus. True, most countries apart from the Nordics bred their own psychos, and certainly the instance of them metered as proportional to the size of the population, the 1985 238 million US nation potentially fostering many more than *exempli gratia* Portugal's ten million citizens. Worse still, no matter how advanced the first world became in terms of technological breakthroughs and social structures, nothing seemed to stem the rate of psychopaths coldly and clinically conducting their trade.

Never a student of sociology, such mortifying facts failed to enter Collins' consciousness until he began to travel abroad on behalf of *Crossroads*. That signalled a demarcation cliff, interacting with locals exposing the not-so-rosy shortcomings of their societies, including incidences of wholesale slaughter. Worse, the aggressors did not bear the hallmarks of a rabid killer, foaming at the mouth, and ambling along with a Frankenstein-like motion. All were quite ordinary in build and facial properties, indistinguishable from the sane in crowds. Consequently, he entered into a period of scrutinising strangers with a jaundiced eye on aircraft and trains, out on the streets, and in concert venues, trying to resolve if they were serial killers. As with all human phases, it petered out, Collins putting his paranoia into perspective.

After skirting around central LA via Pico Gardens and South Park, the Camaro and the Corvette glided along the final part of I10 towards Santa Monica, the city's neon lights and freeway commotion seeming to herald their arrival. An entirely opposite vibe compared to the venerable cities of the Midwest weighed down with Dust Bowl and Great Depression legacies, LA exuded an air of positivity. Any ambition or enterprise seemed possible in California, especially in the City of the Angels. Because of its relative newness, it tarried free from colossal social and municipal baggage, the boulevards and highways squeaky clean, no rotting, brownstone tenement housing and bent eschew streetlamp pillars like in east coast ghettos, a city hall rising resplendent amongst a diffusion of spotless glass and steel skyscrapers, and everything laid out neat and tidy with space to spare, allowing pedestrians to breathe out without whacking a fellow walker.

To Collins, it had always approximated the English garden cities of Letchworth and Welwyn Garden City, only on a much grander scale. Lovingly architected and built in the Edwardian era to accommodate overspill from London, garden cities were idealised model villages detached from the griminess of the Industrial Revolution and *ad hoc* town planning affecting all mature English cities. Most of all, they were imbued with every landscaped facility to make life pleasant for those migrating to the arcadian Hertfordshire countryside. Likewise, Los Angeles shone with elation, her borderlines nettled with rugged, asymmetrical hills, giant forests and the seemingly infinite Mojave Desert, her coastline speckled with flawless beaches, piers jutting out into the Pacific, and rolling waves big enough to carry a surfer from Playa Del Rey to El Segundo. A jewel in the Californian treasure chest, with fabulous weather all year round, containing the world's biggest film production community, more aircraft companies than in any other city on the Earth, and enough nouveau millionaires to out-do a blue-chip investor caucus, LA personified the great American dream. Most people Collins had met from Los Angeles were proud of their city, not in a boastful way but a laid-back manner tinged with confidence. In comparison, he'd talked to many from the north-east and the north-midwest having little regard for their home towns, often castigating them as down-trodden, bleak and dirty, New York, Detroit and Pittsburgh expressly attracting scathing commentary.

Another facet differentiating her from the rest reposed on the demographic statistic, there were more beautiful people in Los Angeles, than in any other major conurbation, Hollywood bearing testament to the fact by hiring many of their stable of alluring actors and actresses from within a fifty miles radius of Ventura Boulevard since the twenties. Back in 1978, Collins had met a galaxy of aspiring starlets and accustomed stars including Candice Bergen, Liza Minelli, Jill St John, Richard Chamberlain and Jeff Bridges, all born in LA, at a party given by Warner

Brothers when Fleetwood Mac's *Rumours* hit ten million sales worldwide. There to interview Mick Fleetwood and John McVie for a *Crossroads* review of the band since their inception eleven years earlier, he became spellbound by the gorgeous brigade, teeth and tits to the fore for the women, groomed locks and suntans for the men. They were all so matter of fact about it, their glowing public image riveting photographers, though Collins knew beneath the posturing and out of sight of the press, immense divides devoured their habitats, claws drawn and tongues spitting sequent from long held grudges and conflicts of interest. Like in the music business where he'd witnessed egos getting bent out of shape and over-ebullient rock artists slapped down by seasoned record company execs, he knew the same mischief and tomfoolery existed in the film business. Nevertheless, it endured as a memorable hiatus trading licks and sharing champers with the gods and the goddesses.

After crossing the Route 66 finish line at Santa Monica Pier, they backtracked, checking into the Palm Motel off Pico Boulevard, before the Collins' circle decamped to Chez Jay on Ocean Avenue for buttered steak and tequila slammers.

"Well, I must say, my dear friends," Gardner opined, "without reservation, it has been a privilege and a blessin' to accompany you for the past few days."

"We liked your presence as well, Wade," Gail advertised.

"Why, thank you, Miss Gail. It brings a dole of gladness to this old heart of mine to commune with venturers having no pre-conceptions or criticisms about my adopted lifestyle."

"It's not what we do with anybody," Collins qualified. "Our intention was, and still is, to take people as we find them."

"Well, that's very laudable, Henry. It's er, not very often in this day and age I run into open-minded rings like yourselves. Most I encounter either grade me with complete disdain, or classify me as a delinquent playboy."

"What are you going to do next, Wade?" Delaney tabled.

"Oh, I'll spend tomorrow with you guys seeing the sights, then I'll head back to Phoenix on Amtrak. I'm of a persuasion to return to the nest for a while. See how the land lies with the family."

Early the next morning, Collins and co breezed out of the Palm Motel in the motors, bearing a few points north of due west.

"Where we headin'," Gardner posed, "Lincoln County Road or Armageddon?"

"That's a line from Dylan's *Senor* on his *Street Legal* album," Collins ascribed.

"Yep. Poses a monumental question, doesn't it?"

"Well, I'd have countersigned the sentiment until recent times, when Gorbachev arrived on the international stage and powwowed with Reagan. Looks like those boys have a collective understanding regarding détente, meaning a massive reduction in ICBMs."

"Amen to that, but additional to a global thermal nuclear exchange, Armageddon has many guises. That devil can transform into monsters near-to as fatal as the hydrogen bomb."

"For instance?"

"I hear tell from a number of informed sources, the benchmark and duration of natural destructive phenomena like twisters broader than Arizona and tsunamis as big as Everest will happen because of manmade gases cloggin' up the atmosphere, and burnin' holes in the ozone layer. Whether it's as catastrophic as they paint, I can't decide. But if it is true, then we're in for some pretty heavy-duty weather patterns, the like of which the world has never seen before. Such cyclopean-sized prodigies could result in more devastation than the A-bombs dropped on Hiroshima and Nagasaki."

"Food for thought. Albeit, to answer you, we're heading for the Los Angeles County Museum of Art on Wiltshire Boulevard, followed by the Hollywood Museum and the Academy Museum of Motion Pictures, then I visualised we'd take a stroll through Griffith Park, Sunset Boulevard and Hollywood Boulevard."

"A lot to see then?"

"Hah, that only scratches the veneer. You really need a week in LA to do it justice."

During an interview with Love guitarist and singer Brian MacLean in England, the LA man had told Collins about his rearing in Holmby Hills, near neighbour Frederick Loewe of the song-writing team

Lerner and Loewe, saluting him as a melodic genius at the age of three, as he doodled on the piano. Influencing his conviction processes, MacLean's mother was an artist and dancer, his father an accomplished architect for Hollywood celebrities Dean Martin and Elizabeth Taylor. His first girlfriend, Liza Minnelli, sung excerpts from *The Wizard of Oz* with him at the piano. Growing up, he became exposed to a multiplicity of art and natural attractions, including the Hollywood Pantages theatre, often used for new film audience testing before going on general release, and the Angeles National Forest, home to a profusion of oak woodlands and rare fauna inclusive of gray foxes and cougars. All in all, his nurturing in the City of the Angels collated with the stuff of legend. During his teens, he had frequented every famous music cathedral on and around Sunset Strip, the Whisky A Go Go, the Trip and the London Fog his nightly backyards, before becoming a balladeer, meeting Byrds Roger McGuinn and Gene Clarke, then forming Love with Arthur Lee. The account left Collins in a state of awe. True, many English rockers, typically the Beatles and the Rolling Stones, could recite similar formative year experiences, but their eventual coalescence into bands happened in grimy, post-second world war backdrops, populated by decaying coffee shops and rock cellars reeking of piss. Driving home to Collins the immense difference between the 'new world' of Los Angeles, and the bombed-out battered and broken English cities, he comprehended MacLean's formative history was emblematic for City of the Angels natives. When he first set foot in LA, after taking a cursory tour around the city, he concluded he'd need a solid week or more to really take in both the natural and manmade attractions.

Late in the day, the English troupe deposited Gardiner at Union Station for his return to Phoenix, the latter furnishing Collins with his family address, and urging him to make contact should there be a second Route 66 expedition.

"Wade, you've been like a shooting star in our midst," Collins eulogised, "flaring briefly with enough energy to imprint us with brio beyond our perceptions."

"Ohh, Henry," he retorted, flinging an arm around Collin's shoulder, "you overpraise me."

"No, he's right," Natasha injected. "You've brought an incandescent element of candour into our trip, we could never have foreseen at its outset."

"Yeah," Delaney added, "you're on the same astral plane as the best of the beats, Wade."

"Oh, my, oh my, you do me too much honour."

"You will always be in our thoughts," Gail assured, "as someone with sound thinking and plain speaking."

"Well, may I say in response, it has been my inestimable pleasure to be in the company of four illustrious fellow travellers."

~ * ~

Returning to Santa Monica, the irresistible Pacific beckoned the English. Joyfully walking beside the ocean in the baking heat, on reaching Venice Beach, they stripped and plunged into the surf, the sea caressing their bodies, drawing out tensions and memory baggage, the liberation so complete, all they could do was laugh and hug and hold each other.

"Say, you guys look like you're throwing off the shackles," a bronzed, heavy-set man with sun-bleached blond hair, attired in Bermuda shorts and a t-shirt proclaiming 'The Governor Sucks' voiced, approaching Collins' guild, still fooling around in the surf.

Shaking his loose hair out of his face, Collins attested, "We're letting out an accumulation of steam."

"That right. My name's Paul Christian. I'm staying at the Marina del Rey Marriott. Down here on business. How about you guys?"

"We've just completed our beat-generation crusade along Route 66," he gaily advertised.

"Wow, it's a long time since I've met anyone doing that jaunt."

His cogs clicking into place, Collins recognised the gent's name. "Are you the same Paul Christian who used to work for CBS?"

"Oohh, as a matter of fact, I am."

"My name is Henry Collins. I'm a journalist for *Performance* magazine."

"So, you're in the music business too?"

"Yes, my buddy as well." Pointing at Delaney still frolicking with Gail and Natasha, Collins explained, "He's an A&R man for Cold Turkey Records."

"You all English?"

"Indeed we are."

"Say, I'd like to chew the cud with you guys. How about we retire to the Marriott's bar?"

"Love to."

After making the remaining introductions to Christian, they sloped off to the nearby Marriott, parking themselves in a booth for five in its robotic equipped bar.

Summoning a waitress, Christian asked, "What'll it be?"

"Oh, beers all round, please," Collins replied.

"Five buds please, honey," he requested to the waitress, "and charge it to room eight-twelve."

"Yes, Mister Christian," she silkily murmured, the flash off her perfect white teeth zinging like cut Dolomites.

"Pretty girl," Delaney complimented as the waitress strode away.

"She should be," Christian insisted. "She's a Hollywood starlet." Facing Collins, he tattled, "So you know my name?"

"You were a mover and a shaker when William S. Paly and Goddard Lieberson ran CBS."

"Yeah, the one gentile amongst a cartel of Jews." He laughed. "Huh, my surname kinda gave it away."

"Rumour had it, you were let go by CBS for exceeding your brief."

"That was the official line. In point of fact, Yetnikof got me fired."

"Walter Yetnikoff, President of CBS Records?"

"Yeah, that's the son of a bitch. You see, I brought in a lot of new rock acts to CBS Records in the late sixties. They really blistered the album charts worldwide, and sequently, I rose to VP level. Yetnikof claimed I wielded too much clout, and threatened the Jewish domination of CBS. The only Jewish exec who supported me was Clive Davis, and they fired his ass under dubious allegations, as well."

"Yes, I've met Clive. Very personable chap."

"One of the best."

"You went to Elektra Records after CBS, didn't you?"

"Uh-huh. Hired by CEO Jac Holzman as VP future artists. That was just fine until Elektra merged with David Geffen's Asylum Records, already owned by Warner Communications. Inevitably, rationalisation determined there were too many VPs and not enough job slots. Geffen is part of the Jewish fraternity, and he saw to it that most of the senior exec redundancies were non-Jewish."

"So you got let go again?"

"You're damned tootin'. Well…I learned my lesson after that. Took time out and wrote a biography of my career in the record business. Then Indie market pioneers Andromeda Records came calling. Their CEO Todd Spencer offered me a VP post. I checked him out. Established he was a gentile, so I accepted. Been with Andromeda for ten years."

"Andromeda signed a lot of the post-punk and neo-psychedelic bands in the early eighties," Delaney interjected.

"For sure, and that's down to yours truly. We're based up in Seattle and posed to sign a whole new raft of local bands similar to Dinosaur Jr and Sonic Youth." Sighing, he annexed, "I was just glad to get away from record companies dominated by Jews."

"I believe," Natasha elucidated, "you suffered at Columbia, and maybe Warner, what the politically correct affiliation categorise as discrimination and racism."

"*Damned* straight, but I've grown to grasp such terms only apply when blacks, Asians and Jews are abused. The same consideration docs not apply to white Christians."

"What brings you to LA?" Gail asked.

"Well, I'll tell ya, because tomorrow it'll be the subject of a press announcement."

"Go on."

"I've been negotiating with a certain major record conglomerate, the same one Elvis signed with after leaving Sun, for the distribution of Andromeda Record products worldwide."

"You mean, RC—"

"*No*, don't say the name," Christian insisted, pushing his hands forward and peering about defensively. "You never know who might be listening." Returning to his previous sanguine posture, he broached, "Back on Venice Beach, you said you've just completed your beat generation odyssey along Route 66."

"All the way from Chicago to Santa Monica Pier," Collins clarified.

"Well, it might interest you guys to know, I did have some dealings with the hipster brigade in the sixties."

"We'd prize you sharing your remembrances with us."

"I was in Denver on behalf of CBS, checking out local folk-rock bands. We'd already signed up Dylan, the Byrds were in the hopper, and we wanted to build up the roster. I'd watched about five to seven outfits over two nights, never really connecting with any of them. About to leave some godforsaken folk club, I can't remember the name, a guy looking like a Leon Trotsky impersonator stood up, went to the microphone and began reciting *Poem from Jail*. He put so much guts into his delivery, I just had to make his acquaintance. Turned out to be Ed Sanders, later known as the bridge between the beat and hippie generations. He told me he was putting together a band to be called the Fugs with fellow post-beat poets come writers, Tuli Kupferberg and Ken Weaver. I'd horsed around with beats in the late 1950s, and read some works by Kerouac and Burroughs, so I knew something about the sub-culture. Back at CBS, I proposed we sign the Fugs, but er...*hah*, as usual, the short-sighted hierarchy didn't want to know, but Folkways did, and they signed them up."

"Didn't Folkways have Ewan MacColl and Woody Guthrie on their roster?" Delaney mooted.

"Damned right, so they had street cred, but that made no difference to the CBS execs and bean counters. Anyway, I kept in touch with Sanders. Needless to say, he was intimate with all the major first gen cats, so I got to parley with Kerouac, Burroughs, Corso and others. Burroughs was the most noteworthy from a professional angle, because he exhibited a want to take his readings into the studio, and work with rock musicians. Again, I tendered to Columbia that we had Burroughs work with Dylan and some rock acts, but they said no, classifying him and the rest of the beat luminaries as anti-American weirdos, freaks and screwballs. Burroughs got his wish via the *Nova Convention*, working with Zappa, Cage and Glass for Giorno Poetry Systems record releases. He even got on the cover of *Sergeant Peppers*."

"What were your impressions of Kerouac and Ginsberg?" Collins asked.

"Jack was the most affable person I met in the sixties, and Ginsberg had his moments. More than ever, I became convinced a marriage between the beat poets and the music industry correlated as a money spinner. Dylan was all for it. The times were right, the younger generation exploring far and wide. An explosion in contemporary music occurred, creating many shades, including folk and country rock, progressive blues and jazz rock, plus cross fertilisation with classical and traditional music on both sides of the Atlantic. But at CBS…" He bared his teeth sarcastically. "…only Davis and me were in tune with the trend. Most of the music fusion acts went to Elektra, Verve and Atlantic, even Capitol, and on your side of the pond, Polydor, Harvest and Island. Naturally, CBS caught on after the Summer of Love and Monterey, which is where I made my mark, but in terms of market perception and kudos, they were deemed to be a follower record company for the underground rock entrants, a bit died in the wool, old fashioned, uncool, and not hip, like for instance Elektra." Hesitating, he attached, "When Jack passed in sixty-nine, I largely lost interest in the beats. Oh, I heard from Ginsberg and Burroughs once in a while, but my heart was no longer in trying to get record companies to take them seriously. Besides, their time hit the downward slope. Other sub-cultures were superseding beatdom and the hippie bohemian lifestyle. But I am sure as hell glad I had the privilege of knowing some of them."

~ * ~

At the crack of dawn, the explorers headed out of LA north-west along the Pacific Coast Highway, Collins and Natasha in the Corvette, its FM receiver booming out REM's *The One I Love* from Radio LAXD, Delaney and Gail in the Camaro. Malibu came and went as did Ventura and Santa Barbara before a contingent layover at Morro Bay for a seafood lunch at a family run cantina specialising in lobster, squid and prawn dishes. What struck the travellers more than any other natural feature became the constant view of the ocean from every nook and cranny of the stretch. Sometimes placid and on other happenings a conflagration of breakers raining down on beaches, it steadfastly caught the eye. Stopping at Rincon Point, they watched a parade of surfers riding waves up to three storeys in height. Most failed to stay upright as they traversed down and across the carrying wall of water, leaving the spectators anxious for their wellbeing, only to see their heads pop up in the swell, after the wave crashed down on the beach. A miracle of human balance and bravery pitted against the awesome supremacy of the sea, they evaluated it took a special kind of person to even attempt the sport, those perfecting it, entering the empyrean of the surfing gods. Another seaward sight often coming into their field of regard centred on dolphins and sharks caught up in the rollers, their darker skin tones visible in the translucent water. Just how surfers and in the case of sharks, predators coexisted in the same time-space continuum became a conundrum, though they failed to see humans and sea life in the same wave. Like staring into a fish tank provides therapeutic and tranquilising benefits to the observer, wave watching accomplished the same boon, the adventurers feeling all tensions drift away leaving them content. But for the need to sustain their extended timetable, they could have happily continued the pastime until dusk.

Reminding Collins of whale watching on Vancouver Island, as he became entranced by the spectacle, visions of the caper emerged. During one of his many band-following tours, he had taken the short flight from Seattle to Victoria on Vancouver Island, hired a car and driven to Otter Point Park to observe bowheads, humpbacks and orcas breaking the surface, their prodigious size dwarfing his preconceptions. Made him fathom how small and puny humans were compared to the kings of the sea.

On they travelled, Harmony, the outskirts of Cambria and San

Simeon flashing by until they stopped at Ragged Point for the night, the invigorating sea air absorbed during the day's run quickly having them retire to their beds, sleepy but blissed out after a light supper and a night cap dose of Wild Turkey.

Chapter 13: Monterey and Cannery Row

Collins had wanted to pay homage at the site of the 1967 Monterey Pop Festival at the Monterey County Fairgrounds while on assignment for *Performance* in Frisco to interview Heart guitarist, the luscious Nancy Wilson, and catch the Minutemen gig at the Old Waldorf. On that occasion, no slack in his schedule negated the desire. He had arrived at San Fran International late from Seattle due to a 737 technical problem before take-off, leaving reduced time to settle into his lodgings at the Hilton and hightail it over to Hyde Street Studios where Nancy was recording backing tracks for an up-and-coming Heart album. Segueing into a round robin drinking bout with studio personnel at a nearby Fisherman's Wharf speakeasy late into the night, it left Collins stretched out and catching zees at the Hilton until past noon the succeeding day. Originally, he'd planned to rise early, drive down to Monterey, do his nostalgic outing, and return to Frisco in time to catch the Minutemen show in the evening. Awaking to the clatter of room service wanting to change his bedsheets, he accepted putting the pilgrimage on hold.

Approaching Big Sur, a world renowned surfing location and Kerouac's accredited name for his ninth novel about resolving the burden of his 'King of the Beats' tag, Collins outlined the Monterey ambition to Natasha.

"After that monumental sixty-seven three-day happening, I assumed it'd become an annual event but alas, nothing has materialised."

"I've read about the Monterey Pop Festival and heard some bootlegs recorded at the shindig. Arguably, the roster was better than Woodstock and both Isle of Wight festivals."

"*Hah.*" He smiled at her. "Well, there's a thing. I've often expressed the same sentiment to colleagues, but few concur with the conclusion."

"Why daddy-o?"

"Two reasons. The Woodstock lore became quickly reinforced because of the worldwide success of the film and triple-album, and for most English music journalists, because the Isle of Wight was home territory, loyalty outstripped professional neutrality. True, Woodstock and the IoW festivals wowed audiences, particularly Hendrix at Woodstock and Dylan at IoW sixty-nine. Obviously, the Who played all three events, and Monterey. But on reflection, what sets Monterey apart was the impact of the British acid-rock outfits and the West-Coast underground psychedelic bands accompanied by a plethora of seasoned blues-rock groups and the mercurial Ravi Shankar set. Another factor for me revolves around Woodstock and the IoW festivals were characterised by huge, spread-out audiences, whereas Monterey gig goers were confined into the much smaller County Fairgrounds. That provided the near-to equivalent warmth between the acts and the audience associated with an in-door gig. You see, Natasha, I've never been a lover of stadium rock and outdoor festivals. I much prefer the intimacy of seeing a band up close in a club like the Marquee and the 100 Club, or a medium-sized auditorium such as the Rainbow and the Lyceum. *Performance* despatched me to report on U2 at Red Rocks in 1983 and the Rolling Stones at Folsom Field Boulder in 1981. Heart were supporting the Stones. That's when I got to interview Nancy Wilson for the first time. Both gigs were outdoor and attracted huge audiences. Though I had a press pass to observe the bands from close quarters, at both junctures I left the hallowed press area, wandering to the back of the crowd and soon substantiated I needed a telescope to see the bands. Worse still, I felt utterly disconnected from the thunder blaring from massive PAs."

"Yes," Natasha corroborated, "I must confess Led Zeppelin at Knebworth seventy-nine was a disappointment, whereas as a kid, I got blown away by them at the Playhouse Theatre."

"Doesn't surprise me."

Reaching Monterey, the convoy made straight for the County Fairgrounds, the ghostly rumbles of Buffalo Springfield, Canned Heat, Quicksilver Messenger Service *et al* still echoing around the deserted arena. If not for the infallible knowledge that the immortal sixty-seven event had occurred, they could have easily assessed the site as just another redundant rock palace devoid of any significant history.

Staring around the setting, noticeably at the stage and the peripheral terraces, the globetrotters were left with an overwhelming impression of emptiness. But for recent history, it equated to stepping into the Pompei amphitheatre or the Rome Colosseum, knowing epochs had passed since the venues were used for gladiatorial games.

Soon an elderly man sprouted from backstage dressed in1930s style overalls, flannel shirt and a straw hat, making his way over to the sightseers.

"You folks on vacation?"

"That's the truth of it," Collins answered.

Taking them in, he tendered, "Tryin' to immerse yourselves in the spirit of sixty-seven?"

"That'd be an apt description."

"Well—" Swivelling on his heels, he took in the scene. "There ain't much left to give credence to the folklore generated by the sixty-seven, world renowned festival. Bin more weddins, community dinners and trade shows held here than rock and jazz festivals. Hell, we've even had cattle auctions and antique fairs."

"A varied history then," Delaney commented.

"I've lived in Monterey all my life. These fairgrounds get a disproportionate amount of publicity compared to the major enterprises forging the town."

"You mean for example," Natasha tested, "when Monterey was a major centre for sardine fishing and canning factories?".

"Damn straight, young lady. I worked in those cannin' factories for over forty-years, until the last closed in 1973. Nearly everyone in Monterey spent their working life either fishin', or cannin' in Cannery Row. *Aahh*—" He scratched his forehead and blew out his cheeks. "Everythin' is finite, and in the end, the sardine stocks became exhausted. Lot of people moved away after that to find work in the countryside, or in the big cities. Compared to the bustling hive of productive activity it used to be, Monterey is now hollow and, like for you folks, has become an en route secondary tourist trap for those venturin' to San Fran or LA."

Remembrance filling his consciousness, he chuckled. "But you should have seen it in the thirties and forties when the sardine beds were still teemin'. There wasn't a more vivacious town in the whole of California. Important people came here to see what all the commotion was about. Steinbeck set two novels in Monterey. They even made a retrospective movie about Cannery Row, though that was long after the final sardine was canned."

"Presumably, you are the fairgrounds caretaker?" Gail submitted.

"That I am. It's the latest in a long line of menial jobs I've done over the past sixteen years, and I'm coming up to seventy-three in November. Canning didn't make me a fortune, but it was regular and dignified work. Some of the jobs I've done since, well—" Again his visage became unambiguous. "Just let's say, they were undignified."

"How about your Fairgrounds caretaker job?" Collins voiced.

"Hah, that lies about midway along the dignified-undignified line."

~ * ~

Wending through the Old Fisherman's Wharf and the San Carlos Beach districts, the Collins ensemble stopped in Cannery Row, the defunct hotbed of the sardine industry the caretaker had passionately eulogised about. One building, clearly a disused factory, displayed the proud name, 'Monterey Canning Company'. Inciting Collins to call up abandoned English car fabricating plants he had seen in the Midlands left to rot and rust, he pondered if the same fate awaited the redundant cannery factories, or whether preservation orders had been placed on them. He knew several University College graduates gravitating to the car industry in various occupations had fallen on rough times when British Leyland had downsized after a series of crippling strikes nurtured by left-wing militants. Some had resumed their careers with other car makers, others finding new pastures in substitute industries. Their melting pot brought home to Collins the fragility of commerce when faced by forces beyond business practices. To reduce risks, his investments were spread into a wide diversity of stocks, but on the instances when an unforeseen catastrophe hit the financial services, retail or manufacturing sectors, he noted the attendant downturn on his return on investment. He'd also recognised music journals were far from impregnable, the *International Times* and *Oz* forced out of business under legislative acts based on their subversive anti-establishment content, main streamers *Disc*, *Zigzag* and *Crawdaddy* ceasing publication, and rumours persisting that *Record Mirror* and *Creem* were about to fold. Even major player *Sounds* were having a rough time in an oversubscribed and competitive market. It made Collins conjecture what he'd do if *Performance* bellied up; seek resumption of his journo career within the rock music genre, migrate to a more general publication where he could adapt his skills to suit their content, or just dip out altogether, and live on his investment earnings. Never one for idling about, and despite furnishing an opportunity to fulfill his art aspirations, he knew the third option only brought jam over a short time period. After that, the lure of productive work would have him seeking employment again.

Taking a stroll along Macabee Beach, they mooned at the adjacent once fertile fishing grounds providing employment for thousands, and making Monterey the subject of artistic and scientific endeavours.

"Nothing lasts, does it?" Gail remarked.

"Very little," Collins agreed. "The out-and-out world is in a capricious state of either natural or manmade flux. Constancy seems to be an anathema."

"Inevitably, what once provided economic boom, always crashes and burns," Delaney augmented. "Every endeavour has its foundation, rise to stardom, and fade into obscurity, Monterey's sardine goldmine no different to an exhausted copper seam, or the demise of sail, superseded by steamships."

"Seems like the nature of everything," Natasha tabled, "from civilisations and industrial giants to the fall of governments and even personal relationships."

"I read philosophy as a supplementary to my economics studies at University College," Collins itemised. "What struck me most, was the recognition that every canon and creed contained weaknesses and imperfections generating doubts in lasting robustness. Made me venerate the absolute futility of life, in that apart from the giants like Shakespeare, Newton and Turner, little survives beyond three score years and ten, the rest of us scurrying around like crazed rats trying to leave an imprint. History either renounces or misinterprets an endeavour's residue, invariably confining it to the archives for the academic's pleasure."

"Plainly, all this is beyond the bounds of the beat's discipline," Delaney insisted. "Though we remain fascinated by them, their spectrum was constrained and insular, all items either cool or square."

"Without doubt," Collins endorsed. "It underscores why there was never a mass take up of their lifestyle, and why it failed to establish prolonged international credentials. Because they were the first subculture to truly kick against the pricks, we romanticise the beats, but their Dionysian customs never convinced the majority. Like students living in an artificial campus bubble supported by the tax-bearing world, the beats behavioural patterns only worked within the realms they defined, never trans-mutating into the mainstream, apart from the curious, like us."

~ * ~

Continuing north along I1 parallel to the Pacific Ocean shoreline, the argonauts became consumed by the juxtaposition of the mammoth seascape and the dappled in a quilt of greens and browns landscape, the former forever trespassing on the latter. In some far-off time, like many worldwide coastlines, the thrashing waves would carve away the coastline to the extent whereby places like Cannery Row became submerged in a perpetual aquatic world, land-based life receding into an ever-shrinking environment.

Whilst with Babette, Collins had taken her to Reculver on the North Kent coast to see the site where Barnes Wallis tested his bouncing bomb for Operation Chastise, the 1943 RAF 617 Squadron assault on the industrial Ruhr Valley dams. She asked him about the decaying Reculver Towers and Roman Fort, later forming part of a medieval church, their northern ramparts and walls missing down a sheer cliff edge. Formed by sea induced coastal erosion, he explained, in 1630 the cliff edge protracted northwards by 500 feet to the shoreline, but under siege, by the mid-nineteenth century erosion had swept inwards, the church's northern perimeter, like much of the village, crumbling and disappearing beneath the waves. Shocked by the apparent rate of the erosion in just two centuries, Babette questioned him about sea defences, Collins replying that during the twentieth century, Canterbury City Council had inaugurated several barriers designed to lessen coastal erosion, but geologists warranted all measures to be an eventual losing battle in favour of the breakers. To illustrate the sea's tidal and wave-power, he reviewed before the dawn of man, England was part of the continent, and over succeeding millennia it created the English Channel. Acclaiming the constancy of coastal erosion, Babette gathered no end resided to the invasion, eventually titanic swaths of land heading for a permanent underwater existence. It drove home to both of them the fragility of life on a planet devoured by adverse weather and climate conditions, typified by erupting volcanos, earthquakes, hurricanes, extreme temperature variations, and brutal seas, man so small and insignificant compared to the natural forces engulfing him.

~ * ~

Bewitching them further, the I1 unearthed further magnificent sea and landscapes as the cavalcade approached Santa Cruz.

"I thought some of the geographies we saw on Route 66 were stunning," Natasha applauded, "but this gorgeous contrast between the ocean and the land has a much more ethereal effect."

"Could it be, unlike land-locked panoramas being static, the waves are in nonstop motion, conveying a dynamic to the vista, like a flowing symphony or even kinetic art?"

"Yes, that's it."

"I always tend to make comparisons using music analogies, seeing objects and spectacles in terms of the harmonies and melodies they emulate. Abidingly, when I look at something for the first time, some musical cadence comes to mind, and as I gaze, I find myself re-playing the song in my head. In the case of what we've been witnessing along the

Pacific Coast Highway, I've found myself introspectively singing *White Bird* by It's a Beautiful Day."

"Because of the escape notion the song generates?"

"Got it in one. Sitting in these mobile prisons on the road, we hunger for the unconditional freedom of movement offered by seabirds and the ocean's waves, just like the caged white bird eager to be set free, or she will die."

"An intriguing perspective. It leads to the supposition, what music do you find to your liking or otherwise?"

"Do you know, Natasha, I've been trying to fathom that impulse all my life. Why am I drawn to some flavours, and find others less appetising?"

"Could be up-bringing, social surroundings, early exposures."

"Yep, undoubtedly true, those factors go a long way to vindicating a person's tastes. But some time ago, I twigged for me at least, it's down to sonority; the vital ringing, vibrancy and resonance hitting the listener's ear in the songs' opening moments that fundamentally determines if the track will be liked or disliked."

"Yes, that perception does make sense."

"It raises the enigma, why do we go back to certain tracks, time after time, from when they first entered our consciousness?"

"For example?"

"The Who's *I Can't Explain* put the hook in me from the opening bar, the chime of Moon's drums interlaced with Townshend's sonic guitar drawing my undivided attention, like iron filings to a powerful magnet. Others include *Louie, Louie* by the Kingsmen, *Strange Brew* by Cream, the Stones version of *Talkin' Bout You*, and the Beatles *Rain*. I could nominate a host of others, but what they all have in common is a less than three-minute framework, jam-packed with pinpointed power and allure, delivered with potency and precision."

"Yes, the Who were still playing *I Can't Explain* early in their set roster for a good five years after it was released as a single. You're right, it is an immutable crowd exciter."

"Whenever I become downhearted about the crap shamming as cantata since the turn of the eighties, I play *I Can't Explain,* Zappa's *Peaches en Regalia,* Talking Head's *Psycho Killer,* Television's *Marquee Moon,* or the Stooge's *I Wanna Be Your Dog,* and they revitalise my faith in rock music."

"There have been some highlights in the 1980s," Natasha argued. "Black Flag, the Jesus and Mary Chain and Primal Scream readily come to mind."

"Quite right, all good bands. I became over-harsh with my condemnation. In fact, there are some additional green shoots, notably in the alternative country-rock segment with the Jayhawks."

"Don't know them."

"The Jayhawks are from Minneapolis, and have solid roots credentials. Their self-titled first album tended to pure country, but the follow-up, recently released *Blue Earth* heralded a root and branch overhaul in favour of searing electric guitar and strong song themes. *Performance* view them to be an outfit with a great future, if they can build on the pedigree of *Blue Earth.*"

"I suppose there's not been a top-notch, blazing country-rock ensemble since the Flying Burrito Brothers."

"No, even Gram Parsons became passive after he left the Burritos. Artists like Neil Young and Steven Stills have flirted with the occasional inclusion of a country-based track on their albums, but in the main, the genre has tarried relatively dormant until the Jayhawks took flight."

"Speaking of country-rock, what's this ditty on Radio FM Santa Cruz?" She turned up the volume.

"Oh...it could be the Long Ryders. Let me listen some more...yeah, it's *Looking for Lewis and Clark* from their *State of Our Union* album. More rock than country, but the band does have a heavy-duty country heritage through their previous incarnation, the Unclaimed."

"Why is it—" She scowled at him. "We always seem to end up talking about music, no matter what the intro subject?"

"I guess it's because music is my constituency of choice.

Routinely, I tend to take dialogues down the assonance avenue. Just goes to show, you've harnessed yourself to a one-trick pony."

"Oh, Henry, quit the modesty line. You know you're better than that."

"Maybe, but when you know me better, you'll find I'm full of self-doubts."

Chapter 14: San Francisco Nights

City of hot-rod angels and heartaches, dusty beach roads, gambling joints and penny arcades, Mission District evangelists rapping out their all-comers-welcome creed, and bill posters at Winterland slapped over last years' gig roster, all epitomised the kinetic city of San Francisco according to Henry Collins when asked to position the metropolis by the curious. Expanding on the eulogy he'd add, neon signs proclaiming the next sky pilot, endless seven-elevens' and coffee houses stacked up and expanding like a concertina, bandits looking for redemption but little by little deteriorating and fading into the background fabric, fire trails devoted to interstate sanctuaries should the worst happen, a city hall caught between conflicting drivers, never sure on which pressure party it should settle, who to accept and who to reject, all echoed a city in flux, never distilling on a single virtue, but a multiplicity of contrary and discordant phenomena.

Before his first sojourn to San Fran, well versed in its idiosyncrasies, Cold Turkey CEO Glen Montague had briefed Collins what to expect. Having dealings with concert promoters, their lawyers, and sundry city officials, Montague had found business protocol to be tinged with personal agendas, and those seeking to make an extra buck off his artists. He'd concluded New York and Chicago were full of shysters and chisellers, out to milk the maximum they could get out of Cold Turkey, but paradoxically, San Fran took the exploitation to new heights. Beneath the veneer of west coast progressive policies, sharks inhabited the rock concert set, preaching love and understanding with benevolent body language, whilst incongruously bearing the greed face and grabbing as much of the concert and concessionaire revenues as possible. Not entirely stupefying Collins, he had found to gain entry to a treasured rock luminary, sometimes palms had to be greased, or courtesies given further down the food chain.

After his band had achieved triple-platinum sales of their first three albums in the US and the UK, Manager Brett Ascot had erected an 'iron-curtain' between English act the Marauders and the press. Zealously guarded by Ascot's minders, the Marauders' main man Scott Furlong had let it be known via a surreptitious conduit, he'd like to talk to *Performance* about the next set of challenges faced by the band, Collins handed the assignment by Editor Max Parish. Knowing the litmus test of the effort required to avoid Ascot's henchmen and tie up with Furlong, Collins had to pay gratuities to both the band's road manager and equipment manager to get a message to Furlong, regarding when and where to meet him. Although the rendezvous went ahead, Ascot got wind of the appointment arranged for noon in the Interview Suite at the Landmark Hotel London. Showing up with his heavies soon after Furlong and Collins settled into their confab, Ascot insisted the meeting be stopped on pain of severe retribution to Collins, meaning a sound drubbing by his flunkies, Furlong springing to his defence and threatening to curtail the Marauders' contract with Ascot. After several heated exchanges between artist and manager, Ascot backed down on the proviso any copy needed to be okayed by him before publication, and *Performance* ran a full-page Marauders advertisement for their forthcoming album, free of charge, Collins agreeing to the deal after consulting Parish. Billed as an exclusive, the increased circulation just about covered the greasing and advertising costs. Not the first or the last time Collins engaged in hush-hush tactics to secure an interview, he accepted beneath-the-counter operations were an integral part of the music industry between artist representatives and the press.

~ * ~

Specialising in world literature, the arts and progressive politics, City Lights Bookstore had been founded by Lawrence Ferlinghetti in 1953. A nexus of erudition and wisdom for beat aficionados, it attracted book buyers and devotees from all over the bohemian world, hence Collins and co aggregating San Fran to their timetable back in London.

Moseying into City Lights, the English contingent saw at least six punters, their heads buried in books and impervious to their presence.

Sauntering over from the counter, a woman addressed the newcomers. "Hi, can I help you?"

"Yes," Collins replied. "I'm Henry Collins with *Performance* magazine. Does Mister Ferlinghetti or Mister Kesey happen to be about?"

"Lawrence is on a lecture tour somewhere on the east coast, and Ken is down in LA."

"Ahh, I see." Dejected by the announcement, his physiognomy swelled into regret. "I was er, hoping to interview them for an article I'm writing entitled, 'The Beats still hold sway over the American underground.' I should have called in advance, but er—" He swung his arm around to encompass his colleagues. "We're on an extended road trip, ambivalent of precisely where we're going to be at any point in time, so er, I conscripted pot luck, hoping either Mister Ferlinghetti or Mister Kesey might be at City Lights when we visited."

"All is not lost," she breezily countered. "Michael McClure is with us today. He's composing *Rebel Lions*, a new collection of poems, and wanted some place to work away from the hubbub of the California College of Arts and Crafts in Oakland. Let me see if he has a few minutes to spare."

Elated by the proposition, Collins gushed, "Ohh, that'd be wonderful."

A leading light amongst a set of notable luminaries in the 1950s beat gen league, McClure had set himself apart when he won the patronage of English playwright Harold Pinter to promote his play *The Beard*. Highly controversial and attracting reviews for and against, the play explores the nature of seduction, portraying an explosive confrontation between platinum-blonde movie star Jean Harlow and baby-faced outlaw with a hair trigger, Billy the Kid. As an inquisitive 1968 teenager, Collins had seen a production of *The Beard* at the Royal Court Theatre. Entranced and startled by the play content in equal measures, it formed one of the mainstay components in his nascent prospection of the beats' world.

"Michael says he can spare you a few moments," the woman

reported on her return.

She led them to the rear of the premises, opening a door and ushering them inside, the trekkers finding themselves in a warehouse stacked to the rafters with publications.

Seeing a man working at a desk, Collins hailed, "Mister McClure."

"That's me," he inveterated, facing the Englishman.

"I'm Henry Collins with *Performance* magazine."

"The rock journal?"

"Indeed."

"You're a long way from home."

"Yes." Pointing to the remainder of the troupe, he informed, "We're stalking in the beat's footsteps. Have completed Route 66 Chicago to LA, and we're heading back to the Windy City via a more northerly carriageway."

"I see." Resting, he then appended, "I gather you want to interview me for an article you are writing."

"If you can spare me some of your valuable time."

Ogling the vacationers, as if checking for valid credentials, he then consigned, "Come on. Let's get comfy."

Taking them deeper into the warehouse inner sanctum, they came to rest in an alcove containing six chairs set up to form a circle.

"We use this nook for group brainstorming." Eyeing Collins, he volunteered, "You want to know my take on the beat movement?"

"In a nutshell."

Launching into discourse, the retrieval came out of him like lightning rods tipped with venom.

"The classic picture painted by the beat gen stenographers often depicts a quixotic regime in which Kerouac, Ginsberg, Burroughs *et al* basked in a Dionysian lifestyle. May have been true for some, but for most slouching into the bohemian habit, life could be tough, cruel and very uncertain."

"In what way uncertain?"

"Let me be specific with an example. You have probably read all the classic beat writers and poets, meaning the three just mentioned plus

Corso, Cassady and Ferlinghetti. You might even have read some of my work, and those real enthusiasts amongst you could have delved into Snyder, Orlovsky, Rexroth and Kesey, but beyond this faction there were and still are legions of good beat writers ignored by the publishing industry. *Hah*—" He grinned. "In my estimation, literary agents are a bunch of egotistical assholes who can't tell sugar from shit. Publishers are much the same. These guys didn't get rich on the output of the published beat gen writers. It's still a niche market. Howbeit, I've read remarkable drafts by totally unknown beat writers having potential mass market appeal, but the publishing industry can't or won't see it. There're too many suited motherfuckers, and not enough Napa Valley wine. Like in a Rene Magritte painting, it's been raining businessmen, fuelled by the quick buck instead of the slow burn. Attitudes have not changed since the nineteenth century. Most publishing traditionalists still gravitate towards the quill and hard copy submissions, even when we're entering an age of computer-based word processing. Hence, all these factors equate with uncertainty."

"What about the people you met during your formative years as a beat gen poet and playwright? Retrospectively, how do you see them?"

"Hhhmm. I have mixed recollections. Some good. Some bad. Some disappointing, even appalling. Any belief system or elected lifestyle panacea has to have elasticity to accommodate the extremities of the genre, but in practice that tolerance is exploited by some, poisoning the central crux of the discipline. Every crusade has its share of reprobates and scoundrels. The cardinal cats attracted some disingenuous humdingers. Hangers-on masquerading as the real deal. Charlatans exploiting the myth for their own ends. Recorders ferreting around for juicy indiscretions to be reported in the mainstream media. Often, that's all the outside world can see. Consequently, the new thing becomes condemned. Without mentioning any names, we had our fair share of parasites and leeches. I don't like anything that slithers, and those sons of bitches slithered like a sidewinder. Some of the upper council tolerated their misdemeanours, but I had no hesitation in calling out the Svengalis and the schemers."

"Why is it in your view beat writers have never enjoyed a

mainstream clientele in terms of book sales in America?"

"Haven't you noticed?" He radiated cynicism. "They're *mad* for Jane Austen!"

"Yes, as a matter of fact, I happened upon a Jane Austen appreciation society in Atlanta a few years ago, when I covered the 1987 Pixies east coast tour. They investigated if I was a Jane Austen fan. Not wishing to offend, and taking the opportunity to test the wit of the colonists, I told them, my cherished Austen novels were *Sense and Sensibility*, *Pride and Prejudice* and Nob and Nob-ability. Decidedly, the latter was made up, and intended to take the rise out of their serious dialogue, but the lewd title flew over their heads undetected."

"*Hah*, I'd love to have been there when you said that," McClure declared, grinning profusely. "Anyway, you obviously take my point, and it's not just the illustrious works of Miss Austen that have the American reading public spellbound. Most dwell fixated by classic pre-1950s works, principally the esteemed eighteenth and nineteenth century English and American cadre. Apart from trashy love stories, puerile fantasies and overblown horror, post the century midpoint, few new works permeate their consciousness."

"Why is that?"

"Because they view the distant past with idealisation, and yearn for a restoration of traditional culture, values and ethics, untainted by any form of modern revisionism. It's the pollyanna principle, and a safety blanket where they feel insulated from modernity. Albeit, modernity is transient. All invention is modern at its time of creation, even in the arts. History has shown most pioneers in their chosen field of endeavour are denounced by the dominant status quo. For instance, the French impressionists became roundly damned by the captains and conductors of the Paris salons, yet at the advent of the twentieth century, the likes of Manet, Cezanne and Monet became arbitrated as visionary ambassadors of the *avant garde*, their fabrications eulogised by art critics as works of greatness."

"So, you're saying with the passage of time, the beat gen oeuvre will be weighed in a more complimentary light by critics, and downline generations might place the works alongside those of Thoreau, Whitman and James."

"I'd not go as far as that, but if history is indeed a valid arbiter, then sometime in the next millennium, you might find Corso and Ginsberg vying for inclusion in the greatest American novelists and poets lists. There's almost a hypnosis, an incantation in Ginsberg's *Howl*, the rhythm of the prose pregnant with mastery. Whenever I begin to doubt the beats' creed, I recap *Howl* and the scepticism is neutralised." He simpered. "Nevertheless, over the past decade, *On the Road* and *The Naked Lunch* have crept into the reckoning. Only time will tell if they and other Kerouac and Burroughs works will join the pantheon of the gods. It's all a matter of perception and gaining mindshare. Dylan has done more to demystify and promote the beat gen than most, but I never calculated the beats to gain nationwide approbation. Our works appeal to misfits on the rim of society, those rejecting the establishment, downright anarchists, and the intellectually curious. That constitutes less than five per cent of the general public, so you'll see why we are near-to a closely barricaded secret, and attain minimal market share."

"What about your own works, Mister McClure?"

"*Hoo!*" He laughed. "I don't think Frost, Pound, Auden, Plath and Eliot are in danger of being unseated from their exalted positions on high by my meanderings. The most I might aspire to is to be judged to be in the same ballpark as Kerouac, Ginsberg, Corso and Ferlinghetti."

"Surely time will be kind to *The Beard* and its sequel *The Sermons of Jean Harlow and the Curses of Billy the Kid*. *Ghost Tantras* and *The Mad Club* should also come into the evaluation."

"So-called seminal works," he self-deprecated. "To-date, I have written thirty-six plays, novels and poem compendiums plus a fistful of songs. Some are better than others, but in terms of acknowledged works, few have attracted lavish praise. I'm a niche writer with a slender guardianship. I always will be."

"Isn't that the fate of most artists in their lifetime?"

"Exactly, and like all scribes, I have an agenda to disseminate through my work."

"How do you mean?"

"All authors are guilty of subliminal indoctrination, designed to stir descent in the discernment of children. But it's psychological warfare. Who is the victim? The child or the author? Those mondo, weirdo freaks out on the periphery will suck the life out of you. They say, let's have a riot. I say no…let's have a revolution. They're like dead canaries in gilded cages. They can't hear the rebel yell, though it's pure ghetto gold."

"That translates as more like philosophy."

"True. You have to appreciate things are unalike here in the New World. We have all the 'old world' vices, plus some new elements of our own invention. Capitalism may have been born in Europe, but America refined it into a monster, and with the warts it has created along the way, America has deconstructed rationalism, and replaced it with much more visceral constructs, based on the self. Ayn Rand had it right in her *The Fountainhead* macrocosm. Under the covers, all Americans want to be Howard Roark, individualists striving for the American dream, the promised land delivering as advertised, meaning a stable employment roadmap, the nuclear family, and mom's homemade apple pie. That in turn dissipates collectivism, and thereby impacts the wholesale acceptance of out-on-the-rim fraternities, like the beats."

"Yeah?"

"Yeah," he confirmed. "I know stuff. I've been around. Seen how the global system works. When you are my age, you might come to the same conclusion. It's like a gifted student of mine at the California College of Arts and Crafts. I told him, you gotta have goals associated with dreams, meaning practice as well as theory germinating society recognition and the capacity to steer development. Our big mistake back in the fifties became hiding our light under a bushel, and staying in the shadows, when we should have affected a front and centre disposition in the literary world, driving it to the beat's hilt, like Charlie Parker did with bebop." Screwing up his features, his climate transposed, his voice becoming sullen. "Then again, maybe we never really got it right, so much aligned to the subjunctive, when it should have been the tangible."

"How do you mean?"

"Like so many artists and writers, we were escaping our worlds. We couldn't cope with them, so we fled into a replacement dimension we created. Oh, we prided ourselves we'd found something better, but it was delusional. All we'd found was something different. Nirvana persevered out of reach." Halting, he squinted at Collins. "Well there you have it, Englishman. I've got no more to add."

"Any advice?

"Advice!" He pondered. "I could say, keep your powder dry or plant your corn seed early in the spring, but I guess you're looking for the profound."

~ * ~

After leaving City Lights, the adventurers took in Coit Tower and the streets where Steve McQueen chased a hood in *Bullitt*, then toured the Russian Hill and Pacific Heights districts before ending up in Golden Gate Park.

Collins had paid homage to the fabled Haight-Ashbury, an epicentre for the mid-1960s counterculture, east of Golden Gate Park, during his first jaunt to San Fran on behalf of *Crossroads* to cover George Harrison's November 1974 concert at the Oakland Coliseum. Earlier in the fifties, the beats had congregated around North Beach, many unable to find accommodation there, turning to the quaint, relatively cheap and underpopulated Haight-Ashbury, their basecamp subsumed into the Summer of Love by hippies in 1967. Collins had researched the locale and uncovered Haight-Ashbury used to be a collection of isolated farms and acres of sand dunes, before completion of the Haight Street Cable Railroad in 1883 climaxing in land grading and the instigation of an upper middle-class homeowner's district. Hit hard by the Great Depression, affluent residents left the declining neighbourhood for green pastures in the Bay Area, their vacated multi-story homes turned into apartments to house workers during World War II, many buildings left vacant at termination of hostilities and later attracting downcast beats. When the Summer of Love took off, attracting ganja-smoking hippies to Haight-Ashbury from all points of the compass, Hunter S. Thompson labelled the district 'Hashbury' in *The New York Times*. Like a moth to a flame, the incomers amassed at Thelin's Psychedelic Shop, a 'head shop' specialising in paraphernalia for the consumption of cannabis, marijuana, and LSD, at that time still legal and affording the hippies access to the drug perceived as a community unifier. Concurrently, progressive San Fran rock bands the Grateful Dead, Jefferson Airplane and many others made Haight-Ashbury their HQ, playing the local theatres and free events in Golden Gate Park, the combination of awareness-altering drugs and psychedelic music having the hippies in ecstasy heaven.

By the time Collins paraded about the mythical locale, it had degenerated into a hard drugs kingdom and been left to rot by the city authorities and the police. Gone were the hippies, replaced by heavy-drug addicts in heroin dens. Pining to catch echoes of the spirit of sixty-seven, all he found amounted to squalor and misery, hope supplanted by debasement, free will by narcotics dependence. Depressed by the scene, he fled to Golden Gate Park, immediately finding a much more cheerful mood prevailed, then onto the Baker Beach seashore, the ozone coming off the sea refreshing him. By the time he headed to the Oakland concert, his caricature of Haight-Ashbury had been filed away in the archive section of his memory.

As the troupe continued their trek around the San Fran peninsula districts, Haight-Ashbury became liberated from Collins deep memory. He knew the locale had been reinvigorated in the early1980s by the coffee shop fraternity and comedy clubs, but refrained from suggesting they took a hike down to Haight-Ashbury, preferring to eternally visualise it in its kaleidoscope Summer of Love pomp.

He had got used to seeing sordidness in the rock-bastion bearing districts of New York, Detroit and Chicago, the formative especially ramming home the cognizance when he spent a week covering the fledgling 1975 rock scene centred around CGBG and Max's Kansas City in South Manhattan for *Crossroads*. Television and the Patti Smith Group were finding their feet with some nihilist rock music honed to perfection at the revered pulpits, Collins interviewing Tom Verlaine about Television's influences and poet-turned-rock-virtuoso Patti Smith about the band's forthcoming debut album *Horses*. Both acts had been fed on a solid diet of the Rolling Stones and the Velvet Underground, Patti adding Arthur Rimbaud to her breeding nutriment intake. Sensing an ascendancy shift in the rock landscape, Collins also attended Ramones, Talking

Heads, and ex-New York Doll, Johnny Thunders and the Heartbreakers gigs. Building on what had been dubbed the 'New Wave', he complemented his comprehension by interviewing former Neon Boys and Television member Richard Hell about his next project, the Voidoids, and David Byrne about how Talking Heads were formed.

Meanwhile, outside of the rock bubble, New York was in social and economic breakdown, Mayor Abraham Beame unable to cover operating expenses or borrow more money, the city facing the prospect of defaulting on its obligations, and declaring bankruptcy. Emerging from the highs of CBGB, Collins became faced by litter piling up in doorways, streets needing a thorough cleaning, muggers running riot, and drug pushers milking the concomitant despair, the disparity between the galvanising energy and invention of the New Wave evangelists and the down and outs begging for fifty cents on 5th Avenue, making him comprehend he inhabited a sub-world insulated from the vagaries faced by most people. Full immersion in the music industry including journalism, certainly at its bombastic and materialistic zenith in the 1970s, could isolate and cushion those inside its luxurious realms from the harsh outside world. The only time they saw Joe Public was at gigs, a forum stimulating excitement and producing happy faces. Little did they realise, once the audience exited the auditorium doors, most receded back into their often glum-face producing decimating domains, Collins only cottoning onto the dichotomy later in his career. Back in New York in seventy-five, absorption in the New Wave discovery obliterated outside America in Collin's eyeline, his concentration completely devoted to recording and reporting on his findings.

~ * ~

In the late afternoon, they checked into Ciro's Motel on Van Ness, Collins writing up and faxing his McClure interview to *Performance*. Then, whilst taking refreshments in Del Mar Deguello, a gin joint first settled in Lombard Street when the gold rush had waned and shipping took stage centre in north-west San Fran, a few blocks from Fisherman's Wharf, Collins and crew were approached by a young woman with fluffy

160

blonde hair, Aegean blue eyes and a peaches and cream complexion.

"Hi, I heard your voices. You must be English," she speculated, her accent drenched in sweetness.

"Indeed we are," Natasha confirmed.

"Are you on vacation?"

"We're on a road trip."

"You don't say. How far are you going?"

"We're heading back to Chicago via Las Vegas."

"I see. My name is Desirae Briscoe."

After Natasha had introduced her companions, Desirae told them she had become homesick, quit her job at Macy's, and wanted to explore the western hinterlands whilst returning home.

"I know this is very forward," she qualified, "but can I bum a lift with you guys back east? I've got money, so I can help pay for gas and I can cover my own expenses." She beamed at them. "I promise I won't be a burden."

"Where's your end destination?" Collins asked.

"Omaha, birthplace of Marlon Brando and Montgomery Clift."

"Well. You're in luck, Desirae. Our course takes us to Omaha on I80." He scanned around his colleagues. "Shall we oblige this young lady?"

They all nodded.

"Oh, that's marvelous," she cooed. "Thank you so much."

"Can't guarantee when we will reach Omaha, other than to say it will be in the next ten to twelve days."

"Suits me," she excitedly chimed. "I'm not up against the clock."

"How long have you been on the West Coast?" Gail scrutinised.

"I came out last year in the early summer. Wanted to find somewhere new to write poetry. I'd lived my entire life in Omaha, even attended the University of Nebraska Omaha to undertake communication studies. I felt stifled, the unmitigated city overwhelming me like a big grizzly tearing apart its prey. Just had to get away. Find a place where I could breathe without the walls closing in on me. I flipped a dime. Heads I'd go east to New York, tails west to San Fran."

"A binary option," Delaney adjudicated.

"Yeah. For me, it didn't matter what side the coin landed on."

"So, you upped sticks for California," Collins submitted, "presumably in the hope of releasing your mental stamp from being bottled up?"

"They say a change is as good as a rest. Incontestably, San Fran is even more packed than Omaha, but the seaboard provides relief. Sometimes I'd go to Muir Beach or Stinson Beach and just gaze at the Pacific stretching out to the horizon." She gawked at Collins. "You can't do that in Nebraska. The only respite from metropolitan Omaha are the prairie cornfields in the Great Plains. As a teenager, I'd roam the plains, but by twenty-two I needed a substitute backdrop. I'd never seen the ocean, and I had a choice of two. Whichever side the dime came down to rest on, I knew I'd be seeing either the Atlantic or the Pacific."

"You mentioned poetry," Delaney reminded her. "Has being out here released the creative valve for you?"

"Yes. As well as the beach areas, I'd also visit the local national parks, and a myriad of art galleries and public buildings, most sparking poem designs. This is a superb film location area as well. I've been up the coast to Bodega Bay where Hitchcock shot *The Birds*, and tracked down some of the landmark buildings he used in *Vertigo*, including the Mission San Juan Bautista. Those junkets also gave me some useful material."

"We have a convergence in common there, regarding *Vertigo*," Collins advised. "During a previous business excursion I made to San Fran, I took the opportunity to check out Fort Point where Madeleine jumps into the bay underneath the Golden Gate Bridge, and Scottie's apartment at Lombard Street. I'd have checked out a bunch of other locales, but I ran out of time."

"Sounds like San Fran provided the poetry results you were seeking, Desirae," Natasha observed.

"Took a while, but yes. Whereas the motifs and words came slowly when I felt smothered in my latter Omaha years, once I'd got into the swing of West Coast life, I had a surge of creation."

"What kind of poetry do you write?" Delaney canvassed.

"It's mainly abstract verse, plus a few rhyming cutlets. If I had to categorise it, I'd place it in the surrealism domain."

"We're going out on the town tonight," Natasha informed. "Do you want to come with us?"

"Thanks for the invitation, but I have a few things to finalise. Where are you staying?"

"Ciro's Motel on Van Ness. We'll be checking out at seven tomorrow morning."

"I'll be waiting for you outside."

Eager to find entertainment, Collins scoured Frisco rock events on a Ciro's lobby flyer. The Saloon, Boz Scaggs' Slim's, the Warfield, and other venues all coming up short on appealing acts. Taking a phlegmatic stance, the wanderers decided to tour Chinatown and the Mission District in search of sustenance and festivity. Leaping out into the San Francisco night, after bathing themselves in chugoku ambience, they docked in Mister Wo's, a Cantonese restaurant specialising in seafood dishes. Splayed out at a round table, whirling ceiling-mounted fans did not completely drown out the Chinatown street brouhaha, shrill oriental voices still faintly audible, passing traffic also registering on their hearing. Taking a gander about unearthed the eating house was plastered in Chinese regalia. If they closed their peepers, they became transported into a Shanghai setting, replete with dragons and Ming vases. Tucking into a plentiful feast washed down with Silk Road Shaohsing Chinese rice wine, they discussed the transformations in the San Fran rock venue scene.

"I know it was before our time, but I gotta say," Delaney insisted, already stoned on a dose of snow he'd ingested at Ciro's, "this city's rock scene is not a patch on what it used to be in Bill Graham's heyday."

"Undoubtedly true," Collins backed. "With the passing of the Fillmore West, the Cow Palace, the Avalon Ballroom, the Matrix, the Ark, and the Straight Theatre, San Fran can no longer claim to be the epicentre of Californian live rock music."

"Before closing earlier this decade, the last truly great bastion was the Old Waldorf on Battery Street, not far from Mister Wo's. I saw Television there in June 1978, well before I landed at Cold Turkey. Took a flying visit to San Fran with a gal I was seeing at the time. Got talking with some dude furnishing me with nose candy, who'd seen Spirit and Iggy Pop at the Old Waldorf. Reckoned it out-blasted anything LA had to offer."

"You're being sentimental," Gail rebuked. "Theatres and clubs come and go. Epicentres of excellence rise and fall. That's the way it's always been with music halls."

"Yes, Gail is quite right," Collins approved. "We're being nostalgic for past glories."

"It's the same for New York." Natasha prescribed. "Though CBGB remains, Max's Kansas City and a whole raft of like rock clubs have disappeared from Lower Manhattan after their prime in the sixties and seventies, hosting Dylan, the Velvets, and the New Wave."

"Again, can't argue with that," Collins sanctioned.

"I suppose," Delaney proposed, "it's natural to pine for familiar objects of the past, and denigrate their progeny."

"It's a human frailty," Collins positioned, "most people guilty of making at some stage of their lives. We feel safe and secure in the known and the proven, whereas the shock of the new often tends to attract revulsion."

"Yes" they all pealed.

Finished with dinner, the voyagers alighted on to Clay Street, once more the cabbalistic night enveloping them, the fragrance of cooking eastern delicacies mixing with stench-tainted steam rising from sewer inspection hatches, a Chinese fire eater mesmerising a gathering crowd with daring feats, the clanging bell of a tram car winging its way along Market Street, tourists craning their necks to see the illuminated apexes of Coit Tower and the Transamerica Pyramid. It all spelt a city in vibrant osmosis, Frisco absorbing the new and blending it in with the established.

Next morning, they found Desirae Briscoe, bag in hand, her features filled with warmth, waiting for them outside Ciro's.

Chapter 15: Las Vegas Bound

As the Vegas bound caravan breezed into Silicon Valley, Desirae in the Camaro with Collins and Natasha, Delaney and Gail shadowing in the Corvette, they all became spellbound by the distinction of global information technology corporate offices and manufacturing plants owned by Fairchild Semiconductor, Intel and others set against the western background towering Redwood State Park mountain range.

"If the San Andreas fault breaks, all this and much more will be under the ocean," Collins informed, "and a new line of beach front properties will meet the Pacific from Santa Rosa to Bakersfield, and on down to Palm Springs and Baja California."

"Yes, it's a real possibility," Desirae elected. "Someone told me, if the tectonic boundary between the Pacific Plate and the North American Plate becomes aggravated by too many concurrent sub-surface tremors, a massive earthquake will induce the land mass disturbance you stipulate. Got me all fired up, so I looked into the history of earthquakes in California at the Larkin Street public library. Because California is a young state, not many records exist. However, Spanish explorers and missions recorded quakes from 1769 onwards, then various settlers carried on the work from 1812 right up to the 1906 San Francisco earthquake, destroying over eighty per cent of the city. Remarkably, it took that momentous event for Washington to acknowledge the seriousness of the problem, eventually setting up the Caltech Seismology Laboratory in the 1920s."

"The first time I flew into San Fran International, the flight was prevented from landing for twenty minutes because of a detected tremor. Afterwards, I made some enquiries and discovered since Caltech commenced operations, they had logged three to four quakes every decade from the San Andreas Faultline, fruiting in injury, death, and gargantuan damage costs running into the tens of millions. It's a key reason why the Silicon Valley computer industry has set up duplicate production plants elsewhere in the US and overseas. If the worst happened, and all the effected industry, commerce and real estate ended up under water, it'd touch off a worldwide economic depression, because of stock market collapse."

"Yes," Desirae backed, "my own research led to the same conclusion."

"Yet all Californians seem either oblivious to the threat," Natasha ratified, "or resigned to their fate."

"It's the same with twisters in the south Midwest and hurricanes crashing into the south-eastern seaboard," Desirae supplemented. "Everybody knows they are coming every year causing immense devastation, injury and lost life, but few move out of the danger zones."

"In Europe," Collins validated, "we live in a relatively benign ecological environment, conveniently forgetting natural disasters are a regular occurrence in other continents. Floods and erosion of coastline are the worst natural events impacting the British Isles, but like here in the US, as a nation we do relatively little to counter the devastation."

"In the end, you can't beat nature," Desirae nominated. "It has greater power than any manmade contrivance. When I was in my early teens, one summer, Omaha suffered a deluge of heavy thunderstorms caused by Nebraska's hot-humid climate, far from moderating bodies of water and mountain ranges. Going on for days, it climaxed in widespread flooding of both the city and surrounding countryside, businesses brought to a standstill, farmers losing crops and the emergency services saturated by calls for help. Eventually, the city administration brought in the Federal Emergency Management Agency to bolster public services, but by then most of the damage had taken place, and over twenty people had lost their lives with many others injured."

"My *God*, that resonates as bad," Natasha babbled.

"Later, it struck me how impossible a task it was to combat such a disaster. It's not as if a ginormous umbrella could be erected above the city, let alone the farmlands. That would just deflect the rain elsewhere. Nebraska has a history of such adverse rain conditions, and no matter how much forward planning was done by the state and city authorities to minimise damage and fatalities, it proves to be totally inadequate, the sheer scale of rain storms overwhelming flood relief provisions within hours."

"Huh, Nebraskans know what is coming," Collins appraised, "but still remain."

"They do," Desirae underwrote. "Begs the question, is there any difference between lemming behaviour, unable to stop mass suicide by diving over the cliff edge, and that of humans?"

~ * ~

Unlike the Chicago to LA section, tagged by a sweeping Route 66 arc, the trek to Las Vegas approximated a dog's hind leg, with frequent deviations north and south about a generally south-east trajectory, passing over the Sierra Nevada's, and through Yosemite National Park and Death Valley on B-roads before hitting Las Vegas. All in all, a two-day junket, with a scheduled stopover at Bishop in the Inyo National Forest.

Festooned with national parks, the greens of northern California contrasted sharply with the browns, reds and yellows of New Mexico, Arizona and southern California, the Camaro and the Corvette passing over hills and dipping into valleys covered in fragrant meadows and sycamore, black walnut and gray pine trees, making the air smell sweet.

Back home, Collins had sought out such places to find tranquillity when the world closed in on him. Even as a young boy, he took refuge in desolate preferably wide-open spaces, where he could gauge his troubles, and put them into perspective against the vastness of space beyond the skies. Quickly perceiving he was but a bonded collection of atoms in the universe, often he'd come away from his sanctuary in an improved mood. When his marriage to Babette soured, it became his biggest hurdle to overcome. Though he never confessed how the failure nagged at him like a thorn in his flesh he couldn't remove, nonetheless, behind his public façade, hurt dug away at him. He had monumentally misjudged Babette. His love for her, blinding him to see her oh-so-obvious flaws. Obsessed with prudence, the upset had made him cautious with girls, his post-

Babette flings kept at arm's length, habitually, Natasha never seeing his true feelings for her.

Crossing Henry W. Coe State Park, his inner vision became transported to the Chiltern Hills, east of Stokenchurch, a darling place to find solitude after the stormier episodes with Babette. Suddenly comprehending the American expedition was acting as a cleanser, even a purifier of the residual torment, in that moment of clarity, he wanted the sabbatical to endure forever, the sheer joy, excitement and comradeship forged between the four travellers way beyond his wildest dreams in London, when he conceived the venture.

Good company from the outset of their meeting, Desirae Briscoe fitted into the English camaraderie like a silk glove over a feathery hand. Never without a smile or a good word, she exuded contentedness at its most glorious. Best of all, her conversational topics aligned perfectly with those of the English, her take on the arts, music and poetry adding a parallel slant to their understandings making for rich dialogue. Fun to be with, and often bewilderingly astute, she also bounced about like a youngster whenever they happened upon colourful people, or a magnificent natural spectacle, her persona flooding the English sensory systems with verve.

They first noticed this when the cavalcade pulled into Turlock for lunch. Congregating around a table in Crowfoot Charlie's, an old-fashioned barrelhouse with a Wurlitzer Jukebox crammed with 1950's classics such as *Twenty-Flight Rock*, *Peter Gunn Theme* and *Be-bop a Lula*.

Examining the menu, they remained indecisive regarding selection, then Desirae piped up, "How about if I order for all of us?"

Collins glanced at the rest of them. "If you know what we'd like, go ahead."

"Carne Asada Tacos for Natasha, Idaho Trout for Gail, Grilled Steak Street Tacos for Kallen and Porterhouse steak with Arugula salad for you."

"And what are you going to have?"

"Swordfish steak."

"Is that okay with everyone?" Collins polled.

They nodded in agreement.

"Tell me, Desirae," Natasha requested, "how did you know I like Carne Asada Tacos?"

"I saw you open your eyes wide, when you clocked it on the menu."

"As simple as that?"

"Uh-hah."

"It's called people watching," Collins informed. "Monitor for obvious transitions in physiognomy and body language when someone is poring over a menu, and it's likely a sagacious observer can judge what appeals."

"That's right," Desirae endorsed. "I learnt to do that when I was a little girl."

"What else did you learn?" asked Gail.

"Always be open to schemes, but never make assumptions."

"Who taught you that?"

"Oh, I just picked it up along the way." She paused. "Come to think of it, I picked up a lot along the way. For example, you can be in love with two people at the same time, your boyfriend and another man. When you're with the boyfriend, you love him. When you are with the man, you love him."

"Irrefutably true," Collins certified, his already high admiration of Desirae further flowering, "but what an odd thing to say."

"Yes," Natasha reinforced, "what made you come out with that?"

"Oh, it just flew off the top of my head. Often, I come out with unpredictable examples."

"Do you have any more pearls for us?" Delaney surveyed.

"Loads, but they usually come out in response to a tabled perplexity."

"What about your poetry?" Gail prompted. "Apart from location stimulation, where does that come from?"

She cogitated for moment, rolling her eyes upwards as if drawing down the answer from heaven. "It started after I read *Alice Through the Looking Glass*. Lot of symbolism in the prose - mirrors, opposites, time running backwards, and the language is festooned in proverbs and axioms. It all made me re-consider the possibility of alternative worlds. That became the source for my early work."

"You mean time and space travel?"

"Yes, and for me going back in time, because—" She hesitated. "Because…I couldn't foresee anything that remarkable in the future, whereas my investigations of the past uncovered many invigorating facts, not just in literature and the arts, but history as well. So, I began to conceive otherly worlds and figments of my imagination." Her manner becoming more forthright, she shared, "Interestingly enough, when I reassessed Alice, I gained the unequivocal standpoint Lewis Carroll was conveying dread as well as fancy."

"All children's stories have an element of horror in them from *Hansel and Gretel* to *Jack and the Beanstalk*," Collins put forward. "Here comes the chopper to chop off your head being typical, and like clowns, I've always rated Punch and Judy to be the stuff of nightmares, grotesque faces with huge, hooked noses and chins. I used to try to visualise the puppeteer, conjuring revelations of some rounded, dwarf-like creature, who secretly ate children."

"Oh, Henry," Natasha shrieked. "*Yuck.*"

"Yuck indeed," Desirae sponsored, "but he's right. Whenever I read children's stories, I got the distinct suspicion of a secondary undercurrent, a message hiding beneath the gloss of the primary text. Made me beg the brainteaser, was the author intending the work to transfer a warning, rather than an apparently innocent tale?"

~ * ~

With the Sun receding from its zenith, after checking into the Golden Wheel Motel in Mariposa, a small town in the Sierra Nevada foothills on the outskirts of the Yosemite Valley, the troupe scampered into the Rideout Saloon, a honky-tonk with a heritage going back to the Californian gold rush.

"Howdy strangers," greeted a white-haired man with an equally white droopy moustache, a big smile, and dressed like a forty-niner, sat at the bar as they entered.

"Hello," Collins responded, congenitally obliged to echo optimism from positivism addressed by the unknown.

"You folks vacationers?"

"Kind off."

"Been in Mariposa before?"

"No, not been our pleasure." He attracted the barman. "Five bottles of Bud please."

"You got it."

"Most people around here drink bourbon, rum or tequila," the barfly informed, sliding off his stool, and closing in on the trekkers.

"Maybe we'll move onto spirits later," Collins conceded, grinning at the kook.

"How long you gonna be here?"

"You ask a lot of q's," Delaney threw into the powwow, his boldness ignited by a recent suction of flake.

"Oh, don't get me wrong, amigo," he begged, his hands defensively pushed forward. "I was just tryin' to be sociable."

"That's fine," Collins approved, signalling Delaney to cool his jets. "What's your name?"

"They call me, the digger, but my real name is Elisha Brooks."

"Why are you called the digger?"

"Well, I'll tell ya, son. I go down to the Mariposa Creek, used to be the Mariposa River way back in the 1849 gold strike, and pan and dig for nuggets. People call me crazy, but I've had a few good finds, big enough to keep me in beans and liquor."

"How long have you been doing that?" Natasha queried.

"Oh, let me see…" He rubbed his bristled chin. "…Must be nigh on ten years. Started just after I buried my wife. Yep, ten years. I quit workin' the Napa Valley vineyards in seventy-nine, and twenty years before that, I worked on the railroads as a steam train driver. Can still remember the old steam trains used by the Sacramento Northern Railway, shuttlin' from Chico to Oakland, and the Central California Traction Company route from Stockton to Lodi. Nothin' like a steam train to get you all excited. But they did away with them, and electrified the tracks. Never the same afterwards. Unlike a steam engine, puffin' and wailin', electric locomotives got no soul."

"I don't suppose," Collins began, "you happened upon the beats during your ventures?"

"*Who?*" he rejoindered, scrunching up his weather-beaten dial.

"They were a literary movement of authors, whose work both explored and fabricated American culture and politics in the post-war era."

"Hah, you don't say."

"Many of them took to the road, often covering the Californian interior on their way to San Fran and LA."

"Well, I pride myself I've been around, seen things and talked to many people, but I don't recall any beats. Hobos and drifters, yeah."

"Sometimes they were seduced by the rambler lifestyle."

"Mmmm, still can't say I ever met a down and out posin' as a writer."

"Nevermind. Forget it."

His optics brightening, he pointed a probative finger. "Say, you folks on your way to Vegas?"

"Indeed we are."

"*Hah,* I've had some rare old times in Vegas, and Reno, tryin' to out-play the one-armed bandits and shootin' craps. Got the wheels to rotate and the dice to roll in my favour quite a few times. Bankrolled my prospecting explorations."

"Is that what you do?" Gail intervened. "Use your winnings to fund the prospecting, and the encashment of gold to fund the gambling?"

"Pretty much so. My kids left long ago for the cities. They don't come back to Mariposa very often, but when they do, we have a matchless old time."

"Can I ask you something?" Desirae posed.

"Go ahead, honey."

"How old are you?"

"Eighty-two and countin'."

"*Wow,* and you're still working."

"Don't know anythin' else. If I didn't work, my toes would curl up within six months."

After dining on spicey orange chicken and shrimp scampi, the wayfarers strolled back along I40 and took a cursory look at the small town. During the gold rush, Mariposa County had boomed into a substantial prospector settlement on the southern end of the mother lobe, Mariposa town a leftover from those heady days, and now a sedate commune, principally filled with private houses and excursionist facilities. Running into similar haunts on their Route 66 expedition, the Collins syndicate had got used to seeing the repercussions of economic variation on townships, some receding into deserts and mountain ranges to the extent whereby they had been classified as ghost towns, bereft of most human survival facilities. Others like Mariposa had transformed from bustling industrial concerns into quiet backwaters, relying on tourist curiosity to sustain them.

Back in their motel room, Collins opened a colloquy with Natasha about Elisha Brooks.

"What's your take on espousing a work-till-you-drop lifestyle, like our genial gold digger?"

"I've never considered it," she divulged, ceasing brushing her hair. "It just seems so far into the future for us, that I can't assign definable features to the concept. My focus is more rooted in the present, and potentially planning for a few years ahead. How about you?"

"Much the same. Nevertheless, as I indicated in Chicago, I do have a nominal ambition to parachute out of journalism, set up an artists' colony, and make the transition from mind art perceptions into canvass images. By then, I should have built up enough kudos in music journalism to go freelance anyway."

"The last part suggests you envisage some gaps in your timetable?"

"Yes, you raise a good point, Natasha. Art and freelance work may not be enough. I'd need other distractions."

"What about more travel, in particular that second US excursion you outlined taking in Graceland *et al*?"

"Though I'm thoroughly enjoying our quest, I'm not sure I could sustain the life for more than say three months, whereas I continue to get kicks out of rock journalism. Additional to the art aspiration and going freelance, I'd need a number of projects, travel inclusive, to absorb the equivalent time I currently devote to my profession."

"Reverberates like a concern for you."

"Increasingly, it is. I'm not one for chilling out on a beach or in a bar for weeks on end. I've got to be active, being challenged, or achieving a goal set by others, or by myself."

"You're very restless."

"Yeah, always have been. Beneath my apparent measured comportment, I'm a hive of perturbation and insecurities."

"*Ohh*…there you go again, Henry, just like on the road to Santa Cruz. I can't conceive you and vulnerability exist in the same space-time coordinates."

"Well as I've said before, I hide it. Unlike Kallen, I can't let my every emotion hang on the outside for all the world to see. It's his cry for help anyway, but don't tell him, I said that."

"So, daddy-o, you intend to soak up your inner turmoil with activity?"

"You got it. As long as I'm pursuing an objective, my inner demons are neutralised, and what you see is what you get."

"Is this Babette legacy?"

"Some, probably most, but even before Babette, I was a driven man."

"How far back?"

"The eleven-plus examinations were the first time I'd been set a demarcation point. After that, more came, not just examinations, but life tests, every junction a Y-shaped crossroad, one path crammed with opportunity, the other a dead end. And the worst of it is, sometimes if I matriculate to the right path, that too is strewn with minefields."

"Like Babette?"

"*Just* like Babette."

"What about your *Magnum* syndrome?" She smirked, signifying her disbelief he could kill someone.

"*Hah*." Grinning at her, he articulated, "I hope I'll be able to restrain the latent desire to waste people incurring my displeasure." He recoiled, controllability coming into his reckoning. "Sometimes it's difficult. I can almost feel my finger wrapped around the trigger, taste the gun smoke after letting loose, see the victim's head blown off."

~ * ~

Though not as dramatic as the Grand Canyon, the Yosemite Valley came close in terms of the breathtaking sight of green forests intermingled with whitey-grey mountains and trickling silvery rivers, the spectrum of their emitted hues and shades splashing the landscape producing a heaven on Earth setting. Could the Garden of Eden have been any more beautiful? Discontinuing several times to photograph the views, the voyagers became awestruck by the majesty of the unspoilt panoramas. Everything appeared pristine as if God had taken special care in sculpting the surroundings, the light limpid, the air sweeter.

"Spinning back down the years," Collins replayed, "this backdrop reminds me of Creux du Van, a rock arena of ginormous proportions with titanic vertical rock faces, surrounding a wide valley basin forest in the Swiss Val-de-Travers region."

"How do you know the Creux du Van?" Natasha sought.

"Babette and I explored the region when we holidayed at Yverdon-les-Bains on Lac de Neuchatel. Just why the remote location became selected evades my memory, but I did recommend Montreux on Lac Leman, site of the legendary Grand Hotel burning down, thereby supplying the kernel for Deep Purple's *Smoke on the Water*. Whilst wandering along the Creux du Van we saw lynx, chamois and ibex mountain goats, and talked about nearby Maison de l'absinthe; the cradle of absinthe, a highly alcoholic spirit popular with numerous artists and writers."

"Such as Van Gogh, Picasso, Lord Byron and Paul Verlaine," Desirae supplied.

"Quite. Somehow that segued into Laudanum, a tincture of opium containing ten per cent opium powder by weight, equal to one per cent morphine, and again beloved amongst the early eighteenth-century artistic community for quelling pain. Thomas de Quincey eulogised his Laudanum addiction in his autobiographical work *Confessions of an*

175

Opium Eater, and bipolar-stricken Samuel Taylor Coleridge composed *Kubla Khan* under the drug's influence. We then discussed how hallucinogens, predominantly lysergic acid diethylamide had stimulated the mid-sixties work of the Beatles, the Doors and many other rock bands intent on using the rock medium as a vehicle to channel otherworldly, inner-space creations."

Cruising amongst the pines and poppies of the Yosemite Valley, Collins used the Creux du Van palaver to recap to Natasha and Desirae how the beats used alcohol and drugs, and why he had refrained from their riveting dependence. Frequently associated with august works of art and literature, and often levied as a prerequisite for artistic enlightenment, copious ingestion of both relaxants and stimulants acted as a subject matter and fuel for the beat writers and poets.

"A notorious heroin addict, Burroughs' books including *Junky* were filled with references to a deluge of illegal drugs," Collins sketched. "Famously, he travelled to South America in search of the mysterious drug Ayahuasca, with the intent of sampling the psychoactive brew to enhance his visionary powers. Whether he savoured the opiate or not, lingers obscure."

"Likewise," Natasha appended, "written with the aid of Benzedrine, bennies to the hipsters, Kerouac's *On the Road* depicted bohemian life, replete with marijuana smoking. No stranger to drugs either, Ginsberg used marijuana and LSD to expand his consciousness, and thereby mould his writing."

"Conclusively hip to the integrated beat generation," Desirae critiqued, "the drugs collective morphed into the counterculture of the sixties, spawning an even brighter wealth of inception, especially in the underground music scene. Albeit, drugs and booze eventually hindered the creative process."

"Undeniably," Collins supported. "Customarily, in his later years Kerouac struggled to crystallise his fancies, and translate them into words, while for Hunter S. Thompson, drugs became a part of his personality. Very possibly exaggerating his drug use for artistic and promotional benefit, the substance abuse tore away at his mind and body, ultimately triggering breakdown."

When Collins and co summed and aggregated the beat gen and counter-culture drug misuses, they concluded the price to be paid for the derived arousal and thrill became a sterile life, characterised by lethargy and lassitude, often culminating in premature death, Collins admitting if he ventured too far down the experimental path, he too could go the same way, the realisation breeding restraint on occasions when the rock world offered him drugs at parties, his consumption never approaching dependency level.

~ * ~

Clearing the Yosemite National Park, the motorcade hit Bishop on I120 just as the sun melted over the Sierra Nevada mountains. Booking into the Creek Motel, the desk clerk told them they had arrived on festival night.

"Yes *sir*," he trumpeted with pride, "it's usually a real humdinger. Plenty of dancin' and booze. Everyone leavin' their troubles behind them, and turnin' loose. Way back when, we used to have a rodeo as the centrepiece of the festival, but all the cowboys have gone."

"It's just the kind of shindig we like," Collins declared.

"Say, if you're lookin' for an eating house, try Ma Winstanley's. It's at the junction of Main Street and East Pine. You can't miss it. It's all decked out in midnight blue, and has a bell tower above it. Used to be the courthouse until the district attorney's office moved to plush accommodation."

Taking the attendant's advice, after freshening up, the wanderers made for Ma Winstanley's, took a corner booth, and ordered dinner.

Scanning about, Collins divined over the years he must have patronised hundreds of like hostelries when performing rock journalist duties Stateside. Invariably coming replete with a chirpy waitress hoping for a big tip, individual portions having a family of four bursting out of their gear, and nondescript, inoffensive background music, he had viewed such eateries to be homely and welcoming.

One time in New York City, whilst covering the Lou Reed concert at the Bottom Line for *Crossroads*, he had slipped into Idaho Harvest, a traditional steakhouse on Spring Street surrounded by delicatessens, fast food joints and chain coffee houses. Unlike the quintessential Bowery, get-em-in, feed em, charge em, then get-em-out, greasy spoons, the steakhouse had adopted a down home, take-your-time ambience, it's décor reflecting pathos for the client, it's staff welcoming and diligent without pressing for immediate choice decisions, or scowling whilst waiting to be asked for the cheque.

During the same stopover, he had interviewed Clive Davis, founder and president of Arista Records. One of the paradigm-shifting, master broker and money manipulator demigods in the American rock movement, in terms of wooing aspiring artists to sign for labels, he had first forged a successful career with Columbia Records, as Paul Christian outlined at the Marina del Rey Marriott, before forming Arista and signing the likes of Lou Reed and the Patti Smith Group. Attending the 1967 Monterey Pop Festival at the insistence of buddy Lou Adler, subsequently Davis signed Big Brother & the Holding Company to Columbia, and went on to gain the signatures of the Electric Flag, Blood Sweat and Tears, Santana and Bruce Springsteen & the E Street Band. Though he knew Davis was capable of displaying a vicious, uncompromising streak to get what he wanted, a prerequisite for success in the highest echelons of the record label business, Collins found the godhead to be courteous and informative when responding to his questions. They met in the Russian Tea Room, an up-market bistro on West 57th Street, popular with record execs and other businessmen, chiefly bean counters. The episode became memorable for Collins, because off the record, Davis expressed a preference for low-key, traditional brasseries, and five-star restaurants such as the Russian Tea Room were just for show amongst the glitterati. Extolling the virtues of Idaho Harvest to Davis, subsequently the Arista President took lunch at the Bowery chophouse and wrote to Collins praising his counsel. A massive feather in the rock journalist's cap, it induced Davis to allow him unique access to his stable of artists, boosting Collins standing at *Crossroads*.

Still in the throes of remembrance, Collins sojourn dissolved when Desirae quipped, "Wouldn't it be good to be able to travel back to the best times you enjoyed in life."

"Wow, that's pretty far reaching," Natasha retorted.

"I know." She scanned around her compatriots. "What about the rest of you?"

"There are some occurrences I'd like to revisit," Gail admitted, "pre-eminently Kingston Fashion School. I effervesced positivity then, thought anything was possible, and I'd make my way in the world of *haute couture*, becoming the next Edith Head, and designing costumes for film and stage stars. How different it turned out to be in reality. I've been struggling ever since graduation, but I've learnt to accept my lot. So yes, Desirae, given the choice, I'd go back to those years in Kingston."

"Oh, count me in," Delaney intoned, his verve at the notion hitting the end stops. "There's no end of cocaine-fuelled trips I'd like to taste again. Boy, when I evoke some the outlandish shenanigans I got up to when I was as high as a kite, before I buckled down to working for Cold Turkey, they seem so astonishing. Now…hah—" He beamed like a James Dean dead ringer. "My habit is much more under control. I still flip out periodically, but not with the frequency I used to do."

"So, you're saying you've lost an attribute?"

"I am, Gail. The thing of it is, if I'd carried on that way, I'd not be here now."

"What about you, Henry?" Desirae solicited.

"Hah." Shining at the conjecture, he admitted, "Like Ray Davies, I yearn for the village green preservation society."

"You mean, how England used to be?" Natasha ticketed.

"Yeah. Since I was a boy growing up in Dunsfold, everything, meaning life, has become more complicated, more testing, and unconditionally, much more regulated. These days I get the feeling of being condensed from all sides into conforming with a lot of pressure cartels' diktats, additional to those of the government regarding how the country should be run. It creates a hunger for divine light to pierce the godless soul of modern life."

"So," Desirae began, "if you had a time machine, you'd go back to Dunsfold and relive your formative years?"

"Dunsfold village hasn't changed in terms of the people, or how they live their lives. It's the reshaping in the metropolitan areas that spook me. My folks used to take me up to London to see the sights, sometimes by road, sometimes on the train to Waterloo. In those days, the A3 was virtually deserted of traffic at the weekend, my father could park his Humber Super Snipe in Kensington Church Street free of charge all day, and the rail cost was pennies. London seemed like a larger version of Dunsfold. As I got into my teens, and began to go to the smoke for a gig or a sporting event with my mates, I began to notice the demographic deviations, and a vast increase in the number of people milling around the streets, most with aggressive physiognomy and not of this nation. That was the beginning of this compression feeling, and with every passing year since, the sensation increases. London is no longer a big village with a traditional semblance and atmosphere. It's more like Detroit or New York at their worst. So, like the Kinks master lyricist, I too yearn for the village green preservation society."

"How about you, Desirae?" Delaney pumped. "After all, you raised the issue."

"Oh, that's easy," she spieled, "on the crest of clocks going backwards, I'd return to my carefree summers in Omaha."

"Why?"

"Because life was simpler than, nothing hidden, everything transparent. I knew where I stood in the lofty shape of things. Everything made sense, everybody kind and considerate. It felt like the Land of Oz."

"And you were Dorothy?" Gail postulated.

"No, just one of the happy bystanders, drenched in the marvel."

"You are *all* fantasists," Natasha condemned, "treading in footsteps worn out by millions before you were even born." She glared at them. "There's no going back."

~ * ~

Pulling into a service station at sleepy Lone Pine, a youngish woman unequivocally of native Indian origin came out of the station's interior to serve the travellers.

"What can I get you?"

"Could you fill up both cars with premium please," Collins requested. Spying about, he noted a small coffee shop by the side of the main building. "Can we get some coffee as well?"

"Sure. Just give me a few minutes to dispense the gas, and I'll be with you."

Stretching, after climbing out of the Camaro and the Corvette, Collin's and co ambled over to the coffee shop, sitting on bar stools adjacent to the counter. Moments later they heard a back entrance door opening, the woman popping up behind the counter.

"What can I get you?"

"Oh, make it coffee with milk all round, please," Collins called.

She set about the task.

"You run this place by yourself?" Natasha nominated.

"I do now," she replied, while still attending to her task. "My husband got hit by an out-of-control truck coming back from Kramer Junction. Sent his pickup rolling off the highway. He ended up killed."

"*Oh*, I'm very sorry," Natasha murmured, embarrassed by her voyeurism.

"Happened three years ago. We'd only been married six months, so having few mutual memories, I've kinda got used to it."

"Nonetheless, it must have been difficult."

"Like other folks experiencing tragedy, I just put it down to bad luck, and carried on."

"Not sure I could do that."

"If you've got no other choice, girl, you would," she insisted, the finality of the statement making the globetrotters uneasy.

"Might I enquire about your tribal ancestry?" Desirae petitioned, intent on updating the subject.

"I'm Cahto Indian of the Laytonville Rancheria. We spring from the Cahto Valley on the Eel River in what is now Mendocino County in North-West California, and can trace our heritage back hundreds of years."

"How come you ended up in Lone Pine?" Delaney queried.

"My husband didn't get on with the tribal elders, so we decided to make out elsewhere. Bought this service station from an old timer. Got it for a song, and did it up with a loan from the bank. Used to be more like a glorified shack, but after modernisation it's making money. It's what keeps me going."

"May I table a philosophical point?" Collins wondered.

She arched her shoulders. "Sure."

"Why is it the indigenous peoples of the United States have little representation in state and national government?"

"I used to tackle my father about the dichotomy," she reviewed, placing five cups of milky coffee on the counter. "He told me treaties signed in the nineteenth century were never honoured by Washington. As to why we don't participate in state and national government, put it down to its alien to our culture. We have our own councils, and within our designated jurisdiction, we can make our own laws, and not be bothered by the federal government."

"Was it down to sheer overwhelming numbers of Europeans, Africans and Asians entering what became the United States why the native Indian nations gave up fighting them?" Gail investigated.

"My father told me our ancestors had the spirit knocked out of them. Though young braves wanted to sustain the battle for our homelands, the chiefs and elders could see the inevitable. He also said when Columbus made land on the east coast, there were eighteen-million Indians in what is now the United States. Over the centuries, wars resulted in a reduction of the Indian population, but the biggest killer was immigrant disease, exemplified by smallpox. That had a far more devastating sequel. By 1870, our population had dropped to less than 50,000. Today, if the census is to be believed, it's about half a million displaced across the United States."

"Dear god," Desirae crooned, "our forefathers have got a lot to answer for."

Back on the road, the atmosphere in the Camaro neared ponderous, Collins, Natasha and Desirae unable to come to terms with what the Indian woman had told them. During his multiple examinations of the United States, Collins had touched on the plight of the indigenous Indians, their centuries-old pickle making him reason, if inward immigration can decimate proud and noble tribes who fought tooth and nail against their oppressors, and still failed due to overwhelming opposition numbers, then it could happen to any indigenous nation, including the English. The ramification appalling him, he retraced the many occasions hostile invasions had either taken place, or been repelled by the English over the past 2,000 years, Hitler the last to attempt a takeover. Then he remembered large scale immigration into England since the early 1950s had dramatically accelerated to the extent whereby undivided parts of cities had been colonised, expunging any trace of English culture, and emphatically, English residents. Could it be that longer term the influx reached critical mass, the English becoming marginalised in their own country, and cascading down the same one-way road to ruination, as per the American Indian nations?

"I feel ashamed," Desirae finally verbalised, breaking the silence.

"Because you are the descendant of European immigrants?" Natasha tested.

"Yes. We don't get taught about how the development of the United States affected the indigenous Indians in our school history classes. It's skimmed over, or watered down to the extent whereby it appears not to have been a monumental catastrophe for the tribes."

"I can empathise with you on that score," Collins credited. "Like American kids, we got our impressions of American Indians from Hollywood. Nine times out of ten they were painted as the bad guys, the hostiles killing the settlers, but that was a convenient lie. All indigenous peoples fight to preserve their culture and their homelands. What that Cahto Indian lady said in a few short sentences, summed up the reality. It's nothing short of slow but sure genocide."

"For sure," Desirae approved. "We are the interlopers. It's their country."

"From investigating world history," Collins began, "I've often finalised strife and loss of life come about when peoples venture outside their own homeland or continent. I'm inclined to say, most of the world's conflict problems are solvable, if everybody went back to their natural constituencies."

"You mean all Europeans back to Europe, all Africans back to Africa and all Asians back to Asia?"

"Yep."

~ * ~

Death Valley became a source of intrigue and fascination to the adventurers way before the I90 took the column to the edge of the National Park. Part of the Mojave Desert bordering on the Great Basin Desert, during the summer, along with the Middle-East and Sahara deserts, it constituted one of the hottest places on Earth, its Badwater Basin the pit of lowest elevation in North America at 282 feet below sea level.

Approaching Death Valley, Collins informed, "We're over the Sierra Nevada mountains now. It's going to be mainly a flat, long, straight road for the next 120 miles, until we reach Death Valley Junction on the east side of Death Valley."

"I'm really looking forward to seeing Zabriskie Point," Natasha revealed.

"You might be disappointed."

"Why?"

"Although it is the stuff of music and film legend, Zabriskie Point is merely a natural landmark in the Amargosa Range noted for its erosional landscape." He glanced at her. "There's no settlement, if that's what you're assuming."

Before he could go any further, Delaney pulled up alongside the Camaro in the Corvette indicating for Collins to stop.

"How about we participate in some breakneck jinx again?" he advocated, as they stood by the road side.

Searching up and down I90, Collins checked for traffic. "Good idea, and there are no speed traps in Death Valley, so we won't get hauled in by a highway patrol sheriff. We'll do it on a long stretch of tarmac."

"Holy Moses, it's hot." Shading his face with a hand, he peered at the lucent celestial sphere. "Very hot. I'm burning up."

"Yeah, temperatures can reach over 130 degrees Fahrenheit. Better be careful. We don't want any mishaps ending in careering off the road. Can't call nine-one-one out here."

"Come on, I'm beginning to bake."

"Me to."

After a few miles of travel, evaporating as if to infinity, the straight road ahead sparked off the surging speed chase, Delaney dropping down from top gear and accelerating past the Camaro, Collins responding in kind, flowers and shrubs carpeting the desert floor, watered by earlier snow melt, rushing by. Similar to viewing a kaleidoscope tube of images, with the cars forming its centrepiece and the desert and sky its walls, as speed increased, the spectacle got more thrilling. Then they hit a dirty section, the car tyres throwing up clouds of dust, Collins blinded by the storm cascading from the Corvette, forcing him to slow and allow Delaney to streak away before flooring the gas pedal when the view ahead cleared. Maintaining a quarter mile gap behind the Corvette, the Camaro equalled its 120 miles per hour speed, the pair barrelling into the shadowy landscape for a further ten miles before Delaney slowed in response to a twisty section, Collins following suit. Similar to the flights of illegal swiftness they had experienced going west on Route 66, what differentiated Death Valley became an intuition of sheer isolation for the speedsters, the absolute stillness and silence of the backdrop acting to forge a vague feeling of insularity, like they had straddled a time barrier into the infinite void.

On reaching Zabriskie Point, they pulled off I90 into a parking lot, then wandered up the trail on foot to the Badlands viewpoint housing a plaque commemorating Christian Brevoort Zabriskie, eventual vice president and general manager of the Pacific Coast Borax Company, a mining combine extensively combing Death Valley for sodium borate in the late part of the nineteenth century and the first few decades of the twentieth century.

"Wow," Desirae gasped, "you can see the unbroken Death Valley flats from here."

"Absolutely," Gail backed. "Perceptions of eeriness and seclusion are even more amplified than when we're motoring. For all we know, we could be the only people in Death Valley, and beyond its boundaries the world might have expired."

"Jesus," Delaney griped, "it's sure as hell baking. I've never been to any place hotter." Touching the plaque to test his theory, he instantly withdrew his finger. "Yep, you could fry eggs on this metal, no problem."

"I was expecting circulating buzzards scanning for carcasses," Natasha reported, "but during the chase, and unarguably standing here, the skies are devoid of the scavengers."

"Maybe it's just too hot for them," Collins insinuated. "We're still in the anvil of the sun. They could fly during the early and late hours of daylight when its cooler."

"Remember what Wade Gardner told us about the uninitiated coming to grief in the Grand Canyon," Gail recollected.

"You mean about patrols recovering the bodies?" Collins solicited.

"Uh-huh." She gazed into the shimmering heat haze bleared distance. "I didn't see any warning signs as we entered Death Valley."

"I'm sure they are there. It's just we weren't looking. Our attention became consumed elsewhere."

"How much water have we got?"

"Plenty, and we're well gassed up. Relax, Gail. We'll be fine. Just got to limit our exposure under direct sunlight, and not become dehydrated."

"Some people live out here," Desirae recounted.

"*What!*" Delaney burbled.

"Yeah, it's hard to believe, but if we went off the beaten track, we might find some camper caravans, even dishevelled shacks."

"Doesn't shake me," Collins reacted. "Some people need complete isolation, and there's the allure of desert purity. Unlike the cities and the towns, Death Valley is clean, free from debris, social and environmental pollution. It holds its own attractions."

~ * ~

As the cavalcade passed along the Amargosa Valley well-worn road, the car occupants frequented Wade Gardner's appraisal of Area 51. Ogling to their left, they knew the mysterious base lay over the mountains and shrubland. Beforehand, Collins picked up the intense secrecy surrounding Area 51 had made it the habitual subject of conspiracy theories, and a central component of UFO folklore, speculators referring to it as 'dreamland' and 'the paradise ranch'.

Lingering on the I95 verge, they ogled in a north-northeast direction.

"Even if we had the time to mount an expedition," Delaney began, "there's every chance we'd be apprehended, and being *aliens* ourselves, apart from Desirae, they'd lock us up and throw away the key."

"Undoubtedly true," Collins supported.

"Gosh, there's not a toot or a bleep to be heard," Natasha observed.

"Yes, it's even quieter than Zabriskie Point," Gail graded.

"Might be unfathomable and uninviting," Desirae advanced, "but there's a certain beauty in the landscape here. All those purples and greys dappled with green produce a quilt-like overlay."

"Yeah, I see what you mean," Delaney praised. "It's almost as if the military have carpeted the outer zone of Area 51 with the seemingly inviting, but it inherently conceals their deepest secrets."

"Considering the whole precept is to make Area 51 impenetrable," Collins repudiated, "isn't that a contradiction in terms?"

"Yeah, *hah*, I'm still on Mount Olympus from that white line fever I took at Death Valley Junction."

"You know," Gail reprimanded, "you miss a lot or misinterpret what you're seeing when you're coked out."

"I know, but I do see things that remain invisible to the rest of you."

Jarred by his peculiar remark, Delaney's compatriots stared at him, meditating if they were missing out on his visions.

Sailplaning overhead, the unmistakable purr of jet engines broke their concentration.

Searching the wild blue yonder, Collins spotted the aircraft to the north of their position. "It's a SR-71 Blackbird."

"The spy plane," Desirae supplemented. "Must be going into Homey."

Sure enough, as the cluster continued to scope the aircraft, it slowed, descended and turned starboard before declining over the horizon.

"Not many people get to see a SR-71," Delaney gabbed.

"Bet it's come from Lockheed's skunk works at Palmdale," Collins stipulated.

"Not Wade Gardner's Aurora flying triangle then," he gibed.

"Oh, I'd not dismiss Aurora lightly. Every secret black-op plane goes through a mystical period. Wouldn't jolt me if in, say ten years' time, the skies are filled with flying triangles."

"Hah, I've fantasised about flying since I was a little girl," Desirae shared. "I mean like Superman."

"Oh, now you're talking," Collins felicitated. "If I could have just one Superman power, it'd be the ability to fly."

"I've always envied birds, explicitly those capable of soaring, because they get a three-sixty view of Earth from the stratosphere. Without wings and a tail, homo sapiens are somewhat impeded to achieve flight."

"It's a matter of each species to their own," Gail put forward. "People can do things that endure as impossible for animals and birds."

"True," Natasha certified, "but the aptitude to fly would be marvellous."

"Hah," Collins chirped, "if we could fly, it'd relieve the bottlenecks on roads, but the skies would be clogged up with humans."

"Government would put highways in the sky," Gail suggested, "and institute speed and height limits."

"Hell's *teeth*," Delaney spat out, "you're right. At the first hint of newfound freedoms, you can always count on bureaucracy to take the joy out of it."

~ * ~

Passing into the interior of Indian Springs as dusk descended on the Mojave, the luminous Las Vegas skyscrapers came into the voyager's view. Billed as the entertainment capital of the world and famous for its mega casino-hotels, the seven-by-twenty-four Vegas gambling business had been in continuous operation since 1906, then illegal, only briefly ceasing for twenty minutes as a mark of respect when Kennedy was assassinated November 22nd 1963. Prior to jetting into O'Hare, Collins had unearthed in the Great Depression years, some of the Dust Bowl huddled masses making for California along Route 66 got wind that construction workers were needed for the Hoover Dam project, less than twenty miles from Las Vegas. Consequently, Vegas avoided economic calamity with the influx of construction workers and their families. Concurrently, Nevada legalised casino gambling and reduced residency requirements for divorce to six weeks, adding to the city's economic boom. When Bugsy Seigel opened the Flamingo in 1946, the first of the super class hotel-casinos, it spelt a geometric rise in the city's fortunes, a further nine like establishments poking above the skyline by the time Collins and co entered Las Vegas.

Anything went down in 'Sin City', from professional sports and ritzy shows to prostitution and drug peddling, most of the businesses Mafia controlled and maintained. In an effort to attract tourists and gamblers alike, some hotel-casinos were torn down and replaced every so often with a fresh shrine to the buck, and new ones added as the Las Vegas city limits crept further out into the desert. Though other industries, including retail and restaurants, contributed to the economy, the ten hotel-casinos with an eleventh, the Mirage due to open November 1989, provided the lion's share of revenues.

Like a virus, gambling was in play twenty-four hours a day, every day, ranging from slot machines, card games including poker and blackjack, craps, roulette and big six wheel. Some went to Vegas for the shows, primarily when Sinatra and Elvis were on the roster, but most were attracted by the gambling, from little old ladies wasting their life savings, prospectors and cowboys wandering in from the desert with a fistful of greenbacks, to recreational punters willing to part with up to 10,000 dollars just for the fun of it, and professional gamblers out to beat the system by fair means or foul. People gambled continuously over breakfast, lunch and dinner, the crunching clank of one-armed bandits and bells and whistles going off heralding a winner constantly crowding the airwaves. Many sat at a cherished slot machine or patronised the same

Baccarat table for days on end, sometimes winning, but mainly losing. And all the time, the deluxe hookers paraded about the gambling dens, dressed to the nines, targeting tricks, preferably rich tricks, meaning successful gamblers, to lure them back to their haunts for very expensive boy-on-girl action.

Collins had been in Vegas to cover one of Elvis's ultimate gigs at Caesars Palace. Part of a *Crossroads* series charting the rise of the king of rock 'n' roll, his degeneration into crass Hollywood movies, followed by middle period rejuvenation, and extended *ad infinitum* Vegas residencies, the gig left Collins close to tears. Colonel Parker had been working Elvis virtually every hour that God sent with two shows a day, seven days a week, for years on end. Gone was the sleek rock icon, his once athletic body swelled by overconsumption of cheese burgers, his sculptured dial bloated by too much alcohol and narcotics, his movements awkward, but sporadically, the voice that had first wowed billions surfaced, and he held a tune together. After the show, if Collins could have got hold of Parker, a hustler and a con-artist only focused on now-money, he'd have strangled him.

Entering the city on I95, the convoy dovetailed onto South Las Vegas Boulevard, otherwise known as 'The Strip', a four-mile stretch of highway flanked by most of the hotel-casinos, plush retail outlets including Frederick's of Hollywood, a myriad of restaurants, McCarran International Airport, and even clip joints. Gambling produced so much revenue for the hotel-casinos that as a punter inducement, they could afford to reduce four and five star rooms, and food and alcohol to one third of New York and LA prices. Like moths to a flame, gamblers played from sun-up to the early hours, the addiction accruing in annual billion-dollar revenues for the city of Las Vegas. Independent of the national economic barometer, war or peace, feast or fowl, people were drawn to the fun city in the desert, often making then losing fortunes. From seaboard to seaboard and from the borders of Mexico and Canada, Las Vegas held a magnetic draw on high plains drifters and gold panners, holidaymakers and gambling professionals. Many kidded themselves they'd set aside a fixed sum for gambling, just like they did for a long weekend in Yellowstone National Park or Niagara Falls. But like the child unable to resist another candy bar when about to be sick, once the budget ran out, they delved into the reserve until that too became depleted. Some lost big time, sacrificing cars, jewellery, property, even businesses to the gambling stakes. Having lost everything, some took their own lives, the cloud busters a conscripted last redoubt before they plunged earthwards. Then there was the Mafia, owners of much of Vegas, and sufficiently in cahoots with the authorities to collect gambling debts without incurring any interference from the police or the state legislature. Rumour had it there were so many weighed-down, bullet-riddled bodies in Lake Mead and Lake Tahoe, that if a drought took hold and the waters receded, a fleet of undertakers were needed to bury the corpses.

After taking rooms at the Desert Rose Motel, the trailblazers dined at El Dorado Cantina, a Mexican restaurant in the rendered old west style, off the Strip, before making for gambling den, the Tropicana, famously used for the filming of *Diamonds Are Forever* and *The Godfather*, amongst a cornucopia of Hollywood products, and replete with boutique stores, flashy restaurants plus a concert theatre and comedy club.

The only member of the Collins party switched on by gambling, Delaney intended to take up residence at one of the many blackjack tables. Steeped in history going back to mid-eighteenth-century France and its burgeoning popularity amongst soldiers during World War One, blackjack had become as popular as poker with Las Vegas punters.

"This may sound dumb, Kallen" Desirae began, "but how is blackjack played?"

"It's very simple. In casino play, the dealer in charge of running the game from shuffling and dealing the cards to handling bets, remains standing, the players seated. When four or more standard fifty-two card decks are used, the cards are dealt from a shoe. Players attempt to beat the dealer by securing a count as close to twenty-one as possible. Card totals greater than twenty-one are busts. Before the deal begins, players place a bet in the form of monetary equivalent chips in the designated area to their front, limits ranging from two to 500 dollars. The dealer then issues one card face up to each player in clockwise rotation, then one card face up to themselves. A second round is then dealt face up, the dealer taking his second card face down. If a player's first two cards are an ace and a picture card or a ten, giving a count of twenty-one, this is a natural or 'blackjack'. When the dealer flips his second card, if it does not result in a natural, the dealer pays that player one and a half times the amount of the bet. If a player has a count less than twenty-one, he can chance requesting further cards from the shoe in an effort to reach near to or hit twenty-one. Minimum stand is a count of seventeen."

"And that's all there is to it?"

"There's a few more details, but I'm sure you get the gist."

"Can I watch you play?"

"Sure. First let me get some chips. I'm feeling confident because I took a line in the rest room a few minutes ago."

Everyone else wandered over to the one-armed bandits and the wheel of fortune, lost a few dollars over the next hour, got bored, then went to the bar and beheld proceedings.

Settling down in a vacant place at one of many blackjack tables, Delaney placed a two-dollar bet, Desirae observing transactions over his shoulder.

Examining his cards, he bayed, "Hit me," the dealer issuing him the next card from the shoe, Delaney's count increasing to twenty. "Stick."

When the residual players had made their own plays, the dealer flipped his face down card, his count totalling nineteen. "Pay twenties," he announced, Delaney collecting his stake plus a further three dollars.

Turning about, he glowed at Desirae.

His luck holding, after fifty minutes play, Delaney had received several blackjack pairings, progressively increased his stake to fifty dollars, and had made a healthy profit of 540 dollars.

"You're doing very well," Desirae congratulated.

"Yep, now for the big one." Making his play, he bet all the 540-dollar chips.

"But Kallen," she yawped, "you could lose all your winnings."

"True, but I haven't lost anything from my set aside budget."

Coming down in his favour after sticking on twenty, the dealer went bust.

"*Holy cow*," Delaney blurted, "I'm on a roll."

Betting 500 dollars for the next game, again he prevailed on twenty, winning 750 dollars.

"Time to get a bit conservative," he announced to Desirae.

For the next game he bet ten dollars and lost.

"Lady luck is turning against me." Smirking at Desirae, he yammered, "*Ahh*, but what the hell. I'm still up, so I'll bet 500 again."

"Oh, Kallen!"

Laying his bet, the dealer dealt him a face card, Delaney goggling at it as the dealer concluded the first betting round. The second round brought him a five.

"Jeepers, I have no option but to play."

He received a three making his count eighteen.

"Damn it, nothing ventured," he droned. "Hit me."

Miraculously, the dealer produced a three from the shoe, making his count twenty-one.

"*Oh boy*," he joyfully bleated, "this could be better than the previous big one."

Finishing dealing to the other players, the dealer then flipped his face down card over, a king. Accumulated to his face up, eight made a count of eighteen. Considering his options for a few moments, his hand hovered over the shoe. He knew to beat Delaney and avoid forking out 750 dollars, he needed twenty-one. Flicking the next card from the shoe, Delaney's eyes fell on a nine.

"*Ohhh!*" He thrust an arm upwards. "He's busted."

"Wow," Desirae gushed, "you're over 2,000 dollars up."

Unbeknown to Delaney, a Tropicana security man dressed in a tuxedo had been watching his efforts.

"Excuse me, sir," he addressed to Delaney, "I need you and your play pal to come with me?"

"*What?*" Delaney yawped, still mesmerised by the blackjack table. "Go away."

"Please sir, don't make a scene. It's in your own interest to come quietly with me."

"I'll do no such thing," he vehemently warranted.

Speaking into a lapel-mounted microphone, the martinet

summoned three more tuxedo-wearing security personnel.

"Come along, sir," instructed the first security man, "I'm sure you don't want to disrupt the game for the other players." Logging Desirae, he augmented, "You too, miss."

"But I was just looking," she countered.

"Do come along," he persisted.

Escorting the duo to an elevator, the mini throng flew up to the Tropicana's top floor. When the doors slid open, Delaney and Desirae were faced by a man sat behind a huge desk in a spacious suite, fixing them with evil intent. Frogmarching them to stand in front of the desk, the security men then stood aside.

"Mister Delaney," the man opened, "my name is Enrico Giordano. I run operations for the Tropicana." Eyeing the gambler again with a distrustful expression, he voiced, "Your luck is just too good to be true. We appraise that you and your partner are counting cards."

"*What!*" he babbled.

"It's a common practice amongst card sharps."

"I can pledge," he yelped, "we were *not* counting cards." Resting abruptly, he squinted. "Just a minute. How do you know my name?"

"You were registered as an alien at Chicago O'Hare on April 29th by the US Immigration and Naturalisation Service."

"That's a government department. How did you get access to the data?"

"Mister Delaney, we have access to everything." Dwelling, he searched Delaney's countenance again. "Right, what are we going to do with you and your partner in crime?"

"She's *not* my partner in crime. Desirae is a friend. This is the first time she's been in a gambling house. She just wanted to see how blackjack is played."

"Maybe so, but how do you account for your phenomenal winning streak?"

"Sheer luck," he defiantly insisted. "I set myself a gambling budget of a hundred dollars. I prophesised losing the lot. Consistently winning definitely surprised me."

"In our business, we deal in chance. Do you know what the

194

probability is of winning twenty-two blackjack hands out of twenty-five?"

"No, I can't bring the index to mind," he indignantly volunteered.

"Over twenty-million to one." He smiled. "Now, either lady luck indeed championed you this evening, or you are operating a system....card counting with your partner."

"As I've told you, my friend has never been in a gambling den before, and I certainly have not got the mental capacity to count cards from a shoe containing four decks."

Considering for a moment, Giordano said, "Let's see." Flicking a switch on a concealed panel in his desk, he engaged a video playback of the Collins gang entering the Tropicana. Shifting the monitor so Delaney could see, he asked, "Who are these people you came with? Fellow card sharps?"

Grinning with incredulity, Delaney rebutted, "You've got it all wrong. Apart from Desirae, who we are giving a lift to Omaha, we're all English wayfarers. We dropped into Las Vegas on our way back to Chicago. We're only here for one night."

"Mmmm. Let's just see." Summoning one of the security guards, he whispered in his ear.

A few tense minutes later, the guard reappeared with Henry Collins in tow.

Beholding Delaney and Desirae, he broached, "What's going on here?"

"Mister Collins," Giordano answered, "I'm Enrico Giordano, VP Operations for the Tropicana. Please do not be alarmed. We are merely seeking clarification regarding your companion's gambling status."

"What do you mean?" Collins queried, breeding a startled mien.

"Mister Delaney tells me, you and your consorts, apart from Miss Desirae, are English vacationers."

"Yes, we are."

"Not professional gamblers then?"

"What on Earth fathered that absurd inkling?"

"Evidently, Mister Delaney is an expert blackjack player."

"He's played before, but I'd not categorise him as an expert."

Hanging back, his tone became more forceful. "What *precisely* are you driving at?"

"Mister Delaney has won a lot of times during his stint at one of our blackjack tables, far more than reasonably anticipated, if just down to luck."

"Sorry, I'm not connecting with any of this."

"Do you gamble, Mister Collins?"

"Apart from losing on your one-armed bandits and wheel of fortune, no. We came to Vegas to absorb the atmosphere. Unfailingly, Mister Delaney chances his arm once in a while, but I'd hardly mark him as an addicted gambler."

"You might be right, but he does have other addictions." Pulling up a video of the restroom and turning the monitor to face the accused again, Delaney saw the image of himself snorting a speedball line. "Taking illegal drugs is a federal offence in the state of Nevada, Mister Delaney. We should really give this evidence to the police, or perhaps, you have an alternative resolution to your quandary?"

"You mean, return my winnings?"

"Yes."

"But I won it fairly and squarely. I did not cheat."

"How much are we talking about?" Collins inquired.

"Twenty-hundred and forty dollars."

"Surely that's chicken feed in the grand scheme of mega revenues gained by the Tropicana in just one twenty-four-hour session."

"Maybe, but we have to deter card sharps. Twenty-hundred and forty dollars can quickly become two-hundred thousand and four-hundred dollars, unless we pull the plug, as we did in Mister Delaney's case."

"You're barking up the wrong tree, Mister Giordano," Collins redressed, grinning. "Delaney might be all kinds of things, but be assured, he has neither the patience nor the mental endurance to be a card sharp. Resonates more like he's had a bit of luck, and you don't like winners."

"Hhmm." Giordano peered at Collins, trying to assess him. "You are logical, but you do not necessarily persuade. We have dealt with hundreds of chisellers, con-artists and crooked gamblers. Like your Mister Delaney, they all claim complete innocence."

"*Look*, with that degree of skulduggery, the Tropicana and the other casinos must keep a log of reprobates." Suddenly, he felt resentment building up inside of him, the Magnum option coalescing in his consciousness, the audacity of the inquisitor percolating a want to blast him to kingdom come. Squeezing his fingers into his palms, he boldly proclaimed, "I'm willing to bet, you will not find Delaney's name or image on such a database."

"Yes, we did check, but there is a first time for everything. That said, you have the note of an honest man, and on this occasion, though his luck is extraordinary, I am willing to take this no further if…you and your pals make a commitment not to gamble anymore this evening, and leave Vegas in the morning."

"What about my winnings?" Delaney interposed.

Curling his top lip provocatively, Giordano yapped, "Take your chips, cash them in, then go."

Still seething with indignation, back at the Desert Rose Motel bar, Delaney griped, "The first time I've ever had a run, and I'm accused of being a grifter!"

"Rough justice, but you got off lightly," Collins corrected.

"What do you mean?"

"It was only a matter of time before your Big C habit caught you out bigtime. That casino tsar could have consigned you to the cops."

"He's right, Kallen," Gail chastised. "Ever since I've known you, you've shot up at least once a day."

"Ohh, *man*," Delaney pleaded, "I only do it for kicks. I'm not dependent on it."

"Then *stop* it," Natasha instructed.

"Alright." He lifted his arms defensively. "I'll cut down, but I can't swear to stop it completely."

"You need a substitute for the white powder," Desirae put forward. "Some other crutch or preferably inert distraction."

"Or better still," Collins appended, "the willpower to fly without a safety net."

Scrunching up his lineaments, Delaney scanned around his

compatriots. Lost for words, for the first time in his life, he felt regret. Aware he furnished an enigma to those within his circle, the knack to engage self-control interminably evaded him. Endlessly promising himself and others, he'd quit the cocaine habit, Delaney's abstinence typically persisted all of half a day before he reached for his stash, or wandered the streets searching for a dealer. This time, it could have ended in a heavy fine, or a custodial sentence, culminating in him being barred from entering the US again, and thereby losing his prized A&R job at Cold Turkey, or any other record label. Under no illusions, Collins knew the possible consequences would distil on his buddy, but despite the temperance, he also distinguished after a brief period of restraint, he'd dive headlong into the nose candy again.

Commonly used as a recreational drug and euphoriant, UK Class A cocaine could be snorted, heated until sublimated and then inhaled, or intravenously injected into a vein. Most readily snorted via a rolled up banknote, invariably Delaney used this method to accomplish an intense feeling of happiness, sexual arousal, and loss of contact with reality, the ingestion consummating in fast heart rate, sweating and the biggest tell-tale signpost, dilated pupils, the effects beginning within seconds to minutes of use, and abiding between five and ninety minutes, dependent upon the amount taken. Sometimes, the repercussions on Delaney translated into physical and mental vanity, chance-taking capping in both abject failure, and like for the blackjack interlude, overwhelming success, the former outstripping the latter by at least fifty to one. Howbeit, whether triumph or fiasco, to Delaney, those were side products, his main aim to rocket into the intoxicating stratospheres. He had told Collins, under the buzz, he could stay hard and pleasure girls for far longer than normal. A benefit not lost on Collins, on the rare instants he had indulged in white line fever, or some other stimulant guaranteed to enhance his sexual performance, he'd found he could be multi-orgasmic within a time period when as a rule, he'd climax just once. Though Delaney craved the heightened sex, like for the attendant over-confidence, again he viewed it as a secondary boon, being as high as a kite, still his principle motive.

That night, with Natasha deep in sleep, Collins revisited the Enrico Giordano encounter, specifically the welling up of the appetite to gun down the Tropicana chief for his unwarranted impertinence. Harlem had not been the first time the hankering for vengeance had permeated to the surface. Previously, other oppressive confrontations not of his making, had manufactured the craving to terminate the culprit, the irrationality of the thirst igniting his concern. They had all been post-Babette. Was it a reaction against miscreants offending his sensibilities, generated by him having to deal with her outlandish conduct without resorting to cutting her head off? Now he wondered if the Magnum had been real, would he have used it?

Early the next morning, the pilgrims swung by Lake Mead and the Hoover Dam before reversing up I11, and taking the I15 out of Vegas heading for Bonneville Salt Flats, the previous night's hang-ups quelled and stored for posterity.

Chapter 16: Bonneville Salt Flats

Still flying around in his mind, as they winged their way along I93, Collins replayed the Tropicana episode, it's facets still crystal clear. If he and Delaney had dug their heels in, the entire touring party could have ended up as fish bait in Lake Mead, the authorities none the wiser. Did life come down to a simple set of go-no go decisions, he hatched, one path leading to oblivion, the other sustaining existence? Never being in a like-situation before, he had no reference to gauge just how near they had come to a premature end. What fazed him more was Giordano and his henchmen looked and behaved like businessmen during the brief instalment in much the same way as he'd experienced with record company execs, concert promoters and band managers. It flowered the notion, when things didn't go the way music industry playmakers wanted, did they also resort to the ultimate solution to rid themselves of pesky irritants? Not uniformly in the same ballpark as casino gambling in terms of annual revenues, nevertheless when the record industry got on a roll as it had done with the rise of the Beatles *et al* in the 1960s and west coast rock in the 1970s, the coffers overflowed into the billions, inflating the egos of those at the top of the management pyramid. As Paul Christian had reviewed at the Marina del Rey Marriott, some of the CBS top brass were not adverse to wielding the axe to get what they wanted. Collins had heard other stories about power-crazed record company moguls using their authority to eliminate management competition. How far did it go when the thorns in their sides refused to budge? Band managers could be just as ruthless. He had heard tell that when manager Don Arden got wind Robert Stigwood was trying to sign his band the Small Faces to the RSO stable of acts, he went around to the Soho RSO offices with a couple of heavies, and had them hang Stigwood upside down outside his fourth-floor office window until he promised to quit. An altogether shrewder operator, Simon Napier Bell proposed to Arden he should manage the Small Faces, with Arden receiving a share of the profits without the hassle of managing the hot-headed group. Receptive to the idea, Arden gave his blessing, saying if the Small Faces didn't accept the deal, he'd break their legs. Magnifying the rapscallion footprint, Collins also knew Led Zeppelin manager Peter Grant had no qualms about employing violence to overcome recalcitrant business partners, some disappearing from the rock scene. Did they end up in Lake Mead? The more he played around with the discernible interconnection between casino and rock business management, the more he became swayed much more went on behind the scenes of his chosen industry than met the eye. The actions of Arden, Grant and numerous CBS execs probably represented a fraction of the power abuses seeping out into the lower echelons of the enterprise. Not wanting the poser to colour his cognition further, he made a conscious decision to park the paradox, maybe frequenting it with *Performance* colleagues back in Blighty.

Much later in the morning, Collins got talking with Natasha and Desirae about American pop-art and rock culture, in particular not-so-obvious significant works, and unobserved casualties falling by the wayside.

"Sometimes," Collins argued, "just because an album is not based on familiar time signatures, themes, motifs and expositions, it doesn't automatically qualify for the bin."

"You're not trying to justify for example, Zappa's endless live guitar dominated panoramas on the *Shut Up 'n Play Yer Guitar* series, are you?" Natasha prompted.

"Not especially, I was considering some other examples."

"Cite an instance?" Desirae prodded.

"Well, like much of modern art, meaning minimalist art, attracting sneers and put-downs from onlookers, you have to listen beyond the obvious. Beefheart's *Trout Mask Replica*, Reed's *Metal Machine Music* and My Bloody Valentine's *Isn't Anything* are examples of gloss cloaking much deeper emotions. Scott Walker's *Climate of the Hunter* is another game changer enlarging rock's vocabulary. Radically opposed to the Walker Brothers sixties hits, he deconstructed the song formula, broke it into sub-elements, then re-assembled them into configurations of his choosing."

"But *Metal Machine Music* is inaccessible," Natasha condemned. "Nothing like the Velvet Underground stuff or Reed's prior solo albums such as *Transformer*."

"Yes, when *Metal Machine Music* was released, we listened to it in the music room at *Crossroads*. Nobody could make head or tail of the recording because it contained no vocals, number arrangements or recognisable structures, and swapped melody and rhythm for modulated feedback and noise guitar mixed at varying speeds by Reed. Some viewed it to be very much La Monte Young inspired. When the *Crossroads* editor called RCA, seeking an explanation behind the bizarre release, an A&R man told him Reed had intentionally placed sonic allusions on Beethoven's *Eroica* and *Pastoral* symphonies to achieve the desired phonic cacophony."

"And so?"

"Took me a while to cotton onto Reed was expressing his emotions in a surrogate medium. Granted, *MMM* tarries impenetrable, but nonetheless it opened up horizons for other experimental musicians. In retrospect, some musicologists have awarded genius, brilliant and sensational status to the work. But these are just words. What's more important is the sentiment behind the work, the discovery of what's in the artist's cognizance."

"You also mentioned rock casualties," Desirae reminded him.

"Indeed I did. Aside from Brian Jones, Morrison and Hendrix, there are innocent bystanders personified by Factory girl Edie Sedgwick."

"Warhol's on and off platonic love interest."

"Yes, Desirae. In many ways Warhol was an agent provocateur invalidating convention, but also using it as a basis for his art. He took ordinary household objects and made them iconic. In reality, he threw America back into its face, and in the process turned the mass assembly line into an aesthetic punchline. Warhol was nuts, touched, half-crazed, call it what you like, but in a very passive way. People took acid to try and project the persona he naturally emitted. However, though listless, he lingered subjectively detached from everything and everybody. He hurt a lot of people, pretending no responsibility for their behavioural revamp after being fed a bitch's brew of false ambitions and debilitating drugs at the Factory, Edie Sedgwick a prime example. She was dippy, but as innocent as snow." Halting, righteousness enveloped his features. "Although considered chic by the mainstream fashion gurus when they learned about Andy Warhol's Factory, within a few years the bettina had become damaged and deemed to be vulgar. Too seedy, too much riffraff, and to many drugs. Notwithstanding, by then Edie had become a basket case."

"There are many more examples," Desirae entreated, "ranging from metaphysical writers' darlings and impressionist artists' muses to those caught up in the maelstrom schemes of frenzied scientists and crackpot politicians. It seems that the outrageously talented need to place one foot on *terra firma* occasionally through their loved ones and partners, and in the process such supporting functionaries become withered and wasted."

"That's a very astute observation," Collins complimented.

"You took the words out of my mouth," Natasha annexed. Swivelling in her front seat, she faced Desirae. "The more you reveal yourself, the more I'm convinced you should add philosophy to your poetry inclination. In fact, I'm surprised you did not major in ideology at the University of Nebraska."

"*Hah*, they were different times, Natasha. Just let's say, back then I hadn't developed an aptitude for reasoning."

~ * ~

Meandering through the Great Basin Desert, with the Snake Mountains to the west and the Great Basin National Park to the east, low-traffic density I93 offered another opportunity for Collins and Delaney to play lightning cat and mouse, the Corvette and the Camaro making graceful, ballet-like manoeuvres around each other for mile after mile whilst keeping an eye on the road ahead for approaching vehicles.

They were slowing back to fifty-five, when Delaney registered a black and white, partially camouflaged by trees on a track to the right of the road. Sure enough, within seconds of the pair careering past the junction, both drivers heard the wail of a siren as the highway patrol car leapt from its lair, blue and red lights flashing.

"Oh, Christ," Collins groaned, "not again."

Trundling to a halt off the highway, the cop car stopping behind the Camaro, Collins and Delaney awaited the inevitable dressing down followed by another spell in jail.

Examining his rear-view mirror, Collins saw a heavily built officer emerge from the black and white, replete with shades. Strolling up to the driver's side of the Camaro, he tapped on the window, Collin's lowering it and noticing the highway patrol man had Officer George Culpepper emblazoned on his badge.

"I might be wrong, but you boys appeared to be decelerating back to the max speed limit when you flew past my radar speed detector."

"Hah, these roads are so straight and long," Collins began, intending to wing it, "that sometimes you can inadvertently drift up to a faster speed than you intended."

"Are you implying you were not decelerating from an illegal speed, when you and your pal registered on my detector?"

"That's about the size of it, officer."

"Let's see your driving license."

On producing the requested document, Culpepper scanned it, then scratched his chin. "This here license was issued in England."

"Yes, we're vacationing in the US."

"That goes for your amigo in the Corvette, as well?"

"Indeed."

"And he's got an English driving license?"

"Correct."

"Just cool your jets for a moment. I gotta call this in to Indian Springs. We 'ain't ever had an English highway offence perpetrator before."

As Culpepper retreated to the black and white, Natasha said, "Let's hope Wade Gardener was right about state police departments not sharing highway offence data."

"Quite."

After a few tense minutes, Culpepper returned to the Camaro. "My chief says to use my discretion regarding your possible speeding offence." Pushing his cap back off his forehead, he leered at Collins. "Can you certify that you and your pal were not speeding recklessly, and as you said, your speed had wandered over the fifty-five miles per hour limit, and when I clocked you, you were returning to the max speed limit?"

"Oh yes, officer."

"And that goes for your fellow ball of fire as well?"

"Absolutely."

"Well, since I'm given to understand that if I handed out speeding tickets to the pair of you and hauled your butts back to HQ, it'd lead to a whole passel of paperwork, I'm prepared to give you the benefit of the doubt."

"Thank you, officer."

"Just make sure you stay to the speed limits in the state of Nevada."

As the black and white slid back onto I93 heading south, Desirae flagged, "You were lucky, Henry. Habitually, the highway patrol cops bust anyone even slightly over the limit."

"For sure."

Arriving at the Camaro, Delaney surveyed, "What happened?"

After relaying on the exchange, Collins concluded, "Somehow, we got lucky. That was the ultimate red-hot race. We've got away with it twice. I don't think our good fortune will hold for a third time."

"I'm surprised we got let off so lightly," Delaney tattled. "I expected at least a fine."

"The gods must be favouring us today, daddy-o."

"Mmmm, I'm not so sure. I've never had any sucker from the deities. Why should they start benefaction now?"

"Ahh, you're being too literal. Just accept it as good fortune."

As Delaney went back to the Corvette, Collins caressed the favourable judgment again. Blinking, he cogitated, 'Maybe Delaney has a point!' Unable to come up with a motivator, he ended up leaving Culpepper's charity in his unsolved mental folder.

Late in the afternoon, the motorcade checked into the Rib Hill

Motel at Ely, a historical Pony Express waystation transformed into the largest city in White Pine County with the unearthing of copper in 1906, though its current population numbered less than five thousand. Sleepy and soporific, the kind of settlement rarely springing into sparky life, Ely's claim to fame rested on being the home to the Nevada Railway Museum. Collins had encountered similar neighbourhoods in California, when driving from major city to major city, following touring bands on behalf of *Crossroads* and *Performance*. Characterised by shrivelling brier, grimy streets and often wooden buildings, they constituted the US arcane hinterland, way off the principal rambling trails, and steeped in late nineteenth and early twentieth century frontiers traditions.

"I doubt the beats ventured into Ely," Delaney consigned over dinner at Cicero Joe's, a Tex-Mex eating house specialising in steak and pepper fajitas, run by Joe Clancy, the gent introducing himself to the diners on their arrival, and telling them, originally he hailed from Dallas.

"You could well be right," Gail backed, her visage filled with sarcasm.

"Yep," Collins propped, "Ely is well away from the well-known beat trails, but then again, so are most of the isolated towns we've seen in California and Nevada."

"And in practice," Natasha insisted, "the swathe of states peripheral to Route 66 have claim to the lion's share of the beat's highways and byways."

"Begs the stumper," Gail initiated, "should we have returned to Chicago on Route 66 taking in some of the outlaying cities we didn't visit on the outbound leg?"

"Then we'd not have met Michael McClure, and more importantly, the vivacious Desirae," Collins propounded, winking at the American girl.

"Ha, ha," Desirae spouted, gleaming like diamonds, "you are too kind."

"It's true," he insisted. "You've affixed an uncommon dimension to our outing, put a fresh slant on our conversations, and most of all, pepped up our sensibilities."

"Praise from Caesar. You'll have me blushing in a moment."

"I don't suppose there's a place to score in Ely," Delaney whooped. "The stash I got in Vegas is nearing exhaustion."

"You've got about as much chance of finding a dealer, as I have of finding a rock venue with Primal Scream top of the bill," Collins retorted. "Your next opportunity will be somewhere to the east of Salt Lake City."

"Who are Primal Scream?" Desirae enquired.

"An indie band, initially influenced by the Byrds before entering a more heavy rock idiom."

"English?"

"No, Scottish."

"Apart from New Order and the Jesus and Mary Chain, I don't know much about 1980s British indie bands."

"Watch out for the Stone Roses from Madchester, that is Manchester. They're a rock band with rave culture overtones. Produced some spellbinding singles, and I heard a pre-release acetate of material for their debut album sent to *Performance* by Silvertone Records last Christmas. Very impressive, Beatles stimulated melodies and jangling Byrds-like guitars."

"Everybody in America loves the Beatles. I first heard them before I went to school. Ever since, for me they have been the yardstick comparison for later bands."

"Yes, though lauded in their active years as the most innovative and influential band of the sixties, it is only in recent times that the Beatles near-to unique significance has been celebrated in wider music circles. I hear tell McCartney, Harrison and Starr assisted by Neil Aspinall are resurrecting a documentary first mooted in 1970 after the Beatles split, in the form of an exhaustive series spanning the band's foundation to its demise, to be broadcast on television."

"The more I listen to the Beatles, the more I realise what unsurpassed musical pioneers they were. I'm no musicologist, but to these untrained ears, their work never fails to come up with something unique to tweak the faculties into appreciating how out on the rim they were with their lyrics, song arrangements and a cacophony of startling instrumentation."

"Unreservedly, Desirae, the Beatles weren't musicians, they were magicians. Put them in a studio with George Martin at the controls and wonderment happened. Arguably, not many came close to the same creative masterminds ballpark."

"What you say is true," Natasha approved, "but on the negative side, sixties rock bands provided the platform for the excesses of seventies and eighties heavy metal merchants."

"Undeniably correct. In comparative terms, if the Beatles have similarities in terms of melody and timbre to Mozart and Bach, then heavy metal's equivalents are Wagner and Mahler, not that I am ridiculing those giants, just setting a benchmark discriminator."

"For a small man, Mozart has cast a giant shadow over the centuries," Desirae applauded.

"When you've quite finished with your fab-four eulogy," Delaney intervened, "I still have the problem of feeding my addiction."

"So, you admit it's an addiction?" Gail jumped in.

"Well, that's too strong a word for it."

"Dependency, then?"

"No. I'm in control of my white rock. But I need to have some on hot standby just in case I need a fix. I get very agitated if I haven't got a stash to hand. It's an insurance policy."

Uncompromising in its finality, Delaney's admission brought the dialogue to an end, the travellers retiring to their rooms at the Rib Hill Motel.

Curled up in bed with Natasha after making love, Collins voiced, "I think we might have stumbled on someone special when we took Desirae into our midst."

"Yeah, she is something. In terms of erudition, that comment about the outrageously talented lays happily alongside much of the philosophy I've read. Difficult to comprehend she is in her early twenties, yet it seems to have flowered post-university based on her adventures."

"Quite. With a mind like hers, I'd be inclined to presuppose she'd fit the higher education lecturer template without any difficulty, and God has blessed her with good looks."

"Mmmm, it's not often beauty and brains coincide."

"Yes. In some ways I wish we'd picked her up far earlier in the tour. Just think what she might have come out with over a period of several weeks in place of a few days."

"I wonder if she fits in with other groups as easily as she fits in with ours? I mean, that in itself is a gift."

"How?"

"Well, to seamlessly dovetail in, she'd need to be studying our body language and what we said from the outset. If I'm right, she made the transition within the first few moments of our meeting her at Del Mar Deguello."

"I won't argue with that." Raising his eyebrows, he said, "We'll have to invite her to London. She'd be a blast amongst the hipster set."

~ * ~

Continuing up I93 the next morning, for mile after uneventful mile, the voyagers hit a series of small townships in the valley between Telegraph Peak and Queen Spring Mountain, their aura and manifestation in common with Ely.

Then out of thin air, after joining the I80 at West Wendover, Bonneville Salt Flats materialised like a mirage to highway traffic, as if white-washed into a two-dimensional singularity as far as the eye could see. A remnant of the Pleistocene Lake Bonneville and the home of land speed records since 1914, a man they met on I93 in a roadside cantina told them, 'The flats are a densely packed salt pan, twelve miles long and five miles wide. For speed merchants and casual trekkers alike, the sight of the gigantic, flat white plain is otherworldly, as if dumped on the Earth by a passing spacecraft, it's sheer quantification and unrelenting presence giving the impression of rank permanence. Often, sightseers have found themselves stranded at its core, unable to determine their geo-coordinates, and thereby the correct direction back to civilisation, the baking sun adding to their fancy of isolation and helplessness.'

Back in the English winter, whilst genning up further on the beat generation, Collins had ascertained a confederation travelling to California from the East Coast had heard about Bonneville Salt Flats from

Denver hobos. Evaluating the spectacle to be ornate desert, they hitched their way west along I80, set up camp in the flats at a location where the highway evaporated over the horizon in the mid-day sun, and became dehydrated when their hipflasks ran out of water. But for a passing speed-freak caravan rescuing them, the wayward beats would have pegged out before stumbling back to I80.

Crashing to the front of Collins' psyche when the Corvette and the Camaro left West Wendover, marking the south-east corner of Bonneville Salt Flats, the remembrance had him contemplating if they'd see any beats wandering the natural phenomena. A few miles later, they pulled off the highway onto the edge of the flats, exited their speed chariots and stared into the shimmering distance, the early afternoon sun blazing down, its rays mirrored off the salt multiplying the heat factor, and driving the ambient temperature to over a hundred degrees Fahrenheit under a cloudless paled-turquoise sky. Returning to the cars, they drove due north for four miles, then stopped and got out, the heat even fiercer than at the flat's south periphery.

"The silence is deafening," Collins pigeonholed, as the troupe shielded their eyes.

"Unquestionably," Natasha endorsed, "it's like we've landed on the moon."

"Though pleasantly tranquillising," Delaney parried. "A prized place to meditate."

"You could literally lose customary perceptions in these surroundings," Gail supplemented. "There are no distractions here. Probably, it hasn't changed since the first indigenous humans came upon it, thousands of years ago."

"Funny you saying that," Desirae began, as they gazed at the Bonneville Salt Flat evanescing over the horizon in the form of the Earth's curvature. "Sometimes, I can't believe humans have ascended that much out of the Miocene epoch period mud, some six million years ago."

"Oh, why do you say that?"

"Well, here we are in the late 1980s, and we still have the same primeval instincts associated with Hominins. We're territorial, egocentric and war-like."

"That's down to the reptilian part of our brain, an inherited legacy from when reptiles ruled the Earth," Collins outlined. "It's the oldest part of the human brain and controls the body's vital functions, typically, heart rate, breathing, temperature and balance. Though the limbic controls behavioural responses, emotions, and with civilisation, value judgments, and the neocortex abstract thought, imagination and consciousness, when we feel threatened, effectively the reptilian overrides standpoints of morality, even fair play, to ensure we react with extreme prejudice to a perceived peril."

"Is that why disparate cultures, religions and nations war with each other?" Desirae probed.

"Despite some latitude for mutual overseas accord, yes. Disparate peoples do not mix and meld together in a competitive environment, especially for jobs and housing, and when the indigenous peoples' culture is threatened. The nearest model free from these dog-eat-dog vices are homogeneous societies epitomised by the Nordics."

"So, morality becomes conflicted by the divergence?" Natasha tendered.

"Mmmm. The only difference between tribes vying for the same cave or carcass, is today the weapons of choice have become much more sophisticated."

"But the justification abides primeval."

"Unerringly, history confirms the motivations to go to war endure the same; dominion, subjugation, land, riches. Some first-world nations have learnt the futility of war results in a zero-sum game with no winners, just amplitudes of losing. Nevertheless, others seeking parity with the top-table players still calculate aggression will prevail."

"As in terrorism?"

"Yes."

"So, it's a matter of universal development, meaning logical precepts. Some nations, cultures or ethnic groups lag behind. They engage in terror to attain what they want, and the top table responds in kind."

"Some never learn," Delaney condemned. "It's a mental deficiency."

"Yes, but how is that explained?" Desirae explored.

"Could be down to eugenics."

"What's that?"

"Eugenics is a set of beliefs and practices aimed at improving genetic quality, and thereby morality," Collins enlightened. "In practice it translates as selective breeding."

"Didn't Plato advance applying selective breeding to Greeks around 400BC?" Delaney queried.

"Indeed he did, but it lay dormant until the nineteenth century when proto-geneticist Francis Galton proposed the first social measures, meant to preserve or enhance biological characteristics based on Darwin's survival of the fittest principle. Later it became coined as eugenics by social anthropologists."

"So, are you saying, for some assortments," Desirae interpreted, "the reptilian mind is still dominating the limbic and neocortex, germinating hostility?"

"Well, that's a social anthropologist or psychologists' explanation. Politicians put a different sentiment on the deficiency."

They fell silent for a few moments, then Gail perceived, "Apart from creating apocalypses for abstract thought, we are going to melt out here."

"Yes, you're right," Collins backed. "Time to bathe ourselves in the cars' air-conditioning."

"Just a minute," Delaney interjected. "We have an ideal opportunity here to test out the max speeds of the motors. That'd be a tremendous high."

"Yes," Collins agreed, "but very risky. We don't have crash hats, and there is nowhere for the girls to shelter while we're flashing across the flats. Besides, the salt would chisel most of the tread off the tyres, rendering them unsafe for road use. If we got pulled up by the feds again, hot water beckons."

"Yeah, you're right. I don't relish another showdown with the local highway patrol sheriff."

Instead of blasting up the Corvette and the Camaro to max speed, the convoy paraded around the salt flats at a steady forty miles per hour, taking in the panoramas before returning to I60 and ploughing on east.

"There's a divergent kind of devastation we're finding compared to the Dust Bowl and depression legacies of the south Midwest," Collins remarked during the journey. "The devastation in the north Midwest is more in the landscape, representing the reverberations of the continents shifting and forming in the Ice Age."

"Evidently, it's more pronounced in California, Nevada and Utah than in Oklahoma and Missouri," Natasha qualified. Deliberating for a moment, she added, "The people are different as well. Whereas there is still a discernible blue-collar working-class tone to cities like St Louis and towns along Route 66, the residents of LA, Frisco and certainly Vegas don't carry Dust Bowl and Great Depression baggage. Sure, there is poverty in these states, specifically in the rural communities, but it's grounded in farming and mining heritage, not inner-city industrial strife." Turning to Desirae, she instigated, "What do you think?"

"I'm no student of the Great Depression and my exposure to the south Midwest is very limited, but what you say does resonate with my impressions. Albeit, I can only really speak for California and Nebraska."

Expanding the text, the powwow participants threw further gems of acquired wisdom into the pot, the heady brew reopened with Delaney and Gail when they briefly stopped to view the Great Salt Lake and Farnsworth Peak to the west of Salt Lake City. Now used to making comments based on their observations, along with Desirae, the English pathfinders found themselves phlegmatic in their sociological deductions, neither making rose-tinted valuations nor nit-picking the disparities they identified.

~ * ~

"If you folks are taking in the Salt Lake City nightlife, you're going to need an alcohol drinking permit," the desk clerk at the Botanical Motel on 1300 South told them when they checked in.

"We'd appreciate that," Collins responded.

Making out five permits discharged by the Botanical Motel in their names, he handed over the warrants.

"Should you want to use the motel's bar, just show your room keys to the bartender."

"Where'd you recommend we can get a good steak?"

"Theodore's at 255 South West Temple in the Hilton Salt Lake City Centre. It's only a few blocks north of 1300 South." Hesitating, he grimaced. "You look like normal folks, so just one final word of advice. Utah is not all conservative Mormon leanings driven anymore. We have an ever-growing gay commune in SLC taking advantage of the state's liberal and diverse politics, and the city's becoming increasingly infected with this infernal AIDS disease. So don't wander into the gay bars in Downtown and Central City. There have been a lot of instances of regular people being attacked by these god-damned freaks and degenerates." Concentrating on the girls, he cautioned, "You young ladies be particularly careful of bulldyke lesbians scouring the streets looking for innocents to have their pleasures with."

Taking the clerk's advice, the adventurers walked to Theodore's, whilst keeping a weather eye out for possible gay assaulters.

"*Holy crap*," Delaney jabbered, "I've never been warned about onslaughts from gays before."

"Intriguingly," Collins contributed, "the first time I went to San Francisco, the then editor of *Crossroads* told me to avoid Canal Street to the north-east of Orange Park, if as he so quaintly put it, I didn't want to get 'rear-ended by an arse bandit'."

"It's a controversial subject in San Fran," Desirae appended. "During my time in the city, the gays were marching and generally causing havoc around City Hall and other government buildings. One time, last year, they took over Golden Gate Park for several days and painted buildings and roads with the rainbow flag, the symbol of gay power. It bossed the tv and FM channels, people calling in wanting to know why the police were slow to disperse them. Then later, they started using a new term to describe their classification; LGBT, meaning lesbian, gay, bisexual and transgender. It all got out of hand, orthodox people clashing with LGBT activists before the mayor finally ordered the city police to intervene."

"I know they congregate as tight-knit collectives in most Western cities including London," Natasha reviewed, "but I've never had any problems with them. Apart from the ones dressing outlandishly to flaunt their sexuality, they are transparent in society. For all we know, one or more of them could have been standing next to us in the motels and gin-joints we've frequented on this tour."

"I knew several men and women at Kingston Fashion School," Gail evoked, "who were open about their gay and lesbian sexuality. Never had any trouble with them apart from one lesbian lecturer who explicitly preyed on the student fraternity. She was an ugly, old trout who liked to be seen with unsure-about-their-sexuality pretty girls in the students' union bar. We all denounced it as sick, pathetic."

"Sounds like the bulldyke in the kennel," Delaney quipped.

"She came onto me once, and I told her in no unequivocal terms to fuck off. She didn't try it again."

"I heard the abbreviation LGBT back in January," Collins advised. "Someone from CBS talked about it to the *Performance* circulation manager. The record industry sees some mileage in catering for this lodge."

"Now you mention it," Delaney remembered, "there's been some similar talk at Cold Turkey under the guise of political correctness."

"*Oh*, political correctness has been around since the early 1970s. It's a front-runner catch-all cliché with lefties. Now and then, it's risen and fallen in the public eye, some of its' perpetrators getting rich on the tenet."

"Looks like it now includes LGBT," Natasha consummated.

"I'm all for fairness and doing unto others as you'd expect from them," Collins specified, "but on each and every occasion, a flavour of PC has been weaponised to gain a foothold, it's led to ideology trumping art and a reduction in freedoms."

"You mean, if a piece of music, an art exhibit or the written word," Desirae interpreted, "does not fit into the PC template, it is condemned?"

"That's about the size of it."

"But that's censorship. It's as bad as fascism and communism. It's the thin end of the totalitarian wedge!"

"True, and there are signs that free speech will be outlawed if it contravenes the PC ethic."

Frowning, she deciphered, "You mean, those who speak out about the iniquity will be ostracised?"

"Indeed they will."

"How is this possible?"

"As the desk clerk told us, the Utah political barometer has become sensitised to agitating, so-called minorities. The exact same thing is happening throughout the Western hemisphere. Politicians no longer ignore them because with mass immigration from the Third World, censuses reveal they form a sizeable proportion of the voting public. It's the axiomatic reason why the record industry is examining the LGBT phenomenon."

"You mean, there are votes to be caught and money to be made?"

"Precisely. As someone once fittingly articulated, I can't remember who, science acts to reassure us, whereas the intension of art, is to disturb us. Whoever said it, didn't bargain for political censoring when an art exhibit, be it music, writing or painting, contravenes the political agenda"

"*Jesum crow*," Delaney hollered, "traditionalists are being used and abused on a grand scale by all these minority factions, and led into the self-sacrificing corral, ready for extinction. It's what PC freaks call ethnic cleansing, isn't it?"

"For sure," Collins okayed, "but keep the recognition to yourself. You never know who might be listening, and ready to dob you in for thought crime."

~ * ~

The Utah valleys between Lewis Peak and Elkhorn Divide took the adventurers into the flatter landscapes and wilderness of Wyoming, home to Butch and Sundance rustling steers along the Wind River and their Hole in the Wall hideaway north of Rock Springs. After the sizzling temperatures of Death Valley and Bonneville Salt Flats, the herculean Wyoming farmlands provided a more temperate climate, Collins and co able to take strolls off I80 into the lush backdrop without a blinding sun hastening their retreat back to the Vet and the Camaro. Welcoming and soft, it felt like a new dawn, each breath they took, fresh and cool, the dust-laden atmospheres of outback Californian and Nevadan shanty towns no longer bugging their nostrils.

Somehow, the light appeared heterogeneous as well, Collins evaluating it as similar to the light at St Ives on Cornwall's north coast, a place he had holidayed at with his parents during his early teens and revisited with Babette. The couple had used the St Ives Bay Hotel as an epicentre for excursions along the coastline taking in Land's End and Penzance, and to strike out into 'Poldark' territory around Kynance Cove, St Agnes Head, Bodmin Moor and Padstow. Immersed in epiphanies of Ross Poldark battling with arch-enemy George Warleggan and evading Captain McNeil's excise troops, they even talked about naming a daughter Demelza after the Winston Thomas created character, but it was not to be.

Chapter 17: The Seasoned Sage

Regrettably, the incidence of meeting next generation beats along the trail substantially dried up after California, the northern option chosen for the explorers return to the Windy City way off the east-west corridor and passages favoured by the early pioneers. City dwellers in their teens and twenties, when not holed up in Mexico or Morocco, the likes of Kerouac, Ginsberg and Burroughs flitted between New York, St Louis, Denver and San Fran, and like for the Collins ensemble, finding Dust Bowl and Great Depression outlasters in downtown gin joints and rickety boarding houses who became zippy characters in their poetry and novels. Devouring the beat oeuvre, from *The Dharma Bums* to *Gates of Wrath*, and *Gasoline* to *Junkie*, Collins had made the connection inflaming his axiomatic want to talk to blue-collar workers, and those on the fringes of society. Predominantly home to lumberjacking, farming and ranching, north-western states from Oregon to Iowa boasted little heavy-duty manufacturing, and thereby less of a blue-collar class. Towering devotion to religion, family values and the stars and stripes also saw to it that disenfranchisement with the American dream rarely raised its head, the prospect of dropping out and becoming a beat or a bum alien to the populace. Thereby the frequency of beats wandering into this vast territory tarried slim to none, apart from those retiring from the game on pretexts of personal drivers or dissolution with the beat credo.

~ * ~

"Time to decide if we're going to call in on Rope Fisher," Collins announced, as they took in Medicine Bow-Routt National Forest from Elk Mountain on I60.

"Who's that?" Desirae tested.

Collins explained about their confab with Luke Berringer in Desert Hill on the outbound leg of the jaunt, including his recommendation they meet with Fisher, positioned as a beat guru.

"Might be our ultimate chance to talk with someone from the first generation," Delaney stipulated, "so it gets my vote."

"Yeah, let's do it," Natasha sanctioned.

"Gail?" Collins prompted.

"Why not. If he's as crabby as Berringer, could be entertaining."

Built on a plain, six-thousand feet above sea level to the south of ice-capped Cheyenne Mountain and domicile to more cowboy legends than downcast ex-beats, Collins had established beforehand that like other Midwest towns and cities, Cheyenne had been founded by the railways, Union Pacific selecting Crow Creek on the South Platte River tributary as a regional headquarters, residents naming the settlement Cheyenne after the native American Indian tribe. An integral part of the wild west, Wyoming attracted its fair share of rustlers and robbers post the American Civil War, Cheyenne acting as a magnet to pull the desperados into dance halls and bars, gunfights being fought with lawman Wild Bill Hickok and Pinkerton agent Tom Horn. Clement during the summer months, temperatures could plunge to minus twenty degrees Fahrenheit in the snowy depths of winter, spring and autumn compressed into short-term transitory periods between inviting warm and bitter cold extremes.

Rope Fisher lived off the CanAm Highway, a few miles north of Cheyenne, in a single-floor wooden house not benefitting from a lick of paint or wood varnish in many decades, its metal chimney maligned with rust and front veranda boards dipping incidental from lack of maintenance. As the Corvette and the Camaro pulled up outside the residence, Collins ruminated if Berringer had given him a bum steer. Could a supposed man of intellect live in such a dilapidated abode?

"Well," he began, as the troupe gawped at the ramshackle habitat, "we've come this far. May as well see if the sage is at home."

Rapping on the front door gained no response. Knocking harder, they heard a gruff voice shout, "*Who* the hell is it?"

"Mister Fisher, Luke Berringer from Desert Hill told us to look you up."

They perceived footsteps crossing a wooden floor, then the front door sprang open to reveal a tall thin man, burnt out from exhaustion, ravaged in the corn, to use a Dylanism. Grey as a seal on top with a corresponding beard and moustache made him look like old father time. Dressed in denim from head to foot and boots badly in need of servicing, the shotgun he carried lay loose in his right hand.

Squinting and rubbing his eyes, he bawled, "You from the IRS?"

"Erm, no," Collins responded.

"City taxation department then?"

"No."

"God damned vultures are always pestering me for money I ain't got." Narrowing his peepers, he raised the gun to eye level pointing it at Collin's head. "Then who the hell are you?"

"Luke Berringer gave us your address, Mister Fisher."

"*Who?*"

"Luke Berringer from Desert Hill, just outside Lake Havasu City in Arizona. He used to know you back in the 1950s."

Cocking his head back, a veil of surprise entered his lineaments. "*Holy smoke*, I imagined that old reprobate had turned up his toes long ago. Still owes me ten dollars-fifty I loaned him for a boarding room in Denver." Lowering the shotgun, he blathered, "Who did you say you are?"

"My name is Henry Collins."

"Good strong name. Go on."

"My friends and I are on a pilgrimage following the beats trail around the west United States. We met with Mister Berringer three weeks back. He told us you were a mover and a shaker in the beat generation movement of the early 1950s."

"So, what do you want from me?"

"We were wondering if you could spare us a few minutes to recount your cognizance of that significant counterculture time."

"A few minutes, *huh*, it'd take longer than that." Scrutinising beyond Collins, he cast a probing glare over the others. "Alright, you all look like civilians. Get your butts inside."

If the outside of the house desperately needed refurbishment, the

Collins cluster viewed its interior to be equally lacking in upkeep, much of the furniture and fittings faded or damaged, carpets around a stone hearth worn to a thread, everything covered in several layers of dust and grime, the only sign of intellect, a shabby record player, and an extensive dresser stacked with singles and albums plus row after row of books.

"I see you're inspecting my retreat," Fisher observed. "Well, I live simply now, with a few refinements, trinkets, memorabilia and such." He pointed to his head, "All I know is in here. If I git worked up, like your arrival worked me up, the adrenalin rush stimulates me. Once the grey matter is whirling, I remember everything, and most everybody." Boring at them with shady optics, he gabbed, "What do you wanna know?"

"We'd be very grateful if you could share with us your recollections of the beats and the adventures you had with them."

"I see." Rubbing his bristled jawbone, he commanded, "You all sit down. There's plenty of seats for everybody." Parking the shotgun in a wall-mounted rack, he swivelled to address his guests. "You must forgive me. I've become cantankerous and suspicious. Comes from too many years living alone."

"Luke said you had a pretty wife," Natasha recalled.

"Sure did." He cringed, his earlier irascibility replaced with remorse. "Hannah passed over ten years ago."

"Ohh...forgive me. I'm so sorry."

"Aahh—" He curled his top lip dismissively. "The love had gone out of our marriage way before I buried her. People change, and not necessarily in directions equitable to their loved ones. The fault and the failing was all mine. Hannah and I met in our early thirties, after we'd both been living on the wild side. That's what forged our union. She wanted more of it, and for a long time, so did I. But when I hit fifty, I began to feel vaguely ridiculous hanging out in fun palaces and barrelhouses, using seven-elevens when we got hungry, and hopping from place to place like homeless refugees. I wanted some roots. Some place we could at least call a base, a home, we could go back to after all the locomotion. She didn't care for that. Hannah was pneumatic, forever verging on the surreal and ethereal, a woman as capricious and elusive as Marilyn Monroe. She wanted to carry on like we were still adolescent teenagers, out to make our mark on the world by rejecting all society values and norms, but for me, the merry-go-round had stopped." Dithering, his demeanour surged into reflection. "You see, where I grew up in Fairmount Park Kansas City, not far from the Missouri river, most folks strived to better themselves. We went skinny dipping in Sugar Creek pretending to be Olympic swimmers, hung around outside Memphis McCoy's on East Eighteenth Street listening to jazz and blues players like Charlie Parker and Dizzy Gillespie, and watched the college baseball teams in the hope of joining them one day. Made us aspirational, but education was not on tap in those days. Coming from poor stock, I found my options were limited. I had high hopes of becoming an automobile engineer and working in Detroit, but I never got the grades required to matriculate for vocational college. I could play guitar and write stories, but Kansas wasn't exactly short of balladeers and fable makers. I got an interview for a junior reporter job with the Kansas City Star. Showed them my stories, but the queue was a mile long, and I was up against college graduates. That said, for some inexplicable reason, they took me. Said I had the necessary instinctive foundation to seek out good copy. But it didn't work out. I was let go with many others when the Star got new ownership. Then after doing a whole bunch of menial jobs way into my twenties, I decided to strike out for Detroit, and hustle my way into Ford or General Motors, start at the bottom and work my way up. I hitched along I70. Only got as far as St Louis when I went into a speakeasy and found a glut of guys reciting poetry and novel chapters. Turned out to be Kerouac, Corso and Cassidy. I got talking with them. Modified my whole perception of life. Made me twig there were alternatives to the mainstream. So, I embraced the beats' idiom, joined their sacred sect, and with Jack's help, even got my stories published by Harcourt Brace. After that, it was all hedonism and enlightenment."

"What was the ambience like?" Delaney quizzed.

"Cars, girls, freight-trains and rock 'n' roll. Hah—" He snickered. "Hannah came along, and we free-wheeled through the late fifties and sixties. We asked ourselves, 'What is the function of an artist?' and answered, 'To reject and rail against the status quo.'"

"*Any* status quo?" Collins posed.

"Yes. No matter what the philosophy or the doctrine, it will have imperfections and contradictions, and that includes the beat confederacy." Conjuring more recollection, he informed, "We took in Monterey and Woodstock, and generally lived for the moment. Somewhere along the way, I got a reputation for being a mahatma, to use a cat's expression, kids seeking edification and direction from me, primarily those with a writing bent. To me, the scenery is always better in books or on the radio than in film or television. It leaves a residual space for ingenuity to build and create. The pictures are better in your own mind. That's what I tried to impress upon them. When Hannah and I first moved here, we got a procession of aspirants knocking on our door, seeking guidance. I told them, follow your nose, keep your standpoint open, and let otherly worlds sweep over your senses. Then and only then, transpose your conceptions into words. Since Hannah passed, I've seen fewer and fewer people. Gotta be honest, I'd had my fill. You see, not all the beats were good eggs. There's only so much disappointment a man can take in his fellow human beings. Made me grouchy and irritable." Ceasing, he blew his nose and turned away, Collins sure he detected a slight whimper. "In more recent times," he reengaged, "I've suffered ill health. Got taken into the Cheyenne Medical Centre two years ago. Underwent an operation to remove a ruptured appendix. They kept me there for over a week taking blood samples. I told them, 'Hell with the amount of blood you people take, I'm beginning to think you're vampires.' Anyways, enough about me."

Wandering over to the dresser, his hand hovered over the middle row of books. "If I'm reading you right, you want to know about the beat generation playmakers. Well, the best of the best were visceral and cathartic, their works purging obsolescence and reaching areas of eloquence hitherto unexplored. Obviously, I knew Kerouac. A lovely man and a first-class writer, taken from us prematurely on October 21st 1969 by the Lord above. His like will never be seen again. Corso is another highly likeable man. He's still with us to the best of my knowledge."

"What about Ginsberg and Burroughs?" Collins tabled.

"Strange man Ginsberg," Fisher categorised, sauntering over to the fireplace. "Never knew what he was musing, but I adored his poetry.

As for Burroughs, if you recount *On The Road*, Kerouac portrayed him as Old Bull Lee. The Bull part stuck, and he could be bullish, meaning bad-tempered. That said, Burroughs is still producing astounding work. During the past few years, I've read *The Red Night Trilogy*, it's first volume, *Cities of the Red Night* is especially good." Pointing to his book shelves, he notarised, "There all up there. Neal Cassidy was another taken before his time. Again, a pleasant fellow, he worked a lot with Kerouac. I have to mention Ferlinghetti as well, so unassuming, so talented. Then there's a bunch of others I met with Hannah along the way. Luminaries such as Gary Snyder and Neal's wife, widow, Carolyn Cassidy. Sweetest folks you could ever wish to meet, and the list goes on. I'm sure you can name them, as well as I can. But er—" He came over all deferential. "What you have to cotton on to is, although Whitman, Thoreau and Emerson were foundation potencies, we were all in awe of Dylan Thomas, and to a slightly lesser extent, T. S. Eliot and W. H. Auden. All those beat gen giants I've reeled off, had a solid grounding in the works of these three twentieth century grandmasters. I caught a public reading of *Under Milkwood* by Thomas and his entourage in Denver. Must have been 1952 when I was green and still finding my way. To say the man had the voice of a titan is an understatement. I'd never heard anything before, or after, coming close to his magnificence, not even Richard Burton, and he was a fine orator. Eliot and Auden were quieter in their readings, but their content survives unsurpassed, the words built into precise phrases, the timbre of the stanzas, neat, everything mapped out to create profound visions. Eliot eulogised Christianity, Auden communism, but both did it in such a charming and persuasive manner, it became difficult not to become a convert. Much as I admire Jack and the others, they remain in a tier down from Thomas, Eliot and Auden."

"Along our sojourn, we met several people having dealings with beat generation members," Delaney indexed. "Some were very negative, saying it had left them with a nasty taste in the mouth."

"Yep, probably true. A follower layer hung onto the shirttails of the vanguard leaders, parasites basking in their reflected light, but contributing little to zilch. Others adopting the beat lifestyle, did it in an exploitative way, hanging out more in clip joints than gin joints. They got us a bad reputation, and that includes Luke Berringer. I don't know what side of his personality he displayed to you, but he was never adverse to causing social train wrecks."

"You mean Luke was devious?" Gail moved.

"Naw, he's too dumb to be devious. More like mischievous. Couldn't resist playing on people's foibles at times. Often it resulted in conflict, bad feeling, discord. Yes, he could be a good companion, throwing some pearls into the beat's melting pot, but like the ten dollars-fifty he still owes me, he's well capable of pulling the wool, then squirming out of his responsibilities. That applied to a lot of the so-called truth and erudition brigade I met on the road and the rail tracks. Kinda tarnished the good works and elan of those giants I've already praised. As my mother always told me, 'It only takes one bad apple to ruin the barrel'. Then again, no one gets away without any pockmarks on their soul. That's been the fate of movements and causes since time immemorial. Lotta people got carried away by the second gen hipsters, meaning the flower-power freaks and gospel scribes. Thought liquid honey dripped from their every utterance, if not their asses, but let me tell you, for every Jimi Hendrix or Jerry Garcia, there were ten-thousand leeches out to exploit that genre for every buck they could screw out of it. Stones found that at Altamont when they hired the Hells Angels as stage security. Despite Hunter S. Thompson's glorification of them, as far as I'm concerned, they are a self-centred, mean bunch of bastards, who'd sell their granny for a joint or a Schlitz."

"What's your opinion of the novelists following in the footsteps of the inaugural beat gen wordsmiths?" Desirae tested.

"Who do you mean?"

"Tom Wolfe for instance."

"Huh, you look a might too young to have read Wolfe."

"I read his *Bonfire of the Vanities* a few years ago, and on that basis checked out *The Kandy-Kolored Tangerine Streamline Baby* from his early career."

"Wolfe made his name as a non-fiction writer, paving the same spheres that Dylan did in his ground-breaking, mid-sixties surrealistic period. There are a number of others, like Joan Didion with *The White*

Album, but these are observers, chroniclers of events as distinct from fiction like Kerouac's *The Subterraneans* and Corso's *The American Express*, and don't get me started on Norman Mailer and Gore Vidal. Sure, they were the same generation as the first beat writers, but their blatant manipulation of American sensibilities, using their media influence based on works like *The Armies of the Night* and *Reflections Upon a Sinking Ship*, milked the countercultures of the fifties and sixties to the extent whereby they were positioned as soap operas and sideshows to the main event, meaning the status quo. *Hell*, that pair used to go hammer and tongue at each other on tv chat shows like delinquent school kids." Wrinkling his nose, he condemned, "Not very becoming for so-called intellectuals. It was the same with Susan Sontag. She wouldn't know class if it got up and bit her on the ass. She just caters for the LCD, yet she's lauded as some kind of libertarian redeemer. But that's down to fashion and deceitful promotion. Just goes to exemplify how politics and the publishing industry manipulate authenticity." Bending forward, he yelled, "You *wanna* know what life's taught me? Well, I'll tell you. Don't believe a god damned thing!"

~ * ~

"What a worthwhile visit," Desirae acclaimed as they returned to the cars. "I've never met anyone like Rope Fisher before. The rhetoric he conveyed in a few short sentences equalled whole life chapters. I could have listened to him for hours, maybe days."

"Yep," Collins agreed. "A very powerful member of the beats' brotherhood in terms of his spoken skills. A natural storyteller."

"Relating to his total life payload, I got the distinct feeling we only scratched the surface. And unlike most seasoned people, his topics were engaging. I found myself rivetted by his every declaration. I think he could have taught us a lot."

"You mean counselling regarding how to conduct our lives?" Natasha questioned.

"I think I do. History is littered with sages and seers, most with little formal education but with a bent for translucent vision. He fell into that category."

"I've come away with the impression he is an original thinker," Delaney recapped, "original in the precept he seems to have distilled pure essence from a hotchpotch of disparate inputs, and come to unequivocal conclusions based on the filtration."

"*Yes*, that's it, Kallen," Desirae propped. "What sets him apart is his capacity to transcend acceptance of the popular viewpoint in favour of what he perceives to be absolute truth." She glowered. "That would have upset a lot of people, because he will have driven a spike through their misconceptions. People don't like the truth. Most exist in a vacuum of half-lies and partial-truths, never settling on out-and-out, unbridled truth because it offends their sensibilities and casts doubt on their adopted credo. You see, I don't believe any tenet is watertight when challenged by its own discrepancies. Every canon I have studied is inherently plagued with paradox and inconsistency. Fisher's lingo cut through the crap, including the beats' shortcomings. He wasn't afraid to call a spade a spade, whereas most people shy away from admitting deficiencies probably because to do so would be testament to an admission of false belief. That in turn is associated with failure, the one minus most people can't stand to bear."

"Hah," Gail began, "there you go again amazing us with your take on the world. Now you've said those things, I'm sure it is intuitively obvious to all of us…but you came out with it first."

"Are you sure you are not a university professor, Desirae," Collins probed, tongue in cheek, "out on a field exercise to observe how mere mortals like us think?"

She beamed. "No."

Chapter 18: A Bolt From the Blue

On leaving Cheyenne, the cavalcade hit I80 again, the field of regard ahead plastered with the edges of the Pawnee National Grassland to the south and the endless golden Prairie to the north. At Pine Buffs, they crossed into Nebraska, latticed by many famous trails, including the Lewis and Clark Expedition, and home to a thousand bleak trapper tales, ginormous cattle ranches and corn farms. With gaps between cities on a par with New Mexico and Arizona, at times the wayfarers felt like they were adrift on an ocean of cornfields and grasslands, only the road setting their course.

"It's easy to see how prairie fever can set in," Natasha commented, as the column swept by mile after mile of unrelenting yellows and greens.

"Some time back," Desirae begun, "I heard tell of a South Dakota farmer-widower who lost it after being marooned in a sea of cornfields. Fleeing to the nearest town, he dumped his tractor and stole a station waggon. They caught him in Rapid City. He said he was on his way to Mount Rushmore to seek advice from the cast-out-of-stone presidents, regarding his isolation. Albeit, he was still done for grand theft auto."

"I'd imagine being alone on a gargantuan farm expanse, must be the same as a sea disaster castaway on a raft, at the mercy of the waves," Collins described.

"The incidence of suicide is much more prevalent in the farming communities of the Prairie states than in the cities," Desirae detailed. "Shotguns are usually the preferred despatch method."

"I understand the perpetual Scandinavian winters also take their suicide toll, people overcome by the constancy of a white landscape and grey sky. I wonder if it applies to desert regimes?"

"Possibly," Desirae cited, "but we'd never know. Desert peoples tend to keep themselves to themselves."

"*Holy cow*," Natasha whooped, "if I'd foreseen it'd lead to a downer, I'd never have brought up the subject of prairie fever."

Bivouacking at the Ponca-Sioux Motel in Big Springs on the Colorado border, presented an opportunity to take in the nearby South Platte River, set in a bucolic wonderland of maples and hawthorns. Finding the locale to be exceptionally tranquil, they felt predisposed to speak in whispers, Delaney chiming in, 'It'd be a delightful place to meditate'. Though appreciating the monastic-like climate after the commotion of Salt Lake City and Vegas, nonetheless, they yearned for the perky dynamics offered by a large metropolis.

Further along I80, they motored into North Platte, a small city at the heart of Nebraska, found lodgings at the Cody Park Motel, then sauntered into nearby Leon's Tacos Bar.

"Passing through?" enquired the barman, a cross in appearance between actors Slim Pickens and Richard Farnsworth in their middle period guises, after Collins had ordered five bottles of Michelob.

"We're on our way back to Chicago after doing Route 66."

"You don't say. It's been a while since I've happened upon anyone exploring the Will Rogers Highway."

"You're familiar with the Mother Road?"

"I used to be. You see, way back when, I had the wanderlust. Did Route 66 myself, hitching from Chicago to LA, then back again." Pausing, he added, "By the way, I'm Leon. This is my bar you're in."

Stepping forward, Delaney congratulated, "You're the first person we've met along the way who can claim that badge of honour."

"Yes," Natasha supported, "we've chanced upon a myriad of Great Depression and Dust Bowl descendants, and the intermittent remnant from the beat generation, but no one who'd taken Route 66."

"Huh, I'm staggered you traded licks with anyone from the beat generation. They've become a rare breed in public."

"Are you a beat gen fan?" Gail asked.

"Oh, some time ago, when I was much younger, and still open to left-field ideas. You see, I was born in Bloomington Illinois, and from age five, I used to stare at the Route 66 sign outside our house on Springfield

Road wondering where it led. Anyway, after high school, I figured it'd be the right time to ride the Main Street of America. Of course, I dropped anchor along the way, got jobs, met people, saw things most folks from Bloomington will never see. Just how I ended up in North Platte Nebraska, I won't bore you with."

"Did you have intentions to track down the beats?" Desirae solicited.

"No, but I heard about them along the way. Made me curious, so I invested in some Kerouac novels. Can't say the beats' lifestyle particularly appealed to me, but I understood why some people were attracted to the sub-culture."

"I don't suppose North Platte has any rock clubs?" Collins tendered.

"Hah, as it happens, there is an outlet on West Front Street, seven blocks east and two blocks north from here." Scanning beneath the bar, he annexed, "I've a leaflet somewhere for Pepper's Den. If memory serves, there's a Nebraska-based band named For Against playing there tonight."

Scurrying to Pepper's Den, Collins and co were pleasantly surprised to find a venue not too dissimilar to LA's Troubadour, the Spine Maidens taking to the stage before the headliners came on, Collins scribbling notes and faxing the gig report to *Performance* from the Cody Park Motel, before joining the others at Leon's Tacos Bar for supper.

"How was the band?" Leon surveyed.

"For Against are a blend of post-punk and dream pop," Delaney advised.

"Dream pop! What's that?"

"Dream pop is a subgenre of alternative rock and neo-psychedelia."

"Hah, you've lost me."

"It emphasizes atmosphere and sonic texture as much as pop melody," Collins articulated. "Common characteristics include breathy vocals, dense productions, and guitar effects such as reverb, echo, tremolo and chorus. Well known examples are Galaxie 500 and the Cocteau Twins."

Brooding, Leon murmured, "I think Pepper's Den put on the Cocteau Twins last year. Seem to recall a flyer to that effect. Anyways, you folks want a tacos supper?"

"Indeed we do, Leon."

Congregating in a wall booth, the gig-goers dissected the event.

"Did you give For Against the thumbs up in your gig report, Henry?" Desirae examined.

"Sure did."

"In retrospect, did you notice," Delaney ticketed, "the Spine Maidens were very much a mirror image of For Against?"

"Yes, I assume they are also from Nebraska, and have caught onto the dream pop band wagon." Frowning, he appended, "By the way, I dialled you disappeared at the break, and came back all bushy-tailed and bright-eyed."

"Yep, er...I managed to find a dealer in the foyer. Hip guy, he said, 'Yeah, I got heroin and coc. Any amount you can count.' So, I flashed the Franklins and acquired 200 milligrams of pearl. Should keep me going until Chicago."

"You know, drugs can be used for purposes other than medical and recreational," Desirae submitted.

"How do you mean?"

"Notoriously, a drugs scheme or maybe it should be categorised as a project with deliverables exists and is run by the CIA."

"To weaponise drug-induced human timebombs?"

"Yes, similar to Jagger and Richards Sister Morphine and Cousin Cocaine, but more like Matron Morphine and Captain Cocaine, it's an altogether more regimented regime, where the users are monitored, and their reactions noted to increasing doses."

"You could end up being a subject, Delaney," Collins quipped.

"Wouldn't bother me. All that free snow!"

Collectively, they shook their heads, but knowing he was a near-to a lost cause, did not reprimand Delaney.

"I get the impression dream pop is on the menu at Pepper's Den regularly," Natasha speculated.

"It's become a popular subgenre worldwide," Gail identified.

"*Hah*, if we'd been here a hundred years ago," Desirae began, "the most popular entertainment would be Buffalo Bill Cody's wild west show."

"Of course, you're quite right," Natasha remarked. "He toured throughout the northern states, west of the Great Lakes."

"Interesting you backtracking to the distant past, Desirae" Collins tattled. "I've noticed before, you have a propensity to shoot off at divergent angles. It's very stimulating. Where does all this unorthodox cogitation come from?"

"Not sure, but I've had the ability to make cosmic-sized jumps in conversation topics from an early age. Something clicks inside concomitant from whatever is being discussed, and I find myself proposing a matter at right-angles to the theme. Often, people find it disconcerting, but within this circle, you all seem to be in tune with the tangential."

"As Henry said back in Cheyenne, you come across more like a philosopher than a poet," Gail suggested, "yet you have no formal training in that discipline."

"No, and it's not even based on good-old, home-spun teachings. It's just a facet that leaps out of me on occasion."

"It's a gift," Collins stipulated. "Cherish it."

~ * ~

On they went, constantly bearing east, the flickering montages of Gothenburg, Lexington and Kearney briefly entering their psyches, everyone high on each other's company, Collins thinking he had made a terrific decision to ride the American freeways, the outbound and inbound legs providing more inamorata than he could ever have anticipated back in London. Then coming upon them unannounced and unprepared for, the unexpected hit them.

Fully absorbed in their own discussions, the campaneros were lunching in Slim's T-Bone Grill at Grand Island just north of I80 when they heard someone say, "Desirae."

Peering over his shoulder, Collins clocked a man attired in a plush suit, accompanied by a nurse dressed in an all-white uniform. Behind them stood two muscular male nurses, also furnished in white. Narrowing his eyes, he then glanced at Desirae sitting opposite him. The blood had drained from her face, her eyes blooming large, her whole being entranced in a catatonic state.

Returning to scrutinize the man, Collins blustered, "Who are you?"

"Yes, *who* are you?" Delaney reinforced.

"We're from the San Francisco Langley Porter Psychiatric Hospital," the suited man explained. "My name is Doctor Forrester."

"What's this got to do with Desirae?" Collins pushed.

"Desirae is an inpatient at the hospital."

"*What!*" he shrieked, pushing back the chair he sat on, and rising to his feet.

"We've been looking for her since she escaped eight days ago."

Glimpsing at Desirae again, Collins stammered out, "I...I don't comprehend this." Noticing his comrades had also entered into a dumbfounded hiatus, he begged, "What's going on?"

"In a moment." Forrester pored over his patient. "Desirae, have you been taking your medication?" She abided stunned. "Desirae." Still no response. Nodding to the nurse, he instructed, "Take Desirae out to the ambulance."

"Now *just* a minute," Collins barked, advancing towards Forrester, images of the Magnum breeding in his mind, his hands clenching up as they did in Giordano's Tropicana suite. "You can't come in here and attempt to apprehend someone without a just cause or authorisation."

Prepared for such a confrontation, Forrester showed Collins a document issued by the California Department of Mental Health, and signed by the chief mental health officer authorising Forrester to take Desirae Briscoe back to the Langley Porter Psychiatric Hospital.

For once in his life bemused by the turn of events, Collins dwelt lost for words. When Natasha prompted him for a response, his inertia persisted.

"Nurse," Forrester repeated. "Look after Desirae."

As the nurse approached her, Desirae shook her head, a low guttural, "Nooo," leaping from her mouth.

Grasping her by the shoulders, the nurse wrestled her up, and started to lead her away by the arm.

"Is that *absolutely* necessary?" Gail blasted, the nurse momentarily adjourning, before Forrester indicated for her to proceed.

"She can be violent," he unambiguously stated. "Best we sedate her before the journey back to San Francisco."

"You've got the *wrong* girl," Natasha insisted. "In the short time we've known Desirae, she's been placidness personified, and never displayed any violent tendencies."

"Schizophrenics exhibit many personalities," Forrester countered.

"*What!*" She gasped.

"Desirae was diagnosed with paranoid-schizophrenia at age eighteen. She can be quite normal for weeks, then descends into psychosis."

"*My god*," Natasha ejaculated. "Poor girl."

"Now that I've mustered my senses," Collins exclaimed, the Magnum back in its metaphorical shoulder holster, his hands unclenched, "could you provide us with some credential proving who you say you are?"

"Certainly." He produced an embossed Langley Porter Psychiatric Hospital identification pass. "I know this must be a shock to all of you." Pressing his lips together as if undecided how open to be, he then offered, "I can tell you what happened, and how we located Desirae."

"Please, go ahead."

"Desirae Briscoe has been an inpatient at Langley Porter for the past three years. What initiated her detention centred around her involvement in the attempted killing of her parents. I only divulge this because it is a matter of public record."

"*Good grief,*" Delaney blurted, his mouth failing to close after the retort.

"Unbeknown to her parents, she must have first become delusional years before the event, her enormous intellect…she's a very erudite and clever young woman…masking off the handicap. The record shows they were not good parents by way of leaving Desirae to her own devices and caring little for her emotional needs. Resentment built up, and she got involved with a man in his early twenties, who wanted to rob the Briscoe house, Desirae agreeing to let him in, if he killed her parents. It all went wrong, the man losing his nerve after purloining Missus Briscoe's jewellery and other expensive items. He shot Mister Briscoe as he slept but completely missed Missus Briscoe sleeping beside him. She screamed and the man fled, then she called nine-one-one for the police and an ambulance. To cut a long story short, when the police investigated, they calculated it must have been an inside job, Desirae implicated because it came to light that she knew the man. Mister Briscoe recovered from his wounds, and the man and Desirae were put on trial. It was only then that it became apparent Desirae had mental issues, and the court referred her to the California Department of Mental Health."

"But she seems so usual," Gail venerated.

"As I say, she can have periods where she appears to be conventional. Nevertheless, the psychosis is always bubbling beneath the veneer, particularly if she's not been taking her medication."

"*Not waving but drowning*," Collins recited.

"Excuse me," Forrester uttered, pursing his lips.

"It's a poem by Stevie Smith. Says everything in the title." Tarrying, he harvested more fancies. "Now I reconsider, when we first met Desirae, she did exhibit a more like drowning than waving carriage in her quest to get to Omaha." Delaying, he then voiced, "What's the significance of Omaha?"

"She had an aunt living in Nelson's Creek Omaha. In her early years, her parents sent Desirae to spend the summer months with her aunt. A time of boundless joy for her, it made up in part for her parent's neglect. Her aunt was very loving."

"Had, and was?" Collins queried.

"She passed last year. Necessarily, we never told Desirae for obvious reasons."

"But she indicated she had to get away from Omaha. She said she'd lived there her entire life, even attended the University of Nebraska, but she felt stifled, the undivided city overwhelming her like a big grizzly tearing apart its prey. She said she had to find a place where she could breathe without the walls closing in on her."

"Location transference," Forrester diagnosed. "It's very common in schizophrenia. In her perception, she told you that yarn in the context of getting away from San Francisco, or more specifically, Langley Porter."

"So how did you find us?"

"Within minutes of Desirae being reported missing, the police were covering the bus and rail station, and checking motels to see if she had got a lift from travellers in transit. Where did you meet her?"

"In Lombard Street at Del Mar Deguello. She wanted to bum a lift with us. Said she had money to cover costs. We were checking out of Ciro's Motel on Van Ness at seven the next day, so she said she'd be outside the motel waiting for us." Furrowing his brow, he investigated, "Where did she get the money for the trip?"

"Amongst other things, her parents sent her money, a lot of money."

"Why?"

"At Langley Porter, we try to allow patients as much everydayness as possible. This includes a small shopping mall within the bounds of the institution, where they can purchase goods. Desirae rarely used the facility. She kept most of the money in her room."

"How did she escape?"

"As I said, Desirae is a clever girl. She duped a maintenance company employee into providing her with a set of overalls and a contractor pass. Once she got through our main gate, she ditched the overalls, and put on civilian clothing from the bag she carried. The overalls were found in a litter bin in Golden Gate Park."

"I wonder where she spent the night before she came to Ciro's?" Delaney tabled.

"Probably slept rough," Forrester supposed. "Knowing we'd be hunting for her, she couldn't check into Ciro's or any other motel. Anyway, the next day, we got a report that a girl fitting Desirae's description was seen with some English tourists getting into a Camaro. The police guessed the car was hired and called around the rental companies. Eventually, we got word that an English party had hired a Camaro and a Corvette from Hertz in Chicago for at least four weeks. We put two and two together and concluded you were heading back to Chicago. The California Police broadcast the car registrations to neighbouring state police and Highway Patrol authorities, all forces on the lookout for the two vehicles. Howbeit, we didn't know your route, so had to wait until we got a positive idea of your whereabouts. Four days ago, we received a call from the Nevada Highway Patrol, saying the Camaro and the Corvette had been stopped by a patrol car on I93. We figured you must be heading for either Denver on I70 or Salt Lake City on I80. Then we got a call from the Utah police saying a circle of excursionists in two cars had been registered at the Botanical Motel Salt Lake City. Well, that confirmed you were on I80, so the Wyoming police kept an eye on you. We knew you'd be passing through Grand Island, so we flew to the regional airport last night, requisitioned an ambulance from a hospital business partner, the rest you know."

"Presumably," Collins postulated, "the police didn't intervene directly on your instructions, because it'd have a bad effect on Desirae."

"Indeed."

Shaking his head, he emitted in a soured tone, "This is all very disconcerting for us, Doctor Forrester."

"You're Mister Collins, are you?"

"Yes."

"We got all your names from the Botanical Motel. They said, you appeared to be the leader of the group."

"We've become very close to Desirae. I speak for all of us when I say, we're concerned for her future welfare. What can you say to reassure us?"

"She will be well-treated, without any penalties to be paid for her absconding. You have my word on that."

"No disrespect intended, Doctor Forrester. But I don't know you."

"You can always check me out with the California Department of Mental Health. They will vouch for me."

"Do you have their phone number?"

Giving Collins the number, he made the call from a phone booth in Slim's T-Bone Grill, then returned to his comrades, raising his eyes indicating Forrester's credentials held water.

"Okay, Doctor Forrester, both you and Langley Porter have a clean bill of health." Turning to his chums, he said, "We have no choice but to accept Desirae has to return to San Fran."

"Can we at least give Desirae her bag out of the Camaro, and say goodbye to her?" Natasha pleaded.

"Go ahead," Forrester sanctioned.

Departing the table they'd been sat at, Collins felt a thud in the pit of his stomach at the prospect of leaving Desirae to her fate. Building an emotion-proof shell around himself since the Babette affair to insulate him from pain, he had managed to avoid heartache. Desirae's circumstances breached the dam. He could feel pathos wallowing up inside, but the last thing he needed was to breakdown in front of Desirae and his confidants, when he knew the girl needed some heartening words, and a smile of encouragement.

Retrieving her bag from the trunk of the Camaro, he hesitantly made for the ambulance, Natasha, Delaney and Gail, a few steps behind him.

Ready to discharge his spiel, Desirae beat him to the draw.

"Don't feel bad about them taking me back," she implored, simpering. "I knew it was inevitable. If they hadn't got me on the road, they'd have been waiting in Omaha. I always knew that, but I just had to experience real freedom with real people for a few days."

He went to speak, but again she was quicker off the mark. "I've a long way to go before they officially let me out. So don't make any promises about staying in contact. It'd be pointless."

"Desirae," he coughed out, "I…"

"It's okay, Henry. Just come and give me a hug. Please, all of you."

They did her bidding, Natasha and Gail turning back with tears in their eyes, the usually implacable Delaney near to white-faced, Collins just about preserving emotional control.

"Goodbye, my English messiahs." She grinned at them. "I nearly made it to Omaha."

Watching her go, Collins whispered, "Jesus, in every dream home a heartache."

Chapter 19: Big Pain, Bad Karma

Consumed in tribulation, Desirae's troubles left the adventurers down and out with the blues for the next few days. Distraught, the night following the Grand Island meltdown, both Natasha and Gail cried themselves to sleep, no comfort from Collins and Delaney quelling their torment, Desirae looming large every time they shut their eyes, the men also close to breakdown.

Despite trying to reignite their up-tempo affectations, and echo on halcyon aspects impinging on them, all endeavours failed after a few minutes of artificially resuming their familiar patter and outlook. Hit badly, Delaney turned to the blow, but no amount of sniffing white powder relieved his hurt, Collins, Natasha and Gail tempted to join him, but resisting the temptation. True, she'd be in good hands, as Doctor Forrester had assured them before the ambulance pulled out of Grand Island, but reservations lingered. Could she overcome her schizophrenic condition and resume a routine life, or would the impediment be lifelong? Such grave misgivings beset the English, Collins and Natasha sharing their notions in the tranquillity of motel bedrooms, Delaney and Gail doing the same. Unlike a physical ailment where the patient usually recovers over a relatively short period, the only time limit on mental disorders was death. The picture of Desirae spending her unabridged life at Langley Porter became a horrific image they'd carry until they passed, the struggle being to grade it against other injurious mishaps, and accept these things happen.

"What I can't resolve," Natasha admitted, lying next to Collins in their room at the Colonial Hills Motel Lincoln, "is Desirae was as homologous to all the other people we have met in terms of lucidity. I have no former experience of mental maladies, my only estimation built from film and novels, and they pulled no punches in terms of abnormalities emanating from those cursed with irrationality and psychosis."

"From what I've gathered over the years, most mentally disturbed people are rational for the majority of the time. It's only when an external force or a knotty remembrance encroaches on their psyche, that the illness manifests itself in terms of incoherent behaviour patterns and violence. I mean hell, Luke Berringer and Rope Fisher came across as being a damned sight more mentally disturbed than Desirae, but I suppose they didn't get involved in potential homicide." Dawdling, he then augmented, "We must have provided a counterpoint setting for Desirae compared to Langley Porter, one whereby she felt completely free in spirit and mind, and thereby acted as regular as the rest of us. I'd go as far as to say, if Forrester had not interrupted our junket, we'd have deposited her in Omaha without a hitch. However, now knowing her aunt had passed, god knows what her reaction might have been when she discovered the loss and found herself alone."

"Yes, maybe she'd have dissolved, and shattered like an overdriven light bulb."

"Maybe, but if Desirae was put into a commonplace environment, she'd be fine. It's because of the crime committed, she's been restrained at Langley Porter."

"It can be argued internment will make her malaise worse."

"Quite. I can only assume at some stage Forrester will assess she's fine to be allowed out for a set time, and that time increased if no breakdowns occur, until she is finally deemed to be liberated from schizophrenia."

"*Holy Moses*, I hope so, but clearly she doesn't trust her parents, and apparently has no other relatives, begging the question, where could she go? Any sidekicks she had before the attempted murder might shun her, and anyway, she might not feel comfortable with them."

"Perhaps she'd go out on the road again, find a sect like us, and take off for all points of the compass."

Not answering, Natasha sighed, Collins comforting her, but similarly plagued with feelings of regret for their friend Desirae Briscoe, his heart sank.

~ * ~

Passing through Omaha only served to amplify the voyager's heartache. An option, should they have taken the I70 Denver route, they intended to apply for tourist permits to visit NORAD, the North American Aerospace Defense Command at Cheyenne Mountain, Colorado Springs, responsible for early warning missile attacks on the US. Failing that, they'd take in Strategic Air Command HQ at Offutt AFB Omaha, birthplace of Enola Gay. Seeing a signpost for Offutt at the junction of I80 with I75, they kept going east, the attractions of Omaha put on hold, possibly, permanently.

Less than forty-eight hours had elapsed since Forrester took Desirae from their chirpy band. It just didn't seem right to swagger around a city she had been aiming for as her journey's end. Close to a funeral cortege, nobody in the Camaro and the Corvette said a word from the moment they entered Omaha city limits on I80. They tried to stare ahead, and wanting to dash across the city, prayed for no traffic jams, all the good vibes built up from Chicago to pre-Grand Island dissipated. Collins hadn't felt so low since his break up with Babette. He'd recovered from that, positioning the failed marriage as nothing out of the ordinary, and with hopes of one day finding a soulmate without hidden personality blemishes. Conversely, he categorised Desirae's predicament as perhaps everlasting, never a time when he got a call out of the blue from her, saying she'd been released into the community fulltime.

Seeking out beat gen relics in the residuum of the pilgrimage became curtailed, nobody that keen to put on a happy face, even if they ran into Ginsberg or Corso. No matter how boisterous with excitement a taproom or juke joint they came to rest in to take sustenance turned out to be, they were imperious to the ambience, their four-way conversations littered with nothingness and quickly decaying into silence. They couldn't wait to be back in Blighty. Maybe then they could gauge the end-to-end furlough, putting the Grand Island cataclysm into perspective, a feat seemingly impossible whilst on American soil.

Formally intending to visit the Japanese Pagoda Shelter in the

Robert D. Ray Asian Gardens, the historic East Village, and the gold-domed State Capital building in Des Moines, instead the vacationers passed them by, their appetite for edification dulled. Instead, they elected to take lunch in Maxwell's Diner, a 1930s in origin, refurbished roadhouse in downtown, hoping the ethos and tenor they'd come to associate with such hostelries would pull them out of the doldrums, at least temporarily. A hope in vain, after ordering sumptuous steaks all round, they quickly regressed into now customary melancholic comportments, no one that hungry to rip into the porterhouses down to the bone.

"If the Desirae revelation had happened at the front end of the trip," Delaney admitted, "I'd have advocated returning home immediately."

"We all would," Natasha supported.

"Her plight makes my own bridges to cross seem tame in comparison," Gail conceded. "I've got all worked up inside so many times about my designs not being chosen by one of the major *haute couture* houses. That seems so selfish and infinitesimally small compared to Desirae's quandary."

"We all could apply the admonishing whip to our bare backs," Collins subscribed. "We don't truly comprehend how good our lives are until we meet someone who could be facing confinement for life, and with little to no opportunity to fulfill her dreams and desires."

~ * ~

The residual of the trip through Iowa and Illinois became a non-eventful slog for the English, the Prairie lands replete with buffalo sweeping by the Vet and the Camaro substantially unnoticed. Kellogg, Iowa City and Davenport came and went, as had York and Lincoln in the stretch between Grand Island and Omaha, without tempting the Collins coterie to do anything other than gas up, find a restaurant, and a motel.

They had planned to deviate off track to Cedar Rapids, north of Iowa City, to visit the Museum of Art containing works by Grant Wood, Marvin Cone and Bertha Jacques, and take in the views of the city from the banks of the Cedar River, perhaps even visit Wood's boyhood home on Turners Alley. Whilst taking lunch in Gunner Ivan's, a watering hole on the outskirts of Iowa City on I80, they discussed the objective.

"Personally, I couldn't care less about Cedar Rapids," Delaney uncompromisingly pronounced. "My bolt is shot. I'm still in the doldrums with the blues. The Big C is doing nothing for me, and all I look forward to is ploughing some A&R furrows at Cold Turkey."

"Gone off the idea of jumping ship for Creation Records?" Collins solicited.

"Yep. I just want to bury myself in something familiar."

"How about you, Gail?" Collins dug.

"Apart from grieving for Desirae, all I've ruminated about since Grand Island is diving deep into my work. I'd postponed much of a new autumn collection for Sherwood Locke before we left England, because it didn't particularly excite me. Now it has the equivalent allure of a Hollywood commission. Like Kallen, I want to immerse myself in work completely, try for a refuge to ease the pain. If I can get locked into the project, it will stop me from straying into Desirae territory during daylight hours. Of course, the nights will be a test. I might get some sleeping pills from my doctor."

"I'm also going for sleeping pills," Natasha advised. "I can just about get off when Henry is beside me, but I know when we're back in London, he won't be with me every night, so I'll need 'Mother's Little Helper' to induce sleep. Unlike you and Kallen, I've not considered work as an antidote for neutralising the Desirae factor." She hunched her shoulders. "I don't think I'll be able to put Desirae into perspective for quite some time, and in my mind, I can't see submergence into any research work at the Natural History Museum, no matter how potentially fascinating, will totally deflect me. I have no wish to be a downer on you three, but I know this will affect me for an indefinite period."

"You seem to be adjusting quite well, Henry," Delaney proposed.

"Not really," he refuted, "I just hide it better, but believe me, I'm in as much inward turmoil with the blues as you are. After the initial shock of Forrester extracting Desirae from our midst, I thought I'd come to terms with it. But during the subsequent days, I've been unable to turn down the empathy dial. If anything, it's gone to a higher plane of consciousness." Halting, he spied around his companions. "The challenge for us is to grade what we witnessed against other outcomes."

"How do you mean?" Natasha interrogated.

"We could have been in a road accident calamity, Desirae ending up dead. At least she's alive and has nothing terminal. She has the possibility of resuming a normal life."

"I know. I suppose the wire in the brain is fostered by the thought of her detainment at Langley Porter."

"Yes, that's it, Natasha," Gail underwrote. "I know she was involved in a potential murder, but given the circumstances budding that clanger, I find it incomprehensible her punishment could be life long."

"Strangely enough, I used to have similar laments for Albert Speer," Collins shared, "when I learnt about the fate of the Nazi hierarchy after the Nuremberg trials in O-Level history. Most of Hitler's captured lieutenants were sentenced to death for war crimes. Speer was given twenty-years, mainly solitary life imprisonment in Spandau Prison. Before release, he served the full term. For some indefinable reason, I felt sorry for him, maybe because two decades of institutional internment seemed as inhuman as the acts carried out by Hitler's henchmen. It was only when Desirae's potential term at Langley Porter became apparent, did Speer's pickle re-enter my mind. She became the surrogate Speer prisoner. Anyway—" He adopted open body language. "What's the remaining consensus on Cedar Rapids?"

"I suggest we keep heading east," Gail delineated. "Cedar Rapids holds no great appeal for me."

"Natasha?"

"No, I can't work up a sweat about Cedar Rapids. It would just beget more bad karma. Visiting the Museum of Art and Grant Wood's boyhood home rings hollow."

Ironically, every time Collins or Natasha turned on the Camaro's FM radio, it seemed to bleat a heart-rendering rock anthem or some sallow ballad, when what they really needed was a solid dose of *I'm Waiting For The Man,* by the Velvets or the Doors *LA Woman* to revitalise them.

Whether they felt a *de rigueur* obligation for sackcloth and ashes in deference to Desirae, Collins could not work out. More inclined to want to fast-forward to a future portal, where her mental incumbrance had been resolved, he pictured a time when freedom beckoned her, she contacted him, and the burden of grief became lifted off their shoulders. Unaccustomed to such heavy-duty qualms, the English felt stranded in the wake of conflicting agents, communication with beat generation survivors achieved but juxtaposed by the downside Grand Island affair. They never saw it coming, Desirae masking off her syndrome so effectively, the possibility of divining an oddment so remote as to be unreal. Like for his stage of eyeing strangers on aircraft and trains, out on the streets, and in concert venues with a jaundiced eye, trying to decipher if they were serial killers after meeting Carrie Carter at Autry Overlook, Collins now imagined he'd adopt the same regime in an effort to detect if they were mental casualties.

Not a pleasant notion, as the caravan continued east, he tried to blot out the sentiment, and wished for happier times.

Chapter 20: Chicago Omnibus

Back at O'Hare International, with the sun setting over America for the final time on their round robin crusade, Collins and co stood outside the departures terminal, watching the skies over Illinois turn from yellow and red to Dylan Thomas's 'starless and bible black'. This was not judgement day, only evening, soft and fair, Lake Michigan's breeze cooling the traveller's angst.

Intoxicated by the ideal, they had blindly crossed the pond, pumped up with visions of a flawless Eden, but were met head-on by glitchy veracity and rampant fact. Not anticipating vicissitudes distilling on assumed certainties, rampant metamorphosis had blighted impressions of America gained from folklore, the inevitability of the ultimate kibitzer; change, and all its adverse ramifications metering out exterminating strokes, wiping out the cowboy, the steam train and great swathes of the Fifth Amendment, the shockwaves felt near and far rankling their preconceptions. A *bete noire* to even the most flexible journeymen, it obliterated their dreamscape, leaving them tumbling down the here-and-now well into the bowels of despair.

Head in hands, reflecting about Wade Gardner, Luke Berringer, Michael McClure, Rope Fisher and a cast of beatnik commentators and Great Depression and Dust Bowl flotsam and jetsam, Collins' volition became overloaded with perturbation. Amelia Hart's beat gen rebuttal, 'They were middle-class college boys playing at being hobos and freight train riders. Sure they understood the subculture and the nature of the people they wrote about, but they knew nothin' about living the life,' struck home more than ever, his appreciation that no counterculture, no matter how seductive approached perfection, heightened. He tried to recall the propitious words delivered by McClure, but they tarried as faded, cloudy and indistinct. Nonetheless, he did remember Homer

Colhoun's, 'You should wind up your quest with a facility to determine what is crucial and what is immaterial.' In view of what occurred in Slim's T-Bone Grill, he now assessed the remark as highly prophetic. He also brought to mind his thinking at the River Hotel Chicago on the first night of their tour. Maybe it'd go like a dream, he'd supposed. Alternatively, he had envisioned the unforeseen might drive them into blank canyons and towering alleys, the unfamiliar having them dig deep to get back on track, or at worst, fighting for survival. In the beginning, the former prevailed, but it stalled in mid-flight, the latter crashing through the good times threshold when Forrester arrived annihilating their cosy world.

Picturing the forlorn rage of growing old that darkens rivers, desert plains and mountain peaks, a shiver swept over him, but most of all, Desirae Briscoe thumped into his machinations, her recurring image swamping all other considerations. He could still see the look of resignation emblazoned in her face as Forrester took her away. He thought of her as a sagacious, sharp-witted beacon of light, burning brightly during those brief few days between San Fran and Grand Island. For one so young, a rare understanding of the human condition flowed out of her like a waterfall. She could have been the mother of illumination they never found.

In the final analysis, the Collins coterie were desolation argonauts, sensing for enlightenment but mainly finding raw tribulation, the plastic coating of modernity and so-called progress failing to heal ancient wounds. America gave them the substance to fire their fantasies, and a trajectory map to feed the senses and stimulate counterculture intellect. Along the way, stark authenticity intervened, purging their souls of surplus hope and conviction. The World had always been terrible and terrifying, the decimating assets nullified by family warmth, societal values and the education system during their formative years. Free to find the rough and the smooth across the Atlantic, the scales of balance had shifted more in favour of grating harshness than idyllic grace. Belligerent euphoria had been superseded by extreme ambiguity stymying ambition, Desirae the innocent amongst the depraved.

They had opted out of their ermine-lined occupations, insulating them from crazy kismet, dipped their fingers into a fiery cauldron, and been scorched for life. It could have happened to them anywhere, but it happened in America, a mythical place in their imaginations where Elvis changed the destiny of popular music, President Kennedy inspired the nation, and the beat generation, principally Kerouac, Ginsberg and Burroughs, reshaped literature into patterns of their choosing.

Under the cold light of assuredness, despite his professional good times Stateside, to Collins, it all seemed like a false dawn, culminating in the unwarranted incarceration of Desirae Briscoe. He wanted to let loose with a real Magnum, but knew it only represented a transitory howl.

Chapter 1: Beginnings

Out of nowhere they came in ever increasing numbers, an infestation multiplying and devouring everything in their path, as if a plague had descended on the northern Occident from a faraway planet. Though great hulking brutes, at first few people really noticed them, their antenna attuned to other frequencies. Those wackadoo ding-a-lings breeding tolerance to their advent accepted them, qualmish fears giving way to notions of magnanimity, the liberality seen as a weakness to be exploited by the invaders. If the harbingers of doom proclaimed their unwelcome entry, their message remained transparent to watchers, most just too predisposed to indifference, or worse, subsumed in apathy.

When casting vision on the newbies, some observers concluded they were unambiguously not of this world and must have come from a faraway, supernova fathered, extragalactic nebula, lightyears from Earth. Howbeit, astronomers had not detected their passage through the Virgo Supercluster and on into the Milky Way before entering the Solar System from some distant star array, possibly beyond the range of Hubble and well outside of the Solar System's interstellar neighbourhood.

~ * ~

Pamela Cavendish inhabited the lexicon of humanity otherwise engaged in making sense of their own lives, thereby she barely registered the newcomers' presence. Consumed with aspirations directed at furthering her architectural career, from newsreel images, she seldom took in how different the aliens were compared to her own kind, her mind saturated in load-bearing stress equations, decorative motif and optimum atrium lighting geometrics.

Grappling to find her touch in her freshman year at the University of Liverpool School of Architecture, subsequently she had bloomed in her sophomore and final years, graduating with a BA (hons) in architectural design and going to work for Teddington & Backersley in Preston as a junior designer. Finding the transition from academia to commerce well within her capabilities spectrum, she easily knuckled down to the demands made on her by the practice, soon originating a distinction for proficiency in her dealings with clients and colleagues. Smart enough to recognise she had merely stepped onto rung one of her career ladder, she avoided falling into the graduate know-it-all trap, instead plumping for measured consideration before opening her mouth in the company of seasoned architects.

Soon after acclimatising to her new environment, whilst socialising with other Teddington & Backersley minions at local hostelry The Stanley Arms, she met Stephen Thornly. Blessed with a plethora of interpersonal skills, he came across to her as erudite personified tempered with a dash of light-hearted witticism.

"So, Miss Cavendish, how are you coping with the real world of business after being cocooned in theory for the past three years?"

"It's tougher than I'd imagined." She grinned, her natural sense of *joie de vivre* pulsing from her being like a lightning rod. "But I'm getting used to the cut and thrust of being on-call beyond contracted hours when a rush job comes in and it's all hands to the pump." She paused, a hint of inquisitiveness seeping from her features. "What about you? Where do you fit into the grownups' domain?"

"Me," Thornly replied. "*Hah*, there's much less to me than meets the eye. You might be disappointed the actuality does not live up to the façade."

"I sense modesty." She pushed his arm. "I can't believe the

substance does not match the frontage. Come on, tell me the worst."

"Very well." Scrunching up his dial, he nailed, "This is the fulcrum at which people are either gladdened or displeased. I wonder which you will be?"

"Go on."

"I'm a correspondent for the *Manchester Evening News*."

"Popularly known as a journo, or disparagingly, a hack."

"Yes."

"I suppose you prepared me for the tremors," she submitted, smiling at him, "because some within your profession have appalling reputations for generating false news, bias and being economical with the truth?"

"My brethren are guilty as charged—"

"But you're different," she cut in.

"I think so."

"What are you doing up here, Stephen Thornly?"

"I have an early morning meeting with BAe Systems at Wharton. The paper is doing a series on the history of defence manufacturers in the North-West. You'd be surprised how many people have been dependent for their jobs on military and civil aerospace contracts traversing the last seventy years, and the trend goes on today."

"I see," she affirmed taking in his visage more fully. When he'd breezed over to subtly separate her from her associates, his lineaments persisted partly hidden in shadows created by roof rafters absorbing the light. Nudging his feet slightly as he last spoke, he had stepped out of the gloom revealing an enticing face with azure optics and wavy blond hair. Just my type, she thought. "So, what's the current hot subject getting the media's attention?"

"Do you read newspapers?"

"I used to glance at the broadsheets in the seniors' common room at school, but since going to university, I only use the web for news feeds, and then infrequently."

"Swallowed up by other concerns?" he ventured.

"Took me a while to find my feet with the study matter. When the penny finally dropped, I kept my focus affixed to the ball. I won't pretend I am a natural when it comes to architectural mathematics. My area of excellence is more in the visionary sphere."

"You mean, the artistic side?"

"I do."

"So, you blithely went around Liverpool and now presumably Preston without much valuation of what's happening beyond your micro-universe?"

"I suppose so."

"Well—" He stood back taking her in. "It might have escaped your notice, Miss Cavendish, but the biggest showstopper claiming front page dominance and coverage in the leader columns is the rise of the invaders in our society."

"You mean, the aliens?"

"Indeed I do."

"Where do they come from?"

"Stargazers have told the world, the Universe comprises thousands of galaxies, each galaxy containing billions of stars, each star orbited by its own planets. Paradoxically, astrophysicists estimate there are more stars in the Universe than there are grains of sand on Earth, but there are more atoms in one grain of sand than there are stars in the Universe, which is to say, the unscalable vastness of the Universe must be capable of conceiving lifeforms totally unimaginable to *homo sapiens*. Although probable, it is not certain, consequently, the interlopers are categorised as beings of indeterminate origin."

"Apart from what I pick up on web podcasts and virtual news feeds, I've never seen one. They're mainly down south, aren't they?"

"Yes, but the Government has given them citizenship rights and they're driving north and west."

"*Really*!" Her phiz flowered into concern. "I'm astonished."

"Westminster has tried to hush it up, but of course all ministerial misdemeanours and controversial policies leak to the press. However, media owners have been warned by the Cabinet Office not to make a big thing of it, so it persists as a word of mouth construct."

At a loss, she confessed, "I'm puzzled why there have been no demonstrations in London."

"Oh there has been, but again the same Cabinet Office injunction applies."

She glowered. "They're intent on keeping it near to a secret?"

"Yes, but ultimately as gossip goes viral, the dam will break and our rulers will encounter a nationwide revolt."

"My god—" Her sensitivities coming online, she narrowed her peepers. "There hasn't been civil war in England since the reign of Charles I and the coming to power of Oliver Cromwell."

"For sure," he agreed, taking the baton. "That contretemps centred on opposing English Protestants and Catholics, and the relinquishment of absolute power from the monarchy to Parliament. This struggle, inextricably culminating in civil war, will centre on the nation wrestling power from legislative collaborators and ridding our shores of the outlanders. Whereas the English Civil War could have gone either way, this just-over-the-horizon battle is heavily stacked against the English people. We could be wiped out altogether."

"Isn't that what is called ethnic cleansing?"

"Yes. And it's been made easy by weak governments endlessly pandering to minority pressure groups in the past. You see, there are no brilliant people anymore, just shades of mediocrity fostered by political correctness. Consequently, the country has degenerated into shambling confusion, making it easy for the English to be subdued by foreigners. They own our businesses, our banks, our service industries, our football clubs, even our newspapers, have immense power in Westminster and are slowly but surely expunging the English from the workplace and bringing in more foreigners to do our jobs."

Gawping at him, she knew what he said to be absolutely true.

Pamela and Stephen soon crossed the friendship barrier, becoming lovers. Hungry for each other, they met whenever work duties permitted, either entwining in protracted acts of sexual bliss at his Belle Vue apartment or her Chadwick Gardens equivalent. Because of her university and work commitments, Pamela had little time to pursue a love life, whereas Stephen had indulged in the pleasures of the flesh since his mid-teens. Never finding a chanteuse to make his heart beat faster, when he got serious with Pamela, he cottoned onto the fact that she affected him in ways he'd not previously experienced. Sure, the evening they met at The Stanley Arms, he'd been attracted by her flowing auburn hair, scintillating cinnamon windows to her soul and comely shape, but as he familiarised himself with her undercurrents, something more transcendental came to light. He felt an overpowering kinship with her, like they'd been cut from the self-same rough diamond. At first. he couldn't place the sensation, then he figured it must be love, real love. From Pamela's angle, what began as an amusing interlude, briskly transformed into strong feelings for him beyond his obvious physical and genial company attributes. She had briefly been in love on two occasions, both in her late teens, neither proving to be the real thing, the letdowns accounting for her prudence with men, and a secondary driver behind her studies and work dedication. Stephen Thornly had effortlessly broken through her cautious barrier, Pamela relaxing into the burgeoning union and finding enjoyment in all their combined ventures. She craved to be with him all the time, the desire metamorphosing into schemes about marriage, babies and a shared abode, Stephen buying into the prospect without hesitation.

Little did the lovers realise, their grand plans would be misshapen by a series of happenings fostered at the national level, significantly impacting the rest of their lives.

Doghouse Blues

So you think you have unexpected issues to resolve? Read about Roger Fraser and you'll soon find your problems pale in comparison!

Roger Fraser is convinced he is cursed by unforeseen situations constantly bringing his integrity into disrepute, especially in social situations.

His family thinks he is gaff prone, but if they could see him in the business arena, they would find Roger is an unassailable trouble-shooter, trampling on Essex boy traders, and solving delicate problems with aplomb.

Join the Fraser family and their assorted band of odd-ball friends and work colleagues, as our hero steers his way through some tricky situations, but nonetheless, always seems to get the rough end of the pineapple and ends up licking his wounds in the doghouse.

Doghouse Blues 2

Roger Fraser, the ever optimistic but perpetually put upon investment banking stock analyst-trouble shooter and occasional rugby player has more work and domestic issues to challenge his sensibilities. He skilfully manoeuvres from one demanding situation to the next, barely managing to extinguish the callous flames of fate seeming to constantly blight his endeavours and bite at his flesh.

During his excursions into shocking social scandals and battling with egotistical megalomaniacs, he endlessly verges on disaster, but somehow always manages to survive. Roger pokes irreverent fun at the new Establishment, single-handedly takes on female dragons, prevails against rampaging supermarket shoppers and trades wisecracks with a Brummy vicar, but invariably finds himself tethered to the doghouse, singing the blues.

Doghouse Blues 3

When it comes to neutralising uppity officials and slaying implacable harridans masquerading as mewling princesses, Roger has no equal in the world of high-finance and within his wife Charlotte's social set.

He survives a no-nonsense outward bound course instructor, boldly engages status quo doyens including an intractable hanging judge and a very persistent spook, avoids being mugged by lazoonland trailer trash, and subdues an autocratic drama teacher.

On a lighter note, Roger dodges the clutches of jailbait schoolgirls, is bedeviled by an overzealous impresario and battles intransigent shrews amongst a plethora of highly contentious and hilarious incidents, but despite his new found remedy, inevitably he winds up in the doghouse, wondering where it all went wrong.

Incident at Lahore Basin

Whilst on business in Pakistan, ex-RAF officer and businessman Dale Latham comes close to death when his helicopter is downed by a ground to air missile. Hospitalised, he meets Chanda Govinda, a persecuted Christian Indian and helps her escape across the Pakistan-India border. Although there is no evidence linking Latham's involvement with Chanda, Muslim zealot police chief Aman aims to imprison him.

With his top-secret knowledge, HMG fear Latham will end up in the hands of Pakistani intelligence. MI6 agent Ross Hunter is dispatched to appraise the situation, and if necessary, liquidate Latham. When Latham is abducted by terrorists, Hunter rescues him, saying that Aman set him up for the ultimate fall. Without evidence, Aman is forced to allow Latham to leave Pakistan, avoiding a bullet from Hunter.

Maggie's Farm

Cody and Carolyn Redford enjoy a carefree lifestyle in Kent County, with friends Gavin and Melanie Maynard. In Cornwall, the Redfords encounter a soothsayer predicting a bleak future for mankind. The foursome then notes some unexplained changes in the behaviour of wild animals and migrating birds, giving credence to the prediction. When a terrorist outrage in South Africa leads to further major atrocities in Israel and India, détente finally fails. Global nuclear war is sparked off by an unforeseen source, resulting in the superpowers exchanging H-bomb punches like drunken boxers. In the midst of survival, Cody Redford becomes aware of the artificial insemination and incubation (AI2) programme, an initiative hatched in the Cold War years to store the sperm of prominent scientists with the objective of using surrogate hosts to factory farm children in a post-holocaust world. Though appalled, nonetheless, he resigns himself to supporting the programme, unaware of the significant down the road consequences to the nature of human life.

About the Author

Clive Radford began writing at school, then university but mainly through subsequent life experience.

His poetry has been published in numerous poetry magazines such as The Journal, The Cannon's Mouth, Poetry Monthly, Poetry Now, Storming Heaven, Poetry Nottingham, Scripsi and Modern Review, plus in many compilations by United Press.

A series of his short stories and poems have been published by Ether Books. The Arts Council has sponsored publication of his novels 'One Night in Tunisia' and 'The Sounds of Silence'. His contemporary satire 'Doghouse Blues' was number one in Harper Collins Authonomy chart and has been awarded gold medal status. It has been published by Black Rose. His spy thriller 'Zavrazin' has been published by Triplicity Publishing. It's companion sequel 'Nexus Bullet' is published by Ex-L-Ence Publishing. His three-book series 'Disclosures of a Femme Fatale Addict' has been published by Wild Dreams Publishing and Miraclaire Publishing. His science fiction novel 'Maggie's Farm', suspense-thriller 'Incident at Lahore Basin', contemporary thriller 'Alpha Centauri' and his satires 'Doghouse Blues 2', 'Doghouse Blues 3' and 'Doghouse Blues Revised and Remastered' are published by Rogue Phoenix Press. Melange Books has published his mystery thriller, 'Monsoon in the Making' and 'The Spiral Staircase and other Novellas', a mix of psychological, modern satire and rite of passage sagas.

'One Night in Tunisia', 'Zavrazin' and 'Nexus Bullet' have all been converted into three-act screenplays. The 'Zavrazin' screenplay is under contract with Story Merchant/Atchity Productions for film production.

Currently, he is crafting a number of works including 'Three Cheshire Boys' a comedic thriller, 'Colby Richmond: The University Years', the coming of age sequel to 'Disclosures of a Femme Fatale

Addict', 'Mozart meets McCartney', a mystery, and 'Wokeland', a dystopian social science fiction.

His work has a distinctive voice setting it apart and appealing to those fascinated by intrigue, and who question status quo accepted views.